Lydia Mendoza's Life in Music /
La historia de Lydia Mendoza

AMERICAN MUSICSPHERES

Series Editor
Mark Slobin

Fiddler on the Move
Exploring the Klezmer World
Mark Slobin

The Lord's Song in a Strange Land
Music and Identity in Contemporary Jewish Worship
Jeffrey A. Summit

Lydia Mendoza's Life in Music / La historia de Lydia Mendoza
Norteño Tejano Legacies
Yolanda Broyles-González

LYDIA MENDOZA'S LIFE IN MUSIC / LA HISTORIA DE LYDIA MENDOZA

Norteño Tejano Legacies

Yolanda Broyles-González

OXFORD

UNIVERSITY PRESS

2001

OXFORD
UNIVERSITY PRESS

Oxford   New York
Athens   Auckland   Bangkok   Bogotá   Buenos Aires   Calcutta
Cape Town   Chennai   Dar es Salaam   Delhi   Florence   Hong Kong   Istanbul
Karachi   Kuala Lumpur   Madrid   Melbourne   Mexico City   Mumbai
Nairobi   Paris   São Paulo   Shanghai   Singapore   Taipei   Tokyo   Toronto   Warsaw

and associated companies in
Berlin   Ibadan

Copyright © 2001 by Oxford University Press

Published by Oxford University Press, Inc.
198 Madison Avenue, New York, New York 10016

Oxford is a registered trademark of Oxford University Press.

Library of Congress Cataloging-in-Publication Data
. Broyles-González, Yolanda, 1949–
Lydia Mendoza's life in music : norteño tejano legacies = La historia de Lydia Mendoza /
Yolanda Broyles-González.
p. cm. — (American musicspheres)
English and Spanish.
Includes index.
ISBN 0-19-512706-4
1. Mendoza, Lydia.   2. Singers—United States—Biography.
3. Tejano music—History and criticism.
I. Title.   II. Title: Historia de Lydia Mendoza.   III. Series.
ML420.M3768B76   2001
782.42162'6872'0092—dc21   00-038534
[B]

1 3 5 7 9 8 6 4 2

Printed in the United States of America
on acid-free paper

Acknowledgments

The work of one is always the work of many. This book was made possible by the strong support of various intersecting communities, individuals, and institutions. Deepest thanks go to my entire family—ceremonial kin and blood kin—most especially to soulmate Francisco González and to my beloved children, Esmeralda Broyles-González and Francisco Guillermo González, *y los tres angelitos también* for all that you mean to me. To you I dedicate this work.

I am grateful to the women whose encouragement and participation helped make this undertaking a reality. *Mil gracias* go to Lydia Mendoza, who powerfully recounts her memories for the benefit of the seven generations to come. The internationally recognized artwork by Estér Hernández imbues the volume with extraordinary beauty and spirit. The exquisite drawings of the 20 symbols from the Aztec calendar are by Verónica Xochitl Valadéz, who represents an emergent generation of gifted artists. María Elena Gaitán lovingly worked with me on the first translation draft when it seemed impossible to render Lydia's eloquent *tejana* speech into English. Marta Paredes painstakingly helped me make editorial decisions. The teachings and ceremonial cycle with Chumash Bear Clan elder and friend Pilulaw Khus (and the entire Bear Clan) always brought insight, spirit, strength, and humor. The women's sweat lodge ceremony with Marsha Hunter Estrada on the Tule Indian ancestral lands allowed me to vision in new ways.

I am grateful to Barrio Libre (39th Street, Tucson, Arizona) and the Yaqui ceremonies that continually inspirit me, my family, and my ancestors. *Abrazos* go to *cantora* Lourdes Matus and to ceremonial leader and border human rights activist José Matus. Andrés Granados Segura (*en paz descanse*) and Xinaxtli hold a special place, as always.

Gracias de todo corazón to my beloved mother, Julia V. Arana, who always sang and sings with me on all our travels and who told me my first Lydia Mendoza stories. To her and my brother Fernando I am also grateful for the experience of regular attendance at the Mexican performance spectacles of the

Million Dollar Theater in Los Angeles during my early childhood years. How could I ever thank all those who have lovingly carried and cultivated *raza* musical traditions across generations—often at great sacrifice?

I acknowledge and deeply thank those who have shared in my daily life and whose presence sustains me: *miles de gracias a Marina y Isaías Guerra (y toda su familia)* for their profound friendship and spirit. The visits from my *tías* across difficult borders (Tía Delfina Rojas, Tía Nelly Aguilar, Tía Tere Chaín, and Tía Juanita Castillo) made all the difference in the world. Special thanks to Gregoria Elias and Vicki Elias. I will always cherish Jayantika (Tita) Das, Satya Bikram (Nanu) Das, and Ram Kumar Das for always welcoming me in kinship. Through you I even came to value the historical irony of being called "Indian." Various cherished presences move within my every day: Laura, Bruce, Layla, Copetón, the owls, brown pelicans, and snowy plovers near these vast nuturing Pacific waters

Women's wisdom nourished this book in different ways. I owe great thanks to the thoughts, words, and deeds of Antonia Castañeda, Estér Hernández, Gloria Anzaldúa, Emma Pérez, María Elena Gaitán, Deborah Vásquez, Rosa Martha Zárate Macías, Olivia Chumacero, Sabine Gross, Roberta Fernández, Guadalupe Castillo, Norma Cantú, Mary Rojas, Deena González, Kum-Kum Bhavnani, Raquel Rubio-Goldsmith, Raquel Mendoza, Karen Maxson, Charity Hirsch (and all WAGE members), Terri Gómez, Paulette Cabugos Mendoza, *a todo el círculo de danzantes, y a todas mis comadres*.

Series editor Mark Slobin nurtured the project and provided much encouragement. I also thank all those involved in this book's production at Oxford University Press. I am indebted to Gerard Béhague and his graduate students and to Estevan Azcona and the raza graduate students at UT Austin. Many thanks to Arturo Madrid at Trinity University. Thank you, Raúl Pérez of Sony Records, for always taking an interest and giving advice. *Muchísimas gracias a* Salomé Gutiérrez and Dyama Gutiérrez of DLB Records in San Antonio, for recording Lydia Mendoza since 1966—and numerous other tejana/o musicians for decades. Special thanks to all of Lydia Mendoza's family—especially her daughters Lydia Alvarado Dávila and Yolanda Alvarado Hernández.

I deeply appreciate the many things I learn from all the students I work with and have worked with. Thank you in particular to Marisol Rodarte Venegas, Noemi García, Edwin López, Gladys Limón, Raquel Hernández, Patti Cárdenas, Benny Torres, Marisol Juarez Moreno, Verónica Barraza, Maribel Amaya, Kristina Elias, Imelda Loza, Beda Gamboa, and Abraham Meza; to El Congreso; to Vista at Williams College; and to MEChA everywhere, particularly at the University of Wisconsin, Madison, where Wunk Sheek and the drumming circle greatly inspirited our gathering. Special thanks to those students who set an example of "¡Si se puede!": Verónica Valadéz, JoAnn Godinez, Verónica Moncayo, and Marisa Flores, as well as their beautiful children.

My thanks go also to the students who read the manuscript with Yvonne Yarbro Bejarano at Stanford University. Librarians Raquel González, Sal Güereña, Patrick Dawson, and Sylvia Curtis always generously helped me. Martha Barajas extended herself above and beyond the call of duty, creating a positive Chicana Studies departmental space. I thank the Institute for Social,

Behavioral, and Economic Research (UCSB) for providing the grant assistance necessary to complete this labor of love.

This book was written in the face of many special challenges: during this time, my *abuelita*—who taught me the old songs and how to dance them— went into spirit. Yet she continues to provide me with invaluable guidance. During this period I also launched a pay equity lawsuit against the University of California. Heartfelt thanks to attorneys Moisés Vázquez, Robert Racine, and Millie Escobedo—and also to President Clinton and First Lady Hillary Rodham Clinton at the White House for honoring my struggle.

Thanks, above all, to Spirit in all its forms.

All my relations!
In tlanextia in tonatiuh!

Contents

About This Book

> With the artistry of her voice and the gift of her songs, she bridged the gap between generations and cultures. Lydia Mendoza is a true American pioneer and she paved the way for a whole new generation of Latino performers, who today are making all Americans sing.

With these words from Pres. Bill Clinton (September 29, 1999) Lydia Mendoza was awarded the National Medal of the Arts in the White House—the highest honor that the nation can pay to a performer. Prior to that, the legendary Lydia Mendoza had been immortalized as one of the most distinguished and towering figures in American music history. In the early 1930s she established her reputation first and foremost as a grassroots idol with a loyal following among U.S.-Mexican migrant farm workers who followed the crops from Texas to Michigan and later to California and the Pacific Northwest as well. Her earliest solo hit, "Mal Hombre" ("Evil Man"), in 1934 made her an overnight star, and that song never waned in popularity throughout her long career. Mendoza's loyal fans nicknamed her "La Alondra de la Frontera" ("The Meadowlark of the Border") and "La Cancionera de los Pobres" ("Singer of the Poor").

By the 1970s Lydia Mendoza had earned national honors from numerous prestigious institutions; the Smithsonian, the National Endowment for the Arts, the White House, and various musician Halls of Fame were among those who acknowledged the singer/musician's contributions. Yet in this memoir those awards receive virtually no mention. Instead Mendoza highlights and places front and center the great teachers in her life: her mother and grandmother. The women of Mendoza's family are the pivots for the family unit as a whole. Her life story is thus an important womanist and woman-centered document.

Mendoza's unique performance and recording career spans two-thirds of the twentieth century, from her earliest recordings, in the 1920s, to the last, in the 1980s. It is no exaggeration to state that Lydia Mendoza's sustained popularity and legendary status remain virtually unmatched by any other U.S.-Mexican

Lydia Mendoza receives the National Medal of Arts (September 1999) at
the White House from President Bill Clinton and First Lady Hillary
Rodham Clinton.

woman of the twentieth century—from any walk of life—and by but few other
American musicians. Lydia Mendoza's voice and 12-string guitar figure prominently as enduring guardians and transmitters of a vast oral tradition of Mexican popular song. She always sang the songs the collective cherished, the songs
of the people, across generations. Invariably she sang by popular demand—
what the people called out to her, that strong ebb and flow of perennial favorite
songs, many of which originated in the nineteenth century, some of which are
more recent. Many of the song forms themselves are even much older. All are
indigenous to the Americas, many to Texas. It is the music that emerged from

the experiences of native peoples (on both sides of the U.S.-Mexico border) within a context of Euro-American westward colonization that greatly accelerated in the nineteenth century.

During her lifetime Lydia Mendoza performed and recorded with different ensemble types: *conjunto norteño* (featuring the button accordion and *bajo sexto* 12-string); mariachi groups (indigenous to the state of Jalisco and featuring violins, trumpets, *guitarrón*, and *vihuela*); and *orquesta* (a derivative Mexicanized version of the big band). Yet she is most closely identified as a lone singer self-accompanied on the 12-string guitar. That kind of self-sufficiency no doubt contributed to her ability to survive and thrive as a musician.

Lydia Mendoza's prominence as a U.S.-Mexican working-class people's idol stems from her sustained presence and long-term visibility within a complex network of social and cultural relations in the twentieth century. The American-born (1916) Mendoza figures among the earliest women recording and touring artists. Like various other grassroots idols, she is loved for her ability to articulate a working-class *sentimiento* (sentiment and sentience) through song—certainly among the most cherished of working-class Chicana/o cultural art forms. Through her vast repertoire and unmistakable interpretive shaping of songs from the oral tradition she became a living embodiment of U.S.-Mexican culture, a symbol of the full spectrum and potential of being, as well as a participant in raza peoples' protracted struggles for survival. On a daily basis, music is an essential practice in the formation and sustenance of *mexicana/o* collective working-class identity. As part of a communal memory system Mendoza's voice provides a shared affirmation of a common experience. Among the most beloved of musical forms are the *ranchera* (lyrical love song), the *corrido* (narrative historical ballads), and the various genres of *música de antaño, huapangos*, and the bolero and others less frequently heard.

In spite of the specificity and depth of her musical roots in the *norteño* (northern Mexican, including Texan) tradition, Lydia Mendoza's voice and musicianship found an avid following across geographies, nations, and generations. Her expressivity rooted in Texas-Mexican soil achieved transnational popularity, reaching deep into the Latin American continent. Mendoza's voice and her popularity spread through her many recordings and live radio performances. Eventually she toured and recorded in various Latin American countries, such as Colombia and Cuba. In a 1943 letter to her, RCA Victor documented the heavy sales of her recorded music in many countries: El Salvador, Guatemala, Venezuela, Colombia, and more.

Lydia Mendoza began her long musical career as a child in the 1920s, singing for pennies and nickels on the streets of downtown San Antonio, Texas. She lived most of her adult life in Houston, Texas, where she was born. The life story of the legendary Lydia Mendoza encompasses a 60-year singing career that included innumerable tours; recordings, including hits; and national awards. Her performing career begins with the advent of the recording industry in the 1920s and continued into the 1980s, when she suffered a stroke that ended her career. Mendoza's legendary status as a Chicana working-class idol continues to this day. She is perhaps the most prominent and long-standing performer within the U.S.-Mexican oral tradition of music.

This book delivers Lydia Mendoza's life story, as told by her. She vividly narrates the particulars of her struggles as a musician, as a woman, as a U.S.-Mexican paving a road for the next generations. In her narrative, Lydia Mendoza also provides a firsthand account of the emergence of an American entertainment industry that took off in the 1920s in tandem with the electronic media: radio, recordings, then television. Mendoza's woman-centered narrative is also a valuable humanistic document, which provides readers with insight—for example—into the spiritual practices and faith of U.S.-Mexican laborers. Lydia Mendoza recounts various miraculous occurrences central to her life. Like millions of others from the same working-class native culture, she consistently puts to the fore her connectedness with the spirit world and with the powers that animate the universe.

In addition to Lydia Mendoza's life-telling, this volume contains an analytical essay that contextualizes and expands on various aspects of her life-telling. (The bibliographical notes provide references for further reading.) In the analytical essay I elaborate on the format of *historia* in which Lydia tells her story and then also provide background that concerns her musical performance life and its relationship to the vibrant Tex-Mex and greater norteño musical traditions. This volume represents a milestone in the writing of music history. It is a befitting monument to the great Lydia Mendoza.

All my relations!
In tlanextia in tonatiuh!

Brief Chronology

1916   Lydia Mendoza is born in Houston, Texas, to Leonor Zamarripa Mendoza and Francisco Mendoza. Lydia is the second-oldest of seven children.

1927–1933   The Mendoza family ekes out a living primarily through street performances and tours.

1928   The Mendoza family constitutes itself as El Cuarteto Carta Blanca (the Carta Blanca Quartet) and begins to perform in the lower Rio Grande Valley. In the same year, they make their first dozen recordings for the Okeh and Odeon labels in San Antonio. Before ever hearing the recordings, the Mendoza family joins the mass agricultural labor migration northward to Michigan. They briefly work as agricultural laborers, until their musical ability is discovered by other workers who pay the Mendozas to sing.

1930–1932   After the onset of the Great Depression, the Mendozas leave Michigan and return to Houston, then San Antonio, where they play for change at Haymarket Square.

1933   Mendoza wins a singing contest and gains popularity through radio performances.

1934–1940   Lydia Mendoza records her first solo hit, "Mal Hombre," on RCA Victor's Bluebird label. Virtually all of her releases become widely popular. In these years, she tours as a solo singer, accompanied by her family's variety show. In 1937 they are booked in California for the first time.

1935–1940   Lydia Mendoza marries Juan Alvarado in 1935. Their first daughter (Lydia Alvarado Dávila) is born in 1935; their second daughter (Yolanda Alvarado Hernández) is born in 1937; their third daughter (María Leonor "Nora" Alvarado Salazar) is born in 1941.

1941–1945	During the Second World War, recording and touring cease because gasoline is strictly rationed.
1947–1954	Mendoza resumes recording and touring with her family variety show. She releases "Celosa," "Amor de Madre," "Pajarito Herido," "Al Pie de Tu Reja," "Besando la Cruz," "Joaquin Murrieta," and other songs that also become hits. The variety show ceases to exist when Lydia's mother dies in 1954.
1954–1987	Mendoza continues touring throughout the United States and Mexico and Latin America. She records with various companies: the Falcón, Ideal, RCA Victor, Columbia, and DLB labels. In the 1940s and 1950s, she begins to perform in theaters. In the 1960s, she begins to also perform at festivals—including the Smithsonian Festival of American Folklife in Montreal—and at university campuses. Her first husband dies in 1961. In 1964 she marries Fred Martínez.
1977–1987	In 1977 Mendoza performs at the inauguration of Pres. Jimmy Carter. In 1982 she teaches as a guest lecturer at California State University at Fresno. At home (in Houston) she continues to perform in small clubs and restaurants and at private parties. In 1982 she also becomes one of the first recipients of the National Heritage Fellowship Award from the National Endowment for the Arts. In 1987 Lydia Mendoza's career ends due to a debilitating stroke.
1991	Mendoza is inducted into the Conjunto Hall of Fame by the Guadalupe Cultural Arts Center in San Antonio.
1999	Mendoza receives the National Medal of the Arts from Pres. Bill Clinton at the White House; this is the highest national award for performers.

Lydia Mendoza's Life in Music /
La historia de Lydia Mendoza

Lydia Mendoza. Graphite drawing by Estér Hernández (1999). Courtesy
Estér Hernández

I

Let's weave that story by telling it

P eople have told me to write my life story, but . . . I don't know. In order to do that I want to be at peace, tranquil, without engagements where I have to leave town and go here and there. No, it's not that I'm a nervous person. But when I have to leave town I worry so much about not forgetting this and that. Then I wish I were already there and back in order to do this thing or another. In short: so many obligations, and I have no peace of mind. So this has been my idea: I told my daughter Nora—because she knows a lot about my life and I can talk with her—I told her, "Look, *mi'ja*, I'm getting the urge to do this."

I've already talked about a part of my life a lot. But I've told it in bits and pieces, you see. It's not woven together in one piece. No. I want to buy some cassettes and tell that story from the beginning: how I started, what it was like, and how my career developed. I want to leave behind my life story, the truth of it. That's the idea I've had. After all of this has been recorded, someone can listen to it, and if they think it's important, it can be written down; if not, then nothing is lost. Don't you think so? That way people don't need to be asking me about my life anymore, nor wasting their time. Bit by bit we'll weave that story by telling it.

Once I shared this idea with a *compadre*[1]—he's a great man. And he told me, "No, *comadre*, don't even think about doing that because people look for morbidity in books."

He said that people are looking for things like whether I had love affairs in my lifetime, or whether I was in love and that sort of thing. Well, frankly, there's been none of that in my life, in all my long life. There's nothing in my life that could interest whoever wants to read that kind of book. But I think he's mistaken, because I just bought a book—it came from Laredo—about the life of María Félix. The truth is that we're all interested in well-known people, right? Who's not interested in knowing how she got started, who discovered her, where she went, or what her beginnings were? We all want to know about a person such as her, right? With all the audiences I've had in all the years, if a book were to be written about my life—I do believe that there will be someone who will say, "I want to know how Lydia Mendoza got started."

3

Lydia Mendoza in 1948. Courtesy U.T. The Institute of Texan Cultures, the *San Antonio Light* Collection

That's what some families have always asked me: How did I get started? Or whether I have a book about my life? What is the history of my music? I think it could be done. Even though I think that if I don't live to see it . . . well, my daughters will. And I would like this book to have photographs and all. I know that if someone is determined to do it, and thinks they can find the money to do this, they can do it. Because it costs money to get it done, you see, like to publish photographs of one's life—like those you see in books. All that, you see?

When I arrived in San Antonio, there were no women singers

 Well, you know there are few women, Mexican women, who have cultivated an uninterrupted career in music and who have dedicated themselves to it body and soul. . . . It's rare, believe me. There are almost none. Nowadays it's much easier to build a career. In those days we didn't have the means. When I began in music—I was about nine years old—we lived in Monterrey, Mexico, and I already played my guitar. The songs we sang at the beginning were from my mother's repertoire. She sang all those songs. She knew them. But I felt like learning more songs, you see, aside from what I had learned from mamá. I just wanted to learn something. But how? There was no way.

Well, I remember once mamá sent me on an errand to buy something or other. She gave me a cent, but what I bought didn't cost a whole cent, and so I bought a piece of gum with the leftover change. That gum was in a little piece of paper that was twisted shut on both ends, and a song was written on that little piece of paper. After I realized this, I bought gum with all the bits of change I could get a hold of. That's how I started up a collection of about twenty or twenty-five gum wrapper songs. And I would look at them: you'd find songs like "La Mocosita," "El Tango Negro," "La Adelita," "Cuatro Milpas," "El Adolorido," "Ladrillo," "Todo Por Tí" . . . so many songs that I can't remember them all. So I would look at those little gum wrappers and say: "I wonder how the melody goes . . ." So many songs, you see, and I didn't know the music. Well, after this story I'll tell you how I learned the melodies. That was in Monterrey about 1926, a year before we came to the United States for good.

But before coming to the United States for good, we were always going back and forth. We'd spend a year in Texas and then a year in Monterrey [Mexico], because papá worked on the railroad; not on the tracks, but rather as a locomotive mechanic. Sometimes they would assign him for a season here or there. We'd be in Monterrey and then, well, "You've got to go to Texas, to the United States."

They'd send him to San Antonio, to Houston, to Beaumont, and so forth. So half of the family were born in Monterrey, like my sisters Juanita and María, and Francisca who died. The rest of us were born here in the United States. Me, a sister—the oldest sister—and the two brothers were born here in the United States. There were seven of us. But Francisca has already died. Francisca is dead, so there are only six of us left.

At the time we were always traveling, you see. A season here and a season there. That's how I first came to San Antonio in 1923. Well. Later we immigrated, in '27, and we lived some time in the Rio Grande Valley. We lived in Kingsville when the ad appeared in *La Prensa* announcing that they needed singers to record. By that time, when we immigrated, papá had already retired from the railroad; he didn't work anymore. We then dedicated ourselves to music, and I loved music.

Cuarteto Carta Blanca at the time of their first recording (1928). *Left to right*: Leonor Zamarripa Mendoza, Lydia Mendoza, Francisco Mendoza, Francisca ("Panchita") Mendoza. Courtesy Lydia Mendoza Collection

I was the, how shall I say it, the principal axis—"Let's keep it up, let's . . ."

At the time I was playing mandolin and mamá played guitar; my sister Panchita played a little triangle and papá a tambourine. We formed a quartet, the Cuarteto Carta Blanca, and we traveled throughout the entire Rio Grande Valley singing for Mexicans, you see. And when papá saw the ad, well, we went to San Antonio. So we recorded in 1928. As soon as we recorded we left San Antonio. As a matter of fact, we didn't even hear any of the recordings.

Someone or other convinced papá that up north [in the United States] we could make us a lot of money with the music we played. Because at that time many people would go there to work in the beet harvest and do other work. Entire Mexican families would go up there. And in all of those places like Detroit, Pontiac, Flint, and other places in Michigan there was no musical entertainment and people were desperate. In those years there was really nothing. Well, I don't know who convinced papá that the music we played would bring us a lot of money up north. So one morning he came and announced to mamá: "Someone told me that up in the state of Michigan, up north, we can make better money than here."

Mamá said—we were very poor and had nothing—mamá said: "Ay, Pancho, you're crazy. How can we go up north if we barely made it here from the valley?[2] How?"

"Oh, I know how we'll go."

And I said, "Yes, papá."

"You and your papá are crazy. How are we going to leave?"

She thought we were nuts. So, nothing more was said about it. Two days later papá arrived with some papers in his hand: "The matter is settled."

"So what is that?"

"Work contracts, papá?"

"Yes, we're going to work the beet fields."

Well you know he went and contracted us! They were recruiting a lot of people. It was the season—in April—when they take people under contract. Contracts to go north. They would travel by train and bus. Well, papá made the arrangements, and mamá said: "Well, don't even think I'm going to spend my time among the weeds up there! Not me, I've never done that. Don't sign me up . . . No!" she said.

"I just contracted myself and two daughters . . ."

It was three of us who were supposed to work.

Well, finally we left. We arrived in Detroit and went on to Flint, Michigan. We arrived there at our place of work. Once there we went to the commissary and papá bought us some pants—those solid blue ones—so we could begin to work in the beet fields, thinning the crops. There were these little plants . . . But what did we know about *that*? Little plants like this with some little leaves which were the beets. The worker's responsibility was to cut all but two leaves, to take off the rest, so that not too many would grow. Just two little leaves. Well, we arrived. So what were we supposed to do? Well, we were supposed to thin plants.

Papá would say, "No big deal. Just leave two leaves on the plant."

But we just didn't know how, you see. We were supposed to take the little plant and . . . oh no, we'd pull too hard—well, we'd uproot the whole plant! We committed mass murder in all the furrows. What did we know!

"Well, I don't know, papá, the whole plant comes out."

"So be careful. Don't be a dummy!"

"See . . . uh . . ."

Well, we never got the hang of it. To make a long story short, the next Saturday we sat outside, practicing and singing like we always did. We were very happy, singing there, when two Mexicans passed by from the other plantation, you see. They stopped and one of them said, "Oh, how beautifully you sing! What are you doing here?"

"Well, brother, we came to work here."

"Well, why don't you go to town? Pontiac is nearby. There's a little restaurant, the only one, a small Mexican inn, and you know, the place gets packed. We all go crazy because there's no entertainment here."

So papá said, "Well, yes, but how will we get there? We have no way to get there."

"Do you want to go?"

"Well of course, let's entertain *la raza*!"[3]

"Well, you know what? If you want to go next Saturday I'll tell an Anglo there on the plantation where we work. He has a little car," he said, "and he's really good people. I'm sure if I ask him to take us, he'll take us."

"Fine, that's fine."

Well, the following Saturday they came and took us. We never returned. They took us there on a Saturday. We sang and sang. You should have seen: they gave us stacks of dollars this high! There were also lots of coins, but mainly piles of dollars—"Sing this one!" "Yes, of course!"

We didn't even name a price, nor did they ask how much. "Here you go!"

And they would put down piles of money, this high, see? So we did really well that Saturday. People would ask us: "Where have you been?" "What are you doing over there?" "Why don't you come stay in town?"

And then papá said, "It's because we have a contract."

"No, no, no," the man said, "many people sign contracts and break them. No one ever looks for those people. If you like, we'll pick you up tomorrow morning. Do you have furniture?"

"No, we don't have anything; just our clothes."

And it was true. We had nothing. Well, the following Sunday they took us to that place. We packed our few belongings, they took us to town, and we never went back. And they didn't look for us.

We stayed there in Michigan for two years. Papá began working right away. We stayed a while in Pontiac and were there when 1929 hit. We lived in Pontiac only about nine months, from April, May, June, July, August, September, October, November . . . almost a year. As soon as the year was up, papá went to Detroit to do the same work. He said he no longer liked Pontiac because there were more raza in Detroit, there were more Mexican people. Papá said to us: "I'm going there to look for work. As soon as I find work, I'll rent a house and we'll go to Detroit."

"That's fine with me," mamá said.

So he left and got work at Ford right away. He found a house and we went to live in Detroit. That's where one of my brothers was born, Andrés, the youngest. And as always we kept up the music. We would sing for the September 16th and May 5th festivities. There was nothing else back in those days, you see. We were the only Mexicans who performed music.

Then the depression hit in '29, and they began to lay people off. Papá was one of the first because he hadn't worked there for long. So when the depression hit, papá said, "We're not staying here. Let's go back to Texas again."

So we returned by car and arrived in Texas in 1930. We arrived at the end of 1930; around October we arrived in Houston. We settled there, because one of my foster sisters lived there. She lived in Sugarland, a town outside of Houston. And we stayed there for part of '30 and '31. We lived in Houston for a year and some months. But in those days Houston didn't have any entertainment, either. Right now, Houston is becoming sort of like San Antonio. Very pretty, lots of ambience, many artists, and everything. But in those days there was nothing. So papá said, "No, let's go to San Antonio instead."

And that's how we arrived in San Antonio in 1932. When we arrived in San Antonio, we always had our music, see. And of course there was more ambience there—at least in those days there was. And there was the Plaza del Zacate [Haymarket Square]. Did you ever hear of the Plaza del Zacate? Where the Mercado is now, that's where the Plaza del Zacate used to be. That's where it was, all outdoors. There was none of what you see there today. There was just

Haymarket Square (Plaza del Zacate) in the years when the Mendoza family played there (1930s). Courtesy U.T. The Institute of Texan Cultures, the *San Antonio Light* Collection

this very big plaza where the vegetable trucks from the valley arrived. They would arrive at midnight, bringing their merchandise. All the retailers at the small stands would go there and stock up, you see. But from seven in the evening to eleven-thirty at night the space was not occupied. That's when they'd set up tables on the outside walkway. There they would sell enchiladas, tamales, chile con carne, and so forth. There were some tables on one side and some on the other and between them a space where cars would enter and stop to listen to the trios of singers. There was nothing but guitar trios. There were no accordions, none of that. Because in those days the accordion was unknown. Just guitars. There were only guitar trios.

So that's where we set up as a group. The singers who were there totaled about fifteen groups in all. Those poor guys would run as soon as a car came in: "What shall we sing for you? 'La Adelita'?" That's because Anglos also came, you see, to have dinner and listen to the music. But we didn't work like that; instead we set up on a corner. There was a lady who had a small stall—she gave us permission to sit there. It was to her benefit since people would come over to where the music was and it was good for business, see. And that's how we eked out a living.

When we started the group there, I already played the violin, and my little sister played the mandolin. I taught María to play the mandolin; mamá, of course, played the guitar, and one of my little brothers played the triangle. And

The Mendoza family played at one of the *baratillos* (cheap food stands) such as this one at Haymarket Square (early 1930s). Courtesy U.T. The Institute of Texan Cultures, the *San Antonio Light* Collection

we sang there. I already knew how to play guitar, because I had learned to play guitar since I was seven years old. My mother taught me. She was the one who taught me.

But initially I didn't even remotely think I had a voice. Nor did I then even dream of becoming a singer, or think I could sing or any of that! I liked music, playing the guitar, instruments. Like I said, I learned the guitar, then the mandolin and the violin, and some piano, by ear. The only instrument mamá taught me was the guitar, but I learned the rest of the instruments by myself. At times when I was home I'd suddenly feel the urge to sing some song, just by myself, you see, to learn some song. And sometimes when our group was out singing I would tell mamá, "Hand me the guitar so I can sing a song."

What I wanted was to be heard. I don't know what was going on in my mind, you see. But before you knew it I began to sing by myself.

So, to make a long story short, there came a time when the whole group hardly sang at all anymore. People would say, "No, we want to hear Señorita Mendoza sing. We want her to sing it . . ."

So then I began to learn many songs. That's how I began singing without at all thinking that I would become a singer or anything like that. I just liked to be heard and I liked to sing.

On one of those occasions—I think—the word began to spread about a young woman who sang well. One night a radio announcer came; he arrived in his car and stopped to listen to us. I was singing at that moment. As soon as I finished singing, he got out of the car and went to speak to mamá: "Ma'am. Mrs. Mendoza, the young lady sings beautifully." He says, "I have a radio program. It's only half an hour, but it has a big audience. And it's the only program we have in San Antonio."

And it's true. It was the only Spanish-language program that existed at the time, you see. His program was called El Programa de la Voz Latina [The Latino Voice Program]. I don't remember the name of the radio station, but this program was the only one of its kind.

So he says: "I'd like to take the young woman to sing a couple of songs for us. She has a very lovely voice, and I assure you she can accomplish something."

"Well, I'm very sorry, sir, but this is how we make a living. If we leave this spot here, what will become of us? This is how we make a living."

"Well, just for one night. She has nothing to lose. It'll be good for her. At least she'll be heard, and it can open up a new future."

"Yes, mamá, I want to go on the radio."

"All right, sir, we'll go."

"OK, I'll come tomorrow, take you both there, and bring you back."

Well, he did take me, and I went and sang. I was happy as a lark because I had sung on the radio. But that wasn't all. About three days later the man came back again. "Mrs. Mendoza," he says, "I've received many requests for Miss Mendoza. They say they want to hear that voice again."

"Well, I'm very sorry, Mr. Cortéz"—that was his name, Mr. Cortéz—"no, we can't do it because we'll lose out."

He says, "What if I get Miss Mendoza a sponsor, an ad that will pay for her air time? That will be a great help for you," he said.

"Well, if they pay her something, yes," she said, "but otherwise, no."

"Well, let's see. I'll let you know."

He went and got me an ad. It paid three-fifty [$3.50], but it had to be all week. In those days it was a huge amount of money, you know. Three-fifty was a lot of money. Everything was much cheaper then . . . We paid a dollar twenty-five for rent. Imagine! Food cost—a pound of meat cost fifteen cents. A bottle of milk was a nickel. Everything was very cheap, so three-fifty was a small fortune. So I finally went and began to sing there. It got to a point where I no longer wanted . . . we no longer went to sing at Plaza del Zacate. He didn't want us to do it anymore.

"No, Miss Mendoza is becoming very famous, she's making a name for herself, and I don't want her singing at Plaza del Zacate for whatever money people give her, no. I'm going to make her a star. I'm going to make her a star because she has a very lovely voice. Just wait and see: I'll help her."

So this man helped us. What he did was to find us little gigs in restaurants. Because in those days there were no bars, no beer yet, nothing. But there were many restaurants or food stores. He booked us for an hour at a food store, and then at a restaurant, and so forth, to the point where I no longer went to the plaza. And then he organized—or looked for a contest, a contest sponsored by El Ferro Vitamina [iron tonic]. I entered and won second place, because some little boys won first. But at any rate I won second place.

Mr. Cortéz said, "No, I want to see you come out on top!"

So he looked for another contest; this time it was sponsored by Pearl Beer. That one did have a sponsor. The contest lasted about three or four months. They eliminated those who had the least number of votes. In the end only three of us were left. Me and two other girls were left, and I won first place.

But, anyway, I don't want to go on about that. What I wanted to tell you is that when I arrived in San Antonio, there were no women singers. No one sang. Many women singers began to emerge during that Pearl Beer contest. Many women singers did come forward then. Among them were Eva Garza—I think you've heard of her—Esperanza Espino, the Fernández Sisters, Rosita Fernández and her sister. Many groups of women singers emerged. Of those women singers, the only one who accomplished something—who made a career but outside of San Antonio—was Eva Garza. When I began to record, she also recorded, but nothing came of it, you see? Later she emerged; she came to public attention when she went on tour with an artist. She toured all the way to New York.

And as I was telling you, almost all the women who emerged in San Antonio during the time I began didn't stick to it; they didn't last very long. Eva Garza was the only one who became famous when she went off with that artist, a so-called Sally Green, I think, a woman who was a fan dancer. She did variety shows and took Eva Garza with her on tour after hearing her sing. And it was on that tour that she went all the way to New York. At the time the group El Charro Gil y Sus Caporales was in New York. They were doing a program in New York. It was then that the variety show with Eva Garza came to town, and I think Eva Garza went to see them at the radio station. There she fell in love with Charro Gil. They both fell in love. Then Charro Gil left the group. The Caporales remained by themselves; Charro Gil took off with Eva Garza and they went on tour. He toured with her to Cuba and other places after they married. The Trío Los Caporales stayed in New York and later became Trío Los Panchos. That's how Los Panchos began, who in fact made a big name and career for themselves to this day, you see. But, as I told you, in San Antonio Eva Garza did not accomplish much.

We toiled and toiled

 Well, let me tell you. What I'm about to say right now I've almost never ever talked about. Or, rather, I've never spoken of it in the many interviews that have been done with me. Like I was telling you, when we returned from the state of Michigan we went to Houston, and then from Houston we moved to San Antonio—that was in the year 1932. I hadn't recorded yet. No one knew who Lydia Mendoza was or anything. Of course, within the artistic community, we were already organized, united; my mother, as well as my siblings, papá, and everyone. We arrived in San Antonio looking for a better means to earn a living, to make a bit more money.

We had a little Ford, an old car. So my father had the idea to do an artistic tour

Lydia Mendoza at age 17, when she first recorded "Mal Hombre" (1933).
Courtesy Houston Metropolitan Research Center, Houston Public Library

as a group, you see. Then mamá prepared my brothers and sisters by teaching them comic sketches and song numbers, with guitars and everything. We organized a little trip to the valley—out toward the Rio Grande Valley—in that little car we had. Without—as I told you—without any contracts. Without anything. We just headed out on an adventure, to see what God would provide [*laughter*].

I remember that in those years the cars had running boards. Do you remember that they had running boards? They called them running boards. Do you know what that is? Well, where you stepped out of the car, it had something that fit like a platform or like a cover, you see. That's where we even carried a mattress, blankets, a petrol stove with one or two burners, pans . . . in short, we were equipped with everything so we wouldn't have problems anywhere we arrived. That's how we took off. We went straight there, driving. We went to the valley, and papá fixed up some cardboards and wrote: "The Mendoza Family. Variety Show. Lydia Mendoza." But at that time no one knew who Lydia Mendoza was. He wrote: "Lydia Mendoza, the guitarist, and the Comic Sketch Variety Show." He made the signs with a thick pencil. All of that was prepared beforehand.

I don't remember anymore what little town we arrived at, and a man said:

"Well, yeah." He said, "there is a little hall if you want to work. Do you have any advertisement?"

"Yes," papá said. "We've got this poster here and everything."

He showed them to him, and we were off to a start. We organized the performance. That's how we did it. Then the man provided us with a room; we unloaded all the stuff we had brought like the little stove, the mattress, and the blankets. We spent the night there. And that's how we toured throughout the entire valley working in little halls. Not in theaters because they wouldn't give us work in the theaters. We started like that in the little halls. Those were our first artistic adventures back in the year 1932. After that, we returned to San Antonio again. It was something small, you see, but we had our little group that could hold its own. And that's how people gave us a chance to work.

We made it through that first adventure traveling with our pillows and our blankets, the mattress and everything, you see. Even a little stove, pots, plates, everything ready for wherever we might stay. But we didn't rent a place because we barely made a few cents from the little show we put on. Not enough to rent a room or a hotel. Instead, we were usually allowed to spend the night right there in the same hall where we performed. So that's where we would set up our dormitory, and the next morning we'd cook whatever we could and eat. Then we would continue on the adventure. Every new place we arrived, papá would ask the person in charge for permission to spend the night. And they would allow us to stay there. We were a family, right? My mother, my siblings, papá, and me. We'd spend the night and the next day the same thing. And that's how we traveled across the whole valley and the little towns, working and gathering a little money. Then we would return again to San Antonio, and the same routine would start all over again.

We would try to hit the little towns where the pickers gathered during the harvest seasons. Especially Fridays and Saturdays. We'd arrive at a little town and ask permission to do a performance at a little restaurant or on a street corner. Often the restaurants wouldn't allow us in. So we'd sing outside, and everyone would gather around. All the people who would come into town to shop on Saturdays. The people were just milling around, since in those days there weren't even any dance halls. There was nothing. It was very different from life today, you see? In those years there was none of that. A dance? Well, no! . . . There was nowhere to dance, and they didn't dance! There were no festivities, no dances, none of that. The poor people who worked would go into town on Saturday just to pass the time. They would just walk the streets, go buy an ice cream, anything . . . Because to make matters worse there was so much discrimination against Mexicans. Mexicans could not enter restaurants. If there was a restaurant, they could not eat there. If they were Mexicans, they were not allowed. If it wasn't a Mexican place, they could not enter that place. They couldn't go in and buy something because they would not be served. Mexicans have always . . . you know. So we would arrive and create a fanfare with our music. We would sit there on a corner, and we would stay there . . . They'd let us use some benches, or whatever. That's where we'd start to sing; people would gather around us and give us whatever they wanted to give. We didn't charge, you see, but we did make good money during the picking season. And that was our existence—earning and struggling in life. That's why I tell you that my career began at the very bottom: working hard and struggling until God finally granted a change in my lucky star. I recorded and our life changed.

But at the beginning, nearly all of '32, we toiled a lot in the towns we toured outside of San Antonio. And there were times when we would even run out of gas. Once I remember we were traveling . . . where were we going? I don't know what town we were going to. We left home before daybreak to go to another town. And on the way, well, we ran out of gas. Papá had money to pay for gas, but there was just one gas station on the road and they didn't want to get up to give us gas. No matter how much we knocked, they wouldn't get up; they refused to get up. Papá would call to them: "We're out of gas, brother."

They ignored us until morning about eight. So we had to wait there until daylight. It was still dark out and it was winter. This was in the month of December, down toward the Rio Grande Valley. What we did was pull over to the side of the road and papá went into the brush to collect branches and firewood. We built a fire and kept warm by the fire until daybreak when they sold us the gas. And we had many experiences like this on the road. All of that during our tours in 1932; we toiled throughout that whole year.

Then in '33 we didn't do very well. We didn't have much work. So we decided it was best to stay in San Antonio at the Plaza del Zacate and try our luck. Everything was fine as long as it didn't rain. When it rained, we didn't make anything. And this was our livelihood, because every day we lived from hand to mouth. I remember we'd collect only about twenty-five to thirty cents per night, because people were really poor. We would sing a song, and my little sister María would go around with a small plate to see if they could help us out. So they'd throw in a cent, two cents, a nickel, a dime. That was it. Then we would leave and arrive home. The next morning, mamá would send me to the store. We would buy a nickel of *masa*, a nickel bottle of milk, a nickel's worth of lard, and so on. That was our daily living. On Saturday and Sunday we'd make enough to pay the rent, which was one twenty-five a week. We paid about five dollars a month, which was cheap, see. And so it went. As I told you, we toiled all of '32 and suffered and suffered. That struggle of ours began since '27— since we immigrated to the United States—1927, '28, '29, '30, '31, and '32. Five years until our luck changed a little in '33.

We immigrated to the United States in 1927. Well, we had been going back and forth, as I told you, many times. But the last time was in '27, because mamá got so tired of coming and going with papá's work. We had been in Monterrey for two years with papá working there.

Then papá says that we're going to the United States. So mamá got tired and said to him: "Look, every year, every two years, there we go again, we have to leave."

Every time we'd arrive at a town, we would settle into a place, a house. We'd buy furniture and everything. And suddenly it was "Let's go!" and everything would come undone and be sold. It was back to the United States again. And we would come here, and then the whole thing would repeat itself. We would begin to work, make a home, and within a year it was back to Monterrey. And that's how it went, you see?

But then, the last time mamá said: "Well, I don't want to go back to the United States to start all over again."

"Come on, let's go; let's go."

"No. I'm tired of traveling like gypsies. We're staying here, or we're going there. If we go, that's fine, let's go. But I'm not coming back. I want to stay here in Mexico, but if you want to go back again to the United States, I'm not coming back here because that's enough, I'm tired," she said. "That business of running around without knowing where my home is."

Us kids liked it better over here on the [U.S.] side. We said: "Come on, mamá, let's go!"

"OK, we're going, but I'm not coming back here."

And papá said, "Yes, yes, that's fine." Papá also wanted that.

So we immigrated and didn't return. Within a year, papá wanted to go back to Mexico. Then mamá said: "No."

"Well then, let's see what you'll do, because I can't get a good job here. I don't want to work on the railroad anymore. Who knows what we'll live on."

"Well, we will make it any way we can," mamá said. "But I'm not going back to Mexico. I already told you that if we came here I was staying here. I wanted to stay in Mexico, but you wanted to come here. Fine."

So that's how we stayed. Papá stopped working [on the railroad], and we devoted ourselves to music. Like I said: from '27 to '33 that's what we did; we toiled and toiled. Some days were good, others bad, and . . . well, that's how those years passed.

I don't know of another musical group like ours. There was none. I think we were the first. Only in San Antonio could you find a musical ambience there in the plaza. But on tour I saw no musicians that traveled like we did. No. Not struggling and touring. Later, after many years some [groups] appeared who would go out on tour. A few little groups. But at the beginning, as I told you how we started—even in the valley when we arrived in '27—there was no music. There was nothing. We traveled across the whole valley, but I never met any groups of musicians. There were no groups. There was nothing. Just us.

Nowadays it's different, and there is a big musical ambience and everything. So many groups have appeared that we don't know what to do with all of them! Every day new accordion players, ensembles, groups of young people appear. There is so much [musical] ambience, so much music. But back in those years there was nothing. Nothing at all. They didn't even like the accordion. They didn't even know it. That came about later.

The accordion didn't make an appearance until—I'll tell you right now—until about 1940. I say someone got the idea to transpose Mexican *ranchera* music to the accordion. Over in New Braunfels [Texas], there are many, many, many Germans, many Poles, many of those peoples. At the time, there was a special radio program in San Antonio—I remember when it started up they used to play only German music. You know, that German music is like polkas. They would play them on accordions, you see. But they were piano-accordions. Then someone got the idea of using one of those accordions like they use now, the *norteño* accordion. The idea of transposing Mexican ranchera music to the button accordion was born and began to develop. So as it developed, the people began to like it. Whichever the first group might have been, the fact is that many groups began to emerge. One of the first was Santiago Jiménez—not the young one but his father. Also Narciso Martínez. Valerio Longoria.

And that's how I began to learn my songs

We always had music at home, and I was born with that talent. Papá bought a guitar for my mother. And what she had inside awakened: her talent, her music. I remember real well. I was about—well, it was in 1920—I was about four years old. I remember that as soon as papá got home from work we would eat dinner, and then me and my little sister would go out to play. As soon as mamá was done, she would take her guitar and sit with papá. The two of them would sing there. And as soon as I would hear the guitar, I'd come there running—I would run and sit at their feet. I inherited that musical gift from my mother. She was the one who taught me, like I told you, and there was always music at home. There wasn't a party where my father didn't take my mother and present her. All my uncles were against papá. They haggled over this music business. They thought that . . . artists were not good people and all that sort of thing, you know. At any rate . . . that's how we always had music at home in that form and I was born with that talent.

I want to finish telling you this so I don't forget it. Let's not forget this. Do you remember that we began to chat about the gum wrapper songs I collected— and that I wondered about the melodies? Well, we lived then in Monterrey in the Bella Vista neighborhood. It was a very poor neighborhood—which is unrecognizable to me now. It has changed a lot. But in those days, there was nothing in that neighborhood. It was very humble, very poor. But my mother's family always lived there. They had their little houses there, and we always lived there. Whenever we lived in Mexico, we'd stay in that neighborhood. So I put together a song collection; I would ask myself how the melodies for those songs might sound.

Well then, where we lived there was a little store where they sold all sorts of things. They even sold beer and wood, and corn and everything, Mexico style, you see? And one Saturday mamá sent me to buy something or other. I was buying that thing—it was Saturday, and there were many people buying. At that moment, four male musicians arrived. One of them had one of those instruments . . . the flute. Do you know it? Well, they're black, you see, it's a black instrument; it's the flute. They had a flute, a double bass, a *bajo sexto*, and a violin. They were elderly gentlemen who came to ask the owner if he would let them play outside, for whatever money people would give them.

Then the owner said to them: "Don't come here to bother me; I can't pay you."

"No, we're not charging you anything; just give us permission."

"No, no. You're going to cause a ruckus here. No, no, I don't want a lot of noise here."

Then I turned to the owner—the elderly owner loved me very much. His name was Don Pablito: "Oh, Don Pablito, why don't you let them play? They aren't charging you anything. Maybe they'll liven up the people here, and you'll get more business. Don't you think so?"

"Oh, this little girl! Well, all right let them play outside."

But I did it with an ulterior motive: to see if I could hear some of those songs I had collected, you see. Well as soon as he said yes, I ran home, dropped off whatever my mother had sent me to buy, and I left. I had a small box where I kept my little gum wrapper songs. I ran. Behind the store there was a sort of little alley, and that's where I stood to listen. And that's where the hubbub of the people began; they began to request songs from the men. They played some of the ones I had. Well, they came back for three Saturdays. On those three Saturdays I stood there transfixed; listening to everything. During those three Saturdays I learned the melodies for the whole collection I had. And that's how I got my start. I was in the dark, alone, you see, because no one paid me much mind. I learned my guitar. I would sit there, but no one paid attention to whether or not I was singing. And I wanted to sing because I already played the guitar.

I was about ten years old; it was '26. I was almost ten. Well, anyhow, I learned my songs and I sang them by myself, without anyone's help. It happened that papá then heard me singing a song. He went to mamá and said, "Listen, Leonor"—they spoke to each other formally (using *Usted*). He said, "Listen, Leonor, guess what? Have you heard Lydia sing? Sounds like she has a voice."

Mamá said, "Oh, really? Well, I'll look into it."

Then one day she called me and said, "Let's see how you sing, *hija*. Let's see. Sing a song."

So I sang one for her; I think it was "La Hija del Carcelero" ["The Jailer's Daughter"]—the first one I learned. So mamá listened to me. Then they began to see that I had a good singing voice. But even then no one imagined—nor did I ever think—that I was to become a singer or anything. So you see how many years it took for me to establish my career. I was devoted to learning, to having a repertoire, and to persisting with the music.

After learning how to play the guitar I learned—right there in Monterrey— to play the mandolin by myself. There was a little neighbor boy who lived across the street. His parents wanted him to learn to play the mandolin. The little boy was always sitting at the window and plucking! He would pluck it and pluck it! But he couldn't make music. I would walk by and watch: "Well, I think I can play that instrument."

I watched him trying to eke out a tune, but the little boy couldn't do it. Then one day I went to my father and said, "Papá I want to play . . . I want to play an instrument I don't even know what it's called. Remember the neighbors' kid across the street?"

"Oh, yes," he says, "the one whose parents want him to play the mandolin."

"Oh, it's a mandolin. Well I can play it, papá."

"Oh, Lydia, you're crazy! Who's going to teach you?"

"Well, I think if I can get my hands on it I can make some music."

"Well, we'll see." That's what he told me.

The next afternoon, papá came home with a mandolin. I don't know where he got it. It was one of those little fat ones, you know. Like mandolins are. He said, "There's your precious mandolin. Let's see how you're going to learn."

Oh, I was so happy to hold it in my hands. Right away I began to sound it out, and I learned quickly: "La Pajarera" ["The Bird Keeper"] was in fact the first piece I learned on the mandolin. I didn't play it real well, but I figured it out. I figured out the chords, you see. And the next day when papá came in the afternoon I told him, "Look, I can already play this piece."

Oh, he was so happy. I did it badly, but he said, "Wow, you do it very well. Well done."

So I pushed ahead, and I learned to play the mandolin by myself. After I learned to play the mandolin, you see, when we immigrated to the United — States, I was already playing it well. And mamá, of course, played the guitar. The years went by, and I learned to play the violin just by watching. I learned without teachers. Just by watching whatever players I could observe.

I see an instrument and I say: I can play it. No one taught me how to play the piano, either. And I didn't find it difficult. When I finally got hold of a piano, I played it. I recently bought an organ, the kind that looks like a piano. And I am practicing. You know, I can really play it! I just put my mind to playing something, and I can play it. It's because I already have a musical sense, you see. That's why no instrument is difficult for me. Even the bass fiddle. Once I went to a party, and I gave it a whirl, and . . . [she laughs a lot].

I remember that my father really loved theater. Back in those years, well, there were no movies, but there was theater. Great variety shows from Mexico came and went. I remember that María Conesa, Virginia Fábregas, and other great theater companies came. Whenever they came, they always performed at the Independence Theater in Monterrey, the largest theater in Monterrey. Nowadays it might be another one, but in those years it was the main theater. And every time a variety show came, well, great performers came. They brought what is called a variety show: singers, popular song shows, dancers, and a bit of everything. At one point I think María Conesa came or Doña Virginia Fábregas. The point is that papá made arrangements to take my mother to the theater. And he always took us two older kids, me and my sister Beatriz. Yes, they would take us too. I guess I was about ten years old. That performance featured a singer doing the song "Mal Hombre" ["Evil Man"], a young woman who sang very beautifully. I don't remember her name. And just from that one time I heard it, I learned the melody . . . the lyrics I think also came in those gum wrappers . . . yes, because otherwise I wouldn't have been able to learn the words very well. But I did learn the melody that night. And that's how I began to learn my songs. As the years passed "Mal Hombre" was always considered one of my songs; because I liked the song, you see. And everyone thinks it's mine because the composer is unknown. No one has claimed it. People say and think that song is mine, but it's not. It's not mine.

In San Antonio they never paid me for my work

 Well, I'll tell you I built my career in San Antonio, and I'm very happy, very content, very grateful. But in San Antonio they never paid me for my work. There was hardly any work there, and they didn't pay. There was nothing. There was a club called El Cubano. Did you ever hear of it? It was a club—I don't know if it still exists—it was upstairs. A club that stayed open until—well, I don't know—they would open until four in the morning. They probably weren't selling drinks at that hour . . . anyway, the owner— called "the Cuban"—once called me to ask if I was interested in working there the whole week. He just told me: "You have to give us a performance at about two A.M. . . . ."

"Well, sure," I told him. "For how much?"

"Well, I'll give you thirty dollars for the whole week."

Imagine! I said, "Thirty dollars for the whole week, sir?" I said, "No sir!"

He said, "Well, look, so and so comes here and the son of so and so."

"Well, find someone else," I said. "I won't do it for thirty dollars, no. I won't even do it for thirty dollars a night. No."

I lived in San Antonio because that's where my husband was raised. When I lived there I always traveled a lot on tour, lots of tours. After my mother died, they would call me for a contract and I would tell them, "Well, the group has broken up."

They would tell me, "It doesn't matter." "If you're willing to come, we'll fix you up with a filler of two or three artists, some dancers, or whatever," they'd say. "But we want you to perform only in movie theaters."

In California I did a tour, you see. I did it with Ramón Gay. Did you ever hear of him? He was an artist in Mexico. Ramón Gay and a trio of—violins—at any rate, it was a trío. I don't remember who the others were. Anyway, that's how I came to California. My daughter Nora used to travel with me then. She was a kid. She was my companion. And that's how I did my tours, you see. But . . . as I was I telling you I always toured. I had lots of work in New Mexico, Colorado, California. I would perform with other artists. But I wouldn't work in San Antonio because they wouldn't pay me.

Now that I live in Houston, however, they call me from San Antonio. I was there recently—when was I there?—well, at the beginning of March they called me from a club. They gave me two hundred dollars for a performance. Now that I'm in Houston, they call me to San Antonio to do performances over there. And they do pay me. But when I lived there they didn't pay me; they didn't want to pay me, you see. Nowadays there's a lot of competition. They'll do a dance and present three, four, five well-known groups, you see. But those groups just play half an hour, and then another group plays for another half hour. And so forth. They pay them a pittance. But, oh well . . . that's how it is.

When I started there in San Antonio, that man—rest in peace, he's dead now—helped me a great deal. He took me to sing on the radio, he organized the contest, and he did a lot of publicity for me. But I didn't make a cent. Just what I made on the radio and the little jobs I found on my own. But after he

Teatro Azteca poster announcing Lidya [*sic*] Mendoza and her variety show (Calexico, California, ca. 1940s). Courtesy Houston Metropolitan Research Center, Houston Public Library

entered me in contests, he'd say: "Well, Lydia, they'd like to meet you at such and such a place."

So I'd go. He was the one who got paid there. He didn't give me one cent. "Well they want you to go visit . . . " who knows where . . .

So there I go all the way to Seguín, Texas. I'd go wherever. He would take me to do a performance, to sing a few songs, and to announce that I was in the contest. I wouldn't make a cent, but he did make money. But I didn't care, be-

The Teatro Nacional in downtown San Antonio, ca. 1940s. Courtesy Zintgraff Collection, U.T. The Institute of Texan Cultures

cause he was helping me. That's why that whole season I worked, I didn't make a cent.

Even when he'd take me to the late shows, he'd say, "There's going to be a midnight show at the movie theater."

At the State Theater, I think. Yes, it was at the State. In those years artists could perform, you see, yet we weren't presented in ordinary performances, but instead after midnight. You'd see the long lines of people but not until after midnight. Lots of artists from Mexico would come, and the impresarios presented them at those movie theaters, especially at the State, or at the Zaragoza, or at the Nacional. But they were always midnight performances.

Well, at the time of that contest he announced: "We have to announce how the contestants are ranked, which are ahead or behind or whatever. I've organized a performance at the State Theater."

Well, all the women who performed got five dollars. I didn't get anything. The next day when I was on the radio, when I went to the program, one of the girls told me about the five dollars. With five dollars you could dazzle people in those days. Everything was very inexpensive. If you went to buy a pretty fancy dress, it didn't cost more than one ninety-eight. Shoes—good shoes that now cost you twenty or thirty dollars—you'd pay a dollar-fifty for them. So with five dollars, well, all the girls went crazy. Even I would have gone crazy.

They said to me: "Hey, imagine! They gave me five dollars!"

I said, "Who gave you five dollars?"

"Well, last night they gave it to us. Didn't you get your five dollars?"

"No, I didn't get anything," I said.

"Well, why not?" they'd ask. "We all got it."

He wouldn't give me anything. Well, it's like I told you. My promoter, he did make money. At the beginning he had an old clunker of a car. I'm talking about his life, not his death. About in a month or two, he already had a new car. And when all the people would see him, they'd say: "Look! Mr. Cortéz with a new car! Well, thanks to Lydia Mendoza."

Yes, the people noticed. And he gave me nothing, you see. But I didn't care, because part of what I am . . . he helped me a great deal.

What I'm telling you about happened a year after I arrived in San Antonio, or maybe less. Because we arrived in '32 and set up at the Plaza del Zacate. This happened in about . . . the beginning of '33. Yes, it was at the beginning of '33 that he discovered me. At the beginning of '33. That's when Mr. Cortéz made my name very famous there, with the contest and all of that, you see. But I didn't make any money. Yet I was happy with the little bit we worked there. I didn't want much . . . and, well, you could see that he helped me a great deal, see.

And then one day I got a contract to perform in Corpus Christi, Texas. I hadn't recorded yet. A manager went, and he heard me. Word of Lydia Mendoza's popularity had spread from San Antonio. They took me to Corpus [Christi] and paid me a hundred dollars a week—we thought it was a fortune! In fact . . . I had never made so much. And that man, he predicted it. He said, "I'm going to see to it that Miss Mendoza makes a hundred dollars a week!"

And it came true. Because that manager from Corpus [Christi] came and took me to perform there. It was a big event.

I don't know how much money the promoter made every time he booked me; that was every single night; don't think it was just once a week. I was on the radio program every night at seven o'clock in the evening, you see. And after the program he would arrive and say: "Lydia, you know some folks want to meet you, over in . . . " who knows where.

"Sure, of course!"

And he would take me—me and my mother, who would go with me.

Like I said, the radio paid me three-fifty. The one who paid me that three-fifty was Mr. García, the owner of Iron Tonic Vitamins. He would give me the three-fifty so I would sing courtesy of the tonic, you see, their ad. And that program was followed by Mr. Cortéz's program. It was for his program that he organized the Pearl Beer contest. And then I told him "But I won't be able to perform with mamá anymore. . ." [at the Plaza del Zacate].

Mamá also told him, "Well, she can't participate in that contest if it means she won't get that money from Mr. García anymore." She said, "That money really helps us."

He said, "No, no, no. He's going to pay Lydia anyway."

As a matter of fact, the girls who participated in the contest didn't like me. They were against me, because they thought I was getting paid and they weren't. So Mr. Cortéz would say, "Well, we pay her because she's sponsored by an ad. If you go and find an ad to sponsor you, then of course you get paid. But you've come for the contest, to see if you can win, right? So you can't be paid. Her, well she's being paid by the ad . . . not by me." he says.

And all of them were fit to be—well, they didn't like me!

As soon as that contest began, well, a lot of people began to say they wanted to meet me. Right after my program I did over the radio, Mr. Cortéz would say, "Well, Lydia . . . they want to meet you."

He would charge them and pocket the money, and he wouldn't give me a penny. So I'm telling you: in that sense he exploited me. Although that business with the contest and all that helped me a great deal because that's when they discovered me and asked me to record. They called me—it was a woman who took me. They went to see me and later I recorded. That's when I started making some money, you see, when I began to record. The family had recorded in 1928. Yes. And after that, six or seven years went by before I had a hit [in 1934].

Yes. But after we recorded as a group in '28 we went north, and we toiled here and there. And we never recorded anything again. As a matter of fact, we never even heard our own recordings. We didn't much worry about that, or anything. We just continued toiling; we went up north, then came to Houston, and finally to San Antonio. That's where I began to sing at the Plaza del Zacate and where I had my first successes. Then when I recorded, that's when our lives began to change, you see; when I began to make money.

In 1934 I recorded the first record. Two months later the company got in touch with me again, because as soon as the "Mal Hombre" recording was released it was a hit. After that first record came out, they showed up again; two months later they were back, signing me onto a new contract and asking me to record more. If they wouldn't have taken me under contract, another company would have snatched me up! So they moved quickly. They came from New York.

It was the Bluebird label, but in reality it was RCA Victor. They signed a one-year contract with my father—with a one-year option. Well, that one-year option turned into ten years. As soon as the contract would near its end, they would send me another one, so I would sign it with another one-year option. And that's how it went on and on. I was tied up with that contract. At one point, a company from California approached me with a contract. But I couldn't sign, you see, because I was already under contract. As soon as the first record came out and began to become popular, that's when lots of people wanted to meet Lydia Mendoza. The contracts began to shower down upon us, you see. Then our life changed.

Yes, our life changed. We had more money to make a better living and to buy clothes. We had barely been eking out a living. I remember very well: for the first recordings they paid me fifteen dollars for each record I cut. The first thing I did was to go downtown with my mother. And mamá said, "Well, what are you going to buy for yourself, hija?"

I said, "Nothing for now."

First I bought shoes for all my little brothers and sisters. My siblings were little, and the shoes were very inexpensive. Shoes cost a dollar. I first bought them shoes because they went barefoot. I also bought them socks and a few clothes.

MARCH 15, 1939.

LIDYA MENDOZA ALVARADO

SAN ANTONIO, TEXAS

Dear Sir: ARTISTS LETTER AGREEMENT

1.   This Letter Agreement will constitute an agreement between you and RCA Manufacturing Company, Inc. (herein called "the Company") for the making of phonograph records.

2.   This Agreement shall remain in effect for a period of ONE YEAR from the date hereof, and during that period you will at mutually convenient times come to and perform at the recording studios of the Company for the purpose of making THIRTY recorded selections, or more than this number if the Company so desires.

        In consideration of this agreement and without further payment than as herein provided, you grant to the Company, its associates, subsidiaries and nominees (1) the right to manufacture, advertise, sell, lease or otherwise use or dispose of, or to refrain therefrom, throughout the world, records embodying the performances to be recorded hereunder, upon such terms as the Company may approve; (2) the right to use your name and photograph and the name and photograph of the Musical Organization, if desired, in connection with the exploitation of said records; and (3) all rights in and to the matrices and records, and the use thereof, upon which are reproduced the performances to be recorded hereunder.

3.   The Company will pay you promptly after the approval of the Master record in complete satisfaction of the rights herein granted and the services to be rendered hereunder by you the sum of TWENTY DOLLARS.

4.   You agree that during the period of this Agreement you will not perform for any other person, party or concern for the purpose of producing phonograph records and that after the expiration of this Agreement you will not record for anyone else any of the selections previously recorded for this Company.

5.   The Company shall have the privilege and option to extend this Agreement from the date of its termination for a period equal to the term of this Agreement by giving to you notice in writing of its exercise of such option and its election to continue. Such notice shall be given to you personally or be mailed to your last known address not less than ten days prior to the said date of termination. Upon the giving of such notice this Agreement shall be continued and extended for such further period upon the same terms as those above set forth.

Standard and All-wave Radio Receivers · Radio Phonographs · Auto Radios · Farm Radios · Broadcast Station Transmitters, Microphones and Associated Equipment · Phonophone Theatre Equipment · Victor and Bluebird Records · Electrical Transcriptions · Marine Radio Equipment · Transoceanic Radio Equipment · Aviation and Police Radio · U. S. Government Radio Equipment · Centralized Sound Systems · Public Address Systems · 16 MM. Sound Projectors and Cameras · Film

A 1939 contract between Lydia Mendoza and RCA Manufacturing Company. Record companies made millions by paying artists a low flat fee and no royalties. Courtesy Houston Metropolitan Research Center, Houston Public Library

I had just enough money; not much left over. Mamá asked me again, "And what are you going to buy for yourself, hija?"

"Nothing. First I'll buy them something, and next time I'll buy something for myself."

And that's how I did it a little at a time. Later I recorded again. This time it wasn't just one record; it was two. So it was thirty dollars. With that money we

Lydia Mendoza records at home in 1938. Courtesy U.T. The Institute of Texan Cultures, the *San Antonio Light* Collection

put in electricity because we had none. We had a kerosene lamp, imagine, and a wood-burning stove. Talk about blistering heat! Well, we went out, and I bought an inexpensive little gas stove. And so on, little by little life began to change, you see. And as time passed, we did better and better and . . . well, God helped us. Our means of living changed, you see. Our father had gotten sick and couldn't work any longer. We were . . . badly off, you see. But everything began to change a little at a time through my recordings, and then later with the jobs that came our way.

I began at the very bottom and with a lot of sacrifices and a lot of toil. But God knows my highest ambition was to make money for my family. It pained me to see my brothers and sisters without clothing. Christmas would come, and the poor little ones would just look at other children who had little toys while they had nothing. So it hurt me, you know, to see my brothers and sisters without the things they could've had. And since I was the oldest . . .

Well, my older sister Beatriz married very young. She didn't want to go on living with us. She had had it and claimed she was tired—she was one of these girls with bad notions. In short she was fed up and was getting married. She married very young: at age fourteen. In fact, she married in Detroit, Michigan. They came with us when we left Michigan. But when we used to toil so hard, she would get angry and say, "You just take Lydia out and you don't let me go out."

Well, she couldn't go out. Who would we leave my little brothers and sisters with? Like Juanita, who was little. She was two years old. And Manuel was also little—all of them. There were three little ones, you see. So the oldest ones—which were me and Francisca—were the ones who went out to sing and make a living. So Beatriz would get angry because we'd leave her; she'd be mad because we never took her out and all that. She was always complaining, even though she was only twelve years old, mind you. Sometimes she'd say that she was going to marry the first man she could find. And that's what happened. We went up north, and in the time we stayed there—1929—she announced she was going to marry a youth she met there. Not really a youth: he was twenty-seven years old and she wasn't even fourteen. He was from Chihuahua. One of those workers who would migrate up north, you see. She met him, they went steady, and she said she was going to marry him. Papá didn't approve. He said no and that if she went off with that man, he would report her and have her sent to juvenile hall.

Then my mother took him aside and told him: "Well, look, Pancho, what good will it do to oppose it?" She said, "She wants to get married. May as well. What will we gain by having her sent here or there? It's up to her. She wants to get married," she said.

And they got married up in Detroit. Not a church wedding, but through the justice of the peace. We came back about the middle of '30. Beatriz had gotten married within two years of arriving up there. She wasn't even fourteen years old yet. And she had her first child up there, in Michigan. Her baby was born at the beginning of, I think . . . 1930, more or less. Then when we were going to come back, the son-in-law said he was thinking of returning to his own country. He, too, had been laid off from his jobs and everything. So they came back when we came back. As soon as we got to Houston, he took off to Chihuahua. And Beatriz left with him and the baby boy.

But, like I'm telling you, she didn't want to keep on toiling with us, and I felt sorry for her. I wanted to rise from poverty. That's why I concentrated on enlarging our performing group—so as to make more money with more musicians, you see. And that's why I taught my sister María to play the mandolin, and then I learned to play the violin. The group got started right there in Houston. That's where we began to come together. That was the second time we organized a group, right? The first group had been the Cuarteto Carta Blanca, yes. Later I organized the other bigger group. So that's the group in which I introduced the violin and other instruments. We also had the sketches, right? We began to organize everything.

My career was not cut off by my husbands (the Mendoza Family)

 I've been married twice, you see. I married my daughters' father in 1935. I had my three daughters. But he died in '61. We were married for twenty-six years. At the beginning, we had some difficulties. But it wasn't because of him; it was on account of his family. Because I was a wife, a married woman, they opposed my continued touring, my working, my performances in theaters . . . Oh, it was a great embarrassment to them. They claimed that it shouldn't be, that once a woman is married, it's her home, and so forth . . . I took it for a year because, well, I got pregnant right away. That's the reason I could no longer work.

But as soon as I had my daughter, I finally convinced my husband. I told him, "Look we're making a big mistake."

It was during that period that my recordings were beginning to take hold and my name began to be known and the contracts and all of that, you see. There was a lot of work. I was being called to sing everywhere. So I said, "Look, here we are barely making a living, but we could live a lot better if I kept accepting these contracts, with my family and all. Look, we can buy our own car."

I didn't even have a car. That was in San Antonio. Well I finally convinced him, and then my in-laws and everyone came at us. But he didn't care. He listened to me, and we began to work.

For seven years we had many contracts. We traveled to California, to New Mexico . . . there wasn't a place we didn't visit. He always went with me. He was a shoe repairman and had been making seven dollars a week where he worked. Well in those times, as I told you, everything was very cheap and we were barely making a living, but we were all right. But if we could remedy that, then why not? Right? So we bought our little car and one for mamá, and we embarked on our tour. Seven years we traveled, me and my two daughters—because first I had Lydia and then I had my other two daughters—Yolanda and María Leonor ("Nora"). We traveled with them those seven years.

It was actually in San Antonio that we worked a lot in the *carpas* [itinerant tent theaters] that were there permanently and others that would come through there, you see. What I'm telling you about happened in '33, '34, '35. There was a carpa called the Carpa Cubana. They had a tent like a huge theater, you see. It featured many performers, trapeze artists, jugglers, dancers, clowns, everything. At one time I sang in that carpa, and so did my family. There was another one, a smaller one that belonged to the García Brothers. But that one stayed in San Antonio. Well, that one doesn't exist anymore, either. Almost all of them have died out. The Carpa García would set it up on the outskirts of

Lydia Mendoza and Juan Alvarado, wedding photo, 1935. Courtesy Houston Metropolitan Research Center, Houston Public Library

town; they would put that carpa in different places in the city. We would also go there to sing. Once they traveled to Corpus [Christi], and we also went to Corpus. As I said, my family and I also had our own variety show. We would all travel in trucks, in trailers, and all that.

All that was before I recorded, you see. Like I said, that happened when we had just arrived in San Antonio, about '32, '33, and '34. Those were the three years when we worked doing that. But after I recorded my first song, which

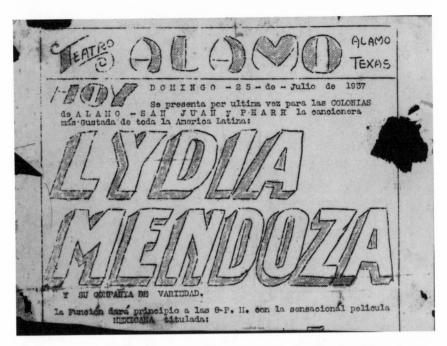

Handwritten Teatro Alamo handbill announcing Lydia Mendoza's tour in South Texas with her variety show (1937). She is billed as "the most popular singer in all of Latin America." Courtesy Houston Metropolitan Research Center, Houston Public Library

was "Mal Hombre," in '34, then we were offered tour contracts to work in theaters and halls. Before then, we pretty much worked in community halls or church halls, because the theaters wouldn't open their doors to us. We had a man who traveled with us and functioned as an agent. He would go to the theaters and propose the Lydia Mendoza Variety Show. But the Anglos—well, they didn't know who Lydia Mendoza was. They didn't know who I was. They never want to take a loss, so they want a performer with a name. I had one, but they didn't know it. So we had that working against us. We dedicated ourselves to [working in] little church halls, or auditoriums owned by mutualist societies.[4] And that's how we fared well as the Lydia Mendoza group—the Mendoza Family Variety Show. So it went until one day we were finally offered a contract from California in '37; we got there by working from town to town.

Like I told you, it was the beginning of our career. We had no means, no money except for what we made playing music, you see. We'd get a job at a little hall, and then we'd make enough to keep going until we'd arrive in El Paso, Texas. We finally would arrive in El Paso, Texas. By luck, that man who traveled with us knew the owner of the Colón Theater real well. He went to see him and to tell him about us . . . Well, this man *was* a Mexican, so he said, "Oh, Lydia Mendoza, of course!"

So in El Paso we didn't work in any halls, but in the theater. We were very successful, thanks to God.

Let's weave that story by telling it

When we finished, our agent told the owner of the Colón Theater: "Mr. Calderón, can you put in a good word for us? You know we've been struggling all along. They don't want to give us work in the theaters because they don't know about the variety show or who Lydia Mendoza is. I would really like to book the variety show in the theaters so that Mexican people . . ."

Because at the time, all they would do was show Mexican movies.

"Yes, of course," he said.

Right away he called Las Cruces, New Mexico. It's near El Paso, you see. And right away they gave us work there at that movie theater. Well, when the gringo owner saw the ticket sales other owners showed up with contracts for other towns. That's how we began to make connections and began to break into the theaters all the way to Los Angeles. We finally arrived in Los Angeles and debuted in the movie house, the theater. We performed there for three days, and thereafter many contracts came our way. We toured for three months. We traveled all the way to San Francisco, Santa Barbara, the whole region . . .

Many impresarios showed up in Los Angeles. They saw the variety show and everything. Right away, one impresario came and booked us. Then another company from San Francisco booked us, and that's how we established more and more of those connections until we had performed for three months. We spent three months here in California. When we finished, we left for Texas, and I think we returned the following year. We came back here often.

We would always perform an hour-and-a-half variety show. Of course, they always showed a movie too, right? They didn't pay us a salary. They gave us 40 percent of what remained after paying movie rental expenses. That was all. They would show a Mexican movie; after the Mexican movie was over, the variety show would go on. We had my brother Manuel with us and my sister Juanita. They would do a comedy sketch. They would joke around, and then they would sing. My sister María was the pianist. She would be down below. She'd play a piece, and then the comedy number would come on. The comedy number lasted about fifteen or twenty minutes. After they finished, María would play another piece while they changed into *charro* and *china poblana* [costumes].[5] They would come out again and perform a dance, be it the Jarabe Tapatío or other Mexican dances. Since María was already at the piano, she would accompany them. After they would finish both their numbers, they would exit and María would play another piece. Juanita would change in a hurry and come out again and sing popular songs. You know, theater songs. She'd sing about three or four songs, for example, like "La Sandunga" or "Espejito" ["Little Mirror"]. *Cuplés* are playful songs, you see. For example, "Espejito" was the one that goes: "Look at me, look at me, look at me, look at me, look at me with your little eyes. I'm looking at a little old man . . ." Something like that, a joke, you see. And also "La Sandunga." So after her three song numbers, Juanita would exit, and then María would follow on the piano. Finally, my brother Manuel would come out and sing two or three songs solo; those were boleros or something else. By then, I was ready to go on. I would come out, sing, and then María was ready to do the duet with Juanita. Then our trio would perform: Juanita, María, and I would sing with two guitars. After the trio sang, mamá and little brother would come out and sing with us. That was

Lydia Mendoza and her family featured on the cover of *Cancionero Acosta*, a songbook (1940s). Courtesy Houston Metropolitan Research Center, Houston Public Library

the finale. We'd sing three or four songs, and that was the end of the party. That was our variety show. It lasted about an hour and a half. When that was over, they would show the movie again. Then later that evening about nine, we would present our variety show again. That's the way it went in all the theaters. Sometimes—like in San Jose or Sacramento—they would take us under contract at dances. But we wouldn't do a complete variety show there, just two or three numbers, and then I would go on. That was it.

Manuel and Juanita would do various sketches; one was called "El Compadre," another "La Tienda," and another "El Muerto Murió." They did many really nice and funny sketches. They weren't risqué or anything of the sort, but those sketches certainly were funny. The two of them had many different pieces, because sometimes we would work two days in the same place, like Phoenix. For example, we would work Friday, Saturday, and Sunday at the Azteca Movie Theater. In Los Angeles we'd be at the Million Dollar Theater and also work at the California Theater. We wouldn't just work one day. We would work three days, the whole three days. Later, we even worked the whole week. That's why we had many different performance pieces, you see.

All of that was my mother's work. She was the one who did all of that. She would arrange the performance sketches, the numbers; she arranged all of that. My mother was the main one behind all of that. That's why when she died, we lost the main axis. Her name was Leonor, like my daughter. Her name was Leonor Zamarripa. But it's like I told you: she was very talented, very intelli-

Manuel and Juanita Mendoza shown in various humorous poses from their vaudeville acts (1930s).

gent, very musically talented. But she wasn't allowed to develop her gifts when she was young. She developed all of that when, shall we say, she could no longer craft a great career. But what she did know, she passed on to her children, you see. She helped me and all my brothers and sisters, see. And, luckily, all of us took to it. We wanted to do it, and we turned out to be good singers and performers in sketches and music numbers, good dancers. Juanita even performed a Spanish number. She danced with those . . . these . . . castanets. Mamá bought her a very large shawl. I don't know where she got it, how she did it. And she made her a type of dress with a fringe, all made from just a *rebozo*. But it had many flowers and wasn't really a rebozo. What do you call those? I

Teatro Azteca (Phoenix) handbill (1956) announcing Lydia Mendoza as "the most beloved singer of all time." Courtesy Houston Metropolitan Research Center, Houston Public Library

don't know. The point is mamá made that dress for her beautifully, all full of flowers. Mamá created that act for her, and my sister danced that number. Mamá always looked for ways to change the numbers within the variety act. We did good work and were very well received at all the movie houses, in all the theaters. Things went well for us. Then I recorded solo in '34. We began to work in '35 and lasted until '41, seven years. By that time, I was already the star. My name was known, see.

We suspended these tours when the war broke out. We arrived in New York in 1941. That was the last tour we did. It was 1941, and rumors of war began to circulate, and then the attack on Pearl Harbor, and all of that. So we could no longer tour. There were shortages of everything: there were no more tires for the cars; there was no gas. And then my husband was being drafted. He didn't go. He wasn't taken away because he was working at a shop where they did a lot of work for soldiers: boots and all those things, you see. They tried to draft him, but the boss told them he needed him for that government work they did there. So that's how he didn't have to go to war. But during those seven years we didn't tour anymore. In '41 I thought everything was over, you see. I still continued singing at parties anyway, there in San Antonio only, but not out of town. No recordings were made, either. But in '47 we began to work again. And we worked like that from '47 until '54 when my mother died.

During all of that I never separated from my daughters. I always had them with me. I would stop working about three months before I had my child. And as soon as my child was born, we went on the road. I would take a woman with me, and she would care for them. But I traveled, since I had my car, and we would arrive and rent a hotel room or an apartment or whatever. I always traveled with my daughters. That's how we traveled. None of my daughters became interested in music. I tell you: you've got to be born with that talent. No matter what it is. You have to be born with it and have that calling for something. And if you don't have it, it's impossible. I even bought a small guitar, because I wanted one of them to . . . but no. None of the three took to singing or playing an instrument. So they just didn't have a musical inclination.

During the seven years of travel that I was telling you about, at the beginning, we had no performance seasons. We would travel and be gone three or four months. Then we'd return to San Antonio to rest. Later, we'd take off in another direction. That's how we traveled. I didn't do it seasonally until my daughters grew older, when they reached school age. At the time, I felt that—or, rather, I didn't want them to be in a situation like mine. I wasn't sent to school. So during the school year I didn't work. I didn't accept contracts during those school months, period. I would get offers, but I would say, "I can't."

I couldn't go, and I didn't. But as soon as school was over, we had our tour ready to go.

One season I went on tour during the school months. We arrived in Los Angeles and got some contracts right away. You know what I did with my daughters? The school year started, and I sent them back. I didn't want them to stay, and they didn't want to stay, either. "No, let's go, mother, I don't want to miss school."

I sent them on the bus all the way to San Antonio to my in-laws. And so they left. Another season I happened to be in Denver, also working; their school year began, and I just had to stay. I wasn't able to send them to Texas, or I don't know what happened. The point is that they began to cry and everything and they said to me: "We'll stay here; let's go to school here."

And they did. During the time I spent in Denver, they went to school there. And that's how I was able to get them to learn something, you see. I would have liked them to have a profession. But no, as soon as they finished, they married

Lydia Mendoza and Fred Martínez on their wedding day (1964). Courtesy
Lydia Mendoza Collection

boys from their own school. They graduated, and they got married. They are
fine, as homemakers. My daughter Lydia had six children. But they're all
grown. She even has granddaughters. Two of her daughters have married, and
the other one is going to be married. Two of the boys are already married. She
just has one left. Yolanda only has three.

I am a great-grandmother because my granddaughters that got married year
before last already have two-year-old little girls. I have two great-granddaughters.
There are twelve grandchildren and two great-grandchildren. So they're all
grown. The oldest grandson, Leroy, turned thirty on the nineteenth of this
month. And there are others after him. The youngest granddaughter is twelve
years old, she's Nora's daughter. Oh, yes, . . . [*she sighs*].

Well, as I was telling you, I became a widow back in '61. And I was left alone,
because all three of my daughters had gotten married. That's when I asked for
work in Denver. I went to Denver, Colorado, to work. There was a man who had
a very big ballroom. They had dances every weekend. So I just called him and
told him I was alone and whether he would give me work. He said: "Lydia,
come." "You'll have a job here for as long as you like," he said.

He paid me more or less, and so I went to Denver. That's where I met my second husband, Fred Martínez. We married in 1964. He's still my husband, you
see. But he doesn't like to travel, he really doesn't like to travel with me. This
business with theaters and airplanes and traveling and so forth . . . he doesn't
like it. He says to me, "If you want to go, go ahead."

But he hasn't been against it, either.

So in this sense I've been lucky, because my career was not cut off by my husbands, you see. I haven't had any difficulties in that regard with husbands being opposed or getting jealous or angry. No. We're happy, thank God. God has brought me even this good luck.

What's upon us is . . . modern times
(San Antonio in the 1920s and now)

 In those years the marketplace in San Antonio was so Mexican. Nowadays it's nice, of course, and so big. But in those days you felt like you were in Mexico. So beautiful. You can't imagine the joy you felt at that Plaza del Zacate, which is now called the Mercado. At the time it was outdoors. And that musical ambience at night! . . . You can't imagine the happiness people felt. The trios playing and singing there. The people selling whatever they sold there. It was something very beautiful. Now everything is so different, so changed. It doesn't at all resemble what it was like during those very Mexican times. The plaza was right there in front of where the Santa Rosa Hospital is now; do you remember where that hospital is now? There used to be rows of trees, and always so many flowers! . . . Now it's all gone! They tore it all down: the pharmacy, the National Theater, the Zaragoza Theater. Everything looked so beautiful. Now it's so . . . I don't know. I don't like San Antonio much now. I liked it better before. There was activity and life at the Mercado twenty-four hours a day. It was full of people.

Nearby was also the Municipal Auditorium. They renovated it instead of tearing it down. Yes, they renovated it. It's gorgeous! It's a historic building in San Antonio. And to think that they wanted to tear it down; but there was opposition and many signatures against it, many. So they didn't let them tear it down. That's what they should have done with the National Theater and the Zaragoza Theater and that León Pharmacy. They were also historical.

I remember our first visits to San Antonio with my parents, about 1923–1924. All of that was so beautiful! Well, people should have protested so that it wouldn't have been torn down! Now the pharmacy is gone; gone are the National Theater and the Zaragoza Theater where great artists performed. They should have left that as well. They tore it all down. The Carta Blanca Restaurant, do you remember? They also demolished the Carta Blanca Restaurant. It was a restaurant downstairs and a hotel upstairs. That's where we stayed when we came to record in San Antonio. Papá called us the Cuarteto Carta Blanca because he really liked Carta Blanca beer. That's why he named our quartet that way.

But it's like I tell you, they tore down the Carta Blanca Restaurant when they renovated and built all that junk. They tore down everything that was so beautiful. But earlier, when we came to record—which was in '28—it was in a restaurant downstairs. One of the main ones. Very big. And upstairs was the hotel. That's where we stayed because papá knew the owner, Mr. Núñez, very

Teatro Zaragoza (Zaragoza Theater), which fell victim to urban renewal (1940s). Courtesy Zintgraff Collection, U.T. The Institute of Texan Cultures

well. About five years later—more or less—it was no longer a hotel upstairs. It was a reception and banquet hall. That's where the San Antonio newspaper *La Prensa* had its anniversary banquets. I think you know him or have heard of Mr. Lozano, from the same family that now owns *La Opinión*, which is in Los Angeles. Well, every year they would have an anniversary banquet for *La Prensa* in that reception hall above the restaurant. They would invite me and my sister to sing every time there was a banquet. I remember that on one of those occasions they also brought José Mojica, the singer. Later he quit performing, after his mother died. He became a priest; he was Father Guadalupe. The point is, though, that they tore all of that down . . . everything on that block. Even the restaurant; and, in fact, a *corrido* [narrative ballad] was written about that. José Morante wrote a corrido where he tells of everything they tore down. All of that which was so beautiful. They put "buildings" there, and they put so much there that it is unrecognizable nowadays. It's no longer the San Antonio that I knew back then in the '20s or '30s when we were there. It's just gone. But the river is very pretty. There is a lot of tourism, you see . . . But I still say: they shouldn't have torn down historic things. So what's upon us is . . . modern times. Modern times.

Look, there is a city I admire very much: Santa Fe. Do you know it? Santa Fe, New Mexico. Well, nowadays it's very modernized. But no, they didn't destroy any part of Old Santa Fe. There's Old Santa Fe and New Santa Fe. There's another town over in New Mexico. Do you know Las Vegas, New Mexico? There's

Portrait of Lydia Mendoza 1983, by Estér Hernández (1999). Courtesy Estér Hernández

another town for you: same thing. The modern part is there. They've modernized the city. Well they did the same thing there. But Old Las Vegas remained as it was. With its *alamedas*, its buildings, its little houses, its restaurants. Like it was in the days when the city began, I think. Old Las Vegas remained the same, but they also have the new one, you see. The same holds true for Puerto Rico with the Old San Juan. It exists as it once was. Oh, a New San Juan, yes! The new city, the modern stuff, the "buildings," the streets, the freeways, and all. But when I went to Puerto Rico, I stayed in Old San Juan. I was there just one day; I worked, and the next day I left. But I got up very early. They put me up in a very lovely hotel: I was on an upstairs floor and had a balcony. From the balcony I admired the little I could see: everything was very beautiful. The streets now are as they were then. For instance, the traffic situation is such that if there is an on coming car you have to wait for it to pass. Only one car fits at a time. And the streets are made of cobblestone. Well, it's divine! It was very beautiful.

And that's what they should have done with San Antonio as well. They should have modernized another area. But the Mercado and all of that, the plaza, they should have left it like it was before. But no. They destroyed everything. What they built there were all the main big stores. They put them right in the center of downtown. Now you go there and you get lost! I lived on a street which I can't even find if I go there now. They turned everything upside down and knocked it down. All you see there nowadays is gringos out on the town.

Musical interlude

 [*Lydia Mendoza sees a Mexican harp in the room and comments.*] Nowadays in Texas you don't hear anyone playing the harp anymore. You did in the past. But nowadays you don't hear it at all. Do you know this waltz "Lágrimas de Vino," ["Tears of Wine"]? [*Lydia sings and accompanies herself on the guitar.*]

The garden you made me dream of
has turned to sorrow.
Ungrateful woman, why do you scorn me?
When you see my tears flow in torrents.
Do you like to see me suffer?
Do you like to see me cry?
Laugh and enjoy, enjoy and laugh,
for I shall love you till I die.

Just to think
that I've lost what I loved so much.
I cry inconsolably.
My only purpose is to wait.
You were going to forge
a new ideal in my mind.
I will form a new ideal in my mind.

And the Eden you made me dream of
has turned to suffering and waiting.
Ungrateful woman, why do you scorn me?
When you see my tears flow in torrents.
Does it please you to see me suffer?
Does it please you to see me cry?
Laugh and take pleasure, take pleasure and laugh,
for I shall love you till I die.

Lydia Mendoza, the teacher

 Lately I've experienced great fulfillment, like during the three-month contract from Fresno [California State University at Fresno] at the college; it gave me a great sense of fulfillment. Over there they called me *la maestra*; "the teacher," they'd say. I would arrive, and the teachers there would come to greet me; they would show me to the office. Then they would take me to class and introduce me. Not just, "Here's Lydia Mendoza."

No. They'd say: "This is maestra Lydia Mendoza, the teacher."

I was treated with great respect. I would gaze upon all the children and think, "My Goodness!" . . . My father never sent us girls to school. He sent . . . only the boys were educated, but not the women. Papá would say—old customs no doubt—he'd say, "Why send girls to school? Just to pick up notions and learn bad habits and be around boys." He thought they'd just grow up and get married and leave . . . What do they need schooling for? That's what they believed in those days. Nowadays I think education is very necessary, right? But in those days parents thought that way. I remember that whole families would take their children out of school to work the harvest. But nowadays: just try to pull them out of school and see if they let you! In those days, papá had friends in San Antonio, not far from the house. There was a man who had eight children, all of them school age. As soon as it was harvest time, they'd take them out of school to work the crops.

So when I went to that program at the university in Fresno I would reflect on how I never set foot at a college, a university, or a school—during my childhood or my youth. And look how far I've gotten as a nobody [*laughter*]! Toward the end of my stay there, I went to do my concert and a talk. Everyone there was a teacher; there were no kids or youngsters there at all. It was a farewell by all the professors. There I was, and they would ask me questions. Everyone was very attentive. So I felt proud as a peacock! I said to myself: "I'm setting foot here without being anyone."

I could never tire, nor do I now tire, of thanking God for all the favors I've received, you see.

When they first called me for that work in Fresno, of course I told them it was an honor that they called me and I felt really happy, but, unfortunately, I don't speak English. So how could I possibly do this job? I couldn't. "Oh," they said, "it's not a problem because we're going to provide you with an interpreter."

And so it was. I always had a young woman with me who spoke Spanish. For example, we would arrive, and they would introduce me to the class. Sometimes they were university students; sometimes they were schoolchildren. They would introduce me, and I would tell them why I was there and that they could ask me questions. They would start to ask questions, you see. They would ask if I was wealthy, whether I had children, whether I liked music a lot, and how I had learned to play. And so forth, you see. All the children would ask many questions. After answering, I would begin to sing them some songs I had learned.

I always took my guitar. Afterward they would look at the guitar and begin to ask how many strings it had, and how, and whether it was difficult to play. Then they'd begin to request songs; sometimes "Cielito Lindo," "La Paloma," or songs they had heard, you see, because they were not Latino children, you see. And that was my work in the schools.

Then they would take me to the universities. As a matter of fact, I spoke not only in Fresno but traveled to many places outside of Fresno. I would only spend one day per week in Fresno. On that day I would perform. Attendance was by invitation only. There we would talk about my history. Teachers went, many people and students went, all grown-ups, no children. Everyone took their books, and they would ask their questions and take notes—I don't know what in the world they took down. But they asked their questions concerning the history of my life, about my music. And that's how it was . . . all of it went very well.

That has been my life and long career (different types of performances, ambiences, and audiences)

 Throughout most of my career I have worked mainly alone. At times with other variety shows, you see. I've toured with two or three other acts. For example, I worked for a time with Chata Noloesca. I worked some places with her. We went to Chicago, Detroit, the Texas Panhandle. But we weren't able to make it to New York because she became ill. There were only three of us on those tours. La Chata, one male colleague, and me. La Chata was a comic, and she'd do her dances. We would hire another person to accompany her. She would perform her sketches and sing and dance. And then I would sing. That was what we did in movie houses and theaters. After her sketch I would come onstage and sing. At the end, she would return to the stage joking and dancing. It was quite a long variety show, long, you see, even though there were only three of us. La Chata, one male colleague, and me. And that's how we did a number of performances. I didn't have a long career with her, no. I didn't hook up with her until I became a widow. In fact, it was she who came to me and offered to help me, so we could perform in some places, you see. But recently, it's been me alone performing these concerts: at universities, colleges, or places where they do Mexican music and all that. I went to Chicago and did a solo program. That's the same way I did a concert in New York, and so on.

Let me tell you something. I want to say that at times I perform for non-Latino audiences like I recently did in New York and Chicago. When they started booking me for those programs—like when I went to Canada, to Alaska—I noticed there were no Latino folks. At the beginning—I won't deny it—I always felt a certain . . . certain fear, a certain apprehension. Since I don't sing in English, I'd always think: "I'm going to perform for an audience and they don't understand me."

Well, I always had a certain fear because what encourages an artist, what

Lydia Mendoza (*long dress*) flanked by famed comedians Chata Noloesca (*right*) and Don Chema (*left*), and other performers in Chicago (1954). Courtesy Houston Metropolitan Research Center, Houston Public Library

gives life to an artist, the main thing is the audience's reaction, the applause. They give you life. And I'd think, "Well, I'm going to a place where they don't understand me. How will that be? I'm going to feel very bad . . ."

I was afraid, in fact. But then I saw the audience's reaction; they received my performance with delight even though they couldn't understand me. My song would end, and they would applaud! I would finish, and the people would stand! In their own language they would tell me they had liked it. Then I began to feel encouraged. Now I perform, and I perform gladly, because I know the audience's reaction will be positive, and that's what gives me life. Like I told you: when you stand on a stage and sing or speak or whatever, it's the audience's reaction that gives you life so that you can continue. And if you notice that they dislike you, or that they don't understand you, or if they don't applaud, then you always feel badly, you see. But that hasn't happened to me, thank God.

Of course, when I'm among Latino people I feel much better because, well, . . . I talk with them, and then they begin to call out to me; or they begin to request songs, and I tell them "I'm going to sing you the first song, but as soon as this one is done you know that I'm here with body and soul with my guitar to sing whatever you want. I'll play whatever you request!"

At the end of the performance I play another fifteen minutes or even half an hour or more, you see, because I don't like to leave audiences clamoring for more.

Falcon RECORDS

LYDIA MENDOZA
"La Alondra de la
Frontera"

•Tres Puñaladas
•Tu Recompensa
•Sin Fe
•Dos Caminos
•Cuando El Destino
•Besando La Cruz
•No Se Ha Perdido Nada
•Viejos Amigos

Lydia Mendoza on a record jacket by Falcón Records (ca. 1940s). Courtesy
Houston Metropolitan Research Center, Houston Public Library

No, I please them. Then I feel better. But even with non-Latino audiences, I
feel very happy anyway. No, I don't feel bad anymore. At first I did, but not anymore.

Nonetheless, it does seem to me that these cultural programs where I've performed, they're too exclusive: they don't advertise on television, on programs,
on radio, or anywhere. I don't know how they do their publicity. On those performance evenings, I feel like no one will come, but the house fills up with people. But you won't see a single ad. None of that. These are just cultural programs they put on to demonstrate a certain music or "folklore." Like the

Letter from President Jimmy Carter thanking Lydia Mendoza for performing at his inauguration (1977). Courtesy Houston Metropolitan Research Center, Houston Public Library

program I performed with in New York; it's a program that showcases the musical "folklore" of many countries. They only put out a kind of events calendar . . . they sent it to me. All the dates are on it: on such a date, they presented music from Japan. On another date, music from India. Then on another day it's the "folklore" of Texas, which is when I was there. That's how they do their music programs. But that's the only advertising I ever saw; no other kind of ad was published. So I don't know . . . over in Chicago there are a lot of Mexican people, but none of them heard about the concert. That type of Mexican programming isn't done for Mexican people.

You see, it's just like when I performed in Santa Barbara, no one . . . no one found out about this performance.[6] In New York a [Mexican] family arrived almost out of breath, they had found out about it somehow . . . How did they find out? . . . I don't know how they found out that Lydia Mendoza was there, and they came running, thrilled to see me in that hall. But beyond that, nobody found out. I don't know how that family found out I was going to be in New York. There was a big audience. But like I told you . . . no Latinos. The same thing happened not long ago in San Francisco at a concert with Flaco Jiménez . . . Yes, there were a lot of people. There were a lot of Latinos, but hardly any Mexicans. But nonetheless, they liked my program very much; and they liked Flaco very much, too.

You know, thank God, I've been lucky that way. Because I've worked in family places, clubs, nightclubs, lounges . . . And you know in those kinds of places, well, there's a lot of people drinking and all that. But to this day, no one has disrespected me. No, not at all. I haven't suffered any disappointment about being mistreated or insulted. No, thank God. I don't know what it's due to. But no one has ever disrespected me. You know, everyone has been very kind to me; I've been shown great affection and respect above all. No matter if they're drunk; they'll ask me for a song, or come up to greet me, or ask me some question. But an insult or the like, I've suffered none of that. The same holds true for the theaters and places like that where I've performed. I've received nothing but affection. I've only experienced good things in those places where I've worked. I have my own way of expressing my music. And I have never been ashamed, nor have I ever refused to perform anywhere. If I'm here and I'm called to a club or a lounge to go and sing some songs, I go. I'm not shocked, nor do I say, "No, that's a crummy place . . ."

So that has been my life and long career. And I'm happy, content, and grateful to the public who has put up with me all these years [*laughter*].

I had a lot of work in Houston. In all of Houston there isn't a club that hasn't called me. For example, I used to start playing on Fridays. I'd do three shifts on Friday, another three on Saturday, and another three on Sunday. Three hours per shift , starting at one in the afternoon. From one to four. Then from five to eight at another place. And then from eight to eleven. I'd do three shifts every Friday, Saturday, and Sunday. In addition, I'd go to other places, mainly birthday celebrations. That was my routine for a period of about fifteen years there in Houston. I moved to Houston in 1964. When I remarried, I didn't stay in San Antonio. As soon as it became known that Lydia Mendoza was in Houston, there wasn't a place that didn't want me to perform. Well, sometimes I would refuse because I didn't have time to go and sing for them. That happens mainly with birthdays where I get hired for two or three hours, and then they ask for another hour, and another hour more, and that's how five or six hours go by. At one party they wanted me to go on until two in the morning. I put my foot down and said, "No, that's it."

Even though there were many people there.

When I go to San Antonio to work, my sisters often tell me, "Ay, Lydia, you have so much spirit. Where do you get the energy to be fixing yourself up, doing your hair, makeup, dressing up, going to the radio station and television stations, and . . ., well, *not me*."

They say they couldn't bear to do it anymore.

"Well, *I can*", I tell them.

Every time I travel to San Antonio and they find out I'm in town, they always invite me to tape a television show. Every time I go, someone's bound to call and ask me to do a program—an interview and then music—on television. But you see, I like it.

Thank God, I still have control over my voice. It hasn't gone . . . you know how when you start getting older . . . perhaps it's the discipline I've kept for so many years that . . . I've got almost seventy years behind me. Controlling the vocal chords is somewhat difficult for many people who get older and can't even talk anymore. Thanks be to God, I can do it. I have control. Like I told you, perhaps it's the practice I've had; I don't know.

Also what gives me energy and bathes my body, you know, are all the good wishes of my audiences: "May God keep you for many years" and "May that voice never end."

All those good wishes I believe enter my system, and that's what keeps me here still hollering at everyone [*laughter*].

That's the artistry: the art of feeling

People have always asked me that question about which are my favorite songs. You know I really can't disregard even one song. I love them all very much. The only songs I don't like are those with insults, see, or with profanities, like that song which says, "Yo fui tu papalote" [I was your plaything].[7] Uh . . . it has that word . . . I just don't like it. There are other songs, for example, the one that says, "Me importa madre" ["I don't give a f***"]. I don't like songs with insults like that. I really like songs about love and rejection a lot, just as long as they're not very insulting, you see. But beyond that . . . I love corridos. I really like boleros, tangos, all kinds, all sorts of songs. This or that song is perhaps my favorite. Sure, because I like it. But at any rate, of all my songs . . . I can't disregard even one of them because I like them all. It doesn't matter what type of song it is.

Now when it comes to music, I can tell you I've been asked a lot about the music of different countries, like Chinese music, Indian, American, and all that. When it comes to musical notes, it all sounds very pretty to me even if I don't understand it. I'm not inclined to say, "Well, I don't like this one or I do like that one."

No. As long as it's music, I like it a lot, even if I don't understand it.

Each song is distinctive—a corrido, a bolero, a song about rejection, a love song, a waltz; all of them. Every single song has its essence, you see. It's not just a matter of opening your mouth and belting it out. You've got to capture the essence of each song. If you don't do that, it just doesn't sound right. That essence flows from one's soul; it's born in the soul. I tell you, when I sing a song—I've said it over and over, and I want to tell you as well—if it's a corrido, I *feel* what happened in that tragedy. I feel it as if it had happened to me. I sing it with that feeling because it's as if whatever happened to the corrido protagonist happened to me. Same thing if I sing a love song. If it's a song about rejection, it's as if the protagonist in that rejection—or whatever—was me. It's instinctive, it flows, I feel it, you see. I'm not forcing anything. It flows from me! The feeling I put into whatever I'm singing comes from deep inside me. I feel it comes from deep within my soul. Like I told you, I live that song. It's like an

Lydia Mendoza (ca. 1950s). Courtesy Houston Metropolitan Research Center, Houston Public Library

actor, you see. It really isn't very easy to stand on the stage and play a dramatic role and just burst into tears. You have to feel what you're doing . . . so that it seems real, you see. If you watch an actor perform and you feel it, it's because she's feeling it. That's why there are great actors, the great artists. That's the artistry: the art of feeling. It's not about doing something just because you want to do it, or about singing a song by just opening your mouth and hollering. No, that's not what it's about! That's not the way. One is born with that art of feeling, and that's what the public and the people value. And that's what creates great careers—it's that talent. Not just anyone can do it. It is a gift you have from God, that's it. It's a God-given gift we carry inside. It's not something you create. You're born with it, touched by the hand of God.

God has certainly helped me in many different ways. For example, many musicians write their songs down in a book because they don't know them by heart. They set up their music stand and have to look at the words when they sing. Not me. I carry them all up here [*points to her head*]. I don't look at any books; whatever I'm going to sing, I've already got it up here. Another example: I can learn three or four songs in one day. When my husband leaves for work, I'm home alone. As soon as I finish my chores and don't have to worry about anything and have a clear mind, I gather my songs and start to memorize them by singing. Once I learn the melody, the song sticks. I don't forget it. Even if it's three very different songs. I learn one and go over it two or three times. Then I set aside the lyrics and sing it by heart, and with that I've learned it. Like I told you, in one day I can learn three or four songs and I won't forget them. They stick with me. I ask myself, how does it work? For example, at times when I'm singing a song and I'll be singing a verse and suddenly the following verse already comes to me. It's already there as if someone were telling me, "This is what's next."

That's how my brain works, you see. I don't forget songs. I don't need to see the lyrics anymore. There are very few singers who sing songs from memory. They have to read it. Not me. I don't forget them. And I know an endless number of songs! I know incredibly many songs!

There are some songs I haven't sung in many years, which I of course do forget. But as soon as I go over them, they come back to mind. But I rarely even forget songs like corridos, for instance, which have so many verses. For example, I sing corridos like "Joaquín Murrieta," "Luz Arcos," "El Contrabando de El Paso," or "Camelia la Tejana." I sing "Luis Pulido" and that corrido "El 24 de Junio," "Jesús Cadena," and "Lucio Vásquez." I know many, many corridos. In fact, I have with me a cassette I recorded with nothing but corridos. People buy that cassette a lot, Mexican people, that is. People buy a lot of my corrido cassettes. I'm about to release another cassette I've just recorded of nothing but corridos.

I've recorded over forty LPs. I have some of them, but most of them I don't have because even when I save one or two for myself, friends come over and say, "I want this one,"

I say, "I don't have it; I've run out."

"Well, give me whatever you have."

"All right, take this one; I'll replace it later."

Later I forget, and of course I never replace it.

My daughter Nora is the one who has all of them. As soon as I get a record [shipment], Nora says, "This one's for me. I'm taking it home, because I know if I don't take it, you'll be left with nothing."

So she does have them. But I don't . . . I only have a couple of them. That's just fine. I wasn't one of those neat or careful people who'd save those records . . . No, I just didn't save them and so the years went by.

The one I did save was the original of "Mal Hombre," the original. But I only have that one because one of my brothers found it when he was shopping at a store in San Antonio and he found it there— I think it was at Sears. They had quite a lot of those old records. This happened when they started to put out those 45s. "Mal Hombre" had been recorded on a 78, on the old records, you see. That's why they were on sale. He found that record there, and one day he came over and said, "Look what I've got here for you."

As soon as I saw it, I put that one away. But that's about all I have. I didn't save them. But with or without records, God has given me great satisfaction. A thing I never expected.

Life . . . that's what has taught me (art across the generations of women)

My grandmother also had a very beautiful voice. She sang very beautifully. Mamá taught me to play when I was seven years old. By the time I was nine, I played the guitar well and we already lived here in the United States. When we returned to Monterrey for a visit, mamá announced that I was already playing the guitar. Oh, it made my grandmother so happy. So she'd have me come over to her place every morning. "Come with me, sweetheart," she'd say.

She would take her guitar—she had a small guitar—and I would take my guitar, and the two of us would sing. Yes, my grandmother and me. But as I said, she never became an artist. She had that talent, and my mother inherited it. But in those days families were so strict that they didn't allow my mother to develop her calling. But after she married papá, her talent awakened . . . But by then she already had children; she didn't pursue a career.

Nonetheless, my mother was an educator in every sense of the word. Later on, she organized the variety show. She was the teacher who trained my brothers and sisters. She always directed us. "All right, you're going to do this, and you will do this other thing." That's how she arranged the musical numbers. She'd find a way to get sheet music, and then she'd go to some teacher who could show María how to play it. María played by ear. She was a great pianist, but she played by ear. She had a very good head on her shoulders and even played with orchestras, in some theaters. For example, we once arrived at a theater where there was an orchestra which accompanied the performers— I believe in Los Angeles. Mamá had my sister listen to what they were going to play. Then my sister played it by ear. So my mother would do all that, and in addition she'd accompany my sisters and brothers, she'd arrange their comic sketches, and all. I don't know how she'd use her imagination to organize the variety show. She'd even design their costumes, and their clothes, too.

Well, I remember how at the beginning when we were going to present our little variety show, my brother Manuel was supposed to appear as a charro, you see, and my little sister as a china poblana dancing the Jarabe Tapatío, I believe, or other Mexican dances. We had no money; there were no means with which to go to Laredo and buy a charro outfit. Well, my mother used her imagination. She went and bought black pants and stitched them on the inside in order to taper them like a charro outfit. Then she sewed a zipper on the side seams. She decorated the whole thing. She went and bought a few dozen very pretty buttons that looked like silver, just like those on charro pants. She took those and decorated it like a charro outfit and then made a little jacket to match. Well, it was a very simple little outfit, but it was a charro outfit. Same thing for my sister Juanita: she fixed her up a Mexican dress. She would use her imagination to make the outfits we needed to wear. After some time passed and we began to make some money, we did go to Monterrey and she bought my brother his real charro outfit. Considerable time passed before that was possible. I'm telling you this to show how mamá organized everything. Everything was in movement by virtue of my mother. She was the mover. When she died, we were left without an artistic director—in a manner of speaking—and the variety show ended.

But, in reality, I was the one who lit the fire and triggered it. First of all, mamá, and then me—both of us made it happen. All of that took off because I loved music. I first learned guitar and later took up the mandolin. Then I

The Mendoza family variety show (1935), featuring Francisca ("Panchita")
Mendoza (*top left*), María Mendoza (*top right*), Leonor Zamarripa Mendoza
(*seated*), Juanita Mendoza (*lower left*), and Manuel Mendoza (*lower right*).
Courtesy Houston Metropolitan Research Center, Houston Public Library

would sing with mamá. So the group began to grow bigger. So at one point I
thought, "Hey, my brothers and sisters should also learn this."

I taught María, who was coming of age, how to play mandolin. And the
darned kid picked it up right away! She quickly learned to play the mandolin.
Then I started in with, "Well, I want to play the violin . . . I really want to."

And I played it! That's how the group continued to grow without any lessons
from teachers or the like. At times, people have asked me whether I have a
trained voice. Well no: it was life, life experience, practice; that's what taught

me the little bit I know, you see. Because no one ever told me, "Do it this way" or "That way," "Hit this note." No, I generated my own ideas from my own intelligence. I just picked up my guitar.

Musical interlude

[*Lydia Mendoza sings "Amor de Madre" ("Mother Love.")*]

In the name of God, give me your blessing,
oh my beloved mother.
At your feet I beg forgiveness
for what you have suffered.

In the name of God, give me your blessing,
gaze upon me I ask,
beloved mother.
Pray to the creator for me.

You who are in the mansion
in that celestial throne,
fill my heart
with a maternal sigh.
A maternal sigh
that will touch my heart,
that will touch, that will touch my heart.

Look, mother, in this world
no one loves you like I do.
Look, a mother's love
shall exist between us two.

You who are in the mansion
in that celestial throne,
fill my heart
with a maternal sigh.
A maternal sigh
that will touch my heart,
that will touch, that will touch my heart.

[*Repeats the first two stanzas.*]

Persevere! Don't hold back; don't give up!
(surrender to music: a whole lifetime)

Throughout my long life, music has been a goal I have pursued; nothing could hold me back. Failures, win or lose, I never said, "No, I'd better do something else."

No, I persisted with music. And that's the beauty of it, you see. I hope that all those who want to accomplish something or who have a particular talent will persevere! Don't hold back; don't give up! Who cares if other singers or other performers emerge: you hold on to your own goal and what belongs to you. You have to decide on one thing and keep on going. If you experience a failure and say, "No, I'd better do some other thing."

You'll never get anywhere that way.

You know, I have a nephew—my sister Juanita's son. And he's a young man of considerable intelligence. God endowed him with great talent. Everything he knows, his considerable education, he obtained it all through scholarships awarded to him for his knowledge, you see. I think they sent him all the way to Hungary, or who knows where. When he started off he wanted to be . . . I don't know what you call those people who study human bones. What do you call those people who know human anatomy? At any rate, that's what he began to study. Then on account of his talent, he was sent way over to Hungary, I believe, or who knows where. He was to complete his studies, you see. Initially he was doing really well. But no, he dropped it. He just didn't continue with it. That's how he has taken on several things; and although he's a highly trained young man who knows a lot he hasn't reached the goal he wanted. He's already thirty-some years old, and he hasn't gotten anywhere. With all his studies, and all he has learned and experienced, he hasn't made a choice. We thought he was going to be some doctor or something. But he hasn't done anything. He has talents. He has studied a lot and hasn't done a thing. Well, I don't think that's good.

Imagine, when I started off, I experienced failures, because everything in this life has its ups and downs. We have to start off facing many hardships and the like, you see. But, nonetheless, I didn't hold back. On the contrary: I wanted to build and expand our efforts—the group, the music, and everything possible in order to push forward. I've spoken about this whenever I've visited schools. I tell parents to help their children to push forward, but [they should] stick to something; don't just start one thing and then drop it; in the end it comes to nothing.

For instance, when we first got started, when I began as a young kid with my family, there were times we would perform and earn nothing. We couldn't even buy food, and we suffered a lot. Sometimes we couldn't even afford to pay the rent. All that sacrifice and suffering just because we wanted to push forward with the music. I could have decided to do something else, but I wanted to stick to it. And then when I was discovered, when people began to know me as a singer, they'd take me to places to perform for people; but they wouldn't pay me even a cent. Nevertheless, I was very happy because I said: "I'm rising; I'm moving ahead."

It's quite easy to say: "I want to be an artist; I want to be this or that, and I want to be successful right away."

But that's impossible. In order for me to finally make a name for myself, to be recognized, it took a long time. We toiled from about 1927 until 1934. How many years was that? About seven years.

We had our share of everything: failures, good and bad times, and all of it. Nonetheless, my day came, and look: God helped me. But we don't all think that way. I've run into people who say, "Well, I want to learn how to play the guitar, I want to sing, and to record, and everything."

Well, it's not that easy. You have to toil a great deal. Nowadays young people have many opportunities, you know. Primarily television, radio, cultural programs, contests, organizations that help them. All of those things are a great help, see. Even in the schools they begin to explore what they like. They have music bands, and teachers instruct them, you know. After that, well, they can continue. But when I started, I didn't even go to school. Well, how could I pick up some learning? And then, in those days there wasn't even any radio, nor other means by which to learn. There was nothing. So whatever I learned, I learned it through my own effort. Out of that willpower. Because the only one who taught me guitar was my mother: my only teacher.

Let the women singers emerge!

 Like I told you, when I first got to San Antonio—in those years—there were no women who sang [publicly] or would dare to sing. There was none of that. I think I was the one who encouraged them. The point is that many women singers began to emerge and then withdrew from singing. I don't know what became of those singers who participated with me in that contest. Like the one who won second place, Lupita Viña from San Antonio. I don't know what became of her, whether she got married or just withdrew. The same holds true for the one who won third place. They didn't do anything: no career or anything. Rita Vidaurri emerged, for example. Do you know her? She's a girl I met when she started off and was twelve years old. She got her start in one of those contests they had at the Teatro Nacional. She won because she sang and played the guitar—the one with six strings. She had a very lovely voice. She began to work and to tour, and so forth. But all of a sudden she vanished. Nowadays she lives there in San Antonio and works in a hospital. So you see, she left the business. Rosita Fernández, another one, the same thing. She never worked outside of San Antonio. In San Antonio she worked a lot singing at the Riverwalk. But she has also retired. The truth is, there are no women singers or artists around who have toured or endured as I have . . . toiling and struggling. Some have married; others have vanished; they've left their career. Right now in San Antonio there are many women singers, many young women who have emerged who sing and everything. But well . . . they never leave town; they haven't done anything. They just stay there.

There are many reasons, many factors, you see? Right close to home, for example: my sisters Juanita and María. They were a duet. My sisters dedicated themselves more to the duet during wartime when they drafted my brother and we couldn't travel. They sang at a club and were very well organized, you see. When we started up touring again in '47, we went to California, and I began to record with Mr. Pelache. I suggested to Mr. Pelache that he also record my sisters' duet.

"No," he said, "I'm really only interested in you."

Well, the second time I recorded with him, I told him again, "Look, I know

Singing sisters Lucia (*left*) and Juanita Carmona (*right*) continued in the
tradition of Lydia Mendoza, playing guitar and singing on Haymarket Plaza
(1941). Courtesy U.T. The Institute of Texan Cultures, the *San Antonio Light*
Collection

what I'm telling you: even if you don't pay them much, I want you to give them
an opportunity."

"All right, Lydia, OK; I'm going to help them out. Let's do a recording."

They recorded it, and I also accompanied them with my guitar, you see. The
duet recording turned out really well. When the record came out, people liked
it a lot. The man put them under contract, and they began to record. When
mamá died, they wanted to continue recording and all. But it happened that
María got married. Juanita also got married right away. So they started having
problems with their husbands. Juanita and María wanted to go on recording.
One of those times they were asked to go do a recording. María's husband did
finally agree to her going, but when it came down to it he said no. There was a
huge mess: would they record, would they not record—I don't know.

María's husband told her, "Well, you married me: it's either your home, your
children, or your career."

And what did María do? Well, she stayed with her children—she had six—
and she withdrew from the business. That's how the duet disintegrated because
of María's husband: and that was it.

Then it turns out that in the end, after so many years of marriage—I think
they lasted about twenty-five years—María's husband gets involved with some

dame; he divorced María and left her. So then María was left disillusioned and sick. So you see he destroyed my sister's career, and to top it off he divorced her. And she is very sick. Imagine; she has colon cancer. Three years ago they wanted to operate on her. She got very sick and went to the hospital. There they told her she had a cancerous tumor in the colon. And in order to prevent its growth they were going to remove it, close her colon, and do a colostomy. She wouldn't have it and left the hospital. And there you have her shriveling in the flesh, skinny, skinny, and very sick. On top of it all, she suffered a disillusion-ment with her husband, who got tangled up with a comadre. In sum: the hus-band divorced her, and María ended up alone. Her children grew up, married, and they don't care about their mother anymore. There she is alone, aban-doned, and sick. Yes. She ended up alone in San Antonio. That's quite a setback to live with.

My brothers are also married and the wives also didn't want them to go on, and so they stayed home. Poor Juanita is also very sick with diabetes. They op-erated on one of her legs, and who knows what they found. And soon they op-erated on the other leg. So you see, for all these reasons they have left their careers.

Let the women singers emerge! I've asked myself: Why hasn't another woman singer emerged in all these years, a woman with a career like the one I've had?

My long career has taken me to many places. I remember the very first time I performed in Mexico. At the beginning of my career, they had wanted me to go there, but I had many contracts here, a lot of work. So I stayed here. The years passed, time passed, and I didn't go [to Mexico] until about 1950-something. A man from California said, "Well, why haven't you gone to Mexico?"

So I told him, "Well I haven't worked over there, nor do I have any connec-tions."

He said to me, "If I get you a contract over there will you go?"

I answered: "Well, maybe."

This is what he did. He went to Mexico and arranged a small contract for a two-week performance at the Esperanza Iris Theater in Mexico. They weren't going to pay me much, but at least I would have the satisfaction of being in Mexico. Of course, they paid for my flight, my hotel, and all. So we settled the terms of the contract and I left.

So upon arriving the director called me and says: "Mrs. Mendoza, I under-stand you're debuting here."

I had top billing. There were other opening acts, but I had top billing.

"Yes sir," I said.

"Well, I want you to know that tomorrow at ten A.M. we're having a general rehearsal here."

I told him: "Well, sir, I never go to rehearsals, because it's not necessary. The fact is that I have my guitar and I accompany myself; my songs are prepared. Just tell me how much time I will be onstage, and that's it."

He said [*she imitates a man's voice*], "No, Mrs. Mendoza, all the artists have to be here, no matter who they are. You also have to be here."

"Very well. I'll go."

Well, I arrived at ten A.M. There I was with my guitar. So they all began rehearsing: the dancers, and this and that. So when that was over the director says: "Lydia Mendoza onstage." I was to go onstage. So I went on.

The man stands up and says to me: "And what are you going to do?"

I said, "Well I'm going to sing . . ."

"With that guitar?"

"Well, yes sir," I said. "This isn't the first time I've done it. I've been doing it for many years." So I explained to him: "I've already performed in California, in New York, and in Los Angeles."

"Oh, yes. But it's very different over there. We're in Mexico here. Our audiences are very demanding and if I introduce you just like that, a woman with a guitar onstage, well, they'll kick our . . . No! God forbid! We can't do that here."

I said, "Well, that's how you contracted me, and that's how I'll go on."

"Can you perform with mariachi accompaniment?"

"Yes, of course." I said. "As a matter of fact, I've even recorded with mariachi."

He says, "Let's see."

Right away, he got the phone and called a very charming young man, very courteous. He was the person in charge of the such and such mariachis. I don't remember. I think it was Miguel Díaz; a very good mariachi. They arrived. Almost instantaneously. Well, they knew who I was but they hadn't met me.

"Yes, of course. We have heard you, but the problem is that we don't know the music you sing."

I said, "Well, we'll have to make the best of it with whatever you know, because the man says I can't just perform with a guitar."

"But that's what you're known for."

"Well, forget it. The director said no."

I told him, "Do you know . . . ?"—I was looking for songs they might know, right?—"Do you know 'Besando la Cruz' ['Kissing the Cross']?"

"Yes, of course."

"And do you know . . . ?"

I named songs I thought they might know. So I rehearsed four songs with the mariachi. The mariachi was going to play with a backdrop curtain, and when another curtain would open I would appear with my guitar. I began with "Besando la Cruz."

Opening night came around, and that's how we did it. First the mariachi walked onstage playing "Besando la Cruz," and then I came out with my guitar, and the audience applauded very much when I began to sing. As soon as I finished that song, hey, the audience began to stomp [*she stomps*] and holler: "Get rid of those jerks! We came to hear Lydia Mendoza with her guitar! We don't want to hear them! We're tired of hearing them! No! No! Let her play alone with her guitar!"

They jumped and kicked and began to ask me for my songs: "Sing us 'Pajarito Herido' ['Little Wounded Bird'] for us!" "We want 'Mundo Engañoso' ['Deceptive World']." "'Celosa' ['Jealous']!"

They wanted songs I hadn't rehearsed with the mariachi. What could I do?

Lydia Mendoza was honored in Juárez, Chihuahua, Mexico, with a parade (1950). Courtesy Houston Metropolitan Research Center, Houston Public Library

The guys just looked at me, and I looked at them. I simply couldn't sing what we had rehearsed. I had to sing what they were asking for. So I began to sing solo. I sang about thirty or forty minutes; everything the audience asked for. And those poor guys just stood there; they couldn't accompany me. That's how it continued the whole week. The audience would tolerate the first song with the mariachi because that's how the show opened: they'd come onstage singing. As soon as they were done, the same thing would happen all over again: the public would scream, "no, get those jerks out of there."

A week later, old four-eyes [the director] says: "Listen, Lydia, I guess it's useless to be paying for the mariachi. This expense is a waste."

"Well, you're the one who wanted the mariachi." I said, "You didn't want me to perform solo. You said they'd throw tomatoes, and that . . . "

He says, "Well, heck, I guess I'd better get rid of them, right?"

"That's your business."

He got rid of them. The second week I went on alone.

That's what happened to me when I went to Mexico. It was in around '54 or thereabouts, you see. I'm telling you, this happened to me with that director who didn't want me to perform solo. At any rate, I went there for two weeks, and I stayed for six months. Because as soon as I was done there, I was offered a contract by a man who toured great artistic caravans throughout Mexico, all with Mexican stars. I had no obligations pending, and I told him, "Yes, of course."

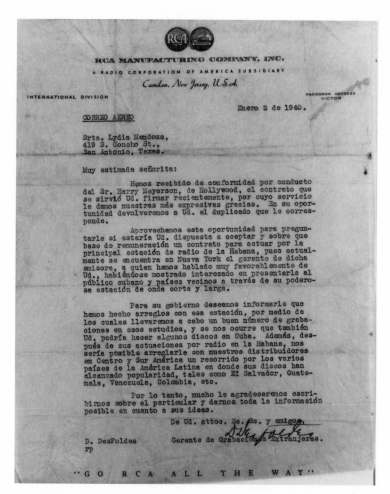

Letter (January 2, 1940) from RCA Victor offering Lydia Mendoza a visit to
Cuba for live radio performances and recordings. They express their
intention to market those records in Latin America, "where your records
have already attained popularity, such as El Salvador, Guatemala, Venezuela,
Colombia, etc." Courtesy Houston Metropolitan Research Center, Houston
Public Library

He says, "We leave this week for Guadalajara."

He paid me well and also paid for all expenses. Without taxes or anything. So
I traveled like that in Mexico for six months, but only in the provinces. And
wherever he presented me, the people already knew me, you see.

I remember a city we went to called Frontera. There were no stage entrances
there, so we had to enter from the front. Included in this very large caravan
were artists as famous as Virginia López, José Alfredo Jiménez, Las Hermanas
Hernández, Mantequilla. It was a caravan with nothing but stars and no fillers.
The audience applauded for everyone, since they knew them [*she applauds*].

[The performers] would enter and step onto the stage. I came on almost at the end. What do you think the people did? They stood up when they saw me come in; they knew it was Lydia Mendoza since I had my guitar; and they received me with a standing ovation. I can't complain. I received a very warm and very beautiful welcome, you see. That's the way it was throughout Mexico. That's the way it's been throughout my long career.

I didn't go to South America until recently. Of course, my recordings became known there since I began [my recording career]. Imagine: a company as big as [RCA] Victor had me under contract for ten years. If the recording stopped, it was only because of the war, when the war broke out. Otherwise, I would have continued recording. They would show up every four months, and I would record four or five records each time. They'd come to San Antonio to record me about three times per year. For them to do that, it meant sales were going very well, you see; my records sold really well. My recordings flooded the entire market.

The last time I was in New York in '41, a South American impresario went to see me. He wanted me to go on tour over there, but he wanted only my solo performance. The reason I didn't go was because he wouldn't take the whole group. If I had gone and left my mother, my brothers, and my sisters alone, they couldn't have made a living; all the contracts we had were with me. Of course, the whole variety show was well liked because it was very well staged, beautiful costumes and everything. But the top billing was, well, you know: my number. And so I told that man, "I'll only go if you take the whole group."

"No. We're just interested in you. We want to put you on television there, on the radio, in cabarets, and also want you to record."

"Well, fine, but I can't go alone."

And I didn't go. God knows I did it so as not to leave my mother alone with my brothers and sisters. That was their livelihood, you see. And I didn't go.

But look, who would have thought that after so very many years I would go to South America? The last time I performed in Chicago—about six years ago—some South American journalists came to see me. They went to my dressing room and greeted me with considerable enthusiasm. They said, "But, Lydia, we thought you were no longer alive! Incredible! You can't imagine the impact your music has and the audiences you have in South America; they want to know you."

"Yes, I've never gone there."

He then says, "I'm sure that if you go there, it will be a great success; audiences adore you."

I told him, "Well, fine. If there's some opportunity to go, of course I'll go."

They had a small tape recorder and I sent a greeting with them, indicating I would probably visit them someday. I sang them some songs, and they took that with them. They published that interview with me in a newspaper down there, you see. The article reported on the interview and the message I had sent.

And that's nothing: I also started to receive correspondence. I got about fifty letters from different people down there who had seen the article in the newspaper. They were delighted and wanted me to visit them. The public just went crazy. Well, it wasn't long before an impresario got hold of me, we signed the

Los Tacónes de Lydia Mendoza (*Lydia Mendoza's High Heels*). Pastel portrait by
Estér Hernández (1999). Courtesy Estér Hernández

contract, and I went to South America. It had an impact on the audiences
down there. They received me with a lot of affection and all. I performed in
Medellín, Colombia, and then in many other towns. I was there for four weeks.
I only bring this up to show how after so many years I got my wish and was
asked to visit South America. The first time I couldn't go, yet after so many
years I was able to go. I went by myself and was very happy there. Well, but of
course . . . life is different over there. But as far as the audiences go, they received me with great enthusiasm.

I really have a lot of faith in the spirits

 I'll tell you, I'm not a religious fanatic: that type of person
who lives in church, and who . . . In the first place, when
you go to the house of God you must go with tranquillity
and devotion. If I go to church, to mass, and I'm thinking,
"Oh, I hope this is over soon because I have to run off to
work here or there . . ."

Then I am no longer with God, so why go? I only go to church, to mass, when
I have tranquillity, when I don't have an obligation pending. If I go there to de-
liver myself to God, I want to be at peace with my prayers: If not, I don't go.
And in any case, whenever I'm at home or wherever I am, before I go to sleep

I say my prayers; I put myself in God's hands; I put my daughters and everyone in God's hands. I always say my prayers before I retire every day, I do that every day in the corner of my house. Sure, I'm Catholic. That was my mother's religion and my grandparents'. But as I told you, I'm no fanatic . . . when I'm at peace and have no pending obligations, then I do go to church. Otherwise, I don't go. Why go if I'm not going to be there with devotion? Diosito is always with me. And, of course, I don't ask him for the impossible or for things. I don't ask for a lot of money or for a car. Of course not. My desires are clean and sincere. Whatever I ask God for, it seems Diosito does grant me. He hears me when I ask him for something for my own good or for someone else's good. God always hears me.

I really have a lot of faith in the spirits. An enormous faith. Even when I'm trying to fall asleep. Sometimes I have insomnia like when I'm about to travel; things start to go through my head: I hope I don't forget this or that, or I better prepare something or other; there's always something. It seems my mind begins to work before I go to sleep. So before I go to bed—when I say my prayers—I invoke the spirits in the heavens to come and watch over my sleep; I ask that I not get insomnia, that I sleep. And you know I really do fall asleep. That's because I do this with great faith.

I'll give you another example: when I want something—how shall I say this?—when I'm sad about something, or if something is going on with my children, or whatever, I always invoke the spirits to free them of whatever it is. And just look: they hear me. I have great faith in the spirits. But it's like I tell you: it has to do with the faith with which the person asks for whatever it is. I don't ask them to let me find some money or to win the lottery. I don't ask for anything like that. I just ask for what's appropriate.

Prayer is a great thing. For instance, when I used to get this pain, I'd invoke the spirits: "Take this pain from me; don't let it continue; let it stop."

And it stopped. Before I know it, that pain has stopped. Who knows: Do they hear me? Or is it the faith with which I ask for something. The point is my wish is granted. And it's the same faith I have when I can't go to sleep. Since I don't like to take sleeping pills, or any of that. So what I do is invoke them, ask them to watch over my sleep. Before I know it . . . I'm asleep. That's why I tell you that I have great faith in the spirits.

My mother would teach us these things

 When my mother realized that my father opposed our going to school, she decided to teach us what little she knew. She began to teach us; she began to buy some blackboards, some pencils, colors, and all. You could say she was the teacher for us when we were growing up. That's why she began to teach us everything, you see.

At the same time, my sainted mother was also a woman who tried to teach us what was right and what was wrong. She used to tell us not to lie: that we better not say something that wasn't true, like give false testimony. For instance, if we claimed that a certain little girl had done something and she hadn't done it—if it was a falsehood—God would punish us. She would tell us many things like parables. What my mother told us in the form of stories has stayed deep within me. told us in the form of a story has stayed deep within me. Once when she was telling us what it meant to give false testimony, to say something untrue, she told us a story. You know this story is very interesting to me. Although many years have passed, I never forget it. She would tell us this like it had really happened.

She'd tell us that once there was a little village where humble people lived. A family lived there, a couple who only had one daughter. The girl was very honorable, hardworking and well mannered. Time passed, and she never married; she remained single. Her mother then died, and shortly thereafter her father also died; and so she lived all alone in her house. So since she was alone by herself, she got a job. She was a young woman who didn't go out anywhere; not to dances nor anywhere else. Just her work and her home, that was all.

It turns out that another family lived across the street from her house, and among them there was one of these women who really likes gossip, idle talk, and looking to see what the neighbor is doing. Once a man came selling something or other. The fact is, he was selling his wares door to door. So he arrived at the home of the gossipy woman, and she bought something from him. At that moment, the young woman left for work all dressed up. She made an impression on the salesman, and he kept looking at her. He was watching her, but she didn't even notice. Then he asked that neighbor woman: "Say, do you know that young woman who just left?"

She answered: "Oh, of course."

"Well, who does she live with?"

I think the stranger liked the young woman. The woman told him: "Well, she's orphaned; her father and mother have already died. She lives there all alone."

"Oh, so she's not married?" he said.

"No, no," she said.

"And what can you tell me about her life?"

"Well, she goes to work and all, but I don't know. I don't think things are right, because she goes out on her own. And you know very well that a young woman who is living alone can't be living a decent life."

What she said against the young woman was malicious. In reality, the young woman was a very serious person: she didn't gossip with anyone or anything of the kind. But the neighbor woman's comments made the stranger wonder. In short, it made an impression on the stranger, who left and never returned.

After some time had passed, the young woman died. She passed away, and the neighbor woman was remorseful. She suffered from remorse because of what she had said against the young woman; in fact, that young woman hadn't done anything wrong. As I was telling you, when the young woman died, the neighbor woman felt great remorse because of the falsehood she had told concerning that poor young woman; she had become remorseful about saying something that wasn't true. And she simply wasn't happy; she was ill at ease and often had dreams of the young woman. So one day she got up and went to church. She went to the priest for confession, and she told him, "Bless me, father, for I have sinned."

She confessed to the priest.

He said: "You bore false witness against that young woman without any reason."

"That's true, and I recognize it," she says, "but that's why I'm remorseful and come to confess so you can assign me penance and forgive me."

"Well, look, my child, I cannot forgive you. You must go see the bishop. Confess to him, tell him what happened."

"Oh, yes, father, I'll go."

The woman went before the bishop, and she tells him the same thing she told the priest.

"Well, my child, I'm very sorry, but I can't forgive what you've done."

"Oh, what shall I do?"

"Your only recourse is to go see the pope. Go see if he can forgive you."

"Yes, of course."

She went to see the pope and confessed. But the pope told her the same thing. "Well what you did was to bear false witness and I cannot forgive you. I can absolve you, but you must do what I tell you."

"Tell me, father," she said.

"Look, go and buy a pigeon or a dove, and kill it. Then choose a very, very windy day, and you go to the highest church tower. Up there you pluck every last feather from that dove; make sure not one is left. Then throw them all to the wind; let the wind take every single one. And then come back."

So she went and did what the pope told her and later returned. "Now I've come so you can absolve me."

He says, "Well, now go and collect every last feather for me."

"But how? . . . but, father, how can you ask me to do the impossible? How can I bring you what you're asking of me? After all, I did choose a very windy day. Where do you think those feathers ended up?"

He said, "Well, where do you think that young woman's honor ended up? So if you bring me every last feather, I will absolve you."

"Father, what can I do?"

He says, "Well, the other solution would be for you to go and beg her forgiveness."

"But how?"

He says, "At midnight all the spirits come out. She will also appear. When you see her coming, go and ask her to forgive you."

"Yes, of course."

And that's what she did. The woman went off and waited until it was midnight. At twelve on the dot, the spirits began to appear as bulky shapes. Among those shapes appeared the young woman. But she came with two children: one she held by the hand and the other in her arms. As soon as the woman saw her, she ran and kneeled before her: "Young woman, I come here to ask your forgiveness. Will you forgive me for what I did?"

"Yes, I forgive you."

The woman was about to leave when the spirit said: "But ask my child for forgiveness also."

She asked the one holding the spirit's hand. "Child, little child, do you forgive me?"

And the little boy said yes. And once again the old woman was about to leave, and the spirit says again, "No, don't leave: you must still ask forgiveness of the baby I carry in my arms."

The little one was about a year old. So she said, "Do you forgive me, child?"

The little child turned to her, and with his finger he signaled, "no." Then she said, "Oh my God!" All the spirits disappeared. "Oh my God!"

And at that very moment, the devil appears. He says: "Well, your body may be thrown to heaven, but your tongue belongs to me."

And that is the end of the story. Don't you think that's interesting? It's intended to put fear into people so they won't go around saying things that are not true, things that damage others, see. And mamá told us this so we would not bear false witness or say things that are untrue. Mamá would tell us many such stories.

Oh, there's something else I want to tell you. This isn't something my mother told me. It's something that happened in the family, you see. The thing is, my father was very jealous with my mother. And my mother was one of those women brought up in the old ways, so to speak. Nowadays the husband tells the wife, "Do this" or "Bring me that."

"Well, do it yourself."

Or they don't do it, right? That's the truth. Not in those days: whatever the boss said—the father—that's what was done. Well, I remember that one Monday morning—this was in 1922 when I was about six years old—my father says to my mother, "Don't forget, Leonor, that you have to go pay the rent."

The man we paid our rent to lived nearby.

"Don't forget."

"No, I won't forget."

"Have the receipt for me by this afternoon."

"Yes, of course, I'll go."

Well, at some point around noon a comadre or friend showed up, and they got to talking and talking. You know. All of a sudden, mamá looks at the clock and sees that it's already three in the afternoon. Papá would come home at four. But she couldn't just tell the woman, "You'll have to leave now because I have to go pay the rent."

Well, there was a man who used to run errands. And mamá told me, "Go tell Don Remigio to come here."

The man came. "Yes ma'am?"

She says, "Look, Don Remigio, please go and deliver my rent for me and make sure they give you the receipt."

"Yes, ma'am, certainly."

The man went, left the rent money, and brought the receipt, and the matter was settled. So finally the woman left and papá arrived.

Papá was one of those men who drank, but he didn't drink in public; instead, he always had his bottle of liquor. He would arrive, sit down, read and take little nips of liquor. After a while, he'd have dinner. So on that day papá arrived, went into the living room, and began to drink his liquor and read the newspaper. So then he calls me over and says, "Lydia, did mamá go drop off the rent?"

Since I already knew what he was like, I already knew what to say and was tuned in to everything. So I told him, "Yes, papá, she dropped it off."

"What dress was she wearing?"

I told him, "Uh, well, a brown one she has."

"Oh, yeah? That's fine; run along now, *mi'ja*."

Well, about an hour later, when papá was drunk, he calls my mother and says: "Leonor, did you drop off the rent?"

She said, "Yes, well, I mean, no, I didn't go."

"Well, did you, or didn't you?"

"Well, no, I didn't go, Pancho, because I had a guest . . . "

My mother hadn't even finished explaining to him or anything when papá lets loose with: "You damned so and so! You're trying to deceive me! I'm not your idiot!"

And he stood up and stumbled toward the rifle. My father always kept a rifle behind the door, and it was always loaded. He claimed it was in case of thieves, or whatever.

At the time, my sister María was a newborn. She was only a week old and mamá always breastfed her children, you see. When mamá saw that papá went to grab the rifle, she knew well that he was going to let her have it, you see. My mother runs and takes the baby in her arms and begins to breastfeed her, see. Just then, my father was stumbling to grab the rifle. No sooner had the baby suckled than she let go and turned blue, blue, blue, as if she had been poisoned. Then my mother screamed at papá, who was stumbling around drunk: "You wretch! Now you've murdered my daughter!!"

Mamá's lament caused him to sober up some, and he even thought he'd fired the rifle. He threw down the rifle and ran to my mother and the baby. The baby, well, she was dead. She had turned blue, blue, blue.

But then right away, they called a doctor. I believe it was papá who went to get him. The doctor comes, looks at her, and says: "Well, what's wrong with this baby girl? It sure looks like she's been poisoned. Well, what happened? This is very serious."

Papá said, "It's because my wife had a fright while she was breastfeeding the baby. The other girls were running around with a pair of scissors and that scared my wife."

"Yes . . . this is like a poisoning, but perhaps even more serious than that."

"Well, that's what happened."

"Well, she's dead."

He pronounced her dead.

In those days they didn't have all those investigations like they do nowadys. At least I didn't see anything of the sort, you see. Next they called my grandmother and my aunts and uncles, right away. So they all came over . . . since the baby had died. In those days the wakes for the dead were done at home: a table was placed in the middle of the living room, and that's where the deceased would be set up, whether it be adult or child. They would set up the deceased, place flowers there, and four candles, one at each corner of the table. That was the custom in those days.

So they set up the table right away because the baby was dead; they placed her body there, with candles and everything. Then within about fifteen minutes, my little sister came back. The baby began to move, and everyone started to scream and cry at the sight of the baby girl moving: they all ran to her. The baby girl came back to life. Right away, mamá took her in her arms, crying with great joy. She had barely come to life for about fifteen minutes when she died once again. Once again, they fetched the doctor. In the end, the doctor came about three times. The last time the doctor said, "Ma'am, this child is dead: She's lifeless. Her heart has stopped. She's dead."

So then they laid her body out for the last time.

And my mother was suffering. Just imagine! Then my mother went into a room we had at the back of the house where she had a trunk. Do you know those big trunks they used to have back then? It was in one of those trunks that mamá stored some clothes, sheets and clean clothes. She had a huge Sacred Heart of Jesus in the living room. Well, mamá went and took it down. I was following right behind her, watching her, and asking myself: What is mother going to do?

My mother was in tears, but she went to the trunk and took out all the clothing; then she placed the Sacred Heart of Jesus facedown at the very bottom of the trunk. On top of that she placed the clothes and closed the trunk. Then she knelt and prayed. She told the Sacred Heart of Jesus that she didn't want to see her daughter suffer any longer. If her child was to be taken, she would give her up willingly and not cry a single tear. She would give her up with all her heart. But were she to remain alive—if mamá were allowed to keep her—those seizures had to stop because she could no longer watch her suffer. She also made some vows. Mamá vowed that if the child was saved she would baptize her and name her María de Jesús. Mamá left the Sacred Heart of Jesus in the trunk and went to the living room. After a few moments, the baby girl returned to life! The moment she came back to life, they baptized her right there at home, and she never had a seizure again. There you have her to this day: alive. This happened in 1922 in Monterrey where María was born. She was just a tiny newborn. I say: this is the faith my mother placed in the Sacred Heart of Jesus. She said she would give up my little sister and wouldn't cry a single tear. So you see it was granted that María live. And to this day María still lives. That goes to show mamá's enormous faith. And it's one of the experiences I never ever forget.

There's another experience which I had myself. What I'm going to tell you happened in 1924. As I told you, my father always worked for a period of time in the United States, and then for another period of time in Monterrey, Mexico. On this occasion we were here in the United States when suddenly papá said we were going back to Monterrey once again. So papá left before we did, in order to put a household together so that by the time we'd get there everything would be ready. Shortly after papá left, about two weeks later, he sent mamá money so she could contract someone with a truck to take us down to Laredo.

You know, every time we'd leave for the other side [Mexico], mamá would stock up on many things: for example, one of those wood-burning stoves, blankets, bathtubs, and . . . It seems to me she even had a mattress or two. She'd take many things along. Finally, she found a man who could take us to Laredo. But the problem was that the truck was one of those flat-bed trucks without side-railings.

The man said to mamá: "Well, if you like I can take you in this truck."

"Fine, that's fine."

"We'll just put the two mattresses on the bottom and the other things on the sides. We'll tie them down securely, and the two girls can sit on top of the stuff. You can sit in the front with the younger children; that's how I'll take you to Laredo."

So we made arrangements to leave.

At the time I had a small dog I loved dearly. Mamá wanted to leave it behind, but I started to cry. She said, "OK, we'll go ahead and take the puppy, but only to Laredo. We have to leave her in Laredo because we can't take her across [the border]."

I accepted that. So we sat down at the very top of the truck; I took my dog in my arms so she wouldn't run off. And that's how we left for Laredo.

In those years, the road from San Antonio to Laredo was not paved, like roads are today, see; it was made of cobblestones and dirt. As such, the truck couldn't go any faster than thirty miles per hour. We must have been nearing Cotula when I started to fall asleep—up there atop the truck. So then the dog jumped out of my arms. Since I was asleep I didn't stop to think where I was and I went after her. I fell down and was out cold in the middle of the road. I had very long hair and it was pulled back with one of those long barrettes with a hook. It was made of metal and about as wide as half a finger. I don't know if you're familiar with those. Well, that metal barrette cut into my head and left a big hole. In any case I was just lying there, and my sister Beatriz started to scream and scream, "Lydia fell off!!Lydia fell off!"

Well, finally the driver noticed. You know, the truck didn't have much power, but it did travel thirty miles per hour. So they had gone some distance before they turned back and picked me up. I was unconscious; I wasn't aware of any-thing. By then we were approaching Cotula. It was there that they took me into some family's home and immediately sent for the town doctor. The doctor came and administered chloroform—they put me to sleep in order to operate and remove the steel barrette from my head, see. Then they sewed me up again. Two days we stayed and then we left.

In spite of everything, I took the dog with me. Mamá wanted to leave it be-hind, but I started to cry. So the truck owner said to mamá: "Look, the child is still very ill, and if you leave the dog here it might affect her."

"Well, I don't know. Let's see what Pancho says"—since papá was named Francisco.[8]

Papá soon arrived. He said: "Well, of course my daughter must keep her dog!"

"But how?"

"Well, I know how."

So we went to the immigration office; there they put the little dog in a cage and sent it by train. In sum: the dog also crossed the border. Well, we all finally arrived at my grandmother's house in Monterrey. Oh, we were all so happy. However, my grandmother was very worried by what had happened to me, because she loved me very much.

Well, shortly thereafter—about two weeks after we settled down in Monterrey—I was brushing my hair one day and noticed that I had soft bulges on both sides of my head. Like balls that you could press. They felt like some type of bag. Then I called out, "Mamá, look, it hurts a bit. What do I have here?"

My mother took a look at those bulges. So she told papá, and they took me to the doctor. The doctor examined me and asked, "What happened here?"

Then mamá told him about the accident I had.

"Oh," he said. "This child had a head injury and this is coagulated blood. That blood didn't come out; it stayed there and formed those bulges. We have to operate. She needs an operation in order to remove that blood."

My mother hated hospitals and was terrified of them and even horrified at the thought of them cutting me open and all. So mamá said, "No."

She was opposed, and the doctor said, "Well, it's the only solution, because that blood can't just stay there."

Once we got home papá said, "Well, let's see what we can do . . . "

But mamá said, "Well, let me think about it."

As soon as we got home from the doctor's, we went to my grandmother's house. My mother arrived in an ocean of tears and said to my grandmother: "Just look, mamá, at what's happening to Lydia's head; and they want to operate on her."

There was a woman at my grandmother's house, an older woman. They began to discuss what the doctor said: that I needed an operation and such. The older woman then says to my grandmother, "Well, you needn't worry so much. My son also suffered such an injury, and he also developed a bulge with coagulated blood. Do you know how he got cured? We took him over to a river where there are many leeches, the kind that suck blood."

She says, "We just put those little animals on him and they sucked the blood out. That's how he got well!"

When I heard that stuff about those little animals, I was horrified at the thought that they might put them on me and that they would suck on me. I got very scared. Leeches? I imagined them to be like rattlesnakes or God knows what. I didn't even know what they might be.

I then took off by myself and went into the bedroom. My grandmother was that kind of woman who keeps her own home altar and with many saints. As soon as you entered her bedroom you'd see the altar and a framed holy image above it. In fact, I didn't know what virgin it was—later I found out that it was Our Lady of the Oak. She has a chapel in her honor in Monterrey. Right outside of Monterrey, she has a little church where everybody goes to adore her. See?

Well, I would see that image every day when I'd go into her bedroom to kneel at her little altar. That image always impressed me, and I would gaze at it a lot. On that occasion when they were talking, I ran to the altar. I entered that little room, the bedroom, saw the image, kneeled, and implored that virgin: "Little virgin, please don't let them put those animals on me. I'm very scared. Heal me!"

I don't remember exactly how I implored her and how I asked her to cure me from this illness. But I didn't want those animals on me. And that's what I did. I didn't say anything to anybody. We finally went home. Two days went by, and my mother was still thinking it over; she didn't want me to be operated on.

As soon as dawn would break I'd say, "I'm going to my grandmother's."

I would go there in order to kneel and implore the virgin—that image I had before me—I'd implore her to save me from those animals. Imagine the faith with which I begged her!

One week passed, and one day I went and washed my hair, was combing myself, and suddenly noticed the bulges were gone; they were gone! As surely as this light is shining! I couldn't feel those bulges at my temples anymore. So I called out to my mother: "Mamá, mamá, *mamacita*, look, come here!"

"What?"

"Look, the bulges are gone!"

"Let's see."

They had just about decided in favor of taking me to that river, see. My mother had a look at me. "But how is that possible?"

Right away we went to my grandmother's house. Mamá said, "Look, mamacita; look at Lydia . . ."

"What? The bulges are gone?"

That's when I told them, "Well, they didn't leave on their own. I petitioned the virgin in your room, grandmother. I begged her to heal me, to take this away. And look: she did take it away."

My grandmother said, "Just look at what faith can do! God and that virgin heard her prayers! It's the Virgin of the Oak that's here in the chapel [in Monterrey]."

Then my mother took me all the way to the little chapel to give thanks and to pray. Later they took me to the doctor, and he was amazed. "It's not possible. She had that blood . . . How did this happen?"

The doctor looked and examined me and said, "Well, the girl is just fine now."

So here you have me: I didn't have the operation. And who saved me? Well, it was the faith that I placed in that virgin, the fact that I begged with all my heart. That's why I say it's faith that makes everything happen.

Another example closer to home: You know about Our Lady of San Juan, don't you? Our virgin whose chapel is in the valley? Well, this happened to me about a year ago. It happened that this finger on this hand got really twisted. I could hardly move it at all. It was bent back totally crooked. If I moved it even a tiny bit, it felt like I was being stabbed with a knife. Well, I would cry because . . . it was extremely difficult to play the guitar. But I also would cry because I love to sew, to make my flowers and outfits, to do things around the house, you see. I couldn't even peel potatoes; I couldn't hold the mop, couldn't mop. In order to wash dishes or to hold a glass, I had to do it like this [*shows how*]. It was quite a sacrifice to have my finger like that. Finally, I went to see the doctor.

My doctor examined me and said: "Lydia, you've severed a tendon, and we have to operate on your whole arm in order to straighten out your finger."

And I said: "Operate on me?" . . .

I was so scared. So one day I implored Our Lady of San Juan. I begged her: "Most holy virgin, you who have worked countless miracles, who have cured so many sick people, hear my petition! I don't want them to operate on my hand. Grant me health. I promise to bring you a little silver finger, or a gold one, or whatever. I'll go to see you. But restore the health of my finger—even if it remains crooked; just stop the pain so I can go about my business."

And look at me! Look at this finger. You see, it's not in perfect shape like the other fingers. You can see a little bone here, see? But it doesn't hurt at all. I can pick up everything, I play the guitar, I can hold scissors . . . I begged the virgin to cure me, for her to take the pain away, even if the finger remained crooked. See, there is a God in heaven. I was spared the operation. The finger isn't perfectly straight, but who cares! It isn't straight but it doesn't hurt. And here I am! So I went to her; I fulfilled the vow I made.

So the fact remains that if you ask for something from the heart and with faith, with a pure faith, your wish will be granted. At least that's how I feel: when I ask for something . . . it is granted to me.

My mother would teach us these things, as I said, from a young age. Even though papá was not Catholic—he didn't believe in anything—my mother was. She taught us to pray and would even send us to church with my grandmother. My father didn't oppose it. He would say, "Well, that's your belief."

But beyond that she would tell us parables about life, about things we should not do. That certainly helped us a great deal. Because our human education begins in childhood. Imagine, these things I'm telling you about—like the story I told you earlier—happened when I was very young. Although we were very little, I've never forgotten them. When you're little, you retain everything deep down. Be they good deeds or good customs: you don't forget them, nor do they leave your heart. Even once you're grown you don't forget.

I also did the same with my daughters. When they were little, I sent them to catechism and to church. Before going to bed at night, I'd teach them good things. Children retain all those teachings.

Nowadays since life has gotten so expensive, and both the mother and the father have to work, the children just go off to school without heeding any *consejos*.[9] You know, they don't learn a thing about that in school. And the mother and father don't have the time to teach them how to behave properly; they're always busy working. They return from work completely exhausted and don't even look after the kids. So the kids grow up on their own. That's why we're seeing such changes among the youth nowadays; it's because they grow up alone.

I remember when I began to travel, the first time I went to Los Angeles and took both my little daughters. I'll never forget a man who worked there as a stagehand. He was an elderly man who saw me with my two daughters and said to me: "It makes me so happy to see you with your daughters . . . those are your daughters, aren't they?"

"Yes, these are my daughters."

"Are those two the only ones?"

"Yes."

He says, "I'm going to give you some advice: don't ever leave them. Never

Lydia Mendoza and her first two daughters, Yolanda (*left*) and Lydia (*right*) (ca. 1940). Courtesy U.T. The Institute of Texan Cultures, the *San Antonio Light* Collection

leave them without your affection and your love, because that's the most important thing to give children. See, I had two daughters, but I got a divorce. Later, since I was always busy working, I forgot about them." He said, "They can't even remember me. Yes, I'm their father, but they feel no affection for me, they don't love me. But it was my own fault; I neglected them. So that's the consejo I give you: don't ever separate from your daughters."

And this is how I did it: when I used to tour, I'd take a woman with me who would care for them. I never left them. I was always with them. So my daughters were well brought up: very sisterly, and very attached to the family. And that's why I tell you that everything depends on what we teach them.

There are all the kinds of things I cultivate, things I believe in. Sometimes I say to myself: "No. Perhaps this thing or that thing is not important."

But perhaps it *is* important. It's like the story I told you about that young woman, about the dove, the feathers, and all . . . When I was at Fresno State University I told that story to the young woman who was my interpreter. I just told it to her in the course of a conversation.

"Oh!" she said. "That story is very interesting."

She also was a teacher in the schools, see. Whenever we'd visit classrooms, I'd seize the opportunity to tell that story. She would translate it into English. I don't know how she told it, what she said, or what meaning she gave it. She'd tell it in English, but the children always paid attention to what she was saying; it looked like they really liked it. They'd sit attentively. I believe that story really might have happened, but I don't know. It must have happened . . . You can't deny that there are far too many people who love to gossip . . . and keep an eye on who's coming and going.

Look, where I live I mind my own business in my own home. I don't get into people's lives here, there. I don't ever spend my time looking to see who went in, who went out. I'm in my own house, and that's that. I know my neighbors, see. We're neighbors, and we greet one another and all. At times they will ask me: "Say, who lives over here? . . . What have they been up to? . . . Did someone visit them?"

I answer: "I don't know a thing, ma'am. Look, I don't know anything."

I don't like to get into problems. I mind my own business at home, and that's it. As it is, I barely have enough time to do my own work. And so, if you get into matters that are none of your business, later on you have to go around picking up the dove's feathers! [*She laughs a lot.*] How interesting that story is, don't you think? Dear holy God. The fact is, one must be very careful.

Musical interlude

[*Lydia Mendoza sings "Nochecita" ("Sweet Night").*]

Surely she cannot forget.
The night was my faithful witness.
Tell me, you who well know,
if what I sing can no longer be.

Refrain
Sweet night, my life went up in dreams
when her love and affection forgot me.
With my heart torn to pieces I now tell you
how I've suffered since I've felt your betrayal.

Although you know that loving you is my delirium,
you mock me and have no compassion.
I love you, and silently adore you,
every night when you hear me sing my song.

Refrain repeats

Other beautiful songs are "Jesusita en Chihuahua," and "Bésame Mucho," and "Noche de Ronda." I also sing "Cucurrucucú Paloma," but I sing it like this [*she sings*]:

They say that all the nights
he'd spend them crying,
they say he wouldn't eat
he'd spend the time drinking.

They swear that heaven itself
would tremble to hear him cry;
how he suffered for her,
that even unto death he called her name.

Ay, ay, ay, ay, ay . . . he'd sing.
Ay, ay, ay, ay, ay . . . he'd wail.
Ay, ay, ay, ay, ay . . . he'd sing
from this mortal passion . . . he was dying.

They say a sad dove
now sings early in the morning
at that empty little house
with its little doors flung open.
They swear that dove
is his very soul
which still awaits her,
hoping for that unfortunate woman's return.

Cucurrucucú . . . dove,
cucurrucucú . . . don't cry.

Stones will never know of love, sweet dove,
they will never know what love is.
Cucurrucucú, cucurrucucú;
cucurrucucú, weep no more, sweet dove.

Or I sing "Margarita" or "El Corrido de Luis Pulido." [*She starts to sing "The Corrido of Luis Pulido."*]

There were many theaters in those years

In those days—in the Lubbock, Texas, area—there was a whole chain of towns, and all of them had theaters. In those years there were lots of people in that territory because there was and still is a lot of cotton. But nowadays it's worked with machines. In those years it was all manual labor in West Texas [the Panhandle]. Since we knew there was good pay and lots of work, lots of cotton, people would flock to the area. That's why all performing groups imaginable were there. Among them Isidro López, Agapito Zúñiga, Andrés Huesca, Valerio Longoria, and Narciso Martínez. I got to know Andrés Huesca pretty well. But we never performed together, because he had his group and I had mine.

At any rate, all those groups were there. And there was work for all of them, because one variety show would arrive, leave, and then another would arrive. We all got work. We'd each get only three days. Three days for us, then the next group, and so forth . . . And you'd work all week; not just Friday, Saturday, and Sunday. No. Because it was just packed with all those people. The groups who

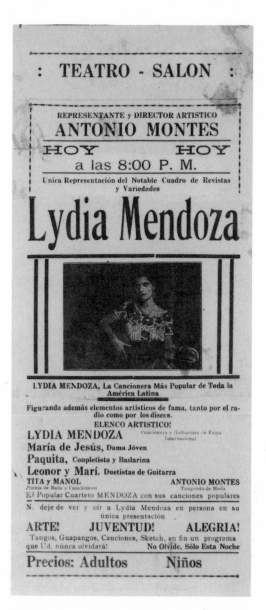

Teatro Salon poster bills Lydia Mendoza as "the most popular singer of all Latin America" (ca. 1940s). Courtesy Houston Metropolitan Research Center, Houston Public Library

played at dances, for example, stayed all week, and there were dances all week. People would work, and still they would go dancing. There was a lot of money. That's where I met Andrés Huesca. He didn't just travel alone with his harp. He had two or three others with him. Most of the time he would play at dance events. He would also do performances in theaters.

People made a lot of money in those years. Those were beautiful days. But when word got out that they were bringing in machines, they stopped hiring people. To this day, there's a lot of cotton and all, but it's all worked by machine. So in that whole territory there's nothing left of those towns which all had theaters. Like the Teatro del Lobo [Wolf Theater], which was a huge beautiful theater; nowadays it's a dance hall. In those theaters they also showed Mexican movies in addition to the variety shows. The owners were [Euro-]Americans, but in all those theaters they showed only Mexican movies. And the same holds true for all the little towns that had theaters: now there's nothing left of that. It's the same thing in the Rio Grande Valley, at the border with Reynosa and Matamoros, which is where we immigrated, through Reynosa. All that territory—beginning from Mission all the way to Brownsville—is full of small towns like Donna, Weslaco, La Feria . . . yes, all of those. The distance between one town and the next is at most seven or eight miles. But even so, there were many theaters in those years I'm telling you about.

After many years passed, after I had established my career, we once again toured that area, but then we did perform in the theaters. We'd work one day in McAllen. Tomorrow in another town. We would work Monday, Tuesday, and Wednesday in those little towns, even though the distance between them was only six or seven miles. We always had work, and we had a very good income. Nowadays you go to the valley, and there aren't any more theaters. In those days they used to show a Mexican movie and afterward have the variety show. And not just my own variety show, but also some big variety shows that would show up. I witnessed variety shows brought by Pedro Infante. Many performing artists from Mexico would come, and all of them toured all those towns: Sara García, Emma Roldán, El Chicote, Tin Tan, and Marcelo. Indeed . . . all those variety shows from Mexico would tour the entire valley because there was performance work every day and in each of those little towns. Entire families would go to the theaters, and there were performances all week.

And even more so during winter when the grapefruit or orange season began. The agricultural season over there is somewhat similar to California. There are huge grapefruit, lemon, and orange plantations. So that when the harvest season arrived, there were lots of people. All of that meant lots of money for the theaters. And then on Friday, Saturday, and Sunday, there were dances, too. The dances were somewhat different. All the musical groups played there.

But nowadays all of that has ended. Well, I believe the dances still go on. But the theaters: that ended ever since television came. As soon as television came, everything started to decline, everything, and so there's nothing left. The fact remains that people don't go to the theater nowadays. But, of course, there are certain places—for example, in Houston—where we do have theaters, but the people go there to see the movies.

For example, just recently in July when I was in Los Angeles, a performance with Togolele was booked. You know who Tongolele is. She is a great dancer. By chance, she was in California, and the producer wanted to book her in a movie theater. But they were also looking for an additional act. They didn't want to feature her alone. So they went to see me—they came with the darned man who paid me four-hundred dollars [*she laughs*] for a performance.

Performers at the Million Dollar Theater in Los Angeles. Lydia Mendoza is flanked by renowned comedians Marcelo (*left*) and Tin Tan (*right*). On the far right is María Mendoza (1950). Courtesy Houston Metropolitan Research Center, Houston Public Library

Well, I was ready to go back home, when he said: "Look, Lydia, don't leave yet because they're going to inaugurate this theater in San Bernardino. And there's plenty of money in it since they've advertised it a lot. Tongolele will be there."

"That's fine," I said.

"We're going to give you one hundred fifty dollars."

"OK. That's fine."

I stayed, and we went to that darned performance. Well, you'll never believe it: fifty people at the most showed up. There were no people! Why? Hard to know. And in spite of the double billing with Tongolele and with me. Then when they said they wanted to take the two of us on tour, I told him, "Not me. Count me out. I'm going home."

I realized that the whole thing was a theater experiment conducted by those producers. Perhaps they only advertised it on the radio. You know that nowadays very few people listen to the radio. Radio listeners are few and far between. Most people watch television. Nowadays if you organize an event like that, a festival, or something like that, what attracts an audience is television advertising. Because everyone watches television. But television is very expensive. One ad can cost thousands of dollars. But like I say: this is what has hap-

Advertisement by the Million Dollar Theater in Los Angeles announcing famed dancer Tongolele and other artists, including Lydia Mendoza (ca. 1950s). Courtesy Houston Metropolitan Research Center, Houston Public Library

pened with the theatrical variety shows in all those towns. They all had the same fate. They had to close the theaters down because people stopped going.[10] They made no money, so they were forced to shut down. Some were turned into dance halls or were completely shut down. You'll notice that in Los Angeles they still advertise Mexican movies. That must mean that there are audiences. But in most towns Mexican theaters fail.

We northerners: nosotros los norteños

What shall we talk about now?

So many musical ideas have been born from all of us northerners[11] up here. We really create music according to our own taste and in our own style: as we like it, and as the audiences like it. So a bolero will suddenly be played in ranchera style; or a corrido is turned into a ranchera or whatever else. The crucial thing is to make change in music. But, of course, it still remains the same: the same essence.

In Texas, for example, they dance a lot of *huapango*[12] but in norteño style.

And they give it a very nice flavor. Also the norteño Mexican polka is different; only the polka idea was borrowed. Someone imagined that it could be transformed into something norteño, different: and they did it. They didn't play it exactly like the Germans play it, see? We adapt the music. I adapt my music.

Take this, for example: I sing the song "La Malagueña," see? "La Malagueña" doesn't go the way I sing it. It has other rhythms, other differences. And I didn't dare sing that song because I knew I wouldn't do it right. But my audiences began to request it a lot. They'd say, "Lydia, why don't you record that song?" and "We want to hear that song with your voice."

Well, at last I took heart, and I recorded it. But I did a recording in which I adapted it to my style. And people have liked it a lot. The same holds true for huapangos, which I don't sing as they are originally sung. "Cucurrucucú Paloma" is a huapango. I can't give it that falsetto that it's sung with. I would say that the flavor of a huapango comes from that falsetto that's used: that change of voice that is used so beautifully. And I can't do that. But in turn I sing in my own style. I don't sing a lot of huapangos. Only "Cucurrucucú Paloma" and perhaps another one. Probably two at most.

I also changed my guitar. Well, when we arrived in San Antonio, all those musical groups had their twelve-string guitars, guitars like the one I've got. But their strings were tuned differently: it's logical that a twelve-string means that it has to have two firsts, two seconds, two thirds, two fourths, two fifths, and two sixths. All pairs tuned the same, like the mandolin which is tuned that way: in octaves, see. It has a very interesting tuning. So I thought: "I'm going to tune my guitar another way."

That's when I got the idea of tuning one string high and one low, and the next . . . and so forth. That's why the sound of my twelve-string is very different. It occurred to me to string it up in a different way. I imagined it would sound more beautiful. For example, the third string is at a certain pitch. If you combine it with a first string, the first string will be higher in pitch than a first string in its normal place. You raise its tuning so it will be at the same pitch as the third. It will sound the same, only an octave higher. The end effect is a different sound. And that's how I have tuned my guitar. That's how I have developed my own ideas; to the limits of my own intelligence, see?[13]

I want to give you another example of the changes I have made. Once I had the opportunity to record an entire LP of nothing but South American music. This happened when I used to record with the Falcón label and the record producer went to Colombia. Over there he did some negotiations with someone— and since I'm known throughout that territory, they suggested to him that I do an entire Lydia Mendoza LP recording of their music. He said: "Well, let's see if we can do it."

And they even gave him an LP which contained the twelve songs they wanted me to record for them.

At some point, Mr. Arnaldo phoned me and said, "Lydia, I have some news for you: in Colombia they want an LP with nothing but their regional songs. But they want them with your voice. I'm sending you an LP today."

So he sent it. And I listened to it. You know, all the music was very beautiful, but in their own style. I couldn't understand it. It would have been impossible for me to adapt my voice to the style of that recording. So I said to this man: "Mr. Arnaldo, I'm very sorry. The songs are very beautiful but—in truth—I won't be able to pull that off."

"No, Lydia," he says. "Adapt them to however you feel them, to however you want to sing them. They don't want you to sing them the same way they do. They want these sung with your voice and in your own style."

Well, so I recorded them; and you should see how nice they sound! On one side I sang what they requested with nothing but mariachi accompaniment, and on the other side it was with my guitar. The collection they sent had songs like—let me see if I can remember: one of them was "Soberbia" ["Arrogance"]; another was "Mis Flores Negras" ["My Black Flowers"]. Not the one I usually sing, but the one that says: "Listen, beneath the ruins of my passions . . ."

"Mis Flores Negras" is a very old song; it also contained "Los Mirlos" ["The Blackbirds"] and some others. All of these are songs from down there, all of them very beautiful. But like I said: I adapted them to my style. And they liked them a great deal. That LP is still for sale in South America. It wasn't distributed here; but when I visited Colombia not too long ago, they had it there. Everybody had bought it.

I also recorded another LP with songs from there. Among them is that song "Serenata de Mayo" ["May Serenade"]. Have you heard of it? It goes like this [*she sings*]:

> The flowers of May have arrived
> with their beautiful aromas
> [*she hums*]
> which go from rose to rose,
> the time shall arrive . . .

See, it's very beautiful. "Serenata de Mayo" it's called. It's a song for Mother's Day. But, like I told you, the version they sent me sounded very different. So I adapted it; I arranged it in *balada* tempo, or like a bolero. It turned out very beautifully. And that's how I've recorded almost all my music, see? I sing it in *my* style; it would be impossible to do it the way they do it somewhere else. And besides, in those recordings of mine I've never liked to sing like or imitate some other artist. I hear a song, I learn it, and then I sing it the way I want to sing it. That has been my musical style: let's say I don't try to imitate what another artist does, see?

I would also claim that I was one of the first people to introduce the norteño polka rhythm to California. This happened when I started to record again after the war was over. I began to work in California in 1947 and then recorded with the Azteca label. This was a very big company which doesn't exist anymore. I had been recording with them for about two years when I suggested that they do norteño accordion recordings. The man from the company said: "No, people don't like that music here."

I told him, "Well, let's try it out. Maybe it will catch on. People aren't very familiar with it, but maybe they'll like it. I know a *conjunto* [accordion ensemble] we can send for."

One of the musicians was Lorenzo Caballero—this man, I don't know if you've heard of him. He's a man who is more or less of my generation. He's a guitarist who had a conjunto, and they played very beautifully. They hardly play anymore. At that time Lorenzo Caballero played the guitar; Juan Viesca played one of those double basses—the *tololoche*—and then there was a bajo sexto. I think that was it. In any case, the owner of Azteca finally said: "OK. Let's try it. If you think so, let's see if people like it. But you'll have to accompany them on the guitar."

I agreed, and he told me: "Get in touch with them."

So I got in touch with Lorenzo, and he said to me, "Yes. We'll go."

So they reached an agreement concerning pay and all that, and that I was going to sit in. Everything was fine. So they named it El Conjunto de Oro de Lydia Mendoza [Lydia Mendoza's Golden Conjunto] A very norteño-sounding group. Well, they finally arrived, and we—I believe we recorded about four records. That's how those norteño recordings began to take off. Since the conjunto carried my name, that helped somewhat in bringing people's attention to it. Well, that music developed a following, and after that point many norteño groups began to record in California.

Lorenzo Caballero's group were excellent performers. Lorenzo was hilarious; he's an artist. Imagine, he plays the guitar with his tongue; he turns the instrument around and fries an egg on top of that guitar. First he would spin it around and then throw some of that flammable liquid on it. What's it called? I can't remember what the devil that liquid was. They would put that liquid on the guitar, then they'd put a frying pan on it and fry an egg. Then they would remove that stuff, and he'd somehow do a somersault from a sitting position. After that, he would play guitar with his tongue—part of some song I don't remember. I think it was "La Paloma" ["The Dove"]; it's a great performance. He himself was like a whole variety show. It's fantastic, except he's so stubborn and he doesn't like to tour or leave town. But as a grand theatrical spectacle he's really good. He's still alive and lives in San Antonio. That's Lorenzo Caballero.

Juan Viesca was one of Lorenzo's partners, the one who played the tololoche. They really did a fantastic number. Viesca with his clowning around on the double bass: he'd spin it and jump around . . . and everything. Now Viesca is semi-retired because last year he had a heart attack, see. But in the theater they were regular clowns. Really great. Now, however, they are retired.

At any rate, I managed to get them to record norteño music in California. Like I was telling you, back then I was one of the people who pushed for norteño music in California. That happened about fifty years ago. Of course, nowadays California is flooded with it. There are conjuntos everywhere. That's for sure. And many accordion conjuntos go to California from Texas.

The Two Great Women of Texas

Nowadays in Texas it's just Chelo Silva and I: the two remaining best-known women still around. When they want a performer, right away it's either Chelo Silva or

Lydia Mendoza (*left*) with singer Chelo Silva (Houston, 1974). Courtesy Lydia Mendoza Collection

Lydia Mendoza. In Texas we're called "The Two Great Women of Texas." That's Chelo and me. Of course, what she sings is very different from what I sing. She sings a whole other . . . a different style of song. But she is a great presence, see. Of course, the poor woman is a bit . . . her voice. It's no longer that voice she had when she got started. I think she's been in the business about twenty or twenty-five years. When she first started, she sang very beautifully; she had a divine voice. But now since she drinks a lot, you see, her voice has been affected by the alcohol. If you hear her talk, you'd think it was a man's voice. The timbre of her voice has changed a lot. Besides that, it isn't just the drinking which has . . . that's not the only thing that has damaged her voice. I would say that a singer has to have a lot of rest. She has to get enough sleep and not stay up late . . . She . . . that's the thing about her, you see? She finishes a performance, people invite her out, and she goes. I never, or hardly ever, accept invitations; unless it's something very special and such. But you won't catch me staying up late or out all night: no.

I can say this because she and I have shared so much. Once we did a show at the Million Dollar Theater [Los Angeles] about three or four years ago. They wanted to expand Vicente Fernández's, and so they sent for me and Chelo in Texas. And we went. When we'd finish our performance . . . well, after I was done I'd go to my hotel room—or to a house where I was staying. Chelo . . . well, people would show up . . . you know, in this theater business there are just so many friends. They'd arrive and say: "Hey, Chelo, we've got a party going . . . come on, Lydia, let's go."

"No," I'd say. "I'm sorry, but I'm not going."

So they'd take off with Chelo. The following day she would arrive right before showtime. She'd arrive, poor woman, disheveled and without having slept. Imagine! She was barely arriving from the party she'd been at. Sometimes she'd show up . . . well, it looked like they'd put her hair up in rollers. Once when she arrived—like always—in a big hurry and right before her turn to go on, they just yanked the rollers out of her hair and didn't even comb her hair out; no, it just fell wherever. She went onstage just like that . . . no makeup, no nothing. That's how she went out to perform. To top it off, she even lost a shoe. All of this on account of her not taking care of herself. She stays up a lot, drinks, and she doesn't rest. So that's why she's already losing her voice. Audiences love her, though. Whenever Chelo Silva comes out onto the stage, the audiences go crazy . . . she's really very well known. But little by little—as is only natural—audiences have become disenchanted when they witness this atrocity of what's happening to her. That's what's happening because she doesn't take care of herself, see? That's what I keep telling her over and over.

It all depends on how you think. You see? Look, look at me. I've been in this business over fifty years. For seven years now, I've stopped carrying the same workload I used to carry, the fast track. But it hasn't been hard for me. Because it all depends on you, on how you think. The same holds true for men. If a man knows how to take care of himself, and not be a party animal and so forth, the same holds true, see? Everything depends on how you think and how you want to be. Because in this line of work . . . you know, there are many options: if you want to drink, stay up all night, live it up and all . . . Not me. I leave my house to go to work. I could say: I'm going to get ready, get dressed, take a taxi and go check out the clubs, spend the night out on the town, hear music, go drinking. I could do that. I'm by myself a lot. But I don't do that because . . . well, I don't like it. As far as I'm concerned, when it comes to resting and sleeping, I'm happy as can be. That's exactly what I want, and I've been that way my whole life, see?

I don't like to stay up late. On television they show some very nice movies and programs, but all of it is aired after midnight. What does occasionally keep me up is those darned soap operas on television. But the only soap I'm watching is the one called *Bodas de Odio* [Wedding of Hatred]. That's all. In Texas it ends at eight-thirty. As soon as it's over . . . I get ready and go to bed. Not my husband. He stays up till midnight watching programs. Not me. As soon as I watch my last program, I close my door and fall asleep, happy as can be. The only times I stay up late are when I'm working.

I say God put us in this world to make something of our lives. To do something of value; not just to exist . . . Like some of my women friends . . . they say they're bored at home, they don't know what to do with themselves. That's why they go out to nightclubs or whatever. When you really want to, there's plenty to do at home. I hunger to be home because when I'm home there aren't enough hours in the day to do so many things. It's like I'm telling you, I dedicate myself to my domestic work, taking care of my own business, my responsibilities. What's more, I sew my own costumes for my performance work. I make the flowers, and then I make the dresses. I rarely buy a ready-made dress or outfit. I like to make my outfits, my dresses, my housedresses, everything. So there's always something to do at home. I tell everyone: we've all come into this world to accomplish something. God meant for us to accomplish something, to occupy our minds with something. To do something of value. That's always been my goal, see? I wish all of us women would think this way.

What more can I ask of life?

 You see, lots of people tell me: "Are you really Lydia Mendoza? . . . No, you can't possibly be. You must be Lydia's daughter, relative; but you can't possibly be Lydia Mendoza because I was a child when I first heard her sing!"

And they ask me: "Excuse me, how old are you?"

As soon as I tell them my age, they say: "Well, then, yes, you are Lydia Mendoza."

Even if I wanted to claim I'm younger, people wouldn't believe me. I have to be able to prove it. But, in fact, I'm proud to say my age because I thank God that I've been given so many years.

You know, when I was introduced in New York, they spoke about many things because they had asked me for all kinds of facts, the whole history and everything, including my age, too. And, of course, they announced it publicly the night I performed. The Latina woman at whose house I stayed told me that the night I was introduced, one of the event organizers came out and said, "This young lady is Lydia Mendoza?"

No, he simply couldn't believe my age. You know that onstage one looks much younger and all. They asked how I could be the woman they were introducing, Lydia Mendoza, the one performing there. But, indeed, that's how it is. I think they'd like to see me with a little cane . . . or with glasses; like a feeble old woman falling down. Sure, of course, those years add up, don't they? That's a lot of years to carry around . . . like it or not . . .

Like recently in New York: I couldn't have imagined that I'd end up there after not having been there for forty-four years. The last time I was there was in 1941! They made a big deal about that in the calendar of events. The *New York Post* also interviewed me the day I arrived. In the interview was asked, for example, when was the last time I had been in New York. All that was a topic of conversation. I'd already been there, but it had been forty-four years since I had visited New York. So many travels in the last fifty years!

Lydia Mendoza at age 76 in front of her home in Houston (1992). Courtesy Yolanda Broyles-González Collection

For example, I also visited Santa Barbara around 1938, yes, actually several times, not just once; we performed in the theaters several times—we toured the whole area. Of course, Texas was the very first territory we toured in those years. And more recently as well, when the theaters were still in operation. They did away with theaters when television came. Like I told you, the whole Texas Valley used to be filled with movie theaters; nowadays there's nothing. We toured that whole region. More recently in Texas I've performed in many places . . . but mainly at festivities, concert halls, auditoriums, or dances. Like

Lydia Mendoza, La Reina Tejana (*Lydia Mendoza, Texas Queen*) (1987). Pastel portrait by Estér Hernández. Courtesy Estér Hernández

Lydia Mendoza at age 60 (1976). Courtesy Houston Metropolitan Research Center, Houston Public Library

on Mother's Day, for example, I'll be in Corpus Christi for three days. I'm already under contract. Austin is another place where I play—do music and talk— for many festivities. Austin is so lovely. Recently I was there again— I don't know if you heard about this—for that Hall of Fame event. Probably a Texas thing, you know. At that event they chose from among two hundred musicians from different parts of Texas. They finally selected one woman from El Paso. And another woman from . . . I think from Dallas. From Houston there was only one: that was me. I was the only Mexican. The three of us were chosen. That was a very beautiful celebration in Austin. And just a year ago we were in California for Cinco de Mayo. But at the moment, I haven't gotten a call for Cinco de Mayo. Nor for September 16, either.[14]

But I can assure you that in spite of my age I still feel lots of enthusiasm, lots of spirit. I'm not going to call it quits, not yet. My husband marvels at this—because he's seventy-two years old, but he's always sick, you see; I believe that's probably why he says, "Goodness, you have so much spirit to sew, to tour, to be among crowds, to sing, and all of that! How do you generate that spirit?"

I tell him: "Listen, I still have life in me."

I feel—thank God I still do—lots of enthusiasm and lots of spirit! Even when I go to bed or wake up, it's with that spirit . . . I open my eyes and, oh, I feel really enthusiastic! I never wake up saying, "Gee, I don't feel like doing anything; I think I'll go back to bed . . ."

You'll never see me that way! I'm always waiting for daybreak, for the new day to dawn so I can go about doing what I need to do. Like I told you, I still feel lots of enthusiasm. Maybe because I enjoy good health, thank God. I hope that . . .

The day after I returned from my last trip to New York, I played for five hours at a party. Because I don't know how to say no [*laughter*]. My daughter gets mad and says, "If the phone rings I'm going to say you're not in."

And I tell her, "Better not, mi'ja. If they call me, I appreciate that they remember me."

And as soon as I say yes to people, she gets mad at me. She says, "Mamá, I don't know why you're killing yourself so much."

"It's a responsibility that I have; it's an obligation," I tell her. "I won't say no to them."

On one occasion I played for five hours, although I had been booked for two. Well, not without a break, of course. But after being there for two hours, I said to the man who hired me: "Well, I've finished playing; now I'm leaving."

"No, don't leave. Stay here for another hour, even if you sing whatever you want to sing, but we want to have your voice here."

Well, like I said: I stayed there for five hours. Let me see: I went at seven and didn't arrive back home until midnight. Although I had planned for only two hours! But the man had a lot of people over, his friends, there at his party. You can be sure they didn't want me to go home! And I held out for five hours. I can tell you I got home dead tired and sleepy. But satisfied and happy. I had a good time, thanks to God; that's just the way I am: once I sit down with my guitar to sing, I'm not the type that can just stop. I keep on going for as long as they request songs. Because, well, I don't know . . . I believe this is one of my responsibilities. I can't say no to people. And like I said: I returned from New York on Sunday, and the next day I went to sing at that man's house. Well, it's just that I like music so much. Whenever I take my guitar and start to sing, I feel happy.

My granddaughters ask me when I'm going to retire from this career. I tell them, "I've already said that I'm going to die singing. In some place where I'm working; right there; that's where I'll die singing."

That's what I've said, and I believe that's the way it will be. I'll be somewhere singing, and my day will come. That's when God will say: "This is it. It's over." [*She laughs a great deal.*]

Oh my God!

But I'll tell you something else: if some illness should come over me someday, some sickness or . . . well, that's fine and I'm ready to go. Because God has already given me quite a few years of happiness and of tranquillity. For example, when my daughter Nora had cancer, she told me about all the tortures she went through, the treatments she went through and everything. That's why I tell her, "Look, mi'ja, I want to tell you that if someday they discover I have cancer, I don't want to be cured."

Because I will not submit to treatments which are going to torture me; I won't put myself through that, be hooked up to machines, or be locked up at home . . . No! I'd rather not be cured! Let God take me, and then it'll be over. It's like I always say: I've already lived many years, and I've fully enjoyed all those years God has given me in good health and with joy. I'm happy. That's why to this very moment I still feel great. Thank God! What more can I ask of life?

—— THE END ——

Lydia Mendoza. Dibujo en grafito por Estér Hernández (1999). Cortesía
Estér Hernández

II

Vamos hilvanando aquella historia: platicándola

Me han dicho que escriba la historia de mi vida, pero no sé... Para hacer eso quiero estar en paz, tranquila, sin compromiso de que tengo que salir para acá o ir pa' allá. No. Yo no soy nerviosa, ¿ves? Pero cuando voy a salir me mortifico tanto de que no se me olvide esto o aquello. Luego quisiera ir y ya venir pa' hacer esto o l'otro. Bueno, tantas obligaciones y no estoy tranquila de mi mente. Entonces esta ha sido mi idea: Le dije a mi'ja Nora, porque ella conoce mucho de mi vida y puedo platicar con ella, le dije: —Mira, mi'ja, me están dando ganas de hacer esto.

Yo ya he platicado mucho una parte de mi vida, pero la he platicado en retazos, ¿ves? No está hilvanada, que vaya derecho. No. Tengo deseos de comprar unos casettes y platicar desde el principio: cómo comencé, y cómo fui desarrollando mi carrera. Quiero dejar platicado todo eso; pero derecho. Esa es la idea que tengo yo. Ya después de grabado todo eso, que alguien la escuche y si cree que es importante, la escribe y si no, pos no hay nada perdido. ¿No crees? Así ya no necesitan estarme preguntando a mí de mi vida, ni perdiendo tiempo. En ratos vamos hilvanando aquella historia: platicándola.

Una vez le platiqué esta idea a un compadre mío que vive en Los Angeles, California; él es un gran hombre. Y él me dijo: —No comadre, ni se anime a hacer eso porque la gente busca la morbosidad en los libros.

Dijo que la gente busca algo como por ejemplo pasajes de mi vida: de que si tuve romances, o estuve enamorada o cosas por el estilo. Pos francamente, yo no tengo nada de eso en mi vida, en toda mi larga vida. Yo no tengo nada de eso que le pueda interesar a quien quiera leer ese tipo de libro. Pero yo creo que él está en un error, porque yo acabo de comprar un libro que me trajeron de Laredo sobre la vida de María Felix. La verdad es que todos nos interesamos por una gran figura, ¿verdad? ¿A quién no le interesa saber cómo comenzó ella, quién la descubrió, dónde estuvo, o cómo fueron sus comienzos? Todos queremos saber de una figura así, ¿no? Tengo yo tanto público y de tantos años que si se llegara a escribir un libro de mi vida creo que habrá alguien que diga: —Yo quiero ver cómo comenzó Lydia Mendoza.

Lydia Mendoza en 1948. Cortesía U. T. The Insitute of Texan Cultures,
Colección *San Antonio Light*

Porque siempre me han preguntado así algunas familias: que cómo
comencé, o que si no tengo algún libro de mi vida, que cómo comenzó la historia de mi música. Yo digo que sí se podría. Aunque pienso que si yo no lo
llego a ver... pos ahí están mis hijas. Y me gustaría que este libro fuera con fotografías y todo. Yo sé que si alguien se propone hacerlo y piensa que puede
obtener dinero para hacer eso, lo puede hacer. Porque se lleva dinero para
hacer eso, ¿ves?, como para publicar fotografías de la vida de uno, así como
esas que están en los libros. Todo eso, ¿ves?

Cuando yo llegué a San Antonio, no había mujeres que cantaran

 Pues fíjate que hay pocas, como mexicanas, hay pocas que haigan labrado una carrera sin interrumpirla, una dedicación en cuerpo y alma. Es raro eso, no creas. No las hay. Ahora una carrera se puede hacer mucho mas fácil. En aquel tiempo no teníamos los medios. Cuando yo comencé en mi música —que empecé yo, digamos cuando tenía yo como unos nueve años— vivíamos en Monterrey y yo ya tocaba mi guitarra. Las canciones que cantábamos al principio eran del repertorio de mi madre. Ella cantaba todas esas canciones, ella las sabía. Y pos, me daba por aprenderme cancioncitas, ¿ves?, aparte de lo que ya había aprendido de mi madre. Quería aprenderme algo. ¿Pero cómo? Si no había la manera.

Sino que me acuerdo de una vez que me mandó mamá a un mandado a comprar no sé qué. Me dió un centavo, pero aquello no costaba un centavo, y compré un chicle con lo que sobró. Ese chicle estaba hecho molotito ves, estaba enredado en un papelito, y ese papelito era una canción. Entonces ya después que me di cuenta de eso, con cada centavo que yo tenía en mi mano compraba un chicle. Así fui haciendo una colección como de unas veinte o veinticinco canciones de puros papelitos. Y los miraba yo. Allí venía, por ejemplo, "La Mocosita", "El Tango Negro", "La Adelita", las "Cuatro Milpas", "El Adolorido", "Ladrillo", "Todo Por Tí" ... bueno, tantos números que no me recuerdo de todos. Entonces los miraba yo esos papelitos, y decía: —¿Bueno pero cómo irá la música? Tantos números, ¿ves?, y yo no sabía la música. Bueno, después de esta historia, te platico como me aprendí la música. Eso fue en Monterrey en 1926; un año antes de venirnos pa' Estados Unidos.

Pero antes de venirnos pa' Estados Unidos siempre íbamos y veníamos, íbamos... Un año estábamos aquí y un año en Monterrey [México]. Porque mi padre trabajaba en el ferrocarril; no en el traque, sino que era el mecánico de las locomotoras. Entonces a veces lo destinaban una temporada acá o allá. Estábamos nosotros en Monterrey [Mexico] y luego, pos que: —Tu tienes que ir a Texas, a Estados Unidos.

Lo mandaban a San Antonio, a Houston, a Beaumont, y así. Entonces la mitad de la familia nació en Monterrey, como mis hermanas Juanita, María y Francisca la que murió. Las otras nacimos aquí. Yo, una hermana —la hermana mayor— y los dos hermanos somos nacidos aquí en Estados Unidos. Fuimos siete. Pero ya murió Francisca. Francisca murió; entonces ya nomás quedamos seis.

Entonces andábamos siempre viajando, ¿ves? Una temporada aquí, una temporada allá. Así fue que estuve en San Antonio por primera vez en 1923. Bueno. Después emigramos en el 27 y vivimos algún tiempo en el Valle [del Río Bravo]. Vivíamos en Kingsville cuando salió el anuncio en *La Prensa* que necesitaban artistas para cantar. Entonces ya pa' ese tiempo, cuando emigramos nosotros, ya mi papá se había retirado del ferrocarril. Entonces nos dedicamos a la música, porque a mí me gustaba mucho la música.

El Cuarteto Carta Blanca durante su primera grabación (1928). *De izquierda a derecha*: Leonor Zamarripa Mendoza, Lydia Mendoza, Francisco Mendoza, Francisca ("Panchita") Mendoza. Cortesía Colección Lydia Mendoza

Yo fui el, cómo te diré, el eje principal: —Que vamos a seguirle, que...

Entonces venía yo tocando la mandolina y mi mamá tocaba la guitarra, mi hermana Panchita tocaba un triangulito y mi papá una pandereta. Formamos un cuarteto, El Cuarteto Carta Blanca, y recorrimos todo el Valle de Texas cantándole a los mexicanos, ¿ves? Y cuando vió ese anuncio mi papá, pues fuimos a San Antonio. Nos dieron las grabaciones en 1928. Y nomás grabamos y nos fuimos de San Antonio. Por cierto que ni oímos ni una de las grabaciones.

No sé quién le metió a mi papá que con la música que traíamos nosotros, allá en el Norte [de Estados Unidos] íbamos a hacer mucho dinero. Porque en ese tiempo se iba mucha gente al betabel y a los trabajos. Familias enteras de mexicanos se iban para allá. Y que en todos los pueblos de por allá, como Detroit, Pontiac, Flint, y otros lugares de Michigan no había nada de diversión de música y que la gente se desesperaba. En aquellos años, pues de veras que no había nada. Pos no sé quién le metió a mi papá, que allá en el Norte con lo que nosotros tocábamos íbamos a hacer mucho dinero allá. Entonces una mañana llega y le dice a mi mamá, dice: —Alguien me ha dicho que allá para el estado de Michigan, para el Norte, nosotros podemos ganar mejor dinero que aquí.

Dijo mi mamá —estábamos muy pobres, no teníamos nada— dice mi mamá: —Ay, Pancho, usted está loco, ¿pos cómo nos vamos, si con sacrificios nos vinimos del Valle, pos irnos al Norte? ¿cómo?

—Oh, yo sé cómo nos vamos a ir.

Y dije yo: —Sí, papá.

—Anda, tú y tu padre están locos, ¿pos cómo nos vamos?

Nos juzgó locos; bueno, ya no se habló más de eso. A los dos días llegó mí papá con unos papeles en la mano: —Aquí está ya resuelto.

—Bueno, y eso, ¿qué es?

—¿Son contratos, papá, pa' trabajar?

—Sí, nos vamos al betabel.

¡Pues fue y nos enganchó! Estaban llevándose a mucha gente. Era la temporada —fue en abril— que se llevaban a gente, enganchaban. Eran los enganches pa'l Norte. Viajaban por tren y bus. Pos ya arregló mi papá, y mi mamá dijo: —Pos *yo* ni crea que voy a ir allá a las hierbas, a hacer eso. Yo no, nunca he hecho yo eso. A mí no me ponga... No.

—Si nomás me puse yo, y a dos hijas...

Eramos tres los que íbamos a trabajar.

Nos fuimos, al fin. Llegamos a Detroit, y a Flint, Michigan. Pos ahí estábamos en la labor y todo. Y allá, pos que es que fuimos a la comisaría y nos compró mi papá unos pantalones, de esos azules seguidos, que pos que íbamos a comenzar a trabajar en el betabel, al desahije. Estaban las matitas... ¿Pero nosotros qué sabíamos de eso, tú? Unas matitas así con unas hojitas que era el betabel. La obligación del trabajador era dejarle nomás dos hojitas a aquella matita y quitarle las que tuviera demás, que no crecieran muchas. Nomás las dos hojitas. Bueno, pos llegamos. ¿Pos que a ver qué íbamos a hacer? Pos que al desahije.

¿Pos qué? —decía mi papá— Nomás vamos a dejarle dos hojitas.

Pero no sabíamos, ¿ves? Teníamos que agarrar la matita y... no, ¡el tirón! —pos nos tráibamos ¡toda la mata! Hicimos un asesinato en todos los surcos. ¿Pos qué sabíamos nosotros?

—Pos yo no sé, papá, pos se viene toda la mata.

—Pos que con cuidado, ¡no sea taruga!

—Mire, que...

Pos nunca dimos con bola. Bueno, como quiera, no te hago largo el cuento. Ya en eso llegó el sábado y nos sentamos allá fuera, pos, siempre practicando o cantando y todo. Estábamos muy alegres, ahí cantando, cuando pasaron dos mexicanos, serían de la otra plantación, otro lugar, ¿ves?, y se pararon. Uno de ellos dice: —Ay, ¡qué bonito cantan ustedes! Pos, ¿pos qué están haciendo ustedes aquí?

—Oh, compañero, pos, nos vinimos al trabajo aquí.

—¿Pos por qué no van pa'l pueblo? Aquí está cerquita Pontiac. Allí hay un restaurantito, el único, una fondita mexicana, y mire, así se pone de gente. Todos nos volvemos locos, pos aquí no hay ni en qué divertirnos.

Entonces dijo mi papá: —Pues, sí, pero ¿pos cómo vamos? no tenemos en qué.

—¿Quieren ir?

—Pos sí, cómo no, ¡pues a divertir a la raza!

—Pos, mire, ¿sabe qué? El otro sábado si quiere ir yo le digo a un americano ahí donde estamos nosotros en la plantación. Tiene un carrito, dice, y es muy buena gente. Yo estoy seguro que si le digo que los lleve, los lleva.

—Bueno, está bueno.

El siguiente sábado vinieron y nos llevaron. Pos ya no volvimos. Nos llevaron allí, fue un sábado. Estuvimos cantando, huuy...mira, ¡nos ponían las pilas así de este tamaño, de puros pesos! Había mucha plata, yo creo, ¿ves?, pero varias pilas de... Que —¡cánteme ésta! —Sí, ¡cómo no!

Ni les decíamos cuánto, ni nos preguntaban. —¡Aquí está!

Y ponían las pilas, así, mira. Bueno, nos fue rete bien ese sábado. Decía la gente: —¿Pos 'onde estaban ustedes? —¿Pos qué están haciendo allá? —decían— ¿por qué no se vienen pa'l pueblo?

Y luego dijo mi papá: —No, pos, es que tenemos un contrato.

—No, no, no, —dicen— si mucha gente hace contratos y se sale y ni los buscan. Si quiere, nosotros mañana domingo vamos por ustedes. Que, ¿tienen muebles?

—No, no tenemos nada; nomás la ropa que tenemos.

Y era cierto eso. Nada. Pos otro día domingo, nos llevaron a aquel lugar. Echamos nuestras cositas que teníamos y nos trajeron pa'l pueblo y ya no volvimos. Y no nos buscaron.

Allá nos quedamos en Michigan... dos años. Mi papá luego luego comenzó a trabajar. En Pontiac estuvimos una temporada y ahí vimos nacer el 1929. En Pontiac vivimos desde abril, mayo, junio, julio, agosto, septiembre, octubre, noviembre... Vivimos como nueve meses, casi el año, en Pontiac. Y luego, nomás pasó el año y se fue mi papá a Detroit a la misma cosa —que ya no le gustó ahí Pontiac, que porque le dijeron que en Detroit había más raza, que había más gente mexicana. Nos dijo mi papá: —Yo me voy a ir y voy a buscar trabajo. Hallando trabajo, rento una casa y nos vamos pa' Detroit.

—Bueno, pos cómo quiera —dijo mi mamá.

Pos se fue y sí, luego luego le dieron trabajo en la Ford. Y ya arregló casa, y nos fuimos a radicar a Detroit. Ahí fue donde nació uno de mis hermanos, el más chico, Andrés. Y nosotros siempre en la misma, con la música. Cantábamos en los 16 de septiembre, 5 de mayo, festividades. Pos no había nada en aquellos años allá, ¿ves? Nosotros éramos los únicos mexicanos que traíamos música.

Ya se vino la depresión del 29 y entonces ya empezaron a rebajar gente. Mi papá fue uno de los primeros, pos, tenía poco... Pero, ya cuando se vino la depresión entonces dijo mi papá: —Pos no, no nos quedamos aquí. Vámonos pa' Texas otra vez.

Pos ahí venimos, en unos carritos, y llegamos a Texas en 1930. Llegamos a fines de 1930, llegamos como en octubre a Houston. Ahí nos instalamos, porque allí vivía una de mis hermanas de crianza; vivía en Sugarland, un pueblo inmediato a Houston. Y ahí nos quedamos parte del 30 y el 31. Vivimos año y meses en Houston. Pero en aquellos años también en Houston no había nada de ambiente. Ahorita está poniéndose Houston algo así como San Antonio. Muy bonito, mucho ambiente, mucho artista, y todo. Pero en aquellos años no había nada. Entonces mi papá dijo: —No, —dice— vámonos para San Antonio mejor.

Y así fue como llegamos a San Antonio en 1932. Cuando llegamos a San Antonio, pos siempre con nuestra música, ¿ves? Y, claro, allá pos había más ambiente. Lo había en aquellos años, como quiera. Y había la Plaza del Zacate.

La Plaza del Zacate durante los años cuando la familia Mendoza tocaba allí (los años 1930). Cortesía U. T. The Insitute of Texan Cultures, Colección *San Antonio Light*

¿No oístes tú mentar eso de la Plaza del Zacate? Onde está actualmente el mercado, ahí estaba la Plaza del Zacate. Ahí estaba al aire libre. No había nada de eso, de lo que se mira ahora, ¿ves? Era nomás esa plaza muy grande que era donde entraban las trocas que venían del Valle con verduras. Llegaban a las doce de la noche, traían su mercancía de ahí. Ahí iban todos los que compraban a menudeo de los puestos chicos, ahí iban y se surtían, ¿ves? Pero de las siete de la tarde a las once y media de la noche estaba libre y ahí es donde se ponían muchas mesas en las orillas, ¿ves? Ahí vendían, pos enchiladas, tamales, chile con carne…y. Estaban unas a un lado y otras al otro lado y dejaban en medio un espacio donde entraban los carros y se paraban ahí a escuchar los tríos de cancioneros. Había puros tríos de guitarras. No había nada de acordeones, ni nada de eso. Porque en aquellos años no se conocía el acordeón. Pura guitarra. Había puros trios de guitarras.

Ahí fue donde nos instalamos nosotros con nuestro grupo. Estos cancioneros que andaban ahí eran por todos como quince grupos. Pobrecitos, nomás entraba un carro, y corrían… —¿Pos, qué le cantámos? ¿"La Adelita"? Porque entraban también americanos, ¿ves?, a cenar, y a oir la música. Entonces nosotros no andábamos así, sino que nos instalábamos en una esquina. Estaba una señora ahí con su puestecito y nos dio permiso de que ahí nos sentáramos. Pos a ella le convenía porque la gente se venía donde estaba la música y le hacían comercio, ¿ves? Y así sacábamos nosotros para vivir.

La familia Mendoza tocaba en un puesto de comida (nombrados "baratillos")
como este en la Plaza del Zacate (principio de los años 1930). Cortesía U. T.
The Insitute of Texan Cultures, Colección *San Antonio Light*

Entonces cuando empezamos ahí el grupo, yo ya tocaba el violín, y mi hermanita la mandolina. Yo le enseñé a María a tocar la mandolina. Mi mamá tocaba la guitarra y un hermanito mío el timbrecito. Y ahí cantábamos. Yo ya tocaba la guitarra, porque yo aprendí a tocar la guitarra desde que tenía siete
años. Mi madre me enseñó. Ella fue la que me enseñó.

Pero al principio ni remotamente pensaba yo que podría tener voz. Ni
soñaba yo todavía con ser cancionera, ¡qué iba yo a cantar ni nada de eso! A
mí me gustaba la música, tocar la guitarra, instrumentos. Porque te digo, yo
aprendí la guitarra, y luego la mandolina y el violín, poquito piano, líricamente. El único instrumento que me enseñó mi mamá fue la guitarra, pero los
demás instrumentos yo sola los aprendí. Entonces, no sé, cuando estaba en
casa me daba de repente por cantar alguna canción yo sola, ¿ves?, de apren-
derme alguna. Y a veces así cuando estábamos el grupo cantando ahí le decía
yo a mi mamá: —Déme la guitarra pa' cantar una canción.

Yo lo que quería era, pos que me oyeran. Yo no sé qué pasaba en mi mente,
¿ves? Pos óyeme, así empecé a cantar yo sola.

Y pa' no alargarte más el cuento, llegó el momento en que ya casi el grupo no
cantaba. Porque: —No, que cante la señorita Mendoza. Queremos que nos
cante la...

Pos ya me empecé a aprender yo muchas canciones. Y así empecé a cantar
yo sin ningún, digamos, sin ningún pensamiento de que yo fuera a ser can-

cionera ni nada. Nomás me gustaba que me escucharan y a mí me gustaba cantar.

En una de esas ocasiones empezó —yo creo— a correr la fama de que ahí había una muchacha que cantaba muy bonito y todo. Una noche llegó un locutor de radio, entró con su carro y se paró a escucharnos. Estaba yo en ese momento cantando. Nomás acabé de cantar se bajó del carro y va y habla con mi mamá: —Señora. Señora Mendoza ¡qué bonito canta la señorita! Sabe que yo tengo un programa de radio. Es únicamente media hora, pero es muy escuchado. Además es el único programa que tenemos en San Antonio.

Es cierto, era el único programa [en español] que había en aquel año, ¿ves? Su programa de radio se llamaba El Programa de la Voz Latina; no me acuerdo de las letras de la estación, pero era el único programa de esos.

Entonces dice: —Me gustaría llevar a la señorita a que nos cante unas dos cancioncitas. Tiene una voz muy bonita, y yo le aseguro que ella puede hacer algo.

—Pues yo lo siento mucho señor, pero éste, éste es nuestro vivir y si nos vamos de aquí, si dejamos esto, pos ¿qué hacemos? De esto vivimos.

—Pos nomás una noche. ¿Qué puede perder? Le hace bien a ella. Sirve de que la escuchan y eso es otro porvenir.

—Sí, mamá, yo quiero ir al radio —empecé yo a decirle.

—Bueno, pos 'tá bueno, señor, pos iremos.

—Bueno, mañana vengo yo, las llevo, y las traigo de vuelta.

Pos sí me llevó, fui y canté yo, felíz de la vida porque había cantado en el radio. Y nada: Pos pasaron como tres días y hay viene el señor otra vez. Dice: —Señora Mendoza, me están pidiendo mucho a la Señorita Mendoza, dicen que quieren volver a escuchar esa voz.

—Pos lo siento mucho, señor Cortéz. —Pos se llamaba ansina, señor Cortéz— No, pero no podemos porque nosotros perdemos.

—Bueno, ¿y qué tal si yo le consigo a la señorita Mendoza un patrocinador, un anuncio que pague por el tiempo que va allá? Pues ya es una ayuda para ustedes —dijo.

—Bueno, pos si le pagan algo, sí, —dice— pero, de otra manera, no.

—Pos ahora verá, yo le aviso.

Fue y me consiguió un anuncio: tres cincuenta [$3.50], pero tenía que ser toda la semana. En aquellos años era un dineral, tú sabes. Era mucho dinero tres cincuenta. Todo estaba más barato... pagábamos uno veinticinco de renta ¡fíjate! La comida costaba... la libra de carne costaba quince centavos. La botella de leche, un nicle.[1] Todo baratísimo, de manera que tres cincuenta era un dineral. Entonces, bueno pos ya fui. Pos empecé a cantar ahí. Bueno llegó al grado de que ya no... ya no quise... ya no fuimos a cantar a la Plaza del Zacate. Porque ya el señor no quiso.

—No, la Señorita Mendoza está haciéndose muy famosa, está agarrando mucho nombre, y a mí no me gusta que esté cantando ahí en ese mercado, ahí en la Plaza del Zacate por lo que la gente le dé, no. Yo la voy a hacer una estrella. Yo voy a hacer de ella una estrella porque tiene una voz muy bonita y ahora verá: yo voy a ayudarla.

Pos a nosotros ya nos ayudó el señor este. Entonces, él lo que hacía era conseguirnos tocaditas en los restaurantes. Porque en aquellos años no había cantinas, no había cerveza todavía, ni nada. Pero, había muchos restaurantes o tiendas de comida. Nos consiguió una hora en una tienda de comida, y en otro restaurante, y así, en tal grado que ya no fui a la Plaza. Y luego, organizó, buscó un concurso, el de un tónico que se llamaba El Ferro Vitamina. Ahí entré yo y gané el segundo lugar, porque unos muchachitos ganaron su primer lugar. Bueno, gané yo el segundo lugar.

El señor Cortéz dijo: —No, yo tengo que hacer que usted triunfe!

Entonces buscó otro programa de la cerveza Perla. Ese sí fue patrocinado; duró el programa como unos tres o cuatro meses. Estaban eliminando a las que tenían menos votos y todo. Al final quedamos nomás tres. Quedé yo y dos muchachas más. Y yo me gané el primer lugar.

Pero, bueno, no quiero seguir platicándote eso. Lo que yo quería decirte es que cuando yo llegué a San Antonio, no había mujeres que cantaran. Nadien cantaba. Pero empezaron a surgir muchas cantantes con el concurso ese de la Perla. Entonces si de pronto surgieron muchas mujeres que cantaban. Entre ellas estaba Eva Garza, yo creo que tú ya la oíste mentar; Esperanza Espino, las Hermanitas Fernández, esta Rosita Fernández y la hermana. Sí, surgieron muchos grupos de mujeres cantando. Que relativamente de esas cantantes, la única que hizo algo —hizo su carrerra pero fuera de San Antonio— fue Eva Garza. Porque cuando yo empecé a grabar, ella también grabó y todo, pero no pasó nada ¿ves? Después ella surgió, resaltó cuando se fue de gira con una artista. Anduvo viajando hasta que llegó a Nueva York.

Y como te decía, casi todas las que surgieron en San Antonio en aquel tiempo que yo comencé, pos no, no siguieron adelante, no duraron gran cosa. Eva Garza fue la única que se hizo famosa cuando ella se fue con esa artista, una tal Sally Green, creo, una bailarina que bailaba con unos abanicos. Trabajaba en la variedad. Ella la vió cantar a Eva y se la llevó, ¿ves? Y es así que en esa gira llegó hasta Nueva York. En ese tiempo estaban en Nueva York El Charro Gil y Sus Caporales. Estaban presentándose en un programa en Nueva York. En eso llegó la variedad con Eva Garza y yo creo que ella los fue a ver al radio. Ahí se enamoró ella del Charro Gil. Se enamoraron los dos. Entonces el Charro Gil se separa del grupo. Se quedaron los Caporales solos y él se fue con Eva Garza. Se fueron en gira. El se llevó a Eva Garza a Cuba y a dondequiera, ya casados. Entonces el trío de los Caporales se quedó en Nueva York, y después se convirtieron en el Trío los Panchos. Así comenzaron Los Panchos, que por cierto se hicieron muy famosos y han tenido una carrera hasta la fecha, ¿ves? Pero ya te digo ahí en San Antonio Eva Garza no hizo nada.

Asi anduvimos afanando y afanando

Pues mira, te voy a decir: Esto que te estoy diciendo ahorita casi nunca lo he platicado. Más bien nunca lo he platicado en tantas entrevistas que me han hecho. Como te digo, cuando regresamos de allá del estado de Míchigan nos fuimos a Houston, y luego de Houston nos

Lydia Mendoza a la edad de 17 años cuando grabó por primera vez "Mal Hombre" (1933). Cortesía de Houston Metropolitan Research Center, Houston Public Library

movimos a San Antonio. Esto fue en el año de 1932. Todavía yo no grababa. Nadie sabía quién era Lydia Mendoza ni nada. Claro que dentro del medio artístico ya estábamos organizados, unidos, tanto mi madre como mis hermanos, mi papá y todos. Entonces llegamos a San Antonio buscando un medio mejor de vida, de cómo sacar más centavos.

Teníamos un carrito Ford, un carrito viejo. Entonces mi padre ideó hacer una gira artística como grupo, ¿ves? Ya mi madre arregló a mis hermanos poniéndoles esketches cómicos y números de canto, las guitarras y todo. Organizamos una salidita para el Valle —allá pa el Valle de Texas— en ese carrito que teníamos. Sin —como te digo— sin ningún contrato, sin nada. Íbamos nomás a la aventura: a ver con qué nos socorría Diós [risa].

Me acuerdo que en aquellos años los carros tenían unas polveras. ¿Te acuerdas que tenían unas polveras? Que les nombraban polveras, ¿no sabes tú qué son? Bueno, donde bajabas tenían algo que se acomodaba como una tarima, o algo que tapaba, ¿ves? Entonces allí cargábamos hasta con colchón, cobijas, una estufa de petróleo con uno o dos quemadores, sartenes... Bueno, equipado de todo ¿ves?, para no tener problemas donde llegáramos. Y así nos fuimos.

Nos fuimos directamente, caminando. Fuimos al Valle y mi papá acondicionó unos cartelones; puso, "Familia Mendoza. Variedades. Lydia Mendoza". Pero pos nadie sabía quién era Lydia Mendoza. El puso "Lydia Mendoza, la guitarrista, y el grupo de Variedades de Sketches Cómicos". El hizo los cartelones con lápiz grueso. Ya listo todo eso.

Pues ya no me acuerdo a qué pueblito llegamos, y le dijo el señor: —Pos sí — dice— ahi está un saloncito si quieren trabajar. ¿Traen anuncios?

—Sí —dijo mi papá— aquí traemos este anuncio y todo.

Luego luego ya le enseñó y empezamos. Se organizó la presentación. Así lo hicimos. Ya el señor nos facilitó un cuarto. Descargamos nuestros cachibaches que llevábamos: digamos la estufita, y el colchón y las colchas y allí pasamos la noche. Así hicimos un recorrido por todo el Valle; trabajando en saloncitos, no en teatros, porque pues no nos daban trabajo en los teatros. En saloncitos así empezamos. Esas fueron nuestras primeras aventuras artísticas, allá por el año de 1932. Luego ya regresamos a San Antonio otra vez. Era algo pequeño, ¿ves?, pero traíamos nuestro grupito para defendernos. Y así nos daban oportunidad para trabajar.

Hicimos esa primera aventura viajando con nuestras almohadas y nuestras cobijas, colchón, y todo, ¿ves? Hasta una estufita y vasijas, platos, todo listo para donde nos quedáramos. Pero no rentábamos lugar porque con la funcioncita que dábamos apenas sacábamos algunos centavitos. No lo suficiente para ir a rentar un cuarto o un hotel, sino que muchas veces en el mismo salón donde nos presentábamos, allí mismo nos dejaban que nos quedáramos. Entonces allí improvisábamos nuestro dormitorio, y otro día en la mañana guisábamos lo que podíamos y comíamos. Luego seguíamos la aventura. En cada nuevo sitio mi papá le pedía permiso al señor del lugar: que si nos podíamos quedar allí esa noche. Y nos permitían que nos quedáramos allí. Pos era una familia, ¿verdad? Mi madre, mis hermanos, mi papá y yo. Allí pasábamos la noche. Y al otro día: la misma cosa. Así recorrimos todo el Valle, y los pueblitos; trabajando y juntando centavitos. Luego nos regresábamos otra vez a San Antonio. Y la misma rutina, ¿ves? Seguía eso.

Procurábamos ir a los pueblitos donde estaban los piscadores en los tiempos en que se venían los trabajos, ¿ves? Principalmente los viernes y los sábados. Llegábamos a un pueblito, y entonces allí pedíamos permiso para poner la función en un restaurantito, o en alguna esquina. Muchas veces no nos dejaban en el restaurante. Pos afuera, allí cantábamos. Y allí se arrimaban todos. Toda la gente que bajaba al pueblo a hacer sus compras el día sábado. La gente andaba allí nomás dándose vueltas; pos, si en aquellos años ni había salones de baile, ni había nada. Era muy diferente a como es la vida ahora, ¿ves? En aquellos años no había nada de eso. Pos no, qué baile, pos no... ¡pos no había dónde y no bailaban! No había festividades, ni bailes, ni nada de eso. La pobre gente que trabajaba salía los sábados al pueblo, pos a distraerse allí nomás: a andar caminando las calles, ir a comprar un helado, algo... Porque hasta eso, había mucha discriminación contra los mexicanos. Los mexicanos no podían entrar a los restaurantes. Si había un restaurante, no podían ir a comer allí. Si eran mexicanos, no, no los dejaban. Si no era un lugar mexicano, no podían entrar a ese lugar; no podían entrar a comprar algo. Porque no. No... no los, no los atendían. Al mexicano siempre lo... tú sabes. Y entonces llegábamos nosotros y armábamos alboroto con nuestra música. Nos sentábamos allí en una esquina, y nos estábamos ahí... nos permitían de ahí unas bancas, o lo que fuera. Allí empezábamos a cantar; se nos arrimaba la gente; y nos socorría con lo que ellos querían. Nosotros no cobrábamos, ¿ves?, pero hacíamos nuestros buenos centavitos en el tiempo de piscas. Y ese era nuestro vivir: a ganar, a luchar en la vida. Por eso te digo que mi carrera comenzó desde muy abajo: jalando mucho, y luchando hasta que al fin Dios me concedió que... mi estrella ya cambiara: grabé, y ya cambió nuestra vida, ¿ves?

Pero al principio —casi todo el 32— afanamos mucho saliendo fuera de San Antonio, a los pueblitos donde íbamos. Y había ocasiones que hasta se nos acababa el gas. Una vez me acuerdo que íbamos —¿A dónde?... no sé a que pueblito íbamos. Salimos muy de madrugada de nuestro hogar para ir a otro pueblo. Y en el camino, pos no sé, se nos acabó el gas. Traía mi papá dinero con qué echarle gas, pero había nomás una gasolinera en el camino, y ellos no quisieron levantarse pa' echarnos gas. Por más que les tocamos, no se levantaron, no se quisieron levantar. Les decía mi papá: —No tenemos gas compañero.

No nos hicieron caso hasta en la mañana como a las ocho. Entonces ahí tuvimos que esperarnos hasta que amaneciera. Todavía estaba oscuro y era en invierno. Fue en el mes de diciembre allá por el Valle. Lo que hicimos fue que nos arrimamos a la orilla del camino, y se metió mi papá al monte a traer leños o maderos. Hicimos una lumbre y allí la pasamos calentándonos en la lumbre hasta que amaneció que nos vendieron gas. Y así... pasamos muchos detalles de esos en el camino. Todo en nuestras giras en 1932, todo ese año del 32 anduvimos afanando.

Y luego ya el 33, pos... no nos fue muy bien. No afanamos mucho. Hasta que mejor nos quedamos en San Antonio, allí en la Plaza del Zacate a lo que saliera, ¿ves? Todo estaba muy bien nomás que no lloviera. Cuando llovía, pos no hacíamos nada. Y eso era nuestro vivir, porque todos los días ganábamos el diario. Me acuerdo que juntábamos nomás de veinticinco a treinta centavos en la noche, porque la gente estaba muy pobre. Cantábamos una canción y se levantaba mi hermanita María con un platito para ver con qué nos socorrían. Pos le echaban un centavo, dos centavos, un nicle, un daime. Era todo. Ya nos íbamos y llegábamos a la casa. Al otro día en la mañana me mandaba mi mamá a la tienda. Comprábamos un nicle de masa, una botellita de leche de a nicle, un nicle de manteca, y era todo. Y eso era nuestro diario. El sábado y domingo sacábamos para pagar la renta que era uno veinticinco por semana. Pagábamos como cinco pesos por mes; pos estaba barato, ¿ves? Y así. Como te digo, afanamos todo el 32 y así anduvimos sufriendo y sufriendo. Esa lucha de nosotros comenzó desde el 27 —desde que inmigramos para Estados Unidos— el 27, 28, 29, 30, 31 y 32... cinco años hasta que ya en el 33 nos cambió un poquito la suerte.

Nosotros inmigramos para Estados Unidos en 1927. Bueno, habíamos ido y venido, como te digo, muchas veces. Pero la última vez fue en el 27; porque mi mamá se cansó de ir y venir con el trabajo de mi papá. Teníamos dos años de estar en Monterrey, México, mi papá trabajando allá.

Entonces mi papá dice pues que nos vamos pa' Estados Unidos. Mi mamá se cansó y le dijo: —Mire, cada año, cada dos años, ai andamos, que nos vamos.

Porque cada vez que llegábamos a un pueblo, formábamos el hogar, la casa, comprábamos muebles y todo. Y luego que, ¡Vámonos! y todo se desbarataba, se vendía. ¡Vámonos otra vez pa' Estados Unidos! Y veníamos acá, y la misma cosa. Empezaba a trabajar, formaba uno su hogar, y al año; pos que nos vamos pa' Monterrey. Y así andábamos, ¿ves?

Entonces, mi mamá la última vez le dijo: —Bueno, pos yo ya no me quiero ir para Estados Unidos para empezar de nuevo otra vez.

—Pos sí, vámonos, vámonos.

—No. Yo ya estoy cansada de andar como los húngaros. Nos quedamos aquí, o nos vamos allá. Si nos vamos, está bueno. Vámonos, pero yo ya no regreso. Yo me quiero quedar aquí en México. Pero si usted quiere irse otra vez pa' Estados Unidos, yo ya no regreso pa'cá. Porque ya, ya me cansé —dice— eso de andar que no sé cuál es mi casa.

A nosotros los chicos nos gustaba siempre más acá de este lado. Decíamos: —¡Pos sí, mamá, vámonos!

—Okey. Nos vamos, pero yo ya no regreso pa'cá.

Y dijo mi papá: —Sí, sí, está bueno. También mi papá quiso.

Ya nos inmigramos, y ya no regresamos. Al año ya se quería ir papá otra vez para México. Entonces dijo mi mamá: —No.

—Bueno, entonces a ver qué hacen, porque aquí yo no consigo buen trabajo. Yo ya no quiero trabajar en el ferrocarril. Y a ver qué vamos a hacer.

—Pos de lo que sea, —dice mamá— pero yo ya no regreso a México. Yo ya se lo dije: que si nos veníamos pa'cá yo me quedaba acá. Yo me quería quedar allá en México, pero usted quiso venirse. Bueno.

Pos así nos quedamos. Entonces ya no trabajó mi papá y nos dedicamos a la música. Ya te digo: desde el 27 hasta el 33. Así anduvimos afanando, afanando. Unos días bien, otros días mal, y... bueno, así pasaron todos esos años.

Yo no sé de otro grupo musical como el nuestro. No había nadie. Yo creo que nosotros éramos los primeros. Nomás en San Antonio se miraba el ambiente de los músicos que andaban ahí en la Plaza. Pero en giras así, yo no vi grupos que anduvieran como nosotros, no. Luchando y trotando, no. Ya después de muchos años surgieron algunos que salían a las giras así; algunos grupitos. Pero al principio, como te digo yo que comenzamos nosotros —inclusive en el Valle que llegamos el 27— no había música, no había nada. Nosotros recorrimos todo aquello, pero yo no conocí grupos. No había grupos, no había nada. Nomás nosotros.

Ahora sí, donde quiera hay mucho ambiente musical y todo. Han surgido muchos grupos, ¡ya no hayamos qué hacer con tanto! Cada día surgen acordeonistas, conjuntos, grupos de jóvenes. Hay mucho ambiente, mucha música. Pero en aquellos años no había nada, nada. El acordeón ni les gustaba; ni lo conocían. Eso vino a surgir después.

El acordeón vino a surgir hasta —ahorita te digo— yo creo que hasta como en 1940. Que digo yo que a alguien se le ocurrió, se le vino la idea de transportar la música ranchera mexicana al acordeón. Allí en New Braunfels viven muchos, muchos, muchos alemanes, muchos polacos, hay mucha raza de esas.

Entonces había un programa especial de radio en San Antonio —yo me acuerdo— cuando se empezó a escuchar... tocaban pura música alemana. Pos ya ves la música esa alemana es como las polkas. La tocaban en acordeones, ¿ves? Pero eran acordeones-piano. Entonces, a alguno se le ocurrió usar un acordeón de botones: de esos norteños. Se le ocurrió transportar la música ranchera mexicana y empezó a organizarse eso. Y ya cuando se empezó a organizar pos empezó a gustar¿ves? Nomás fuera quien fuera el primero y empezaron a surgir cantidades de grupos. Uno de los primeros fue Santiago Jiménez —no este joven— sino el papá. También Narciso Martínez. Valerio Longoria.

Asi fue como fui aprendiendo yo mis canciones

 La música la tuvimos siempre en la casa y yo nací con ese talento. Mi papá le compró una guitarra a mi madre. Y lo que ella tenía dentro, ahí despertó su talento de ella, su música. Me acuerdo muy bien, tendría yo como uno —pos fue en 1920— tenía como cuatro años. Me acuerdo que nomás llegaba del trabajo mi papá, cenábamos, y nos salíamos a jugar yo y mi hermanita. Nomás terminaba mi mamá y se sentaba con su guitarra y con mi papá, los dos cantando ahí. Nomás oía yo sonar la guitarra y allí voy —corría y me sentaba a sus pies. Porque yo heredé eso de la música de mi madre también. Y ella fue la que me enseñó, como te digo. En la casa siempre la música existió. No había fiesta que mi padre no la llevara a mi madre y la presentara. Todos los tíos estaban en contra de mi papá. Que la música, que esto y que el otro. Creían que... de que los artistas no eran buena gente, y todas esas cosas, tú sabes. Pero,... así fue en esa forma como la música la tuvimos siempre en la casa y yo nací con ese talento.

Bueno, te voy acabar de platicar esto para que no se me vaya a olvidar. No se nos vaya a olvidar esto. ¿Te acuerdas que comenzamos a comentar tocante a aquellos chicles que yo... de las cancioncitas que hice una colección, y que me preguntaba yo de la música? Pos vivíamos en Monterrey en la colonia Bella Vista. Una colonia muy pobre —que ahora ya ni la conoce uno— ya cambió mucho. Pero en aquel tiempo, no había nada en esa colonia. Era muy humilde, muy pobre. Allí siempre vivieron los familiares de mi madre. Tenían sus propiedades allí. Y siempre que radicábamos allá, allí vivíamos en esa colonia. Entonces esa colección de canciones que hice yo; me preguntaba yo que cómo iría la música de esas canciones.

Bueno pues en donde vivíamos nosotros había un tendajito donde vendían de todo. Vendían hasta cerveza y leña, y maíz, y todo; al estilo de México, ¿ves? Y un sábado me mandó mi mamá a comprar quién sabe qué. Estaba yo comprando aquello —era sábado y había mucha gente comprando— en eso llegan cuatro señores músicos. Uno de ellos traía de esos instrumentos... la flauta. ¿La conoces? Pues son negras, ¿ves?, es un instrumento negro; es la flauta. Era la flauta, contrabajo, bajo sexto y un violín. Eran unos señores grandes y llegaron a pedirle al señor que si los dejaba que pos tocaran allí afuera, a lo que la gente les diera. Entonces el señor les dijo: —No, no vengan a molestar, yo no tengo con qué pagarles.

—No, si no le vamos a cobrar; nomás denos permiso.

—No, no, se va hacer un relajo aquí. No, no quiero mucho ruido aquí.

Entonces yo voltéo —el viejito dueño me quería mucho; Don Pablito se llamaba: —Ay Don Pablito ¿porque no los deja que le toquen? No le van a cobrar. A lo mejor le animan aquí a la gente, y tiene más negocio. ¿No cree usted?

—¡A qué muchachita! Bueno, pos que toquen allí afuera.

Pero yo lo hice con el interés de ver si oía alguna de las canciones que yo tenía, ¿ves? Pos ya que nos dijo que sí, corriendo llegué a la casa. Dejé lo que me había encargado mi madre, y me fui. Tenía un cajoncito: allí tenía guardadas mis cancioncitas de los chicles. Corrí. Por detrás de la tienda había un callejoncito así, y allí me paré. Y allí empezó el bullicio de la gente, empezaron a pedirles a los señores canciones. Tocaban de las que yo tenía allí. Bueno. Estuvieron yendo tres sábados. Esos tres sábados no me quitaban de allí de atrás, escuchando todo. Pos con esos tres sábados me aprendí la música de toda mi colección que yo tenía. Y así fue como yo empecé. Pues yo como tonta: sola, ¿ves? porque nadie me hacía caso. Yo aprendí mi guitarrra. Yo me sentaba allí pero nadie se fijaba si estaba yo cantando o no. Y yo quería cantar ya, porque ya tocaba la guitarra.

Ya andaba yo en diez años; fue en el 26, andaba en diez años. Bueno, total que me aprendí mis canciones y yo las cantaba sola ya, sin que nadie me hiciera caso. Y en ese inter, una vez me oyó mi papá que estaba cantando una canción. Fue y le dijo a mi mamá: —Oiga Leonor —se hablaban de usted— dice: —Oiga Leonor, ¿Qué cree? ¿No ha escuchado a Lydia cantar? Parece que tiene voz.

Dijo mamá: —¿Sí? Bueno, me voy a fijar.

Entonces un día me llamó mi mamá y me dijo: —A ver que si cantas, hija. A ver: canta una canción.

Ya le canté una, creo que fue "La Hija del Carcelero", la primera que me aprendí. Y ya me escuchó mi mamá. Entonces ya empezaron a probar que yo tenía voz para cantar. Pero aún así nadie se imaginó —ni yo pensé— que iba a ser cantante ni nada. Ya ves todos los años que pasaron para hacer yo mi carrera. Mi empeño era saber; tener repertorio; y luego seguir adelante con la música.

Ya después de tocar la guitarra aprendí —allí mismo en Monterrey— la mandolina yo sola. Había un muchachito de unos vecinos que vivían enfrente. Tenían un chamaco que querían que aprendiera a tocar la mandolina. El muchachito siempre estaba sentado en la ventana y ¡zas que le daba! ¡y zas que le daba! Pero no le sacaba nada. Pasaba yo y me quedaba viéndolo. Y pensaba yo: —Pues yo creo que puedo tocar ese instrumento.

Miraba yo que le buscaba para sacarle pieza; pero no sacaba nada el muchachito. Entonces un día fui y le dije a mi papá: —Papá yo quiero tocar... yo quiero tocar un instrumento que no sé ni como se llama. ¿Se acuerda del chamaco del vecino que vive allí enfrente?

—Ah sí —dice— es el chamaco que quieren que toque mandolina.

—¡Ah! esa es mandolina... Pos yo puedo tocarla papá.

—Ay Lydia, ¡pos 'tás loca! ¿quién te enseña?

—Pues, a mí se me hace que si yo la tuviera en mis manos yo le sacaría algo.

—Bueno ya veremos. —Así me dijo.

Otro día en la tarde, llegó mi papá con una mandolina. Yo no sé dónde la consiguió. De esas panzoncitas, ¿ves? Como son las mandolinas. Dijo: —Ahí 'stá tu dichosa mandolina. A ver cómo vas a aprender.

Ay, me dió un gusto cuando la tuve en mis manos. Entonces empecé luego luego a buscarle y luego luego aprendí. "La Pajarera" precisamente fue la primera pieza que yo aprendí en la mandolina. No bien tocada, pero la saqué. Le saqué las pisadas, ¿ves? Y otro día cuando vino mi papá en la tarde le dije: —Mire, ya toco esta pieza.

Uy, le dió mucho gusto. Lo hacía mal, pero me dijo: —Oh, lo haces muy bien; está muy bien.

Le seguí adelante, y aprendí yo sola la mandolina. Luego que ya aprendí la mandolina, ¿ves?, cuando nos inmigramos pa' Estados Unidos, ya entonces venía tocándola bien. Y mi mamá por supuesto tocaba la guitarra. Luego pasaron los años y empecé entonces a aprender el violín nomás viendo; lo aprendí sin tener maestros; nomás viendo a los que llegué a ver tocarlo.

Yo miro un instrumento y digo: yo puedo tocarlo. El piano tampoco nadie me lo enseñó. Y no se me hizo difícil. Cuando ya llegué a tener un piano en mis manos yo lo toqué. Ahorita lo que me compré fue un órgano, de esos que parecen piano. Y estoy practicando. ¡Vieras que sí lo toco! Nomás se me pone tocar algo y ya lo toco. Es que ya tengo el sentido musical, ¿ves? Por eso ningún instrumento se me dificulta. Hasta el tololoche también. Un día fui a una fiesta, y le di pisadas y,... [se ríe mucho].

Yo me acuerdo que mi padre era muy amante del teatro. En aquellos años pues no había cine, pero había teatro. Iban y venían de México grandes variedades. Me acuerdo que venía María Conesa, Virginia Fábregas y otras grandes compañías. Siempre que venían se presentaban en el Teatro Independencia, el Teatro más grande de Monterrey. Ahora habrá otro, pero en aquellos años era el principal. Cada vez que venía una variedad, pos venían grandes figuras. Traían lo que se nombra variedad: cantantes, cupletistas, bailarinas, y de todo. En esa vez vino, creo que María Conesa o doña Virginia Fábregas. La cosa es que papá hizo arreglos para llevar a mi madre al teatro. Y siempre nos llevaba a las dos más grandecitas, que eramos yo y mi hermana Beatriz. Sí, también a nosotras nos llevaban. Tendría yo pos algunos diez años. Venía cantando ese "Mal Hombre" una cupletista, una muchacha que cantaba muy bonito. Yo no me acuerdo como se llamaba. Y nomás con esa vez que la oí, aprendí la música... la letra creo que también venía en esos chicles... sí, porque de otra manera no podía haberla aprendido muy bien la letra. Pero la música sí la aprendí en esa noche. Así fue como me fui aprendiendo yo mis canciones. Ya después al correr de los años "Mal Hombre" fue la que incluían en lo que yo cantaba. Porque me gustaba la canción, ¿ves? Todos creen que es mía porque nunca ha aparecido el compositor. Nunca la han reclamado. Dicen y creen que esa canción es mía, pero no. No es mía.

En San Antonio nunca me pagaron mi trabajo

 Bueno, yo te diré que yo hice mi carrera en San Antonio, muy feliz, muy contenta, muy agredecida. Pero, en San Antonio nunca me pagaron mi trabajo. No había casi trabajos allí y no pagaban. No había nada. Había un club que se llamaba El Cubano. ¿No lo oíste tu mentar? Era un club —no sé si todavía existirá— estaba en alto. Un club que duraba abierto hasta las... pos no sé, duraba hasta las cuatro de la mañana. Seguro que no sería vendiendo bebidas. La cosa es que en una ocasión me preguntó el dueño —era cubano el dueño— que si no me interesaría trabajar toda la semana ahí. Nomás diciéndome: —Tienes que darnos una presentación como a las dos de la mañana...

—Pos sí. ¿Pero qué tanto paga?

—Pos te doy treinta pesos por toda la semana.

¡Fíjate! —¿Treinta pesos por toda la semana, señor? No, señor.

—No, pos que aquí viene quién sabe quién, hijo de quien.

—Pos, busque otra. Yo por treinta pesos, no. Si ni por treienta pesos la noche. Pos no.

Yo vivía en San Antonio porque allá se crió mi esposo. Siempre que viví en San Antonio salí mucho fuera, muchas giras. Después de que murió mi madre me llamaban, ¿ves?, a los contratos y yo les decía: —Pos, ya el grupo se desintegró.

Me decían: —Pos no importa. Si tú estás dispuesta a venir, te ponemos un relleno de dos o tres artistas, unas bailarinas, o lo que sea. Pero será para presentarte en puros cines.

Aquí en California hice una gira, ¿ves? La hice con Ramón Gay ¿No lo oíste mentar? Era un artista de México. Ramón Gay y un trío de —eran violines— total era un trío; ya no sé quiénes eran. Bueno, y así fui. Entonces viajaba conmigo mi hija Nora; me traiba a Nora. Estaba chamaca. Ella era la que me acompañaba. Y así es como hacía yo mis giras, ¿ves? Es como te digo, por eso es que yo siempre trabajé fuera. Tenía muchos trabajos pa' Nuevo México, Colorado, aquí en California. Me intercalaban con otros artistas. Pero allá en San Antonio, allí no te trabajaba yo porque no me pagaban.

En cambio, ahora que vivo en Houston me llaman de San Antonio. Estuve, ahora —¿cuándo estuve?— pos los primeros de marzo me hablaron de un club. Me dieron dos cientos pesos por una presentación. Ahora que estoy en Houston, me llaman de San Antonio para que vaya a hacer presentaciones allá. Y sí me pagan. Pero cuando yo viví allí no me pagaban; no me querían pagar, ¿ves? Ahora hay mucha competencia. Te hacen un baile allí y presentan tres, cuatro, cinco grupos de nombre, ¿ves? Pero esos grupos nomás te tocan media hora uno y media hora otro. Y así. Les pagan cualquier cosa. Pero, pos... ni qué.

Cuando yo comencé allí en San Antonio, aquel señor —que en paz descanse, que ya murió— me ayudó muchísimo. Él me llevó a cantar al radio, me organizó el concurso y me hizo mucha propaganda. Pero yo no gané ni un centavo. Nomás lo que ganaba en el radio, y los trabajitos así que me buscaba. Pero ya cuando me metió a los concursos comenzó con que: —Pues Lydia, la quieren conocer en tal lugar.

Cartelón de el Teatro Azteca, anunciando Lidya [*sic*] Mendoza y su función de variedades, Phoenix, los años1940. Cortesía Houston Metropolitan Research Center, Houston Public Library

Allá voy. Ahí a él le pagaban. A mí no me daba un centavo. —Pos que quieren que vaya allá quién sabe dónde, que...

Allá voy hasta Seguín [Texas]. Iba a donde fuera. Me llevaban a hacer una presentación, unas cuantas canciones y a anunciar que estaba en el concurso. Yo no ganaba un centavo, pero él sí lo ganaba. Pero a mí no me importaba, porque él me andaba ayudando. Por eso toda esa temporada que yo trabajé; yo no gané un centavo.

El Teatro Nacional en el centro de San Antonio, los años 40s. Cortesía Colección Zintgraff, U.T. The Institute of Texan Cultures

Inclusive cuando dijo: —Va a haber una función de media noche en el cine.

En el cine State, creo, sí, fue en el State. Porque en aquellos años se podían presentar artistas¿ves, pero no los presentaban en funciones ordinarias, sino que después de media noche. Mirabas tú las colas de gente pero después de media noche. Venían muchos artistas de México y los empresarios los presentaban en esos cines: principalmente en el State, el Zaragoza, o en el Nacional. Pero eran siempre funciones de media noche.

Bueno, cuando eso del concurso dijo: —Hay que presentar el cómputo de las candidatas, las que van más adelante, atrás o lo que sea. Ya organicé una función en el cine State.

Ahí, bueno, a todas las que se presentaron les dieron cinco dólares. A mí no me dieron nada. Otro día que estuve en el radio, que fui al programa, me comentó una de las muchachas sobre los cinco dólares. Bueno, cinco dólares deslumbraban a la gente en aquel tiempo. Todo estaba muy barato. Si ibas a comprar un vestido de lujo bonito, no te costaba más que uno noventa y ocho. Los zapatos buenos que ahorita te cuestan 20, 30 pesos, pagabas uno cincuenta. De manera que con cinco dólares, pos, todas las muchachas se volvieron locas. Hasta yo me hubiera vuelto loca.

Me dicen: —¡Ay, pos que fíjate que me dieron cinco pesos!

Decía yo: —¿Quién te dió cinco pesos?

—Pos anoche nos dieron. ¿Qué no te dieron a ti tus cinco pesos?

—No, a mí no me dieron nada —dije.

—Pos, ¿por qué? A todas nos dieron.

Y a mí no me daban nada. Bueno, es como te digo: mi promotor si ganó. Al principio el tenía una carcacha de carro. Hablo de su vida, no de su muerte. Como al mes, a los dos meses, ya traiba carro del año. Y toda la gente, cuando lo miraba decía: —¡Mira, el señor Cortéz con carro nuevo! Pos por Lydia Mendoza.

Sí, la gente lo notaba. Y a mí no me daba nada, ¿ves? Pero bueno, a mí no me importaba, porque parte de lo que yo soy... él me ayudó muchísimo.

Esto que te estoy diciendo fue al año de haber llegado a San Antonio. O quizás menos. Porque nosotros llegamos en el 32 y nos instalamos en la Plaza del Zacate. Esto fue como en el año... a principios del 33. Sí, fue al principio del 33 cuando él me descubrió. A principios del año 33 fue cuando el señor Cortéz hizo mi nombre muy famoso ahí, con el concurso y todo eso, ¿ves? Pero yo no ganaba nada. Pero pues yo me conformaba con lo que, bueno, con lo poco que trabajábamos allí. No ambicionaba mucho... más que me ayudara y él me ayudaba muchísimo, ¿ves?

Luego una vez me salió un contrato pa' Corpos [Corpus Christi, Texas]. Todavía yo no grababa. Fue un empresario y me oyó. Se había corrido la fama de Lydia Mendoza desde San Antonio. Me llevaron a Corpos pagándome cien dólares por semana —¡se nos hizo un dineral!— De manera que... yo nunca había ganado tanto. Y él, este señor lo pronosticó. Dijo: —¡Yo voy a hacer que a la Señorita Mendoza le paguen hasta cien dólares por semana!

Y se le cumplió. Porque fue ese empresario de Corpos y me llevó a presentarme allá. Eso fue una gran cosa.

No sé lo que el promotor sacaba donde él me presentaba; y eso era de todas las noches, no creas que nomás cada semana. Porque yo tenía el programa todas las noches a las siete de la noche en el radio, ¿ves? Y después del programa era cuando llegaba y decía: —Lydia, pos sabe que quieren conocerla, en... quién sabe dónde.

—Sí, ¿cómo no?

Y él me llevaba. A mí y a mi madre que iba conmigo.

Te digo que en el radio me pagaban tres cincuenta. El que me pagaba los tres cincuenta era el señor García, dueño del Tónico Ferro Vitamina. El me daba los tres cincuenta pa' que yo cantara por cortesía del Tónico, ¿ves?, era el anuncio. Y después de ese programa venía el programa del señor Cortéz. Dentro de su programa organizó el concurso de la cerveza Perla. Y entonces yo le dije: —Pero ya no voy a poder estar con mi mamá en la Plaza del Zacate.

Mamá además le dijo: —Pos ella no puede ir a tomar parte en ese concurso, porque si no le van a pagar lo que le paga el señor García —dice— pos esa es una ayuda pa' nosotros.

Dijo: —No, no, no. El como quiera le va a pagar a Lydia.

Que por cierto todas las que tomaban parte en el concurso no me querían; estaban contra de mí. Que porque a mí sí me pagaban y a ellas no. Y decía el señor Cortéz: —Bueno, pos, a ella le pagamos porque está patrocinándola un anuncio. Si ustedes se buscan un anuncio, entonces sí. Pero ustedes vienen al concurso a ver si ganan, ¿verdad? Así es que no se les puede pagar. A ella, bueno le está pagando el anuncio... Yo no —dice.

Y todas estaban que... bueno, ¡no me querían!

Luego cuando comenzó ese concurso, pos empezó a decir mucha gente que quería conocerme. Después del programa que ponía yo en el radio, decía el señor Cortéz: —Pos, Lydia... la quieren conocer...

Les cobraba y él se clavaba el dinero... y a mí no me daba un centavo. Pero ya te digo así en esa forma me explotó. Aunque eso del concurso y todo me sirvió de muchísimo porque fue cuando ya se dieron cuenta y me llevaron a grabar. Me llamaron, me llevó una señora. Fueron a verme y despues grabé. Entonces ya empecé yo a ganar centavos, ¿ves?, cuando empecé a grabar. En 1928 fue cuando grabó toda la familia. Sí. Y ya después de eso pasaron como seis o siete años para resurgir en mi número.

Sí. Porque, después de que grabamos, el mismo 28 nos fuimos pa'l Norte y anduvimos afanando aquí y allá; nunca hicimos nada, ¿ves? Inclusive nunca oímos los discos, no nos preocupábamos por saber de eso, ni de nada. Entonces seguimos afanando y fue cuando nos fuimos al Norte, luego a Houston y por último a San Antonio. Allí fue cuando yo empecé en la Plaza del Zacate a cantar y allí empezaron mis primeros éxitos, ¿ves? Ya que grabé, entonces ya empezó a cambiar nuestra vida, ¿ves?, cuando yo empecé a ganar.

En 1934 grabé el primer disco. Ya para los dos meses estaba la compañía allí, porque nomás salió el disco "Mal Hombre" y fue un éxito. Nomás salió el disco y ellos a los dos meses estaban ahí, contratándome y pidiendo que querían que grabara. Porque si no me hubieran contratado, ¡no hubiera faltado otra compañía que me agarrara! Ellos se adelantaron, luego luego. Vinieron de Nueva York.

Era la compañia Bluebird, pero en realidad era la RCA Víctor. Ellos hicieron contrato con mi papá —por un año, y un año de opción. Pos ese año de opción se convirtió en diez años. Ya nomás se iba a llegar el fin del contrato y ya estaban mandándome otro pa' que lo firmara con otro año de opción. Y así estuvieron y estuvieron. Total que no me dejaron libre. Luego me solicitó una companía de California. Pero yo no podía, ¿ves?, porque estaba en contrato. Luego ya nomás que salió el primer disco y que se empezó a popularizar, entonces ya mucha gente se empeñó en conocer a Lydia Mendoza. Empezaron a llover los contratos, ¿ves? Y cambió ya nuestra vida.

Sí, cambió nuestra vida. Tuvimos más centavos para vivir mejor y ajuariarnos de ropa. Pos estábamos muy escasos de todo. Me acuerdo muy bien que en los primeros discos me daban quince dólares por disco que grababa. Lo primero que hice fue ir al centro con mi madre. Entonces dijo mamá: —¿Pos qué te vas a comprar, hija?

Le dije: —No, ahorita nada para mí.

Primero les compré zapatos a todos mis hermanitos. Ellos estaban chiquitos y los zapatos estaban muy baratos. Costaban un peso. Les compré primero zapatos porque andaban descalzos. Les compré también calcetines y una ropita. Completé muy bien; no quedó gran cosa, y me preguntó otra vez mi mamá: —¿Y tú que te vas a comprar, hija?

MARCH 15, 1939.

LIDYA MENDOZA ALVARADO

SAN ANTONIO, TEXAS

Dear Sir: **ARTISTS LETTER AGREEMENT**

1.   This Letter Agreement will constitute an agreement between you and RCA Manufacturing Company, Inc. (herein called "the Company") for the making of phonograph records.

2.   This Agreement shall remain in effect for a period of ONE YEAR from the date hereof, and during that period you will at mutually convenient times come to and perform at the recording studios of the Company for the purpose of making THIRTY recorded selections, or more than this number if the Company so desires.

In consideration of this agreement and without further payment than as herein provided, you grant to the Company, its associates, subsidiaries and nominees (1) the right to manufacture, advertise, sell, lease or otherwise use or dispose of, or to refrain therefrom, throughout the world, records embodying the performances to be recorded hereunder, upon such terms as the Company may approve; (2) the right to use your name and photograph and the name and photograph of the Musical Organization, if desired, in connection with the exploitation of said records; and (3) all rights in and to the matrices and records, and the use thereof, upon which are reproduced the performances to be recorded hereunder.

3.   The Company will pay you promptly after the approval of the Master record in complete satisfaction of the rights herein granted and the services to be rendered hereunder by you the sum of Twenty Dollars .

4.   You agree that during the period of this Agreement you will not perform for any other person, party or concern for the purpose of producing phonograph records and that after the expiration of this Agreement you will not record for anyone else any of the selections previously recorded for this Company.

5.   The Company shall have the privilege and option to extend this Agreement from the date of its termination for a period equal to the term of this Agreement by giving to you notice in writing of its exercise of such option and its election to continue. Such notice shall be given to you personally or be mailed to your last known address not less than ten days prior to the said date of termination. Upon the giving of such notice this Agreement shall be continued and extended for such further period upon the same terms as those above set forth.

Un contrato del año 1939 entre Lydia Mendoza y la RCA Manufacturing Company. Las compañías de discos hicieron millones pagándole a los artistas una baja tarifa fija y no regalías. Cortesía Houston Metropolitan Research Center, Houston Public Library

—No, —le digo— primero les compro a ellos y pa' la otra ocasión me compro yo.

Y así poco a poco. Ya después volví a grabar. Ya no fue un disco sino que fueron dos. Entonces ya fueron treinta pesos. Con eso pusimos la luz porque no teníamos luz. Teníamos una lámpara de petróleo, fíjate, y una estufa de

Lydia Mendoza grabando un disco en su casa (1938). Cortesía U. T. The Insitute of Texan Cultures, Colección *San Antonio Light*

leña. ¡Hacía un calorón! Pos, fuimos por allí y compré una estufita barata de gas. Y así, poco a poco fuimos cambiando, ¿ves? Y entre más, más... pos Dios nos ayudó. Cambió nuestro modo de vivir, ¿ves? Para entonces papá se había enfermado, y ya no podía trabajar. Estábamos muy mal ¿ves? Pero todo fue cambiando poco a poco todo con mis grabaciones, y también después con los trabajos que nos salían, ¿ves?

Yo comencé desde muy abajito y con muchos sacrificios y muchos afanes.

Pero Dios sabe que mi mayor ambición era ganar más centavos para mi familia. Me daba lástima ver a mis hermanos sin ropa. Se llegaba Navidad y los pobrecitos nomás miraban a los niños con juguetitos y ellos nada. Entonces eso a mí me dolía, si vieras, ver a mis hermanitos que no tenían lo que ellos podían haber tenido. Y como yo era la mayor...

Bueno, mi hermana mayor, Beatríz, se casó muy joven. Ya no quiso seguir con nosotros. Que no, que ya estaba cansada, pos era de estas muchachas de malos pensamientos. Total que estaba cansada, que ya se iba a casar. Se casó muy joven; de catorce años se casó. Y fue precisamente en Detroit, Michigan. También se vinieron con nosotros de Michigan. Pero cuando andábamos afanando mucho ella se enojaba y decía: —Pos nomás a Lydia la sacan y a mí no me sacan.

Pos ella no podía salir: ¿Con quién dejábamos los hermanitos chiquitos? Como Juanita, que estaba chiquita, tenía dos años. Y Manuel estaba chiquito también, todos. Eran tres chiquitos, ¿ves? De manera que las más grandes —que erámos yo y Francisca— éramos las que nos íbamos a cantar y a buscar la vida. Y Beatríz se enojaba porque la dejábamos; que nunca la sacábamos y todo. Siempre vivía renegando y no tenía más que doce años, fíjate. A veces decía que con el primer hombre que encontrara ella se iba a casar. Y así fue. Nos fuimos pa'l Norte, y allá en el tiempo que duramos —el 29— ella dijo que se iba a casar con un muchacho que conoció allá. Que no era ni muchacho: tenía veintisiete años y ella ni catorce. El era de Chihuahua. Era de esos trabajadores que se iban para el Norte, ¿ves? Lo conoció ella, se hicieron novios, y dijo que ella se iba a casar con él. Mi papá entonces se puso renuente: que no, que si se iba con él que la iba a reportar y la metía a la correccional.

Entonces mi madre lo agarró y le dijo: —Pos mire, Pancho, ¿para qué nos oponemos? —Dice— Ella se quiere casar; pos vale más. ¿Qué ganamos con meterla aquí o meterla allá? Allá ella. Ella quiere casarse.

Y se casaron allá en Detroit. No por la iglesia sino por civil. Nosotros nos vinimos a mediados del 30. Beatríz se casó a los dos años de estar allá. No tenía ni catorce años. Y allá en Michigan tuvo su primer niño. El niño nació a principios, creo, del 30, por ahí así. Entonces cuando nos íbamos a venir, el yerno dijo que él no se quedaba, que él como quiera pensaba irse pa' su tierra. También lo habían desocupado de los trabajos y todo. Y se vinieron cuando nosotros nos vinimos. Nomás llegamos a Houston, y de allí de Houston él se fue pa' Chihuahua. Y Beatríz se fue con él y el muchachito.

Pero, es como te digo: ella no quiso seguir afanando con nosotros... y a mí me daba lástima. Yo por mi parte quería resurgir. Por eso me empeñé yo en agrandar el grupo para ganar más centavos con más músicos, ¿ves? Y así por eso le enseñé a mi hermana María la mandolina y yo entonces aprendí el violín. Ahí en Houston precisamente se inició el grupo; fue donde empezamos a juntarnos. Esa fue la segunda vez que se formó un grupo, ¿no? Porque el primer grupo fue el Cuarteto Carta Blanca, sí. Después yo formé el otro grupo más grande. Entonces ya en ese grupo metí yo el violín y se pusieron más instrumentos. También teníamos los esketches, ¿no? Empezó a organizarse todo.

Mi carrera no me la cortaron mis esposos
(la Familia Mendoza)

Yo he estado casada dos veces, ¿ves? Con el padre de mis hijas yo me casé en 1935. Tuve mis tres hijas. Pero él, él murió en el 61. Duré veintiseis años casada con él. Bueno, al principio empezamos a tener algunas dificultades. Pero no era por él, sino por la familia de él. Ellos se oponían a que yo, como esposa y mujer casada, siguiera en giras, trabajando, saliendo a los teatros... Huy, era una vergüenza para ellos. Decían que no, que ya una mujer casada, que su casa, y que... Me aguanté un año porque encargué familia luego luego; por esa razón ya no pude seguir trabajando.

Pero nomás tuve a mi niña y al fin convencí a mi esposo. Le dije: —Mira, estamos cometiendo un grave error.

Fue en ese tiempo cuando empezó a desarrollarse más lo de mis grabaciones y a escucharse mi nombre y los contratos y todo, ¿ves? Mucho trabajo. Donde quiera querían que fuera yo a cantar. Y decía yo: —Mira estamos aquí viviendo una vida, pos pobremente, pero podríamos vivir mejor si yo sigo aceptando esos contratos, con mi familia y todo. Mira, podemos comprarnos nuestro carro.

No tenía yo ni carro. Eso fue en San Antonio. Al fin lo convencí. Entonces mis suegros y todos se nos echaron encima. Pero, pos a él no le importó. El me hizo caso. Y empezamos a trabajar.

Duramos siete años con muchos contratos. Viajamos por California, para Nuevo México... bueno, no hubo lugar que no visitáramos. El andaba siempre conmigo. El era zapatero y ganaba nomás siete pesos por semana donde trabajaba. Pos en aquel tiempo, como te digo, todo era muy barato y la pasábamos pobremente, pero estábamos bien. Pero si podíamos remediarlo, pos, ¿por qué no? ¿verdad? Pos entonces ya compramos nuestro carrito y mi mamá el de ella, y nos lanzamos a la gira. Siete años anduvimos viajando, yo con mis tres niñas —porque tuve la primera, Lydia, y luego tuve mis otras dos niñas, Yolanda y María Leonor ("Nora"). Con ellas viajamos esos siete años.

En San Antonio precisamente trabajamos mucho en unas carpas que había ahí, y otras que llegaban, ¿ves? Esto que te estoy diciendo fue como del 33 al 35. Había una que le nombraban la Carpa Cubana. Tenían una carpa como un teatro muy grande, ¿ves? Traía muchos artistas, trapesistas, malabaristas, bailarines, payasos, de todo. Entonces yo llegué a cantar en esa carpa y mi familia también. Había otra, más pequeña, la de los Hermanos García. Pero esa no salía de San Antonio. Bueno, esa tampoco existe ya. Ya han muerto casi todos. La Carpa García la ponían en áreas allá fuera del pueblo; en diferentes lugares de la ciudad ponían esa carpa. Ahí íbamos a cantar nosotros también. Y luego una vez hicieron un viaje a Corpos [Corpus Christi] y también fuimos a Corpos. Mi familia y yo, como te digo, traíamos nuestra variedad también. Y se viajaba en trocas, en trailers y todo eso.

Eso fue antes de que yo grabara, ¿ves? Fue como te digo cuando recién llegados a San Antonio, como en el 32, 33 y el 34. Esos tres años fue cuando trabajamos en eso. Pero, ya cuando yo grabé mi primer disco, que fue "Mal Hom-

Lydia Mendoza y Juan Alvarado, foto nupcial, 1935. Cortesía Houston Metropolitan Research Center, Houston Public Library

bre" en el 34, entonces ya empezaron a salirnos contratos para giras, para trabajar en teatros y en salones. Que más bién trabajábamos en puros salones de sociedades o salones de la iglesia, porque en los teatros no nos daban entrada. Traíamos a un señor que andaba con nosotros que la hacía de agente. El iba a los teatros y proponía la variedad de Lydia Mendoza. Y los gringos, pos ellos no sabían quién era Lydia Mendoza. Ellos no sabían quién era yo. Entonces ellos nunca pierden; ellos quieren un número de nombre. Yo lo tenía, pero ellos no

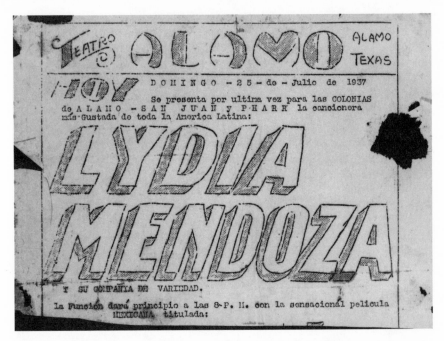

Cartelón escrito a mano. Anuncia la gira de Lydia Mendoza con su función de variedades (1937). La anuncian como "la cancionera más mas gustada de toda la América Latina". Cortesía Houston Metropolitan Research Center, Houston Public Library

lo sabían. Teníamos esa negativa. Pos nos dedicamos a puros saloncitos de iglesia, o auditorios de sociedades mutualistas. Y así nos iba muy bien al grupo Lydia Mendoza y el cuadro de variedades de la Familia Mendoza. Hasta que al fin nos salió un contrato cuando nos hablaron de California en el 37 y nos fuimos trabajando de pueblito en pueblito.

Como te digo, era el comienzo de nuestra carrera. No teníamos nosotros medios, no teníamos dinero más que el que salía de la música, ¿ves? Entonces, se arreglaba algún saloncito, y ya sacabamos pa' seguir más adelante hasta que llegamos a El Paso. Al fin llegamos a El Paso, Texas. Por suerte este señor que andaba con nosotros conocía muy bien al señor del Teatro Colón. Fue a verlo y le habló de nosotros... no pos, este si era mexicano, y dijo: —Oh, Lydia Mendoza, ¡cómo no!

Ahí en El Paso no trabajamos en ningún salón, sino en el Teatro. Tuvimos mucho éxito, gracias a Dios.

Cuando terminamos el agente le dijo al señor del Teatro Colón: —Señor Calderón, —dice— ¿no nos podría usted dar una recomendación? Fíjese que venimos batallando. No nos quieren dar trabajo en los teatros porque no conocen la variedad, ni a Lydia Mendoza. Y pos yo quisiera presentar la variedad en los teatros para que la gente mexicana...

Porque estaban dando puras películas mexicanas.

—Sí, ¿cómo no? —dice.

Luego luego él habló para Las Cruces, Nuevo México. Está cerca de El Paso, ¿ves? Luego luego nos dieron trabajo ahí en el cine ese. Y no, pos el gringo vio la entrada y entonces ya vinieron con contratos de otro pueblo. Así nos fuimos encadenando y fuimos entrando a los teatros hasta que llegamos a Los Angeles. Ya llegamos a Los Angeles, debutamos en el cine, en el teatro. Ahí dimos función tres días, y luego ya nos salieron muchos contratos. Bueno, duramos tres meses. Todo esto anduvimos, Santa Bárbara hasta San Francisco, todo eso...

No pos ahí en Los Angeles llegaron los empresarios. Vieron la variedad y todo. Luego luego llegó un empresario y nos contrató. Después vino otra empresa de por allá de San Francisco y también nos contrató y así se fue encadenando hasta que cumplimos tres meses. Tres meses estuvimos aquí en California. Ya que terminamos nos fuimos a Texas y creo que al siguiente año otra vez volvimos. Estuvimos viniendo muy seguido para acá.

Siempre dábamos una hora y media de variedad. Claro, también pasaban una película, ¿verdad? No nos pagaban sueldo. Nos daban el cuarenta porciento después de sacar el costo de la película. Era todo. Ponían una película mexicana; se acababa la película mexicana y entraba la variedad. Bueno traíamos a mi hermano Manuel y Juanita mi hermana. Ellos hacían un esketch cómico. Vacilaban y luego cantaban. La pianista era mi hermana María. Ella era la que aparecía abajo. Tocaba una pieza y luego aparecía el número cómico. Duraba como unos quince o veinte minutos el número cómico. Terminaban ellos y tocaba María otra pieza mientras que se vestían de charro y china poblana. Ya salían otra vez y bailaban un baile mexicano como el jarabe tapatío u otros bailes mexicanos. Ya María estaba en el piano y los acompañaba. Entonces, ya terminaban ellos sus dos números, se metían y tocaba otra pieza María. A la carrera se vestía y se arreglaba Juanita y salía ella sola a cantar cuplés. Eran canciones, tú sabes, de teatro. Pos cantaba como tres o cuatro. Por ejemplo, había una que cantaba "La Sandunga" o "Espejito". Pero los cuplés son canciones como de vacilada, ¿ves? Por ejemplo, "Espejito" era esa que decía... "Mírame, mírame, mírame, mírame, mírame con tus ojitos. Aquí estoy viendo un viejito..." Algo así, ¿ves?, de vacilada. Y luego "La Sandunga"... Bueno, ya que cantaba sus dos o tres números se metía Juanita, y María seguía en el piano. Por fin salía mi hermano Manuel y cantaba él solo; dos o tres canciones; eran boleros, u otra cosa. Entonces ya estaba yo lista para salir. Salía yo, cantaba, y ya estaba lista María para poner el dueto con Juanita. Después éramos el trío: de dos guitarras, y las voces de Juanita y María. Ya estaba lista pa' salir mi mamá y mi hermanito para cantar con nosotros. Ya ese era el final. Cantábamos tres, cuatro canciones, y ese era el fin de fiesta. Esa era la variedad de nosotros. Duraba como hora y media. Y luego ya que se acababa eso pasaban otra vez la película. Ya más noche, como a las nueve volvíamos a pasar otra vez la variedad. Eso era en todos los teatros. Algunas veces —como en San José o en Sacramento— nos contrataban para bailes. Pero ahí ya no poníamos una variedad completa, sino nomás unos dos o tres números y luego yo. Era todo.

Manuel y Juanita ponían varios esketches; uno que se llamaba "El Compadre", otro "La Tienda" y otro "El Muerto Murió". Tenían muchos esketches. También otro de "La Tienda". Eran muy bonitos, muy curiosos. No eran picarescos ni nada de eso, pero sí eran chistosos los esketches que ponían. Tenían

Lydia Mendoza y su familia en la portada de el *Cancionero Acosta* (los años 1940s). Cortesía Houston Metropolitan Research Center, Houston Public Library

muchos cambios ellos dos, porque había veces que trabajábamos dos días en un lugar como en Phoenix, por ejemplo. Trabajábamos viernes, sábado y domingo, en el Cine Azteca. Y en Los Angeles trabajábamos en el Teatro Million Dollar y también en el Teatro Californian. No trabajábamos nomás un día. Trabajábamos los tres días. Ultimamente trabajábamos toda la semana. Por eso teníamos muchos cambios, ¿ves?

Todo eso era puro trabajo de mi madre. Ella era la que hacía todo eso. Nos arreglaba los esketches, los números; arreglaba todo eso. Mi madre era la principal en todo aquello. Por eso es que cuando ella murió, pos se acabó el eje principal que era ella. Ella se llamaba Leonor como mi hija. Se llamaba Leonor Zamarripa. Pero es como te digo: ella tenía mucho talento, mucha inteligencia, mucho talento musical. Pero no la dejaron desarrollarse cuando ella era joven. Ella vino a desarrollar todo eso cuando ya no podía digamos labrarse una gran carrera. Pero lo que ella sabía lo dejó en sus hijos. Nos ayudó a mí y a los hermanos, ¿ves? Y por suerte que a todos nos gustó. Quisimos hacerlo, y salimos muy buenos pa' cantar y para poner esketch, poner números, para bailar. Si Juanita llegó hasta poner un número español. Bailaba con las, estas... castañuelas. Le compró mamá un rebozo muy grande. Yo no sé de dónde lo... consiguió, cómo lo hizo. Y le hizo como un vestido así de barbas y todo del puro rebozo. Pero tenía muchas flores, no era rebozo... ¿cómo les dicen estos...? Yo no sé. La cosa es que ella le hizo ese vestido muy bonito de puras flores. Mi mamá le puso un número y ella lo bailaba. Mamá buscaba diferentes maneras

Manuel y Juanita Mendoza mostrando varias posturas humorísticas de su función de variedades (1930s).

de cambiar los números de la variedad y todo. Y pos, trabajábamos muy bien. Tuvimos mucha aceptación en todos los cines, en todos los teatros. Nos fue bien. Yo grabé sola en el 34. Comenzamos el 35 y duramos hasta el 41, siete años. Entonces ya la estrella era yo. Pos era el nombre mío el conocido, ¿ves?

Ya venimos a suspender las giras estas cuando se vino la guerra. Llegamos a Nueva York en el 1941. Esta fue la última gira que hicimos. Fue en 1941 y ya, pos empezó a sonar eso de la guerra y luego el ataque de Pearl Harbor, y todo eso. Pos ya no pudimos salir. Se agotó todo; que ya no había llantas para los carros, no había gasolina. Y luego mi esposo lo llamaron para llevárselo. No fue. No le tocó ir por la razón de que él estaba trabajando en un taller donde

Volante del Teatro Azteca (Phoenix,1956) anunciando a Lydia Mendoza
como "la cancionera mas querida de todos los tiempos". Cortesía Houston
Metropolitan Research Center, Houston Public Library

hacían mucho trabajo para los soldados: las botas y todas esas cosas, ¿ves? Lo
llamaron y entonces el patrón les dijo que lo necesitaban por el trabajo que
tenían allí del gobierno. Y por eso fue que no le tocó, que no fue a la guerra.
Pero, durante esos siete años ya no hicimos giras. En el 41 yo ya pensaba que
se había terminado allí todo, ¿ves? Yo como quiera seguí cantando en fiestas,
ahí en San Antonio nomás, pero fuera no. Grabaciones tampoco se hicieron.

Pero ya en el 47 empezamos otra vez a trabajar. Y así anduvimos desde el 47 hasta 1954 que fue cuando mi madre murió.

En todo ese tiempo yo nunca me separé de mis hijas. Yo siempre las traiba conmigo. Me retiraba yo como tres meses antes de tener mi criatura. Y nomás nacía mi niña y a viajar. Me llevaba una señora conmigo y ella me las cuidaba. Como traiba mi carro, llegábamos y rentábamos hotel, un apartamento o lo que fuera. Pero siempre viajé con mis hijas. Así anduvimos viajando. A ninguna de mis hijas les dió por la música. Pos yo te diré que tiene que nacerse con ese talento. Para la música o para lo que sea. Tienes que nacer así y tener esa vocación para algo. Y si no la tienes, es imposible. Yo hasta compré una guitarra chiquita, porque yo quería que alguna de ellas... pero no. A ninguna de las tres les dió ni por cantar, ni por tocar un instrumento. De manera que a ellas no, no les dió por la música.

Los siete años que te platicaba al principio, cuando anduvimos viajando no teníamos temporadas. Viajábamos y nos íbamos dos, tres, cuatro meses. Luego veníamos a San Antonio a descansar. Después seguíamos por otro lado. Así anduvimos viajando. Cuando ya lo hice por temporadas fue cuando crecieron mis hijas y llegaron a edad escolar. Entonces yo pensé que —no quise, más bien— que fueran a estar como yo, que no me mandaron a la escuela. Así que la temporada de escuela yo no trabajaba. No aceptaba contratos en esos meses de escuela y punto. Me salían contratos, pero yo decía: —No puedo.

No podía ir y no iba. Entonces nomás terminaba la escuela y ya teníamos la gira lista para irnos.

Una vez, en una temporada anduve viajando en el tiempo de escuela; llegamos a Los Angeles y luego luego nos salieron unos contratos. ¿Sabes qué hice con mis hijas? Se llegó la temporada de escuela y las mandé. Yo no quise, ni ellas quisieron quedarse: —No, vámonos, mamá, no queremos perder la escuela.

Las mandé en el bus hasta San Antonio allá con mis suegros. Así que ellas se fueron. Otra temporada me tocó estar en Dénver, también en un trabajo, se llegó la temporada de escuela, y pos tenía que quedarme. No pude yo mandarlas a Texas, o no sé qué pasó. La cosa es que pos empezaron a llorar y todo. Y me dijeron: —Pos, vamos a ir a la escuela aquí.

Y sí fueron. El tiempo que estuve en Dénver, fueron a la escuela allí. Y así fue como yo logré que ellas aprendieran algo, ¿ves? Me hubiera gustado que hubieran agarrado una carrera. Pero no, nomás terminaron y se casaron con los mismos muchachos de la escuela. Se graduaron y se casaron. Pos están bien; están en su casa. Mi hija Lydia pos tuvo seis de familia. Pero ya todos están grandes. Hasta tiene nietas. Ya se le casaron dos muchachas, y se le va a casar la otra. Dos de los muchachos también se casaron; ya nomás le queda uno. Yolanda nomás tiene tres y Nora tiene una hija.

Ya soy bisabuela porque las nietas que se casaron el año antepasado ya tienen niñas de dos años. Dos bisnietas tengo. Tengo doce nietos y dos bisnietas. Así es que ya todos están grandes. El nieto mayor, Leroy, ya cumplió treinta años. Y luego siguen los otros. La nieta más chiquita tiene doce años. Es la de Nora. Ay pues sí... [*suspira*].

Lydia Mendoza y Fred Martínez en su día de bodas, 1964. Cortesía Colección Lydia Mendoza

Bueno, como te decía, allá en el 61 quedé viuda. Y quedé sola, porque ya mis tres hijas se habían casado. Entonces fue cuando pedí trabajo en Dénver. Me fui a Dénver, Colorado a trabajar. Había un señor que tenía un ballroom muy grande. Tenían bailes cada fin de semana. Nomás le hablé y le dije que había quedado sola y que si me daba trabajo. Dijo: —Lydia, véngase. Aquí tiene trabajo hasta que usted quiera.

Me pagaba regular y me fui a Dénver. Ahí fue donde conocí a mi segundo esposo, Fred Martínez, que es el actual, ¿ves? Nos casamos en 1964. Pero a él no le gusta viajar, a él sí que no le gusta viajar conmigo. Esto del teatro y de que los aviones y que los viajes, y que... a él no le gusta. Él me dice: —Si tú quieres, anda tú.

Pero él tampoco se ha opuesto. Entonces en ese sentido me tocó suerte, porque a mí, mi carrera no me la cortaron mis esposos, ¿ves? No he tenido ninguna dificultad tocante a eso de que ellos se opongan, o que tengan celos, o que se enojen. No. Contentos, gracias a Dios. Hasta con esa suerte Dios me ha socorrido.

Es que vienen tiempos modernos (San Antonio en los años 20 y ahora)

 El Mercado de San Antonio en aquellos años —bueno, ahorita está bonito, claro, mucho territorio— pero en aquellos años era tan mexicano. Se sentía uno como en México. Tan bonito. No te imaginas tú la alegría que se sentía en esa Plaza del Zacate que te digo que ahora es el mercado. Entonces estaba al aire libre. Y ese ambiente de la música en la noche. No te imaginas tú la alegría que se sentía. Los tríos ahí tocando y cantando. La gente vendiendo lo que vendían ahí. Era una cosa muy bonita. Ya ahora está tan diferente todo, tan cambiado. Ya no se parece a como era en aquellas épocas tan mexicanas. Era la plaza esa que se miraba allí enfrente de donde ahora está el Hospital Santa Rosa ¿Te acuerdas dónde ahora está ese hospital? Antes las arboledas que había allí, ¡y siempre tantas flores que había! ¡Ya no hay nada de eso ahora! Quitaron todo: la botica, el Teatro Nacional, el Teatro Zaragoza. Se miraba aquello tan bonito. Ahora está tan... no sé. Ya no me gusta mucho San Antonio. Me gustaba más antes. En el Mercado había actividad y vida las 24 horas del día. Estaba lleno de gente.

Allí estaba también el Auditorio Municipal. Ese lo renovaron en lugar de tumbarlo. Sí, lo renovaron. ¡Está muy precioso! Es un edificio histórico de San Antonio. Y pensar que lo querían tumbar; pero se opusieron y hubo muchas firmas, muchas. Y no dejaron que lo tumbaran. Así hubieran hecho con el Teatro Nacional, el Teatro Zaragoza y La Botica de León aquella. También eran cosas históricas.

Yo me acuerdo de las primeras visitas que hacíamos con mis papas, que veníamos con ellos a San Antonio. Allá por el año de 1923 ó 24. ¡Eso era tan bonito! ¡Pos hubieran protestado para que tampoco no tumbaran eso! Se acabó esa botica, se acabó el Teatro Nacional y el Teatro Zaragoza donde venían artistas muy grandes. Eso lo hubieran dejado también. Todo eso lo tumbaron. El Restaurante Carta Blanca, ¿te acuerdas? El Restaurante Carta Blanca también lo tumbaron. Era restaurante abajo, y arriba era hotel. Ahí paramos nosotros cuando vinimos a grabar a San Antonio. Pero papá nos puso El Cuarteto Carta Blanca porque a él le gustaba mucho la cerveza Carta Blanca. Por eso le puso a nuestro cuarteto así.

Pero ya te digo, el Restaurante Carta Blanca lo tumbaron ahora que renovaron y que hicieron todo ese mugrero. Tumbaron todo lo que estaba tan bonito. Pero antes cuando nosotros llegamos a grabar —que fue en el 28— abajo era un restaurante. Uno de los principales. Muy grande. Y arriba era hotel. Allí llegabamos nosotros porque papá conocía muy bien al señor Núñez, dueño del restaurante. Después pasaron como unos cinco años o más y entonces dejó de ser hotel. Era salón de recepciones. Ahí tenía sus banquetes el periódico *La Prensa* de San Antonio, en cada aniversario. Yo creo que tú lo conoces, u oíste mentar al señor Lozano, de la familia que ahora son los dueños de *La Opinión* que está en Los Angeles. Bueno, cada año hacían allí en ese salón de recepciones arriba del restaurante el banquete de aniversario de *La Prensa*. En cada

El Teatro Zaragoza en San Antonio fue demolido (los años 1940). Cortesía Zintgraff Collection, U.T. The Institute of Texan Cultures

banquete que tenían nos invitaban a cantar a mi hermana y a mí. Yo me acuerdo que en una de esas ocasiones trajeron al cantante José Mojica. Bueno él después dejó de ser artista cuando murió su mamá. Se hizo padre: Fray Guadalupe. El caso es que tumbaron todo eso... todo lo que había en esa cuadra. También el restaurante, que por cierto hicieron un corrido sobre eso. José Morante hizo un corrido donde habla de todo lo que tumbaron. Todo eso allí tan bonito. Allí pusieron "buildings" y pusieron tanto que ni se reconoce ahora. Ya no es el San Antonio que yo conocí allá por los años 20 ó 30 cuando estuvimos nosotros ahí. Ya no es, pues. Pero está muy bonito el río. Hay mucho turismo, ¿ves?... Pero todavía digo yo: las cosas históricas no debían de haberlas tumbado. Bueno, es que vienen... tiempos modernos. Los tiempos modernos.

Mira, hay una ciudad que admiro mucho: Santa Fe. ¿Tú la conoces? Santa Fe, Nuevo México. Bueno, esa ahora está muy modernizada. Pero no, no, no destrozaron nada de lo que era el Santa Fe viejo. Está Old Santa Fe y Santa Fe Nuevo. Tienes otro pueblo acá de Nuevo México. ¿No conoces tú Las Vegas, Nuevo México? Allí tienes tú otra ciudad, lo mismo. Ha entrado lo moderno, de modernizar las ciudades. Pos ahí hicieron la misma cosa. Pero Old Las Vegas, se quedó tal como es. Con sus alamedas, sus edificios, sus casitas, sus restaurantes. Como era en aquellos años que comenzó, yo creo, la cuidad. Así se quedó Old Las Vegas, pero también tienen la nueva, ¿ves? Pasa lo mismo en Puerto Rico con el Viejo San Juan. Está como era. ¡Ah, el Nuevo San Juan, sí!

Retrato de Lydia Mendoza 1983. Pintura de Estér Hernández (1999). Cortesía Estér Hernández

La nueva ciudad, lo moderno, los buildings, las calles, los freeways, y todo. Pero cuando yo fui a Puerto Rico, yo me quedé en el Viejo San Juan. Estuve nomás un día, trabajé, y otro día salí. Pero me levanté muy temprano. Me pusieron en un hotel hermosísimo; estaba así en alto y tenía un balcón. Bueno de allí del balcón lo poco que pude ver lo admiré, ¡hermosísimo todo! Las calles están como eran. Que por ejemplo, el tráfico que hay allí, si viene un carro de lado opuesto tienes que esperar tú pa' que pase. Nomás cabe un carro. Y las calles son de pura piedra. ¡Bueno, está divino! Es muy bonito.

Y así hubieran hecho con San Antonio también. Hubieran modernizado allá para otro rumbo. Pero acá el mercado y todo eso, la plaza, lo hubieran dejado como era antes. Pero no. Destrozaron todo. Allí pusieron todas esas tiendotas.

Las pusieron allí en el mero centro. ¡Ya tú vas y te pierdes! Yo viví por una calle que ahora que voy, ya no sé ni dónde está. Voltearon y tumbaron todo. Ahora ahí ves puro gringo paseándose.

Pausa musical

[*Lydia Mendoza ve una arpa mexicana en el cuarto y hace un comentario.*] Ahora en Texas ya no se oye tocar el arpa. Antes sí. Pero ahora ya no se escucha para nada. ¿Conoces este vals, "Lágrimas de Vino"? [*Lydia canta con acompañamiento de su guitarra.*]

El vergel que me hiciste soñar
se ha convertido en un triste penar.
¿Por qué ingrata te burlas de mí?
Al ver mis ojos llorar en raudal.
Si es tu gusto el verme sufrir.
Si es tu gusto el verme llorar.
Ríe y goza, goza y ríe,
que yo al fin te amaré hasta el morir.

Tan sólo al pensar
que he perdido lo que tanto amé.
Lloro sin consuelo.
Mi único fin esperar.
Ibas a forjar
en mi mente un nuevo ideal.
Voy a formar en mi mente un nuevo ideal.

Y el Edén que me hiciste soñar
se ha transformado en sufrir y esperar.
¿Por qué ingrata te burlas de mí?
Al ver mis ojos llorar en raudal.
Si es tu gusto el verme sufrir.
Si es tu gusto el verme llorar.
Ríe y goza, goza y ríe,
que yo al fin te amaré hasta el morir.

La maestra, Lydia Mendoza

Últimamente he recibido tan grandes satisfacciones como ese contrato de tres meses que me salió en Fresno [California State University at Fresno] en la universidad, que fue para mí una gran satisfacción. Allá me nombraban "la maestra"; "the teacher", decían. Porque llegaba yo, y salían a recibirme las maestras de ahí; me conducían a la oficina. Y luego ya me llevaban a la clase y ya ahí me presentaban. No como: —Aquí está Lydia Mendoza.

No. Decían: —Esta es la maestra Lydia Mendoza, the teacher.

Unas atenciones muy grandes... Me quedaba yo viendo a todos los jóvenes y pensaba yo: —Chihuahua...

A nosotras mi padre nunca nos mandó a la escuela. Mandó... se educaron nomás los hombrecitos, pero las mujeres no. Decía mi papá —bueno, costumbres antiguas— que para qué iba la mujer a la escuela. Que nomás a aprender ideas y malas mañas y andar ahí con los muchachos. Que al cabo crecían y se casaban, se iban... ¿Para qué querían escuela? Era el concepto que tenían en aquellos años. Actualmente, digo yo, la educación es muy necesaria, ¿verdad? Pero en aquellos años los padres así pensaban. Yo me acuerdo que familias enteras sacaban a sus hijos de la escuela pa' llevárselos a las piscas. Y ahora: sácalos de la escuela a ver si te lo permiten. En aquellos años, papá tenía amistades ahí en San Antonio, no muy lejos de la casa. Había un señor que tenía ocho de familia; de escuela todos. Se llegaba el tiempo de las piscas, los sacaban de la escuela y se los llevaban a los trabajos.

Entonces cuando yo me presenté a ese programa en la Universidad de Fresno pensaba yo: yo nunca pisé —en mi niñez, en mi juventud— un colegio, una universidad, una escuela. ¡Y mira a dónde llegué y sin ser nadie [risa]! Cuando ya iba a terminar todo eso fui a hacer mi concierto y dar la plática. Eran puros maestros y maestras; ahí no había niños, ni chamacos, ni nada. Era una despedida de todos los profesores. Ahí estuve yo y ahí me hacían preguntas. Todos estaban muy atentos. Yo me sentía pos toda regrandota. Pensaba yo: —Estoy aquí pisando un lugar sin ser yo nadie.

No me cansaba, ni me canso de darle gracias a Dios por todo los favores que me ha dado, ¿ves?

Primeramente cuando me hablaron para ese trabajo en Fresno; yo claro les dije que para mí era un honor que me hubieran hablado y me sentía muy contenta, pero que desgraciadamente yo no hablaba inglés. ¿Y, que cómo le iba a hacer yo para hacer ese trabajo? No podía. Y: —Oh —decían— no es problema porque te vamos a poner intérprete.

Y así fue. Traía siempre yo a una muchacha que hablaba español. Por ejemplo, llegábamos y me presentaban en la clase. Había veces que eran chamacos de la universidad, había veces que eran niños de escuela. Me presentaban, yo les decía a lo que iba, y si me querían preguntar algo. Ya empezaban a hacer las preguntas, ¿ves? Me preguntaban que si yo era muy rica, que si tenía hijos, que si me gustaba mucho la música y que cómo le había hecho para aprender a tocar. Bueno... así, ¿ves? Muchas preguntas me hacían todos los niños. Después de que ya contestaba yo, entonces ya empezaba a que iba a cantarles unas canciones, lo que yo había aprendido. Yo siempre llevaba mi guitarra. Ya miraban la guitarra y me empezaban a preguntar que cuántas cuerdas tenía, y que cómo, que si era mucho trabajo tocarla. Luego ya empezaban a pedirme números, me pedían canciones, a veces el "Cielito Lindo", "La Paloma" o canciones que ellos habían oído, ¿ves?, porque no eran niños latinos. Y ese era mi trabajo en las escuelas.

Luego me llevaban a las universidades. Inclusive no solamente en Fresno sino que fuera de Fresno salí a muchos lugares a dar pláticas. En Fresno nomás estaba un día por semana. Era el día en que yo me presentaba. Esto era por invitación solamente. Ahí se hablaba de mi historia. Iban maestros, iba mucha gente y estudiantes, pero ya grandes; niños no. Todos llevaban sus libros, y hacían sus preguntas y apuntaban. Yo no sé que apuntarían. Pero hacían sus preguntas de la historia de mi vida, de mi música. Y así, estuvo muy muy bien todo eso.

Esa ha sido mi vida en mi larga carrera (diferentes tipos de tocadas, ambientes y públicos)

La mayor parte de mi carrera la he trabajado casi sola. A veces con otras variedades, ¿ves? Con dos o tres números más he hecho giras. Por ejemplo trabajé algún tiempo con la Chata Noloesca. Trabajé en algunos lugares con ella. Fuimos a Chicago, a Detroit, al Wes [Texas Panhandle]. Pero a Nueva York no se nos concedió ir porque ella se enfermó. Eramos tres nomás en esas giras. Ella, un compañero y yo. La Chata era cómica y hacía sus bailes. Ocupábamos a otro para que la acompañara a ella. Ponía ella sus esketches y cantaba y bailaba. Y luego yo cantaba. Era todo lo que hacíamos en cines y en teatros. Después del esketch de ella yo entraba y cantaba. Y ya al último, ya entraba ella haciendo bromas y bailando. Hacíamos larga la variedad¿ves, aunque nomás éramos tres. Ella, un compañero y yo. Y así hicimos varias presentaciones. No hice una larga carrera con ella, no. Yo vine a unirme con ella casi cuando quedé viuda. Por cierto que ella fue y se ofreció para ayudarme a que hiciéramos presentaciones en lugares y así, ¿ves? Pero últimamente he andado nomás yo sola en estos conciertos: en universidades, colegios, o lugares donde presentan música mexicana y todo eso. Puesto que fui a Chicago, un programa que hice yo sola. Lo mismo hice un concierto en Nueva York, y así.

Mira te diré. Te diré que a veces me presento así como ahora que estuve en Nueva York y en Chicago, donde el público no es latino. Cuando ya empezaron a contratarme en esos programas —como cuando fui al Cánada, a Alaska— ví que no había gente latina. Al principio, no te lo voy a negar, siempre iba con cierto miedo, cierto temor. Porque como yo no canto en inglés siempre pensaba yo: —Bueno, me voy a presentar en un foro donde no me van a entender.

Pos siempre tenía yo miedo porque el aliciente, la vida del artista, lo principal es la reacción del público, el aplauso. Ahí le dan a uno vida. Pensaba yo: —Bueno, yo voy a ir a un lugar donde no me van a entender. ¿Cómo...? Me voy a sentir muy mal...

Tenía miedo, vaya. Pero al ver la reacción del público, que aunque no me entendían recibían mi actuación con mucho agrado. ¡Acababa mi canción y me aplaudían! ¡Terminaba yo y se paraba la gente! Y en su idioma de ellos me decían que les había gustado. Entonces yo ya empecé a animarme. Ahora ya

Lydia Mendoza (*vestido largo*) a lado de cómicos famosos, La Chata Noloesca (*derecha*) y Don Chema (*izquierda*) y otros artistas en Chicago (1954). Cortesía Houston Metropolitan Research Center, Houston Public Library

me presento, y me presento con mucho gusto, porque sé que la reacción del público es buena y es la que me da vida. Como te digo: cuando tú te paras en un foro, cantando o hablando o lo que sea, la reacción del público es la que te da vida para seguir adelante. Y si miras que te ven mal, o que no te entienden, o que no te aplauden o algo así; entonces siempre te sientes mal, ¿ves? Pero yo no, gracias a Dios.

Claro que cuando estoy entre gente latina me siento mucho mejor porque, eh..., les platico, y luego me empiezan a gritar, o me empiezan a pedir canciones y yo les digo: —Les voy a cantar la primera selección, pero terminando ésta ya saben que aquí vengo en cuerpo y alma con mi guitarra a cantar lo que ustedes quieran. ¡Pídanme lo que quieran!

Al terminar la función les toco quince minutos y a veces hasta les toco la media hora o más, ¿ves?, porque a mí no me gusta dejarlos gritando: —otra, y que otra.

No, yo los complazco. Entonces me siento mejor. Pero aún en otros públicos, yo como quiera me siento muy contenta. No, ya no me siento mal. Al principio sí, pero ya no.

Sin embargo, me parece que en los programas culturales donde me presentan los hacen muy reducidos: no los anuncian ni por televisión ni por programación, ni por radio, ni por nada. No sé cómo hacen ellos sus anuncios. En la

LYDIA MENDOZA
"La Alondra de la
Frontera"

•Tres Puñaladas
•Tu Recompensa
•Sin Fe
•Dos Caminos
•Cuando El Destino
•Besando La Cruz
•No Se Ha Perdido Nada
•Viejos Amigos

Lydia Mendoza en la cubierta de un disco de la compañía Discos Falcón (los años 1940). Cortesía Houston Metropolitan Research Center, Houston Public Library

noche yo pienso que no va haber nadie pero se llena de gente. Pero tú ni miras, ni ves un anuncio público. Nada de eso. Son programas culturales que hacen ellos nomás para enseñar lo que es la música o el "folklore". Como éste al que me llevaron en Nueva York, es un programa que enseña el "folklore" de la música de varias naciones. Hicieron nada más como una especie de almanaque que me mandaron. Ahí vienen todas las fechas: en tal fecha se presentó música de Japón. En otra fecha se presentó música de la India. Después en otra fecha llegó el "folklore" de Texas, que fui yo. Así hacen sus programas musicales.

THE WHITE HOUSE
WASHINGTON

January 27, 1977

To Lydia Mendoza

I deeply appreciate your contribution
to the inauguration. Your appearance in
the free cultural events program marked
an opening of the Nation's Capital to all
Americans. I especially appreciate your
giving the people of our country the opportunity more fully to participate in
the inauguration.

You have set a magnificent example of
what we Americans can accomplish by
sharing our talents and energies with
each other. Thank you.

Sincerely,

Jimmy

Miss Lydia Mendoza
741 Beverly Avenue
Houston, Texas 77017

Carta de el presidente Jimmy Carter dándole gracias a Lydia Mendoza por haberse presentado en la inauguración presidencial (1977). Cortesía Houston Metropolitan Research Center, Houston Public Library

Pero, ese es todo el anuncio que yo vi; no salió ninguna otra clase de anuncio. Así es que no sé... allá en Chicago hay mucha gente mexicana, pero nadie se dió cuenta. Ellos no le llevan las programaciones mexicanas a la gente mexicana.

Pues ya ves, ahora que estuve en Santa Bárbara, nadie... nadie supo de esta presentación.[2] En Nueva York llegó una familia corriendo, que se había dado cuenta.... ¿cómo se dieron cuenta ellos?... No sé cómo se dieron cuenta que estaba Lydia Mendoza en ese lugar, y llegaron corriendo gustosísimos porque me vieron ahí en ese salón. Pues de ahí en más nadien sabía. No sé cómo se dió cuenta esta familia que iba a estar yo allá en Nueva York. Hubo mucho público. Pero ya te digo... latinos, no. Lo mismo pasó hace poco en San Francisco en un concierto con el Flaco Jiménez. Hubo mucha gente, sí. Había mucho latino, pero nomás uno que otro mexicano. Pero ya ves, les gustó mucho mí programa y al Flaco lo quieren mucho también.

Fíjate que, gracias a Dios, he tenido suerte en ese sentido. Porque yo he tra- bajado en lugares familiares, clubs, night clubs, lounges,... Y tú sabes que en esos lugares así, pos, hay mucha gente tomada y todo eso. Pero todavía hasta ahorita, nadie me ha faltado a mí al respeto. No, no. No he sufrido ninguna decepción de que se porten mal conmigo o me digan una grosería. Gracias a Dios que no. Yo no sé a qué se debe. Pero a mí no, a mí no me ha faltado nadie al respeto. Si vieras que todos han sido muy amables conmigo, con mucho cariño y respeto principalmente. No importa que estén tomados; me piden una canción, se arriman a saludarme, a hacerme alguna pregunta. Pero una grosería o algo así: no he sufrido yo nada de eso. Igualmente en los teatros y lugares así que me he presentado. Puro cariño he recibido. Puras cosas buenas me han pasado en esos lugares donde yo he trabajado. Yo tengo mi modo de expresar mi música y todo. Y no me avergüenzo ni me niego a ir a ningún lugar. Si estoy aquí y me llaman de un club o un lounge que les vaya a cantar unas canciones: yo voy. Yo no me escandalizo, ni digo: —No, pos ese lugar no sirve...

Así es que esa ha sido mi vida en mi larga carrera. Y estoy feliz, contenta y agradecida con el público que me ha aguantado tantos años [risa].

Yo he tenido mucho trabajo en Houston. En todo Houston no ha habido un club que no me haya hablado. Por ejemplo, antes yo comenzaba a tocar desde el viernes. Ese día ponía tres turnos, el sábado otros tres, y el domingo otros tres. Tres horas en cada turno y comenzaba desde la una de la tarde. De una a cuatro. Luego de las cinco a las ocho en otro lugar. Y luego de las ocho a las once. Ponía tres turnos todos los viernes, sábados y domingos. Luego había algunos lugares a los que iba, a cumpleaños principalmente. Esa rutina la tuve como por un término de quince años allí en Houston. Yo me vine a Houston en 1964. Cuando me volví a casar otra vez, no me quede en San Antonio. Me vine a Houston. Y allí radicamos. Cuando supieron que yo estaba, que Lydia Mendoza estaba en Houston, no hubo lugar que no me hablara. Bueno, había veces que me negaba porque no tenía tiempo para ir a cantarles. Principalmente en los cumpleaños es donde me contratan por dos o tres horas, y pues, que otra hora más, y que otra hora más, y así se me pasan cinco y hasta seis horas. En un pore [party] querían que le diera hasta las dos de la mañana. Allí sí paré. Dije: —No, ya no.

Aunque había mucha gente allí.

Mis hermanas me dicen: —Ay, cómo tienes ánimo Lydia —cuando voy a San Antonio, que a veces trabajo allá— cómo tienes ánimo de estarte peinando y arreglando, y pintando, y que al radio, y que la televisión, y... pos yo no.

Ellas dicen que ellas ya no podrían aguantar eso.

—Pos yo sí, —les digo.

Cada viaje que hago a San Antonio, saben que estoy allí, y siempre me invitan a grabar un programa en la television. Cada vez que voy, no falta quién me llame para que les ponga un programa —de entrevista y luego uno musical— en la televisión. No pos a mí me gusta, ¿ves?

Gracias a Dios todavía tengo control en mi voz. No se me va... pos tú sabes que ya cuando entra en edad; o será la práctica que he llevado por tantos años que... pos ya con mis setenta años casi encima, para controlar las cuerdas de la garganta, es algo difícil. Muchas personas que entran en edad ya no pueden ni hablar. Yo gracias a Dios que sí puedo hacerlo. Tengo control. Como te digo, será la práctica que he llevado, no sé.

También lo que me da energía y baña mi cuerpo, tú sabes, son todos los buenos deseos de mi público: —Qué Dios la guarde muchos años. Y —Qué esa voz no se le acabe.

Todos esos buenos deseos yo creo que penetran en mi sistema y son los que me tienen aquí todavía gritándoles [*risa*].

Ese es el arte, el arte de sentirlo

 Siempre me han hecho la pregunta de que cuáles son mis canciones favoritas. Vieras que yo no puedo hacer a un lado ni una canción. Todas me gustan muchísimo. Las únicas canciones que no me gustan son como esas de insultos, ¿ves?, de groserías, como esa canción que dice, "Yo fui tu papalote..."[3] ¿Eh?... qué tiene esa palabra... ¡no me gusta esa! Hay otras canciones, por ejemplo, esa que dice, "Me importa madre." Canciones así que insultan no me gustan. Me gustan mucho las canciones de desprecio, pero siempre que no insulten mucho, ¿ves? Pero de ahí en más... los corridos me encantan. Me gustan mucho los boleros, los tangos, de todo, todas las canciones. Hay alguna que otra que pos sé que es mi favorita. Pos sí, porque me gusta. Pero, como quiera, a mis canciones... a ninguna puedo hacerla a un lado. Porque todas me gustan. No importa el tipo qué sea.

Ahora, tratándose de música, te diré también, cómo me han preguntado, de la música de diferentes naciones, como la música china, de los indios, la americana y todo eso. Aunque no la entiendo, tratándose de notas musicales, para mí todo es muy bonito. Yo no tengo predilección, no podría decir: —Pos ésta no me gusta, o ésta sí me gusta.

No. Siendo música, a mí aunque no la entienda me gusta muchísimo, sí.

Cada canción es distinta: un corrido, un bolero, una canción de desprecio, una canción de amor, un vals, todas. Cada canción tiene su gracia, ¿ves? No es nomás de abrir la boca y cantarla y gritarla nomás. Es que tienes que darle el sabor según la canción. Si no se lo das, entonces nomás no sale. Esa gracia viene del alma, del alma viene. Yo te voy a decir que cuando yo canto una canción —lo he dicho varias veces y te lo estoy repitiendo a tí— si es un corrido, yo siento lo que pasó en aquella tragedia. Lo siento como si me hubiera pasado a mí. Lo canto con ese sentimiento porque parece que aquello que le pasó al protagonista de ese corrido, me pasó a mí. Si canto una canción de amor, también. Si es una canción de desprecio, parece que la protagonista del desprecio —lo que sea soy yo. Entonces me nace, me sale, lo siento. No estoy forzando aquello. ¡Me está saliendo! Siento que me sale de acá, aquel sentimiento que yo pongo en aquello que estoy cantando. Yo lo siento que sale de acá del alma. Ya te digo, yo vivo aquella canción. Es como una actriz, ¿ves? No es muy fácil pararte en un foro y hacer un papel dramático, y nomás ponerte a llorar. Tienes que sentir lo que estás haciendo... que parezca que es real, ¿ves? Si ves el papel que está haciendo aquella actriz y si lo estás sintiendo tú es que ella lo está sintiendo. Por eso hay las grandes figuras, las grandes actrices. Ese es el arte, el

Lydia Mendoza (en los años 1950). Cortesía Houston Metropolitan Research Center, Houston Public Library

arte de sentirlo. No es nomás hacer una cosa nomás porque quieres hacerla, ni es nomás cantar una canción y nomás abrir la boca y gritar. ¡No, eso no es! No es el chiste. Ya nace uno con el arte de sentirlo; eso es lo que el público y el pueblo aprecia, ¿ves? Por eso se labran grandes carreras, por ese talento. No cualquiera lo puede hacer. Es un don que Dios te da, es todo. Es un don que ya lo traemos por Dios. Ese no se hace. Se nace con ello porque ya Dios puso su mano en uno.

A mí, Dios me ha ayudado de muchas maneras. Por ejemplo, muchos músicos llevan sus canciones apuntadas en un libro porque no las saben de memoria. Ponen su atril, y están cantando y tienen que estarla viendo. Yo no. Yo todas las tengo aquí [*apunta a la cabeza*]. No te miro ningún libro; lo que voy a cantar ya lo tengo aquí. Otro ejemplo, yo me puedo aprender tres o cuatro canciones en un día. Cuando se va mi esposo al trabajo me quedo yo sola. Ya que termino con todo, ya sin preocupación de nada y mi mente libre, agarro mis canciones y empiezo a memorizarlas, a cantarlas. Ya aprendiendo la música, se me queda la canción. No se me olvida. Aunque sean tres muy distintas, ¿ves? Aprendo una y le doy dos o tres pasadas. Luego hago a un lado la letra y me pongo a cantar de memoria, y ya con eso la aprendí. Como te digo, en un día me puedo aprender tres, cuatro canciones, y ya no se me olvidan. Se me quedan aquí. Pienso yo, ¿cómo puede ser? Por ejemplo, a veces estoy cantando una canción, y apenas canto una frase y ya parece que tengo enfrente lo que sigue. Y lo tengo ya presente como si me dijeran: —Esto sigue.

Así funciona mi cerebro, ¿ves? Las canciones no se me olvidan. Ya no necesito verlas. Es raro el cancionero que te cante la canción de memoria. Tiene que estar viéndola, ¿ves? Yo no. A mí no se me olvidan. ¡Y sé infinidad de canciones! ¡Se muchísimas canciones!

Hay algunas, digamos las que no he cantado en muchos años pos claro que se me olvidan. Pero ya nomás con una repasada que les dé, y vuelven a mi memoria otra vez. Pero como los corridos que tienen tanta letra y todo, no se me olvidan. Por ejemplo, canto "Joaquín Murrieta", "Luz Arcos", "El Contrabando de El Paso" o "Camelia la Tejana". Canto "Luis Pulido", y el corrido "El 24 de Junio", "Jesús Cadena" y "Lucio Vásquez". Sé muchos, muchos corridos. Precisamente aquí traigo un casette que grabé de puros corridos. La gente me compra mucho ese casette; digamos los mexicanos. Me compran mucho los casettes cuando traigo de corridos. Está por salir otro que acabo de grabar de puros corridos.

Sólo de LPs yo creo que tengo más de cuarenta que he grabado. Algunos LPs los tengo, pero la mayoria no los tengo porque cuando guardo uno o dos para mí, llegan así amistades y dicen: —Pos que quiero éste...

—Pos no lo tengo. Se me acabaron.

—Pos de los que tú tengas...

—Bueno, llévate este, después lo guardo.

Después se me olvida y no, no lo guardo.

La que sí los tiene todos es Nora, mi hija. Nomás me llega un disco que mando pedir y luego Nora dice: —Este es mío, yo me lo llevo, porque yo sé que si no me lo llevo, tú te vas a quedar sin nada.

Así que ella sí los tiene, pero yo no; tengo uno que otro. Menos mal. No fui de esas personas curiosas o precavidas que cada vez haya guardado algunos. No, no los guardé y se pasaron los años.

El que conservo es el original de "Mal Hombre". Pero eso lo conservo porque hace cinco años uno de mis hermanos andaba en una tienda en San Antonio y allí se lo encontró —creo que fue en la Sears. Ellos tenían muchos de esos discos viejos. Esto fue cuando empezaron a salir las otras grabaciones del fortyfai' y todo eso. "Mal Hombre" estaba grabado en setenta y ocho, discos viejos, ¿ves? Por eso los estaban dando baratos. Él ahí se lo encontró y llegó un día y dice: —Mira lo que te traigo aquí.

Cuando lo voy viendo, entonces ése sí lo guardé. Pero de ahí en más no tengo. No los guardé.

Pero con discos o sin discos Dios me ha dado tantas satisfacciones. Cosa que yo no esperaba.

La vida es la que me ha enseñado (el arte a través de generaciones de mujeres)

Mi abuelita también tenía muy bonita voz. Cantaba muy bien. Mi mamá me enseñó a tocar cuando tenía yo siete años. Ya pa' los nueve años tocaba bien la guitarra y ya vivíamos aquí en Estados Unidos. Cuando volvimos de visita a Monterrey, llegó mi mamá con la novedad de que yo ya tocaba la guitarra. Uy, a mi abuelita le dió mucho gusto. Entonces no había mañana que no me citara para ir allá con ella. —A ver, véngase, mi'ja —decía.

Agarraba ella su guitarrita —tenía una guitarra chiquita— y yo agarraba mi guitarra y cantábamos las dos: mi abuelita y yo. Pero ella nunca fue artista, como te digo. Ella tuvo ese talento y mi madre lo heredó. Pero eran tan estrictas en ese tiempo las familias que a mi madre no la dejaron desarrollar lo que ella sentía. Pero cuando se casó con papá, pos allí despertó su talento... Pero ya era madre de familia, con sus hijos. Pos ya no hizo carrera.

Sin embargo mi madre fue una educadora en todos sentidos. Ya después surgió eso de que se organizó el cuadro de variedades. Ella era la maestra que fue enseñando a mis hermanos. Siempre nos estaba dirigiendo. Pos que tú vas a hacer esto, tú vas a hacer lo otro. Así arregló los números musicales. Se las ingeniaba para conseguir música escrita, y luego iba con algún maestro para que le enseñara aquello a mi hermana María, que tocaba líricamente. María fue una gran pianista, pero lírica. Era de muy buena cabeza, porque ella llegó hasta a tocar con orquestas en algunos teatros. Como en una ocasión que llegamos a un teatro y estaba la orquesta que acompañaba a los artistas, creo que fue en Los Angeles, ¿ves? Mamá puso a mi hermana para que oyera lo que ellos iban a tocar. Luego mi hermana lo tocó líricamente. Así que mi madre hacía todo eso, y además acompañaba a los muchachos, y les ponía sus esketches cómicos y todo. Yo no sé cómo se las ingeniaba mi madre, pero ella fue la que organizó el cuadro de variedades. Inclusive les confeccionaba su ropa y vestidos también.

Bueno, me acuerdo que al principio que ibamos a presentar el cuadrito de variedades, mi hermano Manuel tenía que aparecer de charro, y mi hermanita de china poblana bailando el "Jarabe Tapatío" u otro baile mexicano. No teníamos dinero. No había medios para ir a Laredo a comprar un traje de charro. Pues fíjate que mi madre se las ingenió. Fue y compró un pantalón negro y de abajo le metió costuras pa' que se entallara como el traje de charro. Luego en la orilla le puso una apertura con un ziper. Aquí todo esto lo adornó. Fue y se compró unas docenas de botones muy bonitos, que parecían de plata, como esos que tienen los pantalones charros, ¿ves? Con esos los adornó como un traje de charro, y luego le hizo su saquito. Bueno, era un trajecito muy sencillo, pero era un traje de charro. A mi hermana Juanita, lo mismo: le arregló su vestido mexicano. Ella se las ingeniaba hasta para hacer los trajes que teníamos que usar. Ya que pasó el tiempo y que empezamos a ganar centavos entonces ya fuimos a Monterrey y le compró a mi hermano su traje de charro completo. Pero para eso tuvo que pasar algún tiempo. Te explico esto porque mi madre fue la que organizó todo aquello. Allí todo se movía por medio de mi madre. Ella era la que lo hacía. Cuando ella murió, pues nos quedamos sin director artístico —como quien dice— y se acabó el cuadro de variedades.

Pero en realidad fui yo quién encendió la mecha, hizo que se formara lo que se formó. Primero mi madre y luego yo: las dos movimos todo aquello. Y todo porque a mí me gustó la música. Yo primero aprendí la guitarra y después empecé con la mandolina. Luego me ponía a cantar con mi mamá. Ya empezó a hacerse aquello más grande, ¿ves? Entonces dije yo: —Pues a Dio', mis hermanos también tienen que aprender.

La función de variedades Mendoza en 1935. Francisca ("Panchita") Mendoza (*arriba izquierda*), María Mendoza (*arriba derecha*), Leonor Zamarripa Mendoza (*sentada*), Juanita Mendoza (*abajo izquierda*) y Manuel Mendoza (*abajo derecha*). Cortesía Houston Metropolitan Research Center, Houston Public Library

A María, que era la más grandecita, le dí clases en la mandolina, ¡y aprendió la fregada muchachita! Pronto aprendió a tocar la mandolina. Entonces yo dije: —Pues yo quiero tocar el violín... quiero tocarlo.

Y lo toqué. Así fue creciendo el grupo sin instrucción de maestros, ni de nada. Hay veces que me han preguntado, que si a mí me educaron la voz. Y no, fue la vida, la experiencia de la vida, la práctica, son las que me han enseñado lo poco que sé¿ves? Porque yo nunca supe de que "dale así o dale asá" o "dale cierta nota". No, yo sola saqué ideas de mi inteligencia. Simplemente tomé mi guitarra.

Pausa musical

[*Lydia Mendoza canta "Amor de Madre".*]

Dame por Dios, tu bendición,
oh madre mía adorada.
Que yo a tus pies pido perdón
por lo que tú has sufrido.

Dame por Dios, tu bendición,
una mirada te pido,
madre querida.
Ruega por mi al creador.

Tú que estás en la mansión
de ese trono celestial,
mándale a mi corazón
un suspiro maternal.
Un suspiro maternal
que me llegue al corazón,
que me llegue, que me llegue al corazón.

Mira madre que en el mundo
nadie te ama como yo.
Mira que el amor de madre
estará entre las dos.

Tú que estás en la mansión
de ese trono celestial,
mándale a mi corazón
un suspiro maternal.
Un suspiro maternal
que me llegue al corazón,
que me llegue, que me llegue al corazón.

[*Repite las primeras dos estrofas.*]

¡No se arrienden! ¡No se queden atrás! (seguir en la música: toda una vida)

En tantos años que tengo, la música ha sido una meta que yo he querido seguir; yo no me arriendaba por nada. Fracasos, o sí ganaba algo o no ganaba, yo nunca dije: —No, yo mejor voy a hacer otra cosa.

No, yo seguí adelante en la música. Y eso es lo bonito,

¿ves? Ojalá que a todas las que quieran hacer algo o tengan algún talento: que sigan adelante y no se arrienden; no se queden atrás. ¿Qué importa que resulten otras cancioneras o más artistas? Tú llevas tu meta, y eso es lo tuyo. Tienes que decidirte por una sola cosa y seguir adelante. Si ves que fracasas y dices: —No, pues mejor voy a hacer esta otra cosa.

Así nunca vas a hacer nada.

Fíjate, yo tengo un sobrino, hijo de Juanita mi hermana. Y él, pues es un muchacho que tiene muy buena inteligencia. Dios lo dotó con mucho talento. Todo lo que él sabe, los grandes estudios, todo lo obtuvo bajo becas que le daban por lo que él sabía, ¿ves? Lo mandaron creo que hasta Hungría, o quién sabe a dónde. Cuando él comenzó, lo que él quería ser era... yo no sé como les nombran a esas personas que estudian los huesos del cuerpo. ¿Cómo se llaman esos que saben la anatomía del cuerpo? Bueno, eso fue lo que él empezó a estudiar. Entonces por ese talento que él manifestaba, lo mandaron hasta por allá, sí creo que hasta Hungría o quién sabe pa' dónde. A hacer sus estudios. Al principio iba muy bien. Pues no; dejó eso. No lo siguió. Así ha emprendido varias cosas, y aunque es un muchacho estudiado que sabe mucho no ha llegado a la meta que él ha querido. Ya tiene treinta y tantos años y no ha hecho nada. Con tanto que ha estudiado, y ha aprendido, y ha practicado, no se ha decidido por nada. Nosotros creíamos que iría a ser algún doctor, o algo. Pos no ha hecho nada. Tiene facultades. Ha tenido mucho estudio y no ha hecho nada. Y eso, pos creo que no es bueno.

Yo, imagínate, cuando comencé, empecé a fracasar; porque todo en la vida tiene sus fracasos. Tenemos que comenzar con muchas penalidades y muchas cosas, ¿ves? Y aún sin embargo, yo no me arriendaba. Al contrario: quería agrandarlo, y lo fui agrandando; el grupo, la música, y todo eso por tal de seguir adelante. Todo esto lo he platicado cuando me ha tocado estar en algunas escuelas. Les digo a los padres de familia que ayuden a sus hijos a seguir adelante, pero que sea en una sola cosa; no nomás comenzar algo y dejarlo, y total no llegar a nada.

Por ejemplo, cuando nosotros comenzamos, cuando comencé yo de chamaca con mi familia, había veces que íbamos a tocar y no sacábamos nada. No teníamos ni para comer, y la pasábamos sufriendo. A veces no teníamos ni para pagar la renta. Todos esos sacrificios y sufrimientos, tan sólo por querer seguir en la música. Yo podía haberme decidido a hacer otra cosa, pero yo quería seguir adelante. Y luego cuando me descubrieron, que ya empezaron a saber que yo podía cantar, me llevaban a presentar a algunos lugares; pero a mí no me pagaban ni un centavo. Sin embargo yo estaba muy contenta porque yo decía: —Voy subiendo, voy adelante.

Es muy fácil decir: —Yo quiero ser artista, quiero ser esto o lo otro y quiero surgir luego luego.

Pero es imposible. Yo para llegar a tener un nombre, y ser reconocida, pasó mucho tiempo. Afanamos como desde 1927 hasta 1934. ¿Cuantos años fueron? Como siete años.

De todo hubo. Fracasos, buenos y malos momentos, y todo eso. Aún así se llegó mi día, y mira: Dios me ayudó. Pero no todos pensamos así. Yo me he topado con gente que dice: —Pues yo quiero aprender a tocar la guitarra, quiero cantar, y también grabar, y todo.

Pues no es muy fácil. Hay que afanar muchísimo. Ahora en los tiempos actuales los jóvenes tienen muchas oportunidades, tú sabes. La televisión principalmente, el radio, programas culturales, concursos y organizaciones que los ayudan. Eso es mucha ayuda, ¿ves? En las mismas escuelas empiezan a ver que les gusta. Tienen sus bandas de música, y los van enseñando, tú sabes. Ya después, bueno, pueden seguir. Pero cuando yo comencé, ni a la escuela fui. ¿Pos qué podía haber aprendido yo? Y luego en aquellos años no había ni radio, ni otros medios para aprender uno. No había nada. Entonces yo todo lo que aprendí, lo aprendí por mi propio esfuerzo. Queriendo. Porque la única que me enseñó a mí la guitarra fue mi madre: mi única maestra.

¡Que surjan las cancioneras!

Como te digo, al principio que yo llegué a San Antonio —en aquellos años— no había mujeres que cantaran o que se animaran a cantar. Nada de eso. Yo creo que yo empecé a animarlas o no sé. La cosa es que empezaron a surgir muchas cancioneras que se retiraron. No sé en qué quedaron las cancioneras que tomaron parte conmigo en aquel concurso. Como la que ganó el segundo lugar, Lupita Viña de San Antonio. Ni sé lo que se hizo: se casó o se retiró. La que ganó el tercer lugar lo mismo. No hicieron nada: Ni carrera ni nada. Surgió, por ejemplo, Rita Vidaurri; ¿la conoces tú? Es una muchacha que conocí cuando ella comenzó y tenía doce años. Comenzó en unos concursos que hubo allí en el Teatro Nacional. Ella ganó porque cantaba y tocaba la guitarra, pero de seis cuerdas. Tenía una voz muy bonita. Empezó a trabajar y a hacer giras así y todo. Pero de repente se apagó. Allí vive en San Antonio y trabaja en un hospital. Ya ves se retiró del ambiente. Rosita Fernández es otra que le pasó lo mismo. Nunca hizo nada afuera de San Antonio. Allí en San Antonio trabajó mucho cantando en el paseo del río. Pero ya también se retiró. La verdad es que no han quedado cancioneras o artistas que hayan hecho giras o que hayan aguantado...lo que yo tuve que afanar y luchar. Unas se han casado, otras han desaparecido; han dejado su carrera. Todavía ahorita en San Antonio hay muchas cancioneras, muchas muchachas que han surgido que cantan y todo. Pero pos... no salen de la ciudad; no han hecho nada. Nomás allí están.

Hay muchas razones, muchas cosas, ¿ves? Sin ir muy lejos, por ejemplo: mis hermanas Juanita y María. Ellas formaron un dueto. Mis hermanas se entregaron más al dueto en tiempo de la guerra cuando se llevaron a mi hermano y no podíamos hacer viajes. Cantaban en un club y estuvieron muy bien organizadas, ¿ves? Cuando empezamos ya otra vez a hacer giras en el '47 fuimos a California y empecé a grabar yo con el señor Pelache. Le sugerí al señor Pelache que grabara el dueto de mis hermanas también.

—No, —me dijo— si a mí me interesa nomás usted.

Bueno, pues a la segunda vez que grabé con él, le volví a decir: —Mire, yo sé

Hermanitas cantantes Lucía (*izquierda*) y Juanita Carmona (*derecha*) continuaron en la tradición de Lydia Mendoza, tocando y cantando en la Plaza del Zacate (1941). Cortesía U. T. The Insitute of Texan Cultures, Colección *San Antonio Light*

lo que le digo. Aunque no les pague mucho, pero yo quiero que les de una oportunidad.

—Bueno Lydia, está bueno, les voy a ayudar. Que me graben un disco.

Se lo grabaron y yo las acompañé también con mi guitarra, ¿ves? Salió el dueto muy bien. Al salir el disco pues gustó muchísimo. El señor las contrató, y empezaron ellas a grabar. Cuando mi mamá murió, pues querían seguir grabando pero tocó que María se casó; y Juanita también se casó luego luego. Entonces empezaron las dificultades con sus maridos. Juanita y María quisieron seguir grabando. Una vez, fueron a pedirles que grabaran. El esposo de María al fin concedió que fuera pero a la hora de la hora le dijo que no. Hubo un laberintazo, que sí grabaron o no grabaron, yo no sé.

El marido de María le dijo: —Pues te casaste conmigo; tu hogar y tus hijos, o tu carrera.

¿Y qué hizo María? Pos se quedó con sus hijos —tuvo seis— y se retiró del ambiente. Así fue como se desintegró el dueto por causa del marido de María, y se acabó.

Y resulta que al fin, al cabo de tantos años de casados —pues yo creo que duraron como veinte y cinco años de casados— que se enreda el marido de María con una vieja; se divorció de ella y la dejó. Pues ya María se quedó desanimada

y enferma. Ya ves, le destruyó su carrera a mi hermana y pa' acabarla de amo-
lar se divorció de ella. Y ella está muy enferma. Fíjate que tiene cancer en el
colon. La quisieron operar hace tres años. Se puso muy mala y fue al hospital.
Allí le dijeron que tenía un tumor canceroso en el colon. Y que para evitar su
crecimiento iban a extirpárselo, cerrarle el conducto y ponerle una bolsa. Ella
no quiso y se les salió del hospital. Y allí la tienes secándose en vida: flaca flaca,
y muy enferma. Además con la decepción que sufrió del marido que se enredó
con una comadre. Total, que el marido se divorció de ella, y María se quedó
sola. Sus hijos crecieron, se casaron, y ya ni les importa su madre. Allí la tienes
sola, abandonada y enferma. Sí. Se quedó sola en San Antonio. Y allí tienes el
trastorno que viven ellas.

También mis hermanos están casados y las esposas tampoco quisieron que
ellos siguieran y se quedaron en la casa. La pobre de Juanita pos también está
muy enferma de diabetes. A ella le operaron una pierna y quién sabe qué le en-
contraron; y luego luego le operaron la otra pierna. Como ves, por todas estas
razones han dejado las carreras.

¡Que surjan las cancioneras! En tantos años ¿por qué no surge una cancionera que haga una carrera como la que he hecho yo?

Mi larga carrera me ha llevado a muchos lugares. Me acuerdo de la primera
vez que me presenté en México. Al principio de mi carrera quisieron llevarme
allá pero tenía yo muchos contratos aquí, mucho trabajo. Entonces, pos, aquí
me quedé. Pasaron los años, pasó el tiempo, y no fui a México sino hasta como
en mil novecientos cincuenta y tantos. Un señor de California dijo: —Pues,
¿por qué no has ido a México?

Ya le dije: —Pos yo nunca he trabajado allá, ni tengo conecciones.

El me dijo: —Si yo te arreglo un contrato allá, ¿vas?

Le contesté: —Pues, pueda que sí.

Así lo hizo. Fue este señor a México y me arregló un contratito de dos semanas en el Teatro Esperanza Iris en México. No me iban a pagar mucho, pero
por lo menos me iba a quedar el gusto de haber estado en México. Y sí me
dieron para mi vuelo, mi hotel, y todo. Pues ya se arregló lo del contrato, y yo
me fui.

Bueno, cuando llegué me habló el director y dijo: —Señora Mendoza, sé que
usted va a debutar aquí.

El número estrella era el mío. Había otros números que iban a abrir pero el
mío era el principal.

—Sí señor —le dije.

—Pues quiero que sepa que mañana, a las diez de la mañana tenemos aquí
el ensayo para todos.

Le dije: —Pues señor, yo nunca voy a los ensayos, porque no es necesario. Al
fin y al cabo yo traigo mi guitarra y yo misma me acompaño; llevo mis
números preparados. Nomás me dice el tiempo que me dan, y es todo.

—Dijo [*imitando la voz del hombre*]: —No Señora Mendoza, aquí tienen
que estar todos los artistas. No importa quién sea. Tiene que estar aquí usted
también.

—Muy bien. Yo voy.

Bueno, pues llegué para las diez de la mañana. Ya estaba yo allí con mi guitarra. Pues empezaron todos a ensayar y que las bailarinas, y que esto y que l'otro. Bueno. Luego que pasó todo dijo el director: —Lydia Mendoza a escena. Que subiera yo. Bueno, subí. Se para el hombre y me dice: —Y ¿usted qué va hacer?

Le dije: —Pues voy a cantar...

—¿Con esa guitarra?

—Pos sí señor —le dije— si no es la primera vez que lo hago; ya tengo tantos años haciéndolo —ya le platiqué —ya me he presentado en California, en Nueva York, y en Los Angeles.

—¡Ah sí! Pero allá es muy distinto: aquí estamos en México. Aquí el público es muy exigente y si yo la presento a usted así nomás... una mujer allí con una guitarra en el foro, pues nos agarran a.... ¡No. Ni lo mande Dios! Aquí no se puede.

Le dije: —Pos, así me contrataron y así toco.

—No pos ¿se puede usted acompañar con mariachi?

—Sí, cómo no. Inclusive he grabado con mariachi.

Dice: —Pos ahorita veremos.

Luego luego agarró el teléfono y le habló a un muchacho muy simpático, muy amable. No me acuerdo quién era. Los mariachis de quién sabe qué. No me acuerdo. Creo que de Miguel Díaz; muy buenos. Llegaron. No pos al momento allí estaban. Bueno, pues ellos ya sabían quién era yo pero no me conocían.

—Sí, cómo no. Ya la hemos oido, pero pos lo duro es que nosotros no sabemos la música que usted canta.

Le dije: —Aquí tenemos que acomodarnos a lo que ustedes sepan, porque el señor dice que no puedo presentarme con la pura guitarra.

—Pero si así la conocemos.

—Pos no; el director dice que no.

Le dije: —Bueno. ¿Saben...? —yo buscando números que ellos supieran, ¿verdad?— ¿Saben '"Besando la Cruz"?

Dijo: —Ah sí, cómo no.

—¿Y saben...?

Y les dije números que pensaba que podían saber. Pos ya preparamos cuatro números con el mariachi. Se iba a abrir una cortina, aparecía el mariachi tocando, y se abría otra cortina y salía yo con mi guitarra. Comencé con "Besando la Cruz".

Pos ya se llegó la noche del debut y así lo hicimos. Salió primero el mariachi tocando "Besando la Cruz", luego salí yo con mi guitarra, y el público me recibió muy bien cuando empecé a cantar. Nomás acabé de cantarla, oyes, y empezó el público a patear y a gritar [patea]: —¡Saquen a esos mamarrachos de allí! ¡Venimos a oir a Lydia Mendoza con su guitarra! ¡No queremos oir eso! ¡Eso ya estamos cansados de oirlo! ¡No! ¡no! ¡Ella sola con su guitarra!

Brinco y brinco, y empezaron a pedirme mis canciones: —¡Cántanos el "Pajarito Herido"! —¡Queremos "Mundo Engañoso"! —¡"Celosa"!

Querían números que ni había estudiado con el mariachi, tú. ¿Pos yo que hacía? Los muchachos nomás me miraban y yo los miraba a ellos. No podía cantar lo que teníamos ensayado. Tenía que cantar lo que estaban pidiendo. Ya les empecé a cantar yo sola. Canté como unos treinta o cuarenta minutos: todo

Lydia Mendoza fue honrada en Juárez, Chihuahua, México con un desfile
(1950). Cortesía Houston Metropolitan Research Center, Houston Public
Library

lo que el público pidió. Y aquellos pobres parados nomás allí; no podían acom-
pañarme. Así nos pasamos toda la semana. El público aguantaba la primera
pieza del mariachi porque así empezaba; ellos salían al foro cantando. Nomás
terminaban y empezaba la misma cosa: el público a gritar que no, que sacaran
a esos mamarrachos de allí.

A la semana dice el viejo cuatro-ojos, el director: —Oiga Lydia, yo creo que
es inútil estar pagando el mariachi. Ese gasto es de oquis.

Dije: —Bueno, pos usted quería mariachi. Dijo que para qué me presentaba
yo sola, que iban a aventarme tomates y que...

Dijo: —Chihuahua... no, yo creo que mejor los despido, ¿verdad?

—Pos es cosa suya.

Los despidió. La segunda semana me presenté yo sola.

Sí, eso me pasó cuando fui a México. Fue como en el cincuenta y cuatro por
allí así, ¿ves? Y ya te digo, eso me pasó con ese director que no quería que me
presentara sola. A fin de cuentas yo iba por dos semanas y me quede seis
meses. Porque nomás terminé allí, y vino a contratarme un señor Vallejo; un
señor que sacaba unas grandes caravanas por todo México con puras estrellas
mexicanas. Yo no tenía compromisos y le dije: —Sí, cómo no.

Dice: —Esta semana salimos para Guadalajara.

Me pagaban bien y además me daban los gastos. Libre de impuestos y de
todo. Pos así anduve seis meses en México, pero pura provincia. Donde quiera
que me presenté la gente ya me conocía, ¿ves?

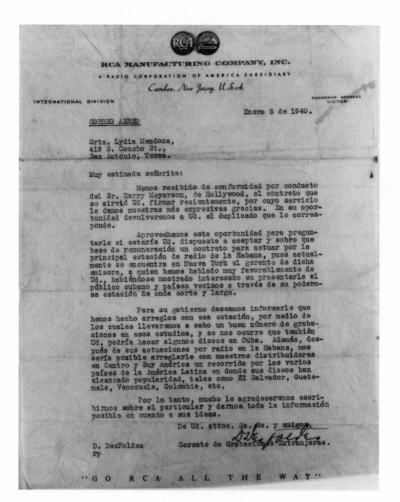

Carta fechada 2 de enero 1940 de la RCA Victor, ofreciéndole a Lydia Mendoza una visita a Cuba para grabar discos y presentarse en vivo en la radio. Expresan la intención de distribuir sus discos en América Latina "donde sus discos han alcanzado popularidad, tales como El Salvador, Guatemala, Venezuela, Colombia, etc." Cortesía Houston Metropolitan Research Center, Houston Public Library

Me acuerdo de una ciudad a la que fuimos, que se llama Frontera. Allá no había entrada para los artistas, sino que teníamos que entrar por enfrente. Iban en esta caravana tan grande artistas tan famosas como Virginia López, José Alfredo Jiménez, Las Hermanas Hernández, el Mantequilla. Era una caravana de puras estrellas y nada de rellenos. A todos les aplaudía el público porque los conocía [*aplaude*]. Entraban allí y directo al foro. Ya casi al último venía yo. ¿Qué crees que hizo la gente? Se paró cuando me vieron entrar; sabían que era Lydia Mendoza, pos iba con la guitarra. Así que se pararon a recibirme. No me puedo quejar, me hicieron un recibimiento muy simpático, muy bonito¿ves? Así fue en todo México. Así ha sido a lo largo de mi carrera.

A Sudamérica no fui hasta hace poco. Desde luego que mis grabaciones fueron conocidas allá desde que yo comencé. Imagínate: una compañía tan grande como lo es la RCA Victor me tuvo en contrato por diez años. Si se pararon las grabaciones fue por la guerra, cuando se vino la guerra. Si no yo hubiera seguido grabando. Ellos estaban allí cada cuatro meses y yo grababa de cuatro a cinco discos cada vez. Ellos venían como tres veces por año a San Antonio a grabarme a mí. Para que hicieran eso, era porque las ventas andaban muy bien, ¿ves? Era mucho lo que se vendían mis discos. Donde quiera se inundó todo con mis grabaciones.

Cuando estuve en Nueva York la última vez, fue un impresario de Sudamérica a verme. El quería llevarme a que hiciera una gira por allá; pero quería nomás el número mío. La razón porque no fui, fue por que no quiso llevar a todo el grupo. Si yo me hubiera ido y dejado solos a mi madre y a mis hermanos, pues no hubieran hecho nada; porque todos los contratos que teníamos eran conmigo. Claro que todo el cuadro de variedades gustaba porque lo teníamos muy bien montado, bonito el vestuario y todo. Pero el número principal era, tu sabes, el mío. Por lo tanto le dije: —Nomás voy si lleva todo el grupo.

—No, pos nos interesa nomás usted. La queremos poner allá en televisión, radio, cabaret, y que grabe también.

—Pos sí, pero yo no puedo ir sola.

Y no fui. Dios lo sabe que lo hice por no dejar a mi madre sola con mis hermanos. Pues de eso vivían, ¿ves? Y no fui.

Pero, mira ¿quién hubiera pensado que al cabo de tantos y tantos años iba yo a ir a Sudamérica? Verás la última vez que me presenté en Chicago con una variedad mexicana —hace como seis años— llegaron a verme unos periodistas que eran de Sudamérica. Fueron a mi camerino y me saludaron con mucho gusto. Dicen: —¡Pero Lydia, si nosotros creíamos que usted ya no vivía! ¡Qué barbaridad! usted no se imagina el impacto de su música y el público que tiene por allá en Sudamérica y que quiere conocerla.

—Pos sí, yo nunca he ido, no.

Dice: —Yo sé que si usted va para allá va a tener mucho éxito; a usted el público la adora.

Le dije: —Bueno, si hay alguna oportunidad, seguro que sí voy.

Ellos traíban una grabadorcita y les mandé un saludo para allá diciéndoles que probablemente un día los visitaría. Les canté unas canciones, las grabaron, y se las llevaron. Esa entrevista que me hicieron salió en un periódico de allá, ¿ves? Hablaban de la entrevista y del saludo que les mandaba.

Y luego deja de eso; empecé también a recibir correspondencia. Me escribieron como cincuenta cartas diferentes personas de allá que habían visto el anuncio en el periódico. Estaban encantados y querían que yo los visitara. Estaba loco todo el público. Pos no faltó un empresario que luego luego se comunicó conmigo, arreglaron el contrato y me fui a Sudamérica. Fue un impacto para el público de allá. Me recibieron con mucho cariño, y todo. Me presenté en Medellín, Colombia y luego en muchos otros pueblos. Estuve allá

Los Tacónes de Lydia Mendoza. Pintura al pastel de Estér Hernández (1999). Cortesía Estér Hernández

por cuatro semanas. Fíjate, me refiero a esto porque después de tantos años se me concedió que me llamaran para que fuera a Sudamérica. La primera vez — en el cuarenta y uno— no pude ir, pero al cabo de tantos años se me concedió. Me fui yo sola y estuve muy a gusto allá. Nomás que pues... es diferente la vida allá. Pero lo que es el público; fue un recibimiento muy grande que me hicieron.

Tengo mucha fe en los espíritus

Voy a decirte que no soy religiosa fanática fanática; de esa gente que nomás vive en la iglesia y que... En primer lugar cuando se va a la casa de Dios, se tiene que ir con tranquilidad y con devoción. Si yo me voy a la iglesia, a misa, y estoy pensando: —Ay que se acabe pronto esto porque tengo que ir a trabajar acá, o allá...

Entonces ya no estoy con Dios ¿y para qué voy? Yo voy a la iglesia, a misa cuando yo estoy tranquila, que no tengo pendiente. Cuando voy a entregarme a Dios quiero estar en mis oraciones tranquila. Si no, no voy. De todas maneras, cuando yo estoy en mi casa, o dondequiera que esté, siempre antes de dormirme hago mis oraciones, me encomiendo a Dios; encomiendo a Dios a mis hijas y a todos. Siempre rezo mis oraciones antes de acostarme. Eso lo hago todos los días, siempre; en el rincón de mi casa. Pero sí soy Católica. Esa era la religión de mi madre y de mis abuelos. Pero es como te digo yo: no soy fanática... cuando tengo tranquilidad, y no tengo pendiente, sí voy a la iglesia. Pero menos, no. ¿A qué voy si no voy a estar con devoción? Diosito siempre está conmigo. Naturalmente no le pido imposibles, ni cosas. No le pido tener mucho dinero, ni tener un carro. No, hombre. Mis deseos son limpios y sinceros. Todo lo que le pido yo a Dios parece que Diosito me lo concede. Me oye cuando yo le pido yo algo para el bien mío o para el bien de alguien más. Dios siempre me oye.

Yo sí deveras le tengo mucha fe a los espíritus. Una grandísima fe... hasta para dormir. Fíjate, a veces me da insomnio cuando voy a salir; me pongo a pensar que no se me olvide esto, o que tengo que preparar aquello; no falta qué. O sea que empieza mi mente a trabajar antes de irme a dormir. Entonces antes de acostarme —cuando hago mis oraciones— invoco a los espíritus del cielo que vengan y velen mi sueño, que no me dé insomnio, que me duerma. ¿Y no crees que sí me duermo? Pero lo hago con mucha fe.

Te doy otro ejemplo: cuando quiero algo —¿como te diré?— que tengo alguna pena, o alguna cosa que les pasa a mis hijas, o algo, siempre invoco a los espíritus para que las libren de aquello. Y mira, me oyen. Yo les tengo mucha fe a los espíritus. Pero es como te digo: es la fe con la que aquella persona pide aquello. Como te digo, yo no me pongo a pedirles que quiero encontrarme dinero, o que quiero sacarme el premio de la lotería. Yo no pido nada de eso. Nomás pido lo justo.

La oración es algo muy grande. La oración. Simplemente como cuando me daba antes una dolencia; yo lo que hacía era invocar a los espíritus:

—Quítenme esta dolencia, que no me siga, que se me quite.

Y se me quitaba. Cuando menos pensaba, aquella dolencia se me quitaba. Pa' saber, ¿me escucharán, o será la voz y la fe con que pido yo aquello? La cosa es que a mí se me concede. Y así también con esa fe cuando no me puedo dormir. Porque a mí no me gusta tomar pastillas para dormir, ni para nada de eso. Cuando se me va el sueño lo que hago es invocar los espíritus que vengan a velar mi sueño... Cuando menos pienso... ya me quedé dormida. Por eso es que te digo que tengo mucha fe en los espíritus.

Mi madre nos enseñaba esas cosas

 Al ver mi madre que mi padre se oponía a mandarnos a la escuela ella decidió enseñarnos lo poco que ella sabía. Entonces comenzó a comprar unas pizarras, unos lapices, colores... de todo. Ella fue, como quien dice, la maestra para nosotros cuando estábamos creciendo. Así fue como ella empezó a enseñarnos todo, ¿ves?

Al mismo tiempo mi santa madre también fue una mujer que procuraba enseñarnos lo que era bueno y lo que era malo. Ella nos decía que no mintiéramos, que no fuéramos a decir una cosa que no fuera cierta; como un falso testimonio. Por ejemplo, decir que alguna niña había hecho algo sin haberlo hecho, que si era un falso, Dios lo castigaba. Nos ponía muchas parábolas así como ejemplos. Se me quedó muy grabado aquello que mi madre nos platicó como cuentos. Y hablando de eso, en una ocasión, platicándonos de lo que significaba levantar un falso, decir una cosa que no era cierta, nos platicó una historia. Fíjate que esta historia para mí es muy interesante. Han pasado tantos años y a mí nunca se me olvida. Ella nos platicaba aquello como algo que había sucedido.

Nos contaba que había un pueblecito en donde vivía gente humilde. Allí vivía una familia, una pareja que tenían únicamente una hija. La muchacha era muy honrada, muy trabajadora y educada. Entonces pasó el tiempo y ella nunca se casó; se quedó soltera. Entre tanto murió su mamá, y luego murió su papá y quedó ella solita en su casa. Bueno, al verse ella sola, pues empezó a trabajar. Era una muchacha que no salía a ninguna parte: ni a bailes ni a nada. Nomás de su trabajo a su casa y era todo.

Resulta que enfrente de esa casa vivía otra familia, y allí había una mujer de esas que les gusta mucho el chisme, hablar, y estar nomás viendo lo que hace el vecino. En una ocasión llegó un agente vendiendo no sé qué. El caso es que llevaba mercancía y andaba casa por casa vendiéndola. Entonces llegó a la casa de la mujer chismosa y ella le compró algo. En ese momento la muchacha, muy arregladita, salió para su trabajo. Al agente le impresionó y se quedó viéndola. La vió y la muchacha ni se dio cuenta. Entonces él le preguntó a la mujer aquella: —Oiga, ¿usted conoce a esa señorita que acaba de salir?

—Sí, cómo no.

—¿Pues con quién vive ella allí?

Yo creo que a aquel forastero le gustó la muchacha. La mujer le dijo: —Pos es huérfana; ya murió su papá y su mamá. Ella vive solita allí.

—Ah, ¿no es casada? —dijo.

—No, no. —dice.

—¿Y qué de su vida de ella?

—Pues sale a trabajar y todo, pero pos no sé. Para mí que no va bien porque se sale sola. Y usted sabe bien que una muchacha ya viviendo sola ¿qué vida buena puede llevar?

Lo que ella estaba diciendo contra aquella señorita fue una maldad. En realidad la muchacha era muy seria; no hablaba con nadie, ni daba lugar a nada. Pero con decirle eso al forastero lo puso a pensar. Al fin ya el forastero se impresionó con aquello, se fue y jamás volvió.

Pasando el tiempo la muchacha aquella se murió. Falleció y la mujer aquella se quedó con el remordimiento. Estaba con aquel remordimiento de lo que había dicho contra la muchacha, porque realmente, aquella muchacha no daba motivo. Bueno, como te decía, cuando se murió la muchacha, le entró mucho remordimiento a la mujer aquella por aquel falso que le había levantado a aquella pobre; le entró remordimiento por decir algo que no era cierto. Y no estaba a gusto y no estaba a gusto, y soñaba mucho a la muchacha. Entonces un día se levantó y se fue a la iglesia. Se fue a confesar con el padre y le dijo:

—Acúsome padre yo cometí un error.

Ella le confesó al padre.

El dice: —Pues si no tenías motivos ese fue un falso testimonio que levantaste tu contra esa señorita.

—Pues sí y lo reconozco —dice— pero por eso estoy arrepentida y vengo a confesarme para que me dé mi penitencia, y me perdone usted.

—Pues mira hija, yo no te puedo perdonar. Tienes que ir a ver al obispo. Confiésate con él, dile tu caso.

—Ay sí padre, yo voy.

La mujer fue ante el obispo y le dice la misma cosa que al padre.

—Pues hija, lo siento mucho, pero lo que tú has hecho, yo no lo puedo perdonar.

—Ay pero ¿qué hago?

—Pos lo único que te puede quedar por hacer es ir a ver al Papa. A ver si él te puede perdonar.

—Sí, cómo no.

Fue a ver al Papa y se confesó. Y el Papa le dijo la misma cosa: —Pues lo que tu hiciste fue levantar un falso testimonio y yo no te puedo perdonar. Sí puedo absolverte, pero tienes que hacer algo que te voy a decir.

—A ver dígame padre —dice.

—Mira anda y cómprate un pichón o una paloma, y la matas. Luego escoge un día que esté haciendo mucho pero mucho aire y te subes a la torre más alta de la iglesia. Allí le quitas a la paloma una por una todas las plumas, que no le quede ni una. Las avientas, las dejas que se vayan, que se las lleve el aire, todas, todas, todas. Y luego, vienes.

Pues fue e hizo lo que le dijo el Papa y después volvió. —Ahora sí, ya vine a que me absuelva —dice.

—Pues ahora, vas y me trais las plumas una por una.

—Pero cómo... pero padre ¿cómo me pide usted lo imposible? ¿Cómo voy a traerle eso que me pide? Pos si escogí un día que hacía mucho aire. ¿Pos a dónde cree que hayan ido a dar esas plumas?

—Pues ¿a dónde crees que habrá ido a dar la honra de esa señorita? Así que si me traes todas las plumas yo te absuelvo.

—Padre, ¿pero qué hago? —dice.

—Pues la otra solución sería que fueras y le pidieras perdón a ella.

—¿Pero cómo?

—A las doce de la noche salen todas las ánimas. Ella tiene que salir también. Cuando la veas venir anda y pídele que te perdone.

—Sí, cómo no.

Pues así lo hizo. Se fue aquella señora, y esperó que dieran las doce de la noche. A las doce en punto empezaron a salir las ánimas, los bultos. Entre aquellos bultos venía la muchacha. Pero venía con dos niños: uno de la mano y otro en brazos. La mujer nomás la vio, corrió y se le hincó: —Niña, niña, vengo aquí a que me perdones. ¿Me perdonas por aquello que yo te hice?

—Sí, yo te perdono.

Ya se iba cuando la ánima dijo: —Pero pídele también perdón a mi niño.

Al que traiba de la mano: Le dijo: —Niño, niñito, ¿me perdonas?

Y el muchachito le dijo que sí. Y otra vez ya se iba la vieja y vuelve a decirle la ánima: —No, no te vayas; te falta pedirle perdón a mi niño que traigo en los brazos.

El chiquito era como de un año. Y le dijo: —¿Me perdonas niño?

Volteó el niñito y con el dedito le dijo que no. Y entonces: —¡Válgame el santísimo! —Se desaparecieron todas las ánimas. —¡Válgame el santísimo!

Y en eso sale el diablo y dice: —Pos tu cuerpo será tirado pa'l cielo, pero tu lengua es mía.

Y se acabó el cuento. ¿Verdad que está interesante eso? Eso es para atemorizar a las personas para que no digan cosas que no son ciertas, que perjudiquen a los demás, ¿ves? Y eso nos lo platicó mi madre para que no levantáramos falsos, o dijéramos lo que no era cierto. Muchas cosas así nos platicaba mi madre.

Ah, te quería platicar algo más. Esta cosa no me la platicó mi madre. Es algo que pasó en la familia, ¿ves? Pues fíjate, la cosa es que mi padre era muy celoso con mi madre. Y mi madre era de esas señoras criadas a la antigua, como quien dice. Hoy en día el marido le dice a la esposa: —Haz esto. O: —Me vas a traer esto.

—Pos hazlo tú.

O no lo hace, ¿verdad? Es la verdad. En aquellos años no. Lo que el jefe, el padre, decía, eso se hacía. Bueno. Me acuerdo que un lunes en la mañana —esto fue el 1920 cuando tenía yo como seis años— le dice mi padre a mi madre: —No se le olvide Leonora que tiene que ir a pagar la renta.

Vivía cerca de nosotros el señor al que le pagábamos la renta.

—No se le vaya a olvidar.

—No, no se me olvida.

—Pa' la tarde me tiene que tener el recibo.

—Sí, cómo no, sí voy.

Bueno. En eso, como a medio día llegó una comadre o amiga y empezaron plática y plática, tú sabes. De repente mamá ve el reloj y se da cuenta que ya eran las tres de la tarde. Mi papá llegaba a las cuatro. Y a ella le daba pena decirle a la señora: —Váyase porque tengo que ir a dejar la renta.

Entonces allí había un señor que hacía mandados. Y me dijo mi mamá: —Anda háblale a don Remigio que venga pa' 'ca.

Y vino el señor. —¿Sí señora? —dice.

—Mire, don Remigio, hágame favor de ir a llevarme la renta y que le den el recibo.

—Sí, señora.

Fue el señor, dejó la renta y le trajo el recibo a mi madre, y se acabó. Bueno, por fin se fue la señora y llegó mi papá.

Mi papá era de esos señores que tomaba, pero no tomaba en la calle sino que siempre tenía su botella de trago. Llegaba y se sentaba, empezaba a leer y le daba sus traguitos a la bebida. Ya al rato cenaba. Pues ese día llegó mi papá, se metió a la sala, y empezó a tomar su trago y a leer el papel [periódico]. En eso me habla a mí, y dice: —Lydia, ¿fue tu mamá a dejar la renta?

Y yo ya conociéndolo como era, yo ya sabía qué decir y estaba muy atenta en todo. Entonces le dije: —Sí papá, sí fue a dejarla.

—¿Que vestido llevó?

Le dije: —A pos uno café que tiene.

—¿Ah, sí? Bueno. Está bueno, váyase mi'ja.

Bueno, cómo a la hora, cuando ya estaba mi papá más tomado, le habla a mi madre y le dice: —¿ Leonor, fue a dejar la renta?

—Sí, bueno, digo no, no fui.

—Bueno, ¿sí o no?

—Bueno, no, no fuí Pancho, porque tuve una visita...

Pos si ni acabó mi madre de decirle el motivo o lo que fuera cuando se suelta mi papá: —Hija, ¡de quién sabe qué! ¡que usted trata de engañarme! ¡yo no soy su pendejo!

Y se levantó trastabillándose directamente a la carabina. Siempre mi padre tenía detrás de la puerta una carabina, y siempre la tenía cargada. Decía que si por los ladrones, o lo que fuera.

En ese tiempo estaba recién nacida mi hermana María. Tenía apenas una semana de haber nacido y mamá siempre criaba a sus hijos, ¿ves? Cuando mamá vió que papá corrió a agarrar la carabina pos sabía bien que le iba a tirar, ¿ves? Corre mi madre y agarra la niña en los brazos y empieza a darle el pecho, ¿ves? Mientras tanto mi padre allá, trastabillándose fue a agarrar la carabina. Tan pronto como la niña tomó el pecho inmediatamente lo soltó y se puso así, mira: negra, negra, negra, así como envenenada, ¿ves? Entonces mi madre le tiró el grito a papá que andaba borracho: —¡Infeliz! ¡Usted ya me mató a mi hija!

Con el grito de mamá el salió de su borrachera. Creyó que había disparado. Aventó la carabina y corrió a donde estaba mi madre con la niña. Pos la niña estaba muerta. Se puso negra, negra, negra.

Pero luego luego trajeron a un doctor. Creo que mi papá lo fue a traer. Viene el doctor, la mira y dice: —¿Ay pos qué tiene esta niñita? Pues parece estar envenenada. ¿Pues qué pasó? Esto es algo serio.

Dijo mi papá: —Es que mi esposa se asustó cuando le estaba dando de comer a la niña. Las otras chamacas andaban corriendo con las tijeras y ella se asustó.

—Pues sí, es envenenamiento... pero esto es algo más que eso; es algo más fuerte —dijo.

—No pos, así fue.

—Pues está muerta.

Y el doctor dió fe que la niña estaba muerta.

En aquellos años no había tantas investigaciones como ahora. Pues digo: yo no ví nada de eso, ¿ves? Entonces lo que hicieron fue llamar luego luego a mi abuelita y mis tíos. Y allí vienen todos... pues que la niña se había muerto. En aquellos tiempos, los muertos se velaban en casa: ponían una mesa en medio de la sala; allí arreglaban y tendían al muerto, fuera niño o adulto. Lo tendían, le ponían flores y cuatro velas; una en cada esquina de la mesa. Esa era la costumbre en aquellos años.

Bueno, luego luego pusieron la mesa porque la niña estaba muerta; la tendieron allí con sus velitas y todo. Entonces como a los quince minutos mi hermanita volvió a la vida. Se empezó a mover la criatura y todos empezaron a gritar y llorar al ver a la niña moverse: todos corren a verla. Volvió a la vida la niña y luego luego la agarró mamá, llorando con mucho gusto. Pos apenas duró unos quince minutos con vida y se volvió a morir. Volvieron a traer el doctor. Total que trajeron al doctor como tres veces. La última vez dijo el doctor: —Señora, esta niña está muerta: No tiene vida. El corazón no le trabaja. Está muerta.

Por fin la tendieron por última vez.

Y mi madre sufriendo, ¡imagínate! Entonces mi madre se fue a un cuarto que teníamos atrás de la casa donde tenía mi madre una petaca. ¿Tú conoces esas petacas [baúles] grandotas que había antes? En una de esas petacas tenía mamá alguna ropa alzada: las sábanas y la ropa limpia. En la sala tenía un [Sagrado] Corazón de Jesús grandote. Fue mamá y lo descolgó. Y yo detrás de ella, viéndola, y pensando, ¿Qué irá a hacer mamá?

Mi madre con sus lágrimas se fue a la petaca y sacó toda la ropa: al mero abajo de la petaca puso boca abajo al Sagrado Corazón de Jesús. Luego volvió a guardar la ropa y cerró la petaca. Después se hincó y oró. Le dijo al Sagrado Corazón de Jesús que ella ya no quería estar viendo sufrir a su hija. Que si se la quería quitar, de todo corazón se la daba, y no le lloraría ni una lágrima. Que se la daba de todo corazón. Pero que si se la iba a dejar; entonces, que ya no le dieran esos ataques, porque ella ya no quería verla sufrir. También hizo unas promesas. Mamá pidió que si se salvaba la niña —que si se la dejaba— la iba a bautizar y le iba a poner María de Jesús. Ya dejó el corazón de Jesús en la petaca y se fue para la sala. ¡De repente vuelve la niña a la vida! En ese momento cuando volvió en sí la bautizaron allí en la casa. ¿Ves? Jamás le volvió el ataque. Allí la tienes. Vive. Esto pasó en 1922 en Monterrey donde nació María; estaba recién nacidita. Yo digo: esto es la fe que mi madre puso en el Sagrado Corazón de Jesús. Le dijo que se la entregaba a mi hermanita y que no le lloraría ni una lágrima. Visto está que le concedió que no se muriera. Porque María vive todavía. Eso te muestra la fe tan grande de mi mamá. Esta es una de las experiencias que a mí no se me olvidarán jamás.

Hay otra experiencia que me pasó a mí. Lo que te voy a contar sucedió en 1924. Como te decía, mi padre siempre estaba una temporada en Estados Unidos, otra temporada en Monterrey. En esta ocasión estábamos aquí en Estados Unidos, y luego de repente dijo mi papá que nos íbamos a Monterrey otra vez. Bueno, primero se fue mi papá para arreglar la casa, para que cuando llegáramos nosotros estuviera todo listo. Ya nomás se fue papá y como a las dos semanas le mandó dinero a mi mamá para que contratara a alguien con una troca para llevarnos hasta Laredo. Verás, siempre que nos íbamos para el otro lado mamá se ajuariaba de muchas cosas. Por ejemplo, hasta llevaba una estufa de esas de leña, cobijas, baños; hasta un colchón o dos, me parece. Se llevaban muchas cosas. Pues anduvo buscando y al fin encontró un señor que nos podía llevar a Laredo. El problema era que la troca era de esas que nomás tienen la tarima, no tenía barandales, ¿ves?

El señor dijo a mamá: —Pues si quiere yo la puedo llevar aquí.

—Bueno, está bien.

—Nomás ponemos los dos colchones abajo, y las cosas alrededor; las amarramos muy bien, y las dos niñas pueden irse sentadas arriba. Usted se va enfrente, se va usted con los niños más chiquitos; así los llevo a Laredo.

Bueno se arregló el viaje para irnos.

Entonces yo tenía una perrita que quería mucho y mamá quería dejarla, pero yo empecé a llorar. Ella dijo: —Bueno, vamos a llevar a la perrita pero nomás hasta Laredo. La tenemos que dejar porque no podemos pasarla.

Bueno yo me conformé con eso. Entonces ya nos sentamos mero arriba; yo agarré mi perra en los brazos, para que no se me fuera a ir. Pues así nos fuimos a Laredo.

En aquellos años, la carretera de San Antonio a Laredo no era de asfalto, como las de ahora, ¿ves? Era de piedra y tierra; por lo tanto la troca no podía correr más que a treinta millas por hora. Ya iríamos llegando cerquitas de Cotula cuando yo me empecé a quedar dormida; allá mero arriba. Entonces se me soltó la perra de mis brazos. Por estar yo dormida, no pensé en dónde estaba y me dejé ir a agarrarla. Me caí y me quedé tirada a medio camino. Yo tenía mi pelo largo y lo llevaba agarrado con un broche de esos largos de ganchito. Pero era de lámina y ancho como la mitad del dedo. No sé si tú los conocerás. Bueno, pues ese fierro me cortó aquí mero arriba de la cabeza y me hizo un agujero, ¿ves? El caso es que yo me quedé tirada, y mi hermana Beatríz empezó grite y grite: —¡Se cayó Lydia! ¡Se cayó Lydia!

Y por fin el señor se dió cuenta. Verás que la troca no era muy fuerte, pero sí iba a treinta millas. Pues ya iban lejos cuando se devolvieron a levantarme. Pues yo estaba inconsciente; no me dí cuenta de nada. Para entonces ya estábamos cerca de Cotula. Allí me metieron en una casa de una familia y luego luego trajeron al doctor del pueblo. El doctor vino y me puso cloroformo; me durmieron para poderme operar y sacarme el fierro de la cabeza, ¿ves? Bueno, me cosieron y todo. Bueno. Allí estuvimos dos días, y a los dos días ya nos fuimos.

A pesar de todo, la perra me la llevé. Mamá la quería dejar, y yo empecé a llorar. Entonces le dijo el señor de la troca: —Mire, la niña está muy enferma y si deja la perrita aquí, a lo mejor se le va a atrasar.

—Pues yo no sé. A ver que dice Pancho —porque mi papá se llamaba Francisco.

No pues ya llegó mi papá y dijo: —No, pos mi'ja tiene que llevarse su perrita.

—¿Pos cómo?

—Pos yo sé como.

Ya fuimos a la imigración; allí echaron a la perrita en una jaula y se fue por el tren. Total que la perra pasó [pasar la frontera] también. Al fin llegamos todos a Monterrey muy contentos a la casa de mi abuelita. Mi abuelita sí muy apenada por lo que me había pasado a mí, porque ella me quería mucho.

Bueno, al poco tiempo —como a las dos semanas de estar ya instalados en Monterrey— un día que me estaba yo peinando sentí aquí en los dos lados de la cabeza una bolas. Así como pelotas y se sumían como si fueran bolsas. Entonces grité: —¿Mamá mire, me duele poquito; ¿qué tengo aquí?

Ya vió mi madre que tenía esas bolas. Pos ya le dijo a mi papá, y luego luego me llevaron con el doctor. Me vió el doctor y dijo: —¿Pos qué pasó aquí?

Ya mamá le platicó el accidente que yo había tenido.

—Ah, —dijo— entonces, esta niña se golpeó la cabeza y tiene allí sangre molida. No salió esa sangre; se le quedó allí y se le hicieron esas bolas. Tenemos que operarla. Necesita operación para sacarle esa sangre".

Mi madre, pos era enemiga de los hospitales; era un horror ir al hospital, y mucho más que me cortaran y todo eso. Mi mamá dijo: —No.

No quiso. Entonces dijo el doctor: —Pues es el único remedio porque esa sangre no puede quedarse allí.

Cuando llegamos a la casa mi papá dijo: —Pos, a ver qué hacemos, qué...

Pero mi mamá dijo: —Pos voy a pensarlo.

Nomás llegamos de con el doctor, y nos fuimos a la casa de mi abuelita. Llegó mi madre hecha un mar de lágrimas, y le dice a mi abuelita: —Mire mamá lo que pasa con Lydia, con su cabeza, que tienen que operarla.

Estaba allí con mi abuelita una señora, una viejita. Ellas empezaron a platicar allí de lo que decía el doctor: que necesitaba operación y todo. La viejita le dice a mi abuelita: —¿Pues pa' qué se apuran tanto? Mi hijo también se dió un golpe y también se le hizo una bola de sangre molida. ¿Y sabe cómo se alivió? Lo llevamos allá a un río donde hay muchas sanguijuelas de esas que chupan la sangre.

Dice: —Nosotros le poníamos esos animalitos y ellos le chupaban la sangre molida. ¡Así se alivió!

Entonces cuando yo oí eso de los animalitos, a mí me dió horror pensar que me los iban a poner y que me iban a chupar acá. Sentí mucho miedo. ¿Sanguijuelas? Me imaginé yo que serían algunas víboras, o sabrá Dios qué. Pos no sabiá yo ni qué eran.

Entonces me retiré yo de allí de la familia y me fui a la recámara. Mi abuelita era de esas señoras que tienen su altar y tienen muchos santos. Al entrar a la recámara, allí luego luego tenía su altar enfrente y un cuadro arriba. Por cierto que yo no sabía ni qué virgen era, después supe que era la Virgencita del Roble; ella tiene su capilla en Monterrey. Allí fuera de Monterrey tiene su iglesita donde va toda la gente a adorarla, ¿ves?

Bueno. Miraba yo ese cuadro todos los días que entraba yo a su recámara a hincarme allí, al altarcito. Me impresionaba ese cuadro, y yo lo miraba mucho. En esa ocasión cuando estaban platicando: corrí y me fui al altar. Entré al cuartito aquel, a la recámara, vi el cuadro, me hinqué, y le pedí a esa virgen: —Virgencita, no permitas que me pongan esos animales. Yo tengo mucho miedo, ¡cúrame!

Bueno, ya ni me acuerdo cómo le imploré, ni cómo le pedí a la virgen que me curara de esto; pero yo no quería que me pusieran esos animales. Bueno, así pasó. Nomás yo lo supe, ¿ves? Al fin nos fuimos a la casa. Pasaron dos días, y mi madre seguía pensándolo; no quería que me operaran.

Pero nomás amanecía y yo decía: —Voy con mi abuelita.

Iba a hincarme, a implorarle a la virgen, a aquel cuadro que miraba yo, a implorarle que no permitiera que me pusieran esos animales. Pero fíjate nomás: ¿con qué fe se lo pediría?

Bueno, pasó como una semana y un día me lavé el pelo, y me andaba peinando, y ya no me toqué aquello. ¡Ya no había nada! ¡Cómo ésta luz que nos alumbra! Ya no me toqué nada aquí cercas de los sentidos, aquellas bolas. Entonces le grité a mi madre: —¡Mamá, mamá, mamacita, mire, venga pa'cá!

—¿Qué?

—Mire, ya no tengo nada.

—A ver.

Ya estaban decidiéndose a llevarme al río ese, ¿ves? Y que me va viendo mi madre: —¿Pero cómo va ser posible?

Luego luego nos fuimos allá con mi abuelita.: —Mire mamacita, mire, fíjese que Lydia...

—¿Pero cómo? Ya se le quitaron.

Entonces ya les platiqué yo: —Pos no se me quitó sólo. Yo le pedí a la virgencita que tiene Ud. allí en su cuarto, Abuelita. Le pedí que me aliviara, que me quitara esto. Y mire: ella me lo quitó.

Mi abuelita dijo: —¡Mira ves lo que es la fe! ¡Cómo la oyó Dios y la oyó esa virgen! Pos es la Virgen del Roble que tenemos aquí en la capilla.

Entonces mi madre me llevó hasta allá a la capillita a dar las gracias y a rezar allí. Después me llevaron con el doctor, y se quedó sorprendido el doctor: —No puede ser posible. Esa sangre que ella tenía... ¿Cómo fue?

El doctor me vió, me examinó, y dijo: —Pues no, la niña ya no tiene nada.

Y aquí me tienes: no me operaron. ¿Y quién me salvó? Pues fue la fe que yo puse en aquella virgen, lo que yo le pedí con todo mi corazón. Por eso digo que es la fe con la que logra uno todo.

No vayamos muy lejos: Tú conoces a la Virgen de San Juan, ¿verdad? La virgencita que tenemos en la capilla que está en el Valle. Bueno, verás, que te voy a contar. Esto me sucedió hace como un año. Resulta que el dedo de esta mano se me puso bien bien torcido. Sin poder moverlo casi para nada. Así, así, se me dobló mi dedo. Nomás lo movía un poquito y sentía que me clavaban un cuchillo allí. Bueno, yo lloraba porque... la guitarra la tocaba con mucho sacrificio. Pero yo lloraba también porque a mí me encanta coser y estar haciendo mis flores, mis trajes, estar haciendo cosas en mi casa, ¿ves? No podía pelar las papas, ni podía agarrar el mapiador, mapiar.[4] Si tenía que lavar los trastes, agarrar un vaso, pos tenía que hacerlo así [*demuestra como*]. Bueno era un sacrificio: tener el dedo así.

Al fin fui a ver al doctor. Mi doctor me vió y dijo: —Lydia, se le ha soltado un tendón y tenemos que operarle aquí a lo largo del brazo para enderesarle su dedo.

Y yo pos dije: —¿Operarme?

Y tenía tanto miedo. Pos un día le imploré a la Virgen de San Juan. Le pedí: —Virgen santísima, tú que has hecho tantos milagros, que has curado a tantos enfermos, oye mi súplica. Yo no quiero que me operen la mano. Dame mi salud. Te prometo llevarte un dedito de plata, o de oro, o de lo que sea. Yo voy a verte. Pero dame la salud de mi dedo, aunque no se me enderece de atiro, nomás que no me duela; que yo pueda hacer mis cosas.

Y aquí me tienes, mira el dedo. ¿Ves? no lo tengo como este otro, mira. ¿Ves cómo se me nota allí un hueso? Pero no me duele pa' nada. Agarro todo, toco la guitarra, agarro las tijeras... Yo le pedí a la Virgen que me lo curara aunque no me quedara derecho, pero que se me quitara esa dolencia. Mira, allí está Dios del cielo. Me salvé de que me operaran. ¿Que no me quedó derecho? ¡qué me importa! No está derecho, pero no me duele. Y aquí me tienes. Pos fui a verla, fui a pagarle la manda que le prometí.

De manera que si lo pides de corazón y con fe, con una fe limpia, se te concede lo que pidas. Al menos así siento yo; cuando yo pido algo... se me concede.

Mi madre nos enseñaba esas cosas, ya te digo, desde chiquitas. Aunque mi papá no era Católico —el no creía en nada— mi madre sí. Ella nos enseñó la oración. Inclusive nos mandaba a la iglesia con mi abuelita. Mi padre no se oponía a ello. El decía: —Bueno, es tu creencia.

Pero aparte de eso, ella nos contaba parábolas sobre la vida, de cosas que no debíamos hacer. Eso pos nos ayudó mucho. Porque la educación comienza cuando uno está niña. Fíjate, estas cosas que yo te estoy platicando, como la primera que te conté pasaron cuando estaba yo chiquita. Estábamos todos chiquitos y no se me han olvidado. Sí cuando uno está chiquito, todo se le queda grabado adentro. Las buenas acciones y las buenas costumbres no se te olvidan, ni se te salen del corazón. Aunque crezcas y seas grande eso no se te olvida.

Yo también con mis hijas hice lo mismo. Cuando estaban chiquitas las mandaba a la doctrina; las mandaba a la iglesia. Antes de acostarnos siempre les platicaba, les enseñaba cosas buenas. Y todo eso se les va quedando a los niños.

Ahora ya con eso de que la vida está tan cara, y que tienen que trabajar la mamá y el papá: los hijos sin más consejos nomás se van a la escuela. Tú sabes que en la escuela no aprenden nada de eso. Y para los buenos modales, pos, no tienen tiempo la mamá y el papá; siempre están ocupados trabajando. Llegan de sus trabajos bien cansados, y ni se ocupan de los hijos. Y ellos van creciendo solos. Yo creo que a eso se debe el cambio que ha habido en la juventud de ahora; es porque ellos crecen solos.

Yo me acuerdo cuando empecé a viajar, la primera vez que fui a Los Angeles que llevé a mis dos niñas, chiquitas, ¿ves? Nunca se me olvida un señor de los que trabajaban allí en los foros. El era un señor grande que me vió con mis hijas y me dijo: —Ay, mire qué alegría me da verla con sus hijas. ¿Son sus niñitas verdad?

—Sí. Son mis hijas.

—¿Nomás esas tres tiene?

—Sí.

Dice: —Yo le voy a dar un consejo: nunca se separe de ellas. Nunca deje de darles su cariño y su amor; porque eso es lo principal para los hijos. Mire, yo tuve dos hijas pero me divorcié. Luego por andar trabajando, me olvidé de ellas. Ellas no se acuerdan de mí. Sí, soy su padre, pero no me tienen cariño, no me tienen amor. Pero yo tuve la culpa; me desentendí de ellas. Ese es el consejo que yo le doy: que nunca se aparte de sus hijas.

Y así lo hice. En las giras que hacía, yo llevaba a una señora que me las cuidara. Yo nunca me separé de ellas. Siempre con ellas. Y crecieron mis hijas bien: muy hermanables y muy apegadas. Y por eso te digo que todo es lo que uno les enseña.

Estas son cosas que tengo yo, ¿ves?, que creo. Para mí a veces me digo: —No, pos no tiene importancia esto o aquello.

Lydia Mendoza con sus primeras dos hijas, Yolanda (*izquierda*) y Lydia (*derecha*) en los años 1940. Cortesía U. T. The Insitute of Texan Cultures, Colección de el *San Antonio Light*

Pero a lo mejor que sí tiene importancia. Es como esta historia que te platiqué de la muchacha esa, de la paloma, las plumas y todo eso... Cuando estuve en la Universidad de Fresno se la platiqué a la muchacha que me interpretaba; se la conté nomás platicándola.

—¡Ay!! —dijo ella— ese cuento está muy interesante.

Ella también daba clases en las escuelas, ¿ves? Yo aprovechaba —cuando íbamos a clases así— para contar esa historia. Ella les traducía al inglés. No sé en que sentido, no sé cómo lo platicaba ella o lo que les decía, ¿ves? Les decía aquello en inglés, pero los niños siempre ponían atención a eso que les platicaba ella; parece que les gustaba, ¿ves? Se quedaban atentos. Yo creo que esa historia puede haber sucedido; pero no sé. Ha de haber pasado eso, ¿ves? No me negaras tú que hay demasiadas personas que les gusta mucho el chisme... y estar viendo quién llegó y quien salió.

Yo allí donde vivo, mira, yo vivo muy aparte en mi casa. Yo no te doy cuenta de quién vive aquí o quién vive allá. Yo nunca me estoy fijando quién entró o quién salió. Yo estoy en mi casa, y se acabó. Conozco a mis vecinos, ¿ves? Somos vecinos, nos saludamos y todo. Hay veces que me preguntan: —¿Oiga pos quién vive allí?... ¿qué hicieron?... ¿llegó alguien?

Les digo: —Yo no sé nada señora. Mire, yo no sé nada.

A mí no me gusta meterme en dificultades. Yo en mi casa y total. Tiempo me falta pa' hacer mi quehacer. ¡Así es que si te metes en lo que no te importa después tienes que andar recogiendo las plumas de la paloma [*se ríe mucho*]! ¡Qué interesante está esa historia! ¿verdad? Ay Diosito santo. Así que hay que tener mucho cuidado.

Pausa musical

[*Lydia Mendoza canta "Nochecita".*]

Como se podrá olvidar.
Noche mi testigo fiel.
Dime, tú que sabes bien
si lo que canto yo ya no puede ser.

Refrain
Nochecita que de ensueños fue mi vida
cuando su amor y su cariño me olvidó.
Con el alma en mil pedazos yo te digo
lo que he sufrido al sentir tu decepción.

Aunque sabes que el amarte es mi delirio,
tú te burlas y no tienes campasión.
Yo te quiero, y en silencio he de adorarte
cuando escuches en las noches mi canción.

Refrain repeats

Otra canción bonita es "Jesusita en Chihuahua", "Bésame Mucho" y "Noche de Ronda". Yo les canto, por ejemplo "Cucurrucucú Paloma", pero yo la canto así [*canta*]:

Dicen que por las noches
nomás se le iba en puro llorar,
dicen que no comía
nomás se le iba en puro tomar.

Juran que el mismo cielo
se estremecía al oír su llanto;
¡cómo sufrió por ella!
que hasta en su muerte la fue llamando.

¡Ay, ay, ay, ay, ay!... cantaba
¡ay, ay, ay, ay, ay!... gemía
¡ay, ay, ay, ay, ay!... lloraba,
de pasión mortal... moría.

Que una paloma triste
muy de mañana le va a cantar,

a su casita sola
con sus puertitas de par en par.

Juran que esa paloma
no es otra cosa más que su alma,
que todavía la espera
a que regrese la desdichada.

Cucurrucucú... paloma,
cucurrucucú... no llores,

Las piedras jamás, paloma,
¿qué van a saber de amores?
Cucurrucucú, cucurrucucú;
cucurrucucú, paloma, ya no le llores.

O canto "Margarita" o "El Corrido de Luis Pulido". [*Comienza a tocar "El Corrido de Luis Pulido".*]

En aquellos años . . . había muchos teatros

 En esa época —por allá por Lubbock, Texas— todo aquello era una cadena de pueblos y todos tenían teatros. En aquellos años había mucha gente por ese territorio porque había —y hay— mucho algodón todavía. Pero ahora ya lo trabajan con máquinas. En aquellos años era pura mano de obra en el Wes de Texas.[5] Entonces, como ya estabamos enterados de que se pagaba bien allí y había mucho trabajo, mucho algodón, se llenaba de mucha gente. Entonces todos los grupos musicales habidos y por haber: estaban allí. Entre ellos Isidro López, Agapito Zúñiga, Andrés Huesca, Valerio Longoria, Narciso Martínez. A Andrés Huesca, por ejemplo, lo conocí muy bien. Pero nunca trabajé yo con él, porque él andaba con su grupo, y yo andaba con el mío.

Bueno, todos estabamos allí. Y para todos había, porque entraba una variedad, salía, y luego entraba otra. A todos nos daban trabajo. Nomás tres días nos daban. Tres días nosotros, y luego el siguiente, y así...Y se trabajaba toda la semana; no nomás viernes, sábado y domingo. No. Porque así era el gentío que había. Los grupos que tocaban para bailes, por ejemplo, se quedaban toda la semana, y toda la semana había baile. La gente trabajaba, y como quiera se iba a los bailes. Había mucho dinero entonces. Fue allí donde yo conocí a Andrés Huesca. No andaba nomás él solo con su arpa. Traiba otros —como dos o tres más— con él. Casi la mayor parte del tiempo él tocaba más bien como en bailes. Pero hacía presentaciones en teatros también.

Sí, se ganaba mucho dinero en aquellos años. Estaba todo muy bonito en aquel tiempo. Pero cuando ya empezaron el rumor de que iban a entrar las máquinas, pos ya nomás no ocuparon gente. Hasta la fecha hay mucho algodón y todo, pero todo se trabaja con máquina. Y en todo aquel territorio ya no

Cartelón del Teatro Salón nombra a Lydia Mendoza "la cancionera mas popular de toda América Latina" (los años 1940). Cortesía Houston Metropolitan Research Center, Houston Public Library.

queda nada de aquellos pueblos que había de puros teatros. Como por ejemplo el Teatro del Lobo, que era un teatro grandísimo, hermoso; en la actualidad es un salón de baile. En esos teatros también daban películas mexicanas además de las variedades. Eran americanos los dueños, pero en todos los teatros daban puras películas mexicanas. Y así sucesivamente, en todos los pueblitos que tenían teatros: ya no hay nada de eso. Igualmente pasa en el Valle de Texas, allá para fronteras con Reynosa y Matamoros, todo eso que fue el area por donde inmigramos, por Reynosa. Todo ese territorio —comenzando desde Mission hasta Brownsville— todo eso está lleno de pueblitos: Donna, Weslaco, La Feria... Bueno, todos esos. La distancia que hay de un pueblo a otro es a lo más siete u ocho millas. Y aún así, en aquellos años de los que yo te estoy diciendo, había muchos teatros.

Cuando ya pasaron los años, después que hice yo mi carrera, volvímos a recorrer todo aquello, pero entonces sí en los teatros. Trabajábamos en Mc-Allen. Mañana en otro pueblo. Trabajábamos lunes, martes y miércoles en esos pueblitos, aunque la distancia fuera nomás seis o siete millas. De todos modos se trabajaba y teníamos muy buenas entradas. Ahora vas al Valle y ya no hay teatros. Antes daban una película mexicana y después la variedad. Y no solamente la variedad mía, sino que también iban grandes variedades. Yo llegué a presenciar variedades que llevó Pedro Infante. Venían muchos artistas de México y todos ellos recorrían todos esos pueblos; Sara García, Emma Roldán, El Chicote, Tin Tán y Marcelo. Sí, esas variedades de México recorrían todo el Valle porque se trabajaba todos los días y en cada pueblito. Las familias iban a los teatros y había función toda la semana.

Y luego más en el invierno cuando se venía la temporada de la toronja o la naranja. Porque la agricultura allá es algo parecido a lo de California. Hay plantaciones grandísimas de toronja, de limón, de naranja. Así que cuando se venía la temporada de los trabajos pos había mucha gente. Todo aquello traiba un dineral a los teatros. Y luego, viernes, sábado, y domingo, los bailes. Los bailes eran algo distinto. Tocaban todos los conjuntos.

Pero ya todo eso se acabó. Bueno, los bailes yo creo que todavía siguen. Pero los teatros, eso se acabó desde que entró la televisión. Ya cuando entró la televisión pues se fue decayendo todo y todo, y... ya no hay nada. El caso es que ahora la gente no va a los teatros. Bueno, hay ciertas áreas, por ejemplo, en Houston sí tenemos teatros pero la gente va a ver las películas.

Por ejemplo, nada menos ahora en julio que estuve en Los Angeles se organizó allí una presentación con Tongolele. Tú sabes quién es Togolele. Ella es una gran bailarina. De casualidad ella andaba en California y el promotor quiso presentarla en un cine. Pero también andaban buscando un relleno, ¿ves? No querían nomás llevarla a ella sola. Entonces me fueron a ver a mí, con el dichoso señor que me pagó cuatrocientos pesos [se ríe] en una tocada.

Bueno, pues yo ya me quería regresar y dijo: —Mira Lydia, no te regreses todavía porque va a ser el estreno de ese teatro en San Bernardino. Y va a haber muy buena entrada, pues está muy anunciado. Va a ir la Tongolele.

—Bueno, pues —dije.

—Te vamos a dar ciento cincuenta a tí.

—Bueno, está bueno.

Me quedé y fuimos a la dichosa función. Pos no vas a creer, si entraron cincuenta personas fueron muchas; ¡No fue gente! ¿Por qué? Ve tú a saber. Y eso que nos anunciaron a Tongolele y a mí. Luego que querían hacer una gira con nosotras les dije: —Yo no. Conmigo no cuenten. Yo me regreso.

Artistas en el Teatro Milion Dollar en Los Angeles. *De izquierda a derecha*: el famoso cómico Marcelo, Lydia Mendoza, el cómico Tin Tan y María Mendoza (1950). Cortesía Houston Metropolitan Research Center, Houston Public Library.

Yo comprendí que eran experimentos teatrales de los promotores. Quizás lo anunciaron nomás por el radio. Tú sabes que hoy en día muy poca gente oye radio. Son contadas las personas que lo oyen. La televisión es la que miran más. Ahorita un evento de esos, un festival, o algo así, lo que levanta es que se anuncie por televisión. Porque la televisión todos la miran. Pero la televisión es muy cara, ¿ves? Cuesta miles de dólares por un anuncio. Ya te digo: esto es lo que ha pasado con las variedades de teatro en todos los pueblos. Así les pasó a todos. Tuvieron que cerrarlos quizás porque la gente no iba. Como no tenían entrada forsozamente tuvieron que quitarlos. Algunos los hicieron salones, o los cerraron de a tiro. Pos ya ves simplemente en Los Angeles, todavía anuncian las películas mexicanas. Para que hagan eso, es que tienen público, ¿ves? Pero en la mayoría de los pueblos es un fracaso en el teatro.

Publicidad del Teatro Million Dollar (Los Angeles) anunciando la famosa bailarina Tongolele y otras artistas como Lydia Mendoza (los años 1950). Cortesía Houston Metropolitan Research Center, Houston Public Library.

Nosotros los norteños

¿Qué más platicaremos, tú?

Han nacido tantas ideas musicales de nosotros los norteños de por acá. Hacemos la música a nuestro gusto y a nuestro estilo: como nos gusta, y a como le gusta al público. Entonces ya un bolero lo hacen al estilo ranchero; o el corrido lo hacen ranchera o lo que sea. La cosa es hacer cambio en la música. Pero pues sigue siendo la misma, el mismo sentimiento.

En Texas, por ejemplo, bailan mucho huapango, pero al estilo norteño. Y le dan un sabor muy bonito. También la polka mexicana norteña es diferente; nomás agarraron la idea. Se les ocurrió que la podían trasformar en algo norteño, algo diferente, y lo hicieron. No lo tocaron exactamente como la toca el alemán, ¿ves? Uno adapta la música. Yo adapto mi música.

Por ejemplo, mira, allí tienes tú: yo les canto "La Malagueña" ¿ves? "La Malagueña" no es así como yo la canto. Tiene otro ritmo y otras diferencias. Y yo no me atrevía a cantar esa canción porque yo sabía que yo no lo iba a hacer bien. Pero, mi público empezó a pedírmela mucho. Me decían: —Lydia, ¿por qué no la grabas? Y: —La queremos oír en tu voz.

Bueno, al fin me animé, y la grabé. Pero la grabé adaptándola a mi estilo. Y les ha gustado mucho. Igualmente, el huapango yo no lo canto como debe de ser. "Cucurrucucú Paloma" es un huapango. Yo no le puedo dar ese falsete que le dan. Yo digo que el gusto de un huapango es el falsete que se da: el cambio de esa voz que se le da tan bonito. Y yo no puedo hacerlo. Pero en cambio yo la canto a mi estilo. No canto muchos huapangos. Nomás "Cucurrucucú Paloma" y no sé qué otro. Si son dos es mucho.

También cambié mi guitarra. Bueno, cuando llegamos a San Antonio todos esos grupos de música traían sus guitarras dobles, guitarras como la que traigo ahora. Pero traían sus encordaduras de otra manera: es lógico que una guitarra doble quiere decir que tiene que tener dos segundas, dos primeras, dos terceras, dos cuartas, dos quintas y dos sextas. Todas iguales, como la mandolina está ensordinada así. ¿Ves? tiene muy curiosa la encordadura. Entonces dije yo: —Bueno, pos yo voy a encordar la guitarra de otro modo.

Me nació la idea de poner una cuerda alta y una bajita, y otra... y así. Por eso el sonido que da mi guitarra es muy distinto. Me nació la idea de encordarla diferente así. Se me figuró que sonaba más bonito. Por ejemplo: la tercera cuerda está afinada a cierto tono. Si combinas esa cuerda con una cuerda primera, esa primera estará afinada más alta que si estuviera en su lugar normal. Le subes la afinación y tendrá el mismo tono que la tercera. Será lo mismo. Solo que una octava más alta. Entonces te da un sonido diferente. El efecto final será un sonido diferente. Y así es como tengo yo afinada la guitarra. Así, yo sola me fui dando ideas; pos nomás hasta donde llegaba mi inteligencia, ¿ves?

Te voy a dar otro ejemplo de los cambios que he hecho. En una ocasión yo grabé un LP completo de pura música de Sudamérica. Esto pasó cuando estaba yo grabando con discos Falcón y el gerente de los discos fue a Colombia. Por allá tuvo algunas pláticas con alguien y como ya me conocen en todo ese territorio le sugirieron que grabara con Lydia Mendoza un LP de pura música de ellos. El dijo: —Bueno, pues vamos a ver si podemos hacerlo.

Y le dieron inclusive un LP grandote donde venían todas las doce canciones que querían que yo se las grabara.

Pues ya me habló el señor Arnaldo, y me dice: —Lydia, te tengo una buena noticia; en Colombia quieren un LP grabado con puras canciones de por allá. Pero las quieren con tu voz. Aquí te lo mando.

Ya me lo mandó y me puse a oirlo. Oye: pues toda la música estaba muy bonita. Pero al estilo de por allá. Yo no le entendía, no. Era imposible que yo adaptara mi voz a como estaba aquello grabado. Entonces yo le dije a este señor: —Señor Arnaldo, lo siento mucho. Las canciones están muy bonitas pero —la verdad— yo no voy a poder hacer esto.

—No Lydia —dice— adáptelas a como usted las siente, y como usted quiera cantarlas. Ellos no quieren que se las cante igual. Quieren estas canciones en su voz y al estilo de usted.

Oyes pues se las grabé, ¡si vieras que bonitas! Por un lado se grabó lo que querían con puro mariachi; y por el otro lado así con mi guitarra. En esa colección que me mandaron venían, ahorita te digo... a ver si me acuerdo. Una de ellas era "Soberbia", otra era "Mis Flores Negras". No ésta que canto yo sino esa que dice: —Oye, bajo las ruinas de mis pasiones...

Es una canción muy vieja "Mis Flores Negras"; también venía "Los Mirlos" y otras tantas; puras canciones de allá, ¿ves?, todas muy bonitas. Pero como te digo, yo las adapté a mi estilo. Y les gustó muchísimo. Ese LP todavía se está vendiendo allá en Sur-América. Aquí no lo distribuyeron; pero ahora cuando yo fui allá, lo tenían. Todos lo habían comprado.

También grabé otro LP que hice de canciones de allá. Y entre ellas grabé esa, "Serenata de Mayo"; ¿la has oido? esa que dice [*canta*]:

> Ya llegaron las flores de mayo,
> con sus aromas más preciosas
> [*tararea*]
> que están de rosa en rosa,
> el tiempo ha de llegar...

Es muy bonita, ¿ves? "Serenata de Mayo" se llama. Es una canción para el Día de las Madres. Pero ya te digo, esa me la mandaron muy diferente. Y yo la adapté, la arreglé como en tiempo de balada, o bolero. Salió muy bonita. Y así es como yo he grabado casi toda mi música ¿ves? Yo la canto al estilo mío; imposible hacerlo como lo hacen allá. Además en tantas grabaciones que tengo, nunca me ha gustado cantar o imitar como canta algún otro artista. Yo oigo la canción, la aprendo, y luego la canto como yo quiero cantarla. Ese ha sido el estilo de mi música: como te digo, no trato de hacerlo como lo hacen otros artistas, ¿ves?

Además, casi puedo decirte que yo fui una de las primeras que introdujo el ritmo de la polka norteña en California. Esto pasó cuando yo empecé a grabar otra vez después de que se acabó la guerra. Empecé a trabajar en California en 47, y entonces grabé con Marca Azteca. Esta era una compañía muy grande que ya no existe. Verás, tenía yo como dos años de estar grabando con ellos cuando les sugerí la idea de que grabaran con acordeón norteña.[6] Y me dijo el señor de la compañía: —No, esa música no gusta aquí.

Yo le dije: —Bueno pues vamos hacer algo. A lo mejor gusta. Es cierto que no la conocen muy bien y a lo mejor sí les va a gustar. Yo conozco a un conjunto norteño y podemos mandarlo traer.

Uno de ellos era Lorenzo Caballero. Yo no sé si tú lo conoces. El es un muchacho que es casi de la época mía. Es un guitarrista que tenía su conjunto y tocaban muy bonito. Ya casi no tocan. En aquel tiempo era la guitarra de Lorenzo Caballero; era Juan Viesca con un contrabajo de esos —un tololoche— y era un bajo sexto. Creo que nomás. El caso es que el dueño por fin dijo: —Pues está bueno; si usted cree, vamos a ver si acaso les gusta. Pero usted los acompaña con la guitarra.

Le dije yo que sí. Y me dice: —Bueno, comuníquese con ellos.

Ya me comuniqué con Lorenzo y me dijo: —Sí, sí, vamos.

Pues ya se arreglaron de precio y todo, y que yo iba a ayudarles. Bueno, está bueno. Y le pusieron por nombre El Conjunto de Oro de Lydia Mendoza. Así, muy norteño. Bueno por fin vinieron ellos y creo que grabamos cuatro discos. Así empezaron a surgir esas grabaciones norteñas. Como traiba mi nombre el conjunto, eso ayudó un poquito a que la gente se fijara. Pos empezó a gustar. Y ya después de allí pa'cá empezaron a grabar muchos grupos norteños en California.

El de Lorenzo Caballero era un grupo buenísimo para el teatro. Lorenzo era un chango; es un artista. Fíjate, toca la guitarra con la lengua, la voltea y guisa un huevo arriba de la guitarra. Primero la volteaban y luego le echaban de ese fluido que arde, ¿cómo se llama? No sé qué diablos era ese fluido que le echaban. Total que ponían un sartén y guisaban un huevo arriba de la guitarra. Luego ya le quitaban aquella cosa, se sentaba así no sé cómo y echaba una maroma. Y luego toca un pedacito de canción en la guitarra con la lengua. Creo que "La Paloma"; era fantástico su número. Bueno, él solo era toda una variedad. Es fantástico; nomás que es muy terco y no le gusta hacer giras ni salir. Pero como número de espectáculo fuerte es muy bueno. Todavía vive y está en San Antonio. Así es Lorenzo Caballero.

Juan Viesca era un compañero de Lorenzo, él que tocaba el tololoche. Bueno, hacían un numero fantástico. Viesca con sus monadas del contrabajo: ya le da vuelta, ya brinca... y todo. Lo que es Viesca pues ya se ha retirado un poco porque hace uno o dos años le dió un ataque de corazón, ¿ves? Pero eran unos payasos para el teatro. Buenísimos. Pero, pues ya se retiraron.

En todo caso conseguí que grabaran música norteña en California. Ya te digo, en aquellos tiempos yo fui una de las que los animó a que entrara lo norteño a California. Eso sucedió hace como unos cincuenta años. No, pero ahora está inundado California de música norteña. Donde quiera hay conjuntos norteños, eso sí. También de Texas vienen muchos conjuntos de acordeón para California.

Las Dos Grandes de Texas

Hoy en día en Texas somos nada más Chelo Silva y yo; las únicas dos de más nombre que hemos quedado. Que quieren un número: luego luego dicen Chelo Silva o Lydia Mendoza. En Texas nos dicen Las Dos Grandes de Texas. Somos Chelo y yo. Claro que lo que ella canta es muy distinto, muy diferente a lo que yo canto. Ella canta otro... otro estilo de canciones. Pero es una gran figura ella, ¿ves? Bueno, pobrecita, ella ya está poco... de su voz. Ya no es aquella voz que tenía cuando ella comenzó. Yo creo que ya tiene como 20 ó 25 años en el ambiente. Cuando comenzó, cantaba muy bonito, tenía una voz divina. Ahora, como toma mucho, ¿ves? su voz se le ha hecho aguardientosa. Tú hablas con ella y crees que es un hombre. Ya le cambió mucho su timbre de voz. Además de eso, no solamente es la tomada, el trago, lo que la..., no es eso solamente lo que le ha trastornado su voz. Una cantante, yo digo, debe tener mucho descanso, tiene que dormir sus horas, no desvelarse... Ella... es lo que tiene, ¿ves?

Lydia Mendoza (*izquierda*) con la cantante Chelo Silva (Houston, 1974).
Cortesía Colección Lydia Mendoza

Termina una función y la invitan y se va. Yo nunca, o casi nunca, acepto invitaciones; solamente que sea algo muy especial y todo. Pero ¿yo? desvelarme o amanecer: no.

Y yo lo digo, porque he convivido con ella. Una vez fuimos a una presentación al Million Dollar [Los Angeles] hace como tres o cuatro años. Quisieron reforzar la variedad de Vicente Fernández, y nos mandaron traer de Texas a Chelo y a mí. Y venimos. Cuando terminábamos... bueno yo terminaba y me iba para mi hotel o a una casa donde me estaba quedando. Y ella... pues llegaban ahí personas... tú sabes, en esta cosa del teatro hay muchas amistades. Pos llegaban que: —Chelo, fíjate que tenemos una fiesta.... vamos Lydia.

—No, —les decía— yo lo siento, pero yo no voy.

Bueno, pos, se llevaban a Chelo. Otro día llegaba Chelo ya casi pa' comenzar la variedad. Llegaba, pobrecita, toda despeinada y bien desvelada. ¡Imagínate! Apenas venía de la parranda en que había estado. Y había veces que llegaba...pues yo creo que le habían puesto los rollers.[7] Una vez, como siempre, llegó a la carrera y ya seguía ella. En un dos por tres le quitaron los rollers y ni siquiera le arreglaron el pelo, no, nomás se lo alborotaron. Bueno, salió así... sin maquillaje ni nada. Así salió a presentarse. Y para colmo hasta se le salió el zapato. Pero todo eso a consecuencia de que ella no se cuida. Se desvela mucho, toma y no descansa. Entonces, por esa razón ella ya está perdiendo su voz. El público la quiere mucho, ¿ves? Nomás saliendo Chelo Silva y el público se vuelve loco... Ella tiene mucho, mucho nombre. Pero como ya es natural ya poco a poco se empieza a decepcionar el público al ver la atrocidad de lo que está pasando con ella. Esto sucede porque ella no se cuida, ¿ves? Y es lo que yo vivo diciéndole.

Todo depende de cómo piense uno, ¿ves? Mírame a mí. Yo tengo más de cincuenta años en esta carrera... Hace como unos siete años que he dejado yo de llevar ese tren de vida que llevaba de mucho trabajo. Pero, para mí no ha sido nada difícil. Porque todo depende de uno, como uno piense. Igualmente le pasa al hombre. Si el hombre se sabe cuidar de lo mismo de no andar parrandiando y todo eso, es la misma cosa, ¿ves? Todo depende de cómo piense uno y cómo quiera ser. Porque en este ambiente, tú sabes, hay de todo: si quieres tomar, desvelarte, tener juergas y todo. Yo no. Yo me salgo de mi casa a trabajar. Pos yo podría decir: me alisto, me visto, agarro un taxi y me voy a conocer los clubs, a pasar una noche alegre, oyendo música y tomando. Podría hacerlo. Ando por acá sola. Pero no lo hago. Porque... pos, no, a mí no me gusta eso. A mí, tratándose de descansar y de dormir, soy feliz de la vida. Eso es lo que yo más quiero y toda mi vida he sido así, ¿ves?

No me gusta desvelarme. En la televisión pasan unas películas y programas muy bonitos, pero todo pasa después de las doce de la noche. Lo que más me hace desvelar son las ingratas novelas esas de la televisión. Pero ya la única que miro yo es esa "Bodas de Odio". Es todo. En Texas a las ocho y media se acaba. Ya nomás se acaba esa... me arreglo, y yo a dormir. Mi esposo, no. El se queda hasta las doce de la noche viendo programas allí. Yo no. Yo ya nomás miro mi último, cierro mi puerta y me duermo, feliz de la vida. Mis desveladas vienen cuando tengo que trabajar.

Pos yo digo que a este mundo Dios nos mandó a hacer algo en la vida. Hacer algo de provecho, no estar ahí nomás... Como algunas amiguitas mías... dicen que se desesperan, que en la casa, no saben qué hacer. Por eso se salen a los clubs o qué sé yo. Cuando uno quiere, hay mucho qué hacer. Yo tengo hambre de estar en mi casa porque cuando estoy en mi casa, si vieras cómo se me hace el día chiquito pa' hacer tantas cosas. Es como te digo: yo me dedico a los quehaceres de mi casa, a todo lo mío, mis obligaciones. Ya además de eso, la hechura de mis trajes que yo misma me los hago para mi trabajo. Confecciono las flores y luego hago los vestidos. Sean vestidos o trajes yo raramente me compro un vestido hecho. A mí me gusta hacerme mis trajes, mis vestidos, mis batas para la casa, todo. De manera que en la casa siempre hay qué hacer. Yo les digo: es que todos hemos venido a este mundo a hacer algo. Dios nos mandó a hacer algo, a ocupar nuestra mente en algo. A hacer algo de provecho. Esa ha sido siempre mi meta. ¿ves? Ojalá y que todas las mujeres pensáramos así.

¿Que mas puedo pedirle a la vida?

 Ya ves que mucha gente me dice: —¿Es usted de verdad Lydia Mendoza?... no, no puede ser usted. Usted ha de ser alguna hija de Lydia, una parienta, pero ¡no puede ser Lydia! porque yo estaba chiquita cuando la oí por primera vez.

Y me preguntan: —Perdone, ¿cuántos años tiene? Ya nomás les digo la edad que tengo y dicen: —Ah, pos sí, sí es Lydia Mendoza.

Aunque quisiera decirles que tengo menos años, ¡no me creerían! Tengo que comprobarlo. Pero no; yo orgullo tengo de decir la edad que tengo, porque doy gracias a Dios que me ha dejado vivir tantos años.

Sabes que cuando me presentaron en Nueva York pos, claro, hablaron de todo porque me pidieron muchos datos, así con historia y todo y la edad que tengo. Claro que eso lo anunciaron la noche que me presenté. Me dijo la señora latina con la que me estaba yo quedando que cuando me presentaron dijo uno de los promotores de la fiesta aquella: —*This young lady is Lydia Mendoza?*

Que no quiso creer la edad que yo tenía. O sea que en el foro se mira uno mucho más joven y todo. Dijeron que cómo podía ser yo la mujer que estaban anunciando, Lydia Mendoza, la que se estaba presentandose ahí. Pos sí, así es. Yo creo que me quieren ver con un bordoncito... O con unos anteojos; ya como una viejita cayéndome. Oye, pos ya los años, ya, ya son muchos ¿no? Son muchos años encima de uno y aunque uno no quiera.

Como ahora en Nueva York; ni me esperaban y allá fui a dar después de cuarenta y cuatro años que no iba yo para allá. ¡En el 41 fue la última vez! Y eso lo anunciaron mucho en el programa. El *New York Post* me entrevistó también ese día que llegué. En la entrevista me preguntaron, por ejemplo, que cuándo había sido la última vez que estuve en Nueva York. Todo aquello se comentó en esa entrevista en Nueva York. Porque yo ya había estado allá, pero de eso hacía cuarenta y cuatro años que había visitado a Nueva York. ¡Tanto viajar en los últimos cincuenta años!

Tambien estuve por ejemplo en Santa Bárbara como en el 38, sí, pero vine varias veces, no nomás una vez; estuvimos varias veces en los teatros; todo esto viajamos. Claro que Texas fue el primer territorio que recorrimos en aquellos años. Y últimamente también, cuando todavía existían los teatros. Pues después se quitaron los teatros cuando comenzó la televisión. Como te dije, todo el Valle eran puros cines antes; ahora ya no hay nada. Pero todo eso lo recorrimos nosotros. Últimamente en Texas me he presentado en muchas partes, pero son a festividades. En salones, en auditorios o bailes. Como ahora para el día de "Mother's Day," el Día de las Madres voy a estar en Corpos [Corpus Christi] tres días. Ya estoy contratada, pues. Otro lugar donde también visito mucho en festividades —así de música y de plática— es en Austin. ¡Austin, tan lindo! Ahora hace poco también fui —no sé si habrás tú oido— a eso del Hall of Fame. ¿Será de Texas? sí. Ahí escogieron de entre doscientos, de diferentes puntos de Texas, ¿ves? De El Paso escogieron una. Y otra de...creo que de Dallas. De Houston, nomás una: yo. Y era la única mexicana. Las tres fuimos elegi-

Lyida Mendoza a la edad de 76 años frente a su casa en Houston (1992).
Cortesía Colección Yolanda Broyles-González

das. Muy bonita que estuvo esa fiesta en Austin. Hace apenas un año que también estuvimos en California para el Cinco de Mayo. Pero hasta ahorita no me han llamado para el Cinco de Mayo; ni para El Dieciséis de Septiembre tampoco.

Pero yo sí te voy a decir que aunque tenga la edad que tengo, yo me siento todavía con mucho gusto, con mucho ánimo. Yo no me decaigo por nada, todavía. Mi esposo se admira — porque él tiene setenta y dos años, pero él vive enfermo, ¿ves? yo creo que probablemente por eso me dice: —Ay, cómo tienes ánimo de estar ahí cociendo, de salir en giras, de andar en esos bullicios, estar cantando y todo eso, ¿cómo te animas?

Lydia Mendoza, La Reina Tejana (1987). Pintura al pastel por Estér Hernández. Cortesía Estér Hernández

Lydia Mendoza a la edad de 60 años (1976). Cortesía Houston Metropolitan Research Center, Houston Public Library

Le digo yo: —Oyes, yo todavía tengo vida.

Yo me siento —gracias a Dios todavía hasta ahorita— con mucho gusto y mucho ánimo! Yo me acuesto y me levanto con un ánimo... Abro mis ojos y, ¡ay pos con mucho gusto! No me levanto con: —Ay, no, pos no tengo ganas de nada. No, yo me voy a acostar...

¡Nunca me miras tú así! Yo siempre estoy deseando que ya amanezca, que llegue el día para ponerme a hacer lo que tengo que hacer. Ya te digo, tengo mucho gusto todavía. Será porque tengo buena salud gracias a Dios. Ojalá y que...

Mira, después de volver de mi último viaje a Nueva York, al día siguiente toqué por cinco horas en una fiesta. Porque yo no sé decir que no [*risa*]. Mi hija se enoja y dice: —Si suena el teléfono yo le voy a decir que no estás.

Y yo le digo: —Vale más que no mi'ja. Si me llaman, agradezco que se acuerden de mí.

Y ya que les digo que sí,ella se me enoja. Me dice: —Mamá, yo no sé para qué te estás matando tanto.

—Es un deber que tengo, es una obligación, —le digo yo— yo no voy a decirles que no.

Una vez toqué cinco horas aunque iba nada más por dos. Bueno, no seguidas ¿no? Pero esta vez después de dos horas le dije al señor que me contrató: —Pues ya le toqué, ya me voy.

—No, no te vayas. Quédate una hora más, aunque nomás cantes lo que tú quieras cantar, pero aquí queremos tener tu voz.

Pos ya te digo: allí me estuve cinco horas. Ahorita te digo: Me fui a las siete; y a las doce de la noche vine a dar a la casa. ¡Y eso que nomás iba por dos horas! Pero el señor tenía mucha gente, amistades allí en su fiesta. ¡Pos cúando me iban a dejar ir pa' la casa! Y me las aguanté. Te digo que llegué cansadísima y muerta de sueño a la casa. Pero satisfecha y contenta. La pasé bien, gracias a Dios. Porque así soy yo. Ya sentándome con mi guitarra a cantar, yo no soy de las que puedo parar. Yo le sigo a como ellos van pidiendo y pidiendo las canciones. Porque, pues no sé... creo yo que es un deber mío. Yo no puedo decirles que no. Ya te digo que llegué de Nueva York el domingo, y al otro día me fui a cantar allá ya con el señor ese. Y pues es que me gusta a mí mucho la música. Con mi guitarra me pongo a cantar y soy feliz.

Me preguntan mis nietas que cuando me voy a retirar ya de esta carrera. Les digo yo: —Ya lo he dicho antes que yo voy a morir cantando. En algún lugar donde yo esté trabajando; allí, allí voy a terminar yo cantando.

Así lo he dicho, y yo creo que así va a ser. En un lugar en que yo esté, que ya se me llegue la hora, y esté yo cantando. Entonces dirá Diosito: —Pos hasta aquí, y se acabó. [*Se ríe mucho.*]

¡Ay Dios mío!

Pero sí, también te digo una cosa: que el día que a mí ya me llegue un malestar o una enfermedad o algo de eso... pos bueno, ya estoy resignada. Porque ya bastantes años me ha dado Dios de felicidad y de tranquilidad. Por ejemplo, cuando mi hija Nora tuvo el cáncer, me platicó todos los martirios que pasó, lo qué le ponían y todo. Por eso yo le digo a ella: —Pos mira, mi'ja, yo si te digo que si un día a mí me descubren que tengo cáncer, yo no me voy a curar.

Porque yo no me voy a poner en tratamientos que me estén martirizando, y que me estén poniéndome fierros y teníéndome encerrada... ¡No, yo mejor no me curo! Que Dios me lleve y se acabó. Al cabo, como les digo, yo ya he vivido muchos años, y todos esos años que Dios me ha dejado los he disfrutado en muchos aspectos, y en salud y en alegrías. Estoy contenta. Por eso es que yo todavía hasta ahorita, me siento muy bien. ¡Gracias a Dios! ¿Qué más puedo pedirle a la vida?

—— FIN ——

III

Background and analysis

Much of the oral tradition is concerned with the universe of power and the interface between that universe and the world of mortals. Cautionary, prescriptive, descriptive, metaphysical, and mythic narratives tell us how we must behave as individuals and as societies in the face of the Great Mysterious that surrounds and fills all that is.

Paula Gunn Allen,
*Grandmothers of the Light: A Medicine
Woman's Sourcebook*, p. 21

It is when the western nation comes to be seen, in Conrad's famous phrase, as one of the dark corners of the earth that we can begin to explore new places from which to write histories of peoples and construct theories of narration.

Homi Bhabha,
Nation and Narration, p. 6

My "stories" are acts encapsulated in time, "enacted" every time they are spoken aloud or read silently. I like to think of them as performances and not as inert and "dead" objects (as the aesthetics of Western culture think of art works). Instead, the work has an identity; it is a "who" or a "what" and contains the presences of persons, that is, incarnations of gods or ancestors or natural and cosmic powers.

Gloria Anzaldúa,
Borderlands / La Frontera, p. 67

Yo no canto porque se,
ni porque mi voz sea buena.
Canto porque tengo gusto
en mi tierra y en la ajena.

"El quelite,"
ranchera song, oral tradition

Participation in this historia

 I consider it is necessary and ethical for me to historicize my position as "voice" and participant in this project, as "listener" (interlocutor) with Lydia Mendoza. Given the limitations of space, I must be brief.[1] Lydia Mendoza delivered this *historia* (her history, her life-telling) to me from a sense of *confianza* (trust) between us. All talk is relational and circumstantial. What Lydia Mendoza performed was no doubt in some measure a reaction to me as a woman and as a member of the same ethnic group; she also spoke from the position of what she knew about me and in light of the circumstances that surrounded us. The confianza between us outweighed our differences. The age difference worked in favor of generating historia.

The sense of confianza was related to the fact that I had lived for six years in San Antonio and my life had intersected in various ways with Lydia's. For example, I happened to be the next-door neighbor of Gloria Méndez, friend and comadre of Lydia's daughters Yolanda Alvarado Hernández and Lydia Alvarado Dávila. In San Antonio our paths crossed occasionally; I kept up on Lydia Mendoza through Gloria. In 1982 I videotaped a live performance by Lydia Mendoza on the streets of San Antonio.

Several months after we moved to Santa Barbara, I received that memorable phone call from Lydia Mendoza: she announced to us her impending arrival and performance in Santa Barbara (1986) and she asked if she could stay at our house. I was thrilled to welcome the legendary Lydia Mendoza, whose music I had known since childhood—along with many stories about her. It was during those days in 1986 and during our conversations that she ultimately flowed into historia, asked me to taperecord it, and extended her visit. As *mexicana*/Chicana/raza women we converged on a common ground of gender, shared class affiliations, shared musical traditions, and other shared elements of culture, including the Mexican language and spiritual practices. At the time, my family lived in a very small apartment stuffed with musical instruments. Lydia Mendoza also knew my husband as a musician and knew that I at times participated as a musician with him. Perhaps she spoke part of her historia to the musician in me. There was much common ground.

Commonalities *and* differences shaped our collaboration. My status as a university professor was a point of social difference—as was my knowledge of English. In Lydia's eyes, however, these differences were also assets: I had access to and knowledge of the world of publishers and print.

We recorded at a small table in front of the home altar whose spirit-world images—ranging from the Guadalupana to photos of deceased ancestors—generated further confianza and flow between us. Musical instruments were everywhere. Feeling at home, she insisted on cooking the meals herself. Together we watched the final installments of the Mexican soap opera *Cristal*, which at that time held in its grip broad segments of the (raza) population (including me and many of my friends and family). Lydia Mendoza sat majestically before the TV in her *chanclas y bata* (old slippers and robe). On April 27,

Lydia Mendoza with Yolanda Broyles-González on April 27, 1986, in Santa Barbara, California, the day Mendoza completed her *historia*.

1986, she finished telling the last story in the volume and signaled for me to turn off the recorder. "Ya terminé" ("I have finished"). The certainty and finality of that statement intrigued me. Perhaps at that time I did not understand historia the way I do today. After finishing the historia we stayed up talking until late into the night and went to bed at midnight. Two hours later my labor pains began, and my first child, Francisco Guillermo, was born within hours. Lydia's (and my) timing had been impeccable.

What Lydia Mendoza performs in her life narrative and through her songs is a composite re-creation, a collective and individual reconstruction called historia. Like other histories from the working class, hers is necessarily a useful narrative. It enables survival, distance, inspiration, and even freedom from what could easily become crippling and life-threatening social circumstances. That historia is charted and driven by the forward-looking need to recall, remember, and reenact essential customs and rituals that sustain both physical survival and humanistic development into the future. Historia is a central tool of Chicana humanism. It is raza humanism codified and transmitted in oral cultural practices across generations.

To date, Lydia Mendoza's historia is the first and only sustained Chicana working-class life narrative *performed* in the oral tradition and transposed into print culture.[2] Lydia Mendoza was the driving force in initiating this historia. She envisioned this project as a book and approached me with that vision and with a sense of urgency. Over the course of 10 days I taperecorded what she chose to narrate concerning her long life. In retrospect, her narrative reveals her *presentimiento* of the end of her career. Shortly after finishing this life narration, Lydia Mendoza suffered a debilitating stroke that ended her long performance life. In the intervening years, I tended first to the completion of my book *El Teatro Campesino / Theater in the Chicano Movement* while Lydia Mendoza underwent a long period of rehabilitation. Although Mendoza lost the ability to play instruments and sing, she recovered her speech and memory gradually, although not fully. We resumed our collaboration in 1992, yet now of a different nature: over the next few years I transcribed the tapes, looked for and negotiated with publishers, and reworked the "spoken" manuscript. Lydia was not at home with the minutiae of my transposition of her spoken words to the print medium. Although I involved her, met with her, and presented to her, page by page, the emergent fine-tunings of the transcribed historia, she entrusted me with the reworking process. Perhaps that was an extension of the same sense of confianza that first led her to me and which grew over the years. Mendoza never changed her historia by adding or deleting anything substantial; nor did she ever put pen to paper. For her eightieth birthday (in 1996) in Houston, Texas, I presented her with the final version. She lived in her native Houston until 1999, when she moved to San Antonio.

Lydia Mendoza proposed this project to me after having been interviewed by innumerable persons over the years. The one existing book publication (interviews compiled as *Lydia Mendoza: A Family Autobiography*[3]) interlaces Lydia Mendoza's interview segments with interview segments from members of her extended family: her second husband and a dozen other speakers (all but one are male). They cover an immense range of topics, The experience of those interviews—of being interrogated as an informant—triggered her desire to orally "write" her own book, to assume narrative control, to deliver what *she* considered memorable. She wanted to perform her own life story not as a respondent to externally imposed ethnographic questions and not as one of many voices within an extended family but on her own terms: self-configured and shaped as a direct reflection of her own human agency and mexicana/Chicana working-class subjectivity. Mendoza's gifts as a musician certainly match her gift of *buen hablar*, her speaking talents as a storyteller. She is as much a maestra of historia as of music. As an elder, she exercised narrative control and was always very clear on what *she* wanted to leave for future generations. This work is neither conceived nor assembled by means of the conventional ethnographic question/answer dynamic, in which a researcher shapes/influences narratives by means of "leading" questions. Those questions seek to extract "material" from human subjects—materials then shaped by the ethnographic imagination.[4]

Lydia Mendoza's desire to bequeath this historia is also related to her knowledge of popular books on the lives of idols such as María Félix, Pedro Infante, and La Tigresa. Such books have always circulated in Mexico and the borderlands. By motivating the writing of this book, Mendoza willed her presence and authority, as well as her rightful place on the borderlands of print culture and oral tradition.[5] For a full discussion of my roles in negotiating the movement between orality and print culture, see the final section in this chapter. In what follows I discuss the social powers of music; Mendoza's place within the norteño performance repertoire; her performance of historia, her life-telling;

and my guiding principles in transposing her orally performed *historia* to the print medium.

Lydia Mendoza and the social powers of music

Lydia Mendoza's unique performance and recording career spans three-fourths of the twentieth century, from her earliest recordings in the 1920s to the last in the 1980s. It is no exaggeration to state that Lydia Mendoza's sustained popularity and legendary status remain unmatched by any other raza woman of the twentieth century—from any walk of life. Her prominence as a U.S.-Mexican (and Latin American) working-class people's idol stems from her sustained presence and long-term visibility within a complex network of sociocultural relations across time. Fans love Mendoza, like various other grassroots idols, for her ability to articulate a working-class *sentimiento* through song—certainly among the most cherished of working-class Chicana/o cultural art forms. Through her vast repertoire of songs from the oral tradition she became a living embodiment of U.S.-Mexican culture. She is a symbol of the full spectrum and potential of being, as well as a participant in raza people's protracted struggles for survival. The powers of music within daily life and the formation of Mexican working-class community identity in the United States is little understood. On a daily basis, music is an essential practice in the formation and sustenance of *mexicana/o* collective working-class identity. Mexican/Chicana/o culture is not unique in having the oral tradition of music as a central fact of daily life. However, its megapresence and omnipresence within the raza cultural matrix may be unique. As a communal memory system it provides a shared affirmation of a common experience.

I have at times thought of Lydia Mendoza as a powerful labor organizer and/or *curandera* (healer), for she has served as a collectivizing and galvanizing force for raza laborers and as a voice of collective self-power. Later she extended her influence to the incipient middle class and other ethnic groups as well. Her voice and guitar have been prime conduits in consolidating a collective consciousness and social healing for raza farm and factory laborers, for railroad and mine workers, for the army of migrant labor. These are the people who have crisscrossed the United States and Mexico in the mass migrations that began in the twentieth century and extend into the twenty-first. The music performed by the itinerant Lydia Mendoza has transcended physical and temporal boundaries, serving as a multivalent bonding counterforce to the disintegrative forces of displacement, uprooting, exile, migration, and Euro-homogenization/assimilation that emanate from elitist Euro-American institutions and transnational capital, as well as from the repressive nation-states and their bureaucracies. As a traveling public singer, she offered her voice and interpretive genius as a vital nexus and bridge among raza dispersed across national and state borders. In the age of global capital, formerly stable communities and identities have disintegrated and then regrouped in new configurations, in part through the invisible web of music. Lydia Mendoza's love songs, for example, have provided a common ground and bonding agent for diverse raza peoples in the United States and Latin America. Through her recordings and life as an itinerant performer, which began in the 1920s, Lydia Mendoza established a far-flung auditory community and helped create a transnational circuitry and supranational cohesion that often superseded the "imagined community" of nation-states. It is the homeland constituted in song.

Raza musical roots—as well as the larger aesthetic and historical contexts for understanding the social powers of music—extend through tens of thousands of years, predating the arrival of Europeans. Although there has been conversation and exchange among musical languages in the Americas, such as during the colonial regimes of the last two centuries, indigenous systems of musical languages remained a constant in raza musics. For many thousands of years in what is today the Americas, songs have been vessels or transmitters of knowledge—scientific, spiritual, historical, and social. Since time immemorial, songs have healed, narrated history, summoned powers from the spirit world, and expressed beauty and the full range of human sentiments. In more recent times, music's changing social powers—akin to those of laughter, prayer, storytelling, and dance—have both lightened the burden and articulated the diverse collective consciousness of workers. As food for the soul, mind, spirit, and body these musical powers provide vital energy for ethnic self-identification and working-class survival and triumph amid the dehumanizing conditions of colonialism and its changing labor markets in which workers are regarded as less than human. The self-affirming nature of music has remained a constant since antiquity, as expressed in the Nahuatl expression: "Only through song does our pain on earth subside."[6]

The crucial nexus of song—the communal values, knowledge, and working-class sentimiento that attach to that artistic expression—cannot be quantified and as yet has not been satisfactorily translated into analytical terms. Lydia Mendoza's visibility and stature, as well as her lifetime dedication to songs from the raza memory storehouse, pose a challenge to researchers and students interested in how U.S.-Mexicans have traditionally constructed meaning for themselves. The omnipresent nexus of song forms is an intuitively and deeply understood and felt commonality of shared (and contested) meanings, a common ground of collectivity, self-empowerment, and identity formation. Raza cultural systems of representation are everyday sites of re-creation and regeneration. Songs are thus generators of a resilient and profound humanness, of human endurance and survival. They are as vital as the weekly paycheck.

Autonomous domains of self-power

 As I discuss elsewhere,[7] the presence and strength of oral culture and performance within the Chicana/o lifeworld —particularly as it pertains to women—is among those realities least understood and theorized within academic circles, which largely privilege the inert objects and is-

Lydia Mendoza portrait by Estér Hernández. Courtesy Estér Hernández

sues of print culture. The entire interlocking network of oral culture—a unified as well as contradictory and heterogeneous network of cultural practices—is very much in need of holistic critical elaboration. Although there is no lack of writing on Chicana/o "folklore," virtually all studies are piecemeal and focus on one oral performance form or practice and not on the body of oral performance practices as an organic system of interrelated and mutually sustaining practices within living social contexts. The work of Charles L. Briggs is one notable step toward a more holistic and contextualized conceptualization.[8]

To understand the importance and centrality of a working-class idol like Lydia Mendoza we need to put the social scientific discourses of economic materialism in a broader context. We need to enhance our understanding of raza low-income laborers beyond the material dimensions or the dynamics of economic determinism; authors of those discourses must learn to converse with the human soul/mind and heart. How do we account for the survival of peoples under the harshest of social circumstances of the last two centuries? How do we account for the profound humanism and humanistic philosophies of economically marginalized native peoples, a humanism transmitted across generations and in the face of genocidal social realities? Sheer survival against insurmountable odds (by those who managed) has been as much (if not more) a function of song, faith/prayer, storytelling, and dance as of wage labor, union organizing, and political activism.[9]

The social powers of music and faith/spirituality as instruments of humanistic growth, maintenance, and survival undergird and traverse Lydia Mendoza's life-telling. Thus she illustrates the truth of our mothers and grandmothers: that the lived existence of low-income Mexicans and other indigenous peoples encompasses material dynamics always *in conjunction with* multiple lifesaving, life-giving, and life-defining emotional, cultural, and spiritual dynamics, which I call autonomous domains of self-power.[10] These are the powerful sites of mediation, restoration, self-empowerment, self-centering, transcendence, and humanization. For blue-collar workers, the daily encounters with dehumanizing and alienating strategies of capitalist control are not counterbalanced exclusively (sometimes not at all) by workplace resistance and struggle. In the lives of the so-called working poor all is not struggle at the workplace, resistance against power holders, subversion, and coping mechanisms.[11] Many academic conceptualizations of low-income workers tend to imagine a world that wedges "workers" between the reductive dualisms of dominance/opposition; victimization/liberation. These standard top–down bipolar terminologies imply a reactive vision of human subjects struggling and moving vis-à-vis a hugely imagined "hegemony." Peoples of color (and other communities in poverty) are often cast in analytical terminologies that signal powerlessness and an overriding dependency relationship vis-à-vis capitalism, which "disenfranchises," "marginalizes," "subjugates," "dominates," "exploits," and otherwise "victimizes."[11] Thus terminologies tacitly replicate the ideology and momentum of capitalist imperatives. This is not to in any way deny the dire realities of working too hard for very little money. However, we need to perceive other fields, types, and relationships of power. Part of what Lydia Mendoza demonstrates in her life narrative is that raza are so much more than wage laborers or national subjects. Particularly the daily life practices of many women reveal those autonomous domains of self-power within which women perform cultural rituals and practices of self-definition, self-power, and self-centering that at the same time mediate, invert, or deflect realms of negative social power. As examples of those autonomous domains of self-power I would highlight Lydia Mendoza's traditional relationship to the spirit world (*los espíritus*); to the Creator, Dios, as a sustaining power of the universe; to faith as a moving force; to the powerful expression of music; and her relationships to other women. These autonomous domains constitute her center, her innermost core, her life foundation, her human power and most profound social meanings. Those self-constitutive *relationships* comprise what Anzaldúa refers to as the process of re-creating "the godwoman in me."[12] Many raza women move within these autonomous domains of self-power, those cultural spaces that enable both the symbolic airing and/or resolution of social contradictions *and* a dynamic self-power *outside* of those contradictions. The discussion of strategies for social transformation at times tends to cast transformation as an outward event (directed hierarchically) and not one that begins within individuals. Women's autonomous domains of self-power, however, can enable social transformation from within. Gandhi, one of the masters of social transformation, envisioned such a social transformation: "You must become the change you want to see in the world."[13]

Women's traditional autonomous domains of self-power—spirituality, community ties, music, dance, healing practices, cooking, childbearing, the loving relationship to the land, and more—need to be understood first in and of themselves, on their own terms, and in relationship to one another before they can be further contextualized (but not exclusively defined) within the bipolar field of dominant/reactive power relations which tend to be privileged in established hierarchical models of academic discourses.[14] Seen from the perspective of these autonomous domains of self-power, capitalism is the margin and the autonomous domains of self-power form the core of people's lives, the ways people express their needs, passions, and desires. The notion of a "dominant culture" becomes surreal. When we understand music in this way, we may perceive how its powers (like those generated by spiritual practices or storytelling, for example) can intermittently eclipse the nation-state, capitalism, or corporations as primary objects of identification or affiliation for some raza peoples. Some recent research—notably that by Devon Peña—perceives and theorizes women's autonomous spaces and theorizes the "inventive force," self-power, and agency of "marginal" *maquiladora* women workers.[15]

Lydia Mendoza and generations of blue-collar U.S.-Mexican communities have constructed and lived a broader and richer spectrum of reality than what we know within the narrow confines of the sociopolitically repressive world of patriarchy, the "isms" (racism, classism, and sexism), ecocide, and homophobia and under the umbrella narratives of nation-states. Thus any attempt to situate Lydia Mendoza (and the millions who live in similar circumstances) strictly within the academic discourses of economic and historical materialism produces an understanding much like that of a pickpocket who beholds a saint and only sees her pockets. Academic myopia has indeed been staggering: university research has produced absolutely nothing concerning Lydia Mendoza, not even one lengthy article, not one book-length study. Nor is she even mentioned in any of those many volumes written about the working-class populations who idolized her across generations. The same holds true for the host of other pan-Mexican popular idols since the turn of the century—such as Lucha Reyes, Chelo Silva, Agustín Lara, José Alfredo Jiménez, David Zaízar, and Cantinflas, to name only a handful—largely ignored in academia. Even when newer academic disciplines (such as ethnic studies) attempt to "right" the Eurocentric/male-centered record or expand the base of ethnic knowledge at the university, the research produced at times suffers from a gender-and-class-based bias that tends to replicate the jargon, theories, research questions, and disciplinary paradigms of the established Eurocentric disciplines. The social powers of Lydia Mendoza as a beloved performer and cultural focal point have not been studied or understood even amid all the talk and writing on "identity" and identity formation. Much of the writing on identity formation is not grounded in empirical research, in living familiarity with communities, in first-hand experience, or in popular cultural practices. Only Gloria Anzaldúa, in her brilliant borderlands writing, which defies all categories and disciplines, identifies Chicana/o norteño musics as one of the chief forces of identity formation and pays very brief yet intense homage to Lydia Mendoza as "one of the great border *corrido* singers" and as "a singer of the people," indicating that "folk musicians and folk songs are our chief cultural myth-makers, and they made our hard lives seem bearable."[16] It is time to study those "chief cultural myth-makers."

Lydia Mendoza has meant many things to many people of different social classes and regions. For stoop laborers and those in the sweatshops, the miners, smelters, and railroad workers—whose migratory routes she traveled as a performer from earliest childhood until old age—she became the first "star" who rose from among the ranks. In her lifetime, she has carried various epithets that fans fondly coined for her: La cancionera de los pobres (Singer of the poor), La gloria de Tejas (Glory of Texas), and La alondra de la frontera (The meadowlark of the border)—each highlighting important attributes of class origins and affiliation; of geographic place; of the immense pride people projected and project onto her; and of her musical artistry: her woman's voice as beautiful and migratory as a "lark" whose songs and physical presence transcend unnatural national boundaries.

For generations Mendoza's voice has resounded in many modalities, ranging from the denunciatory corrido, which inverts power, race, gender, and sexual relations in the borderlands (and far beyond), to the most intimate of love songs, which celebrate human subjectivity. Her voice and body have channeled the collective voices of the people in her capacity as a musician *de talón* (literally, "on her feet"). *De talón* directly references the oral tradition of song on the go, on its feet or *talónes* (heels). Lydia Mendoza was trained as a child in that ancient oral tradition of *música de talón*: the trade of wandering street musicians who commingle among their principal audience: poor people who socialize on the streets and (more recently) in restaurants on a day off from work. Thus Mendoza was obliged to master the repertoire of the oral tradition, singing by heart those songs the people requested; weaving and mending the cloth of raza culture, of that shifting collective consciousness enacted in the circle of songs.

She continued the practice of singing traditional songs by popular demand to the very end of her career, even when she was invited to sing in concert halls or at the White House. In her native Houston, Texas, she had her steady gigs in small working-class neighborhood restaurants and bars, as well as at private parties. What she sang was intimately linked to what the people needed, wanted, and requested to hear in that time and place. She prides herself on knowing hundreds of songs by heart: songs requested over and over throughout her career of almost 70 years. Of course that musical flow is by no means static: some new songs would come into the repertoire, and others would be forgotten.

Lydia Mendoza was important not only as a legendary voice but also as a performer of visual spectacles on tour. She was not only among the first recording artists but also among the earliest touring entertainers in the United States. Her flashy performance dresses and extraordinary hand-crafted jewelry are breathtaking works of art that she designed and sewed—hand-sequined, hand-

Lydia Mendoza in 1947 at age 30. Courtesy Houston Metropolitan Research Center, Houston Public Library

beaded, all spectacularly colored and decorated with designs that announced her ancient cultural roots in the Americas. The shimmering and highly symbolic sequined eagle and serpent, for example, covered some of her attire, such as the backs of her flowing black capes. She also emblazoned that symbol on the front of many of her dazzling red, white, and green dresses, marking the enduring presence of indigenous Mexican culture. The very sight of her was magical and could awaken a populist frenzy and collective pride in Mexicans. Her body, a billboard of Mexicanness, bravely flaunted those boldly sequined, flowered, brightly colored dresses even through historical periods in which public displays of Mexicanness targeted you for governmental harassment and/or deportation by Euro-American officials. She proclaimed Mexicanness throughout historical periods when signs that read: NO DOGS, NO MEXICANS were the rule along the migrant worker routes. Lydia Mendoza traveled thousands of miles, from town to town, in such perilous times as the 1930s, with its cycles of mass deportations of raza by the U.S. government, and the 1950s, with its infamous Operation Wetback. Her flamboyant performance attire as well as song style and repertoire loudly proclaimed a mexicana politics of place and of belonging for native people officially deemed as not belonging to the United States—and targeted for deportation and "repatriation."[17] As she set off touring with her family, singing in the native poetics and harmonies of the lost homeland, Lydia Mendoza affirmed the ancient legacy and presence of indigenous Mexican peoples while also resisting the English-speaking hegemony. Her voice and the communal repertoire of song symbolically reclaimed and remapped the United States as Mexico—particularly the Southwest, which was part of the Mexican nation until 1848.[18] In some ways, Lydia Mendoza is a precursor of the new circuits, networks, and flows of culture and politics that George Lipsitz maps for contemporary popular musics (albeit not norteño) in the postindustrial age— musics "which both respond to the imperatives of place at the same time that they transcend them."[19]

If Chicanos/Native Americans in the nineteenth century survived the violent westward expansion by Euro-Americans and the transformation into a permanent underclass; if raza survived the bloodthirsty gold rush and the new slave laws (such as California's statutes that legalized raza slavery in the 1850s and 1860s);[20] if raza farm laborers and factory and railroad workers survived the inhumane work conditions of the twentieth century, we must consider the social powers of music in these processes. Lydia Mendoza remains a towering figure within that legacy of survival that encompasses not only physical definitions of survival but also the cultural/emotional/spiritual dimensions of self-power. She embodies the continuance of a deep humanistic/ethical legacy that resonates in popular raza expressions that denote those desirable qualities of higher consciousness and dignified action. Expressions such as "Es muy gente" ("ser gente") encapsulate an ancient philosophy about "humanness." The concept of being human, of becoming human, and concern for the ethical ways that qualify as "human" have ancient roots in the Americas and are intimately linked to Nahuatl Aztec humanistic concepts and ideals such as "In ixtli in yollotl" (a wise countenance and strong heart or "making face, making soul"). That concept espouses the vital link of the mind and the heart (centers of movement), the connection of theory and practice. Mexican/Latina/o indigenous culture regards music as a humanizing force or also as an alternative force in the face of evil and difficult circumstances. Both the ancients and Mendoza describe song as a gift from a higher source, as a mediatory power that connects the divine with humans:

> ¡oh, Dador de la vida!
> Con cantos das colores
> con cantos sombreas
> a los que han de vivir en la tierra . . .[22]

[O Life-Giver!
Through songs you give color
through songs you give shade
to those who inhabit the earth . . .]

Similarly, a contemporary popular expression denotes music's powers of purification and self-defense: "Quien canta, sus males espanta." (Whoever sings expels their troubles.) No wonder that the Aztec deity Huitzilopochtli instructed his migratory people to sing: "Wherever you go, you shall go singing." Yet the universe of song is not merely a cathartic place. Since before colonization, music has ranked among the most prominent of self-constitutive practices and domains for raza peoples. Songs are invaluable and key resources in which communities theorize, rehearse, codify, and transmit what Mikhail Bakhtin has called "the unofficial truth about the world"[22]—the marginalized knowledges of raza in the Americas. Those knowledges encompass a broad spectrum that ranges from everyday human values in the face of adversity, to the diverse knowledge about gender relations or sexual relations found in the *canciónes rancheras*, to the historical and humanistic knowledges of corridos, to the verbal play and cultural allusions of *arrullos* (lullabies), and to the spiritual knowledge of hymns and *alabanzas* (song chants). The flow of song in Chicana/o communities functions as an autonomous domain of self-power or forum where the collective airs a host of contending ideas, ideologies, interests, values, love configurations, tragic circumstances, humorous situations, social analysis, the gamut of emotions, and memory of roots in the land. This explains, for example, the ongoing tradition of song and countersong that exists in the barrios, whereby a popular song (the canción ranchera) on immigration like "Jaula de Oro" ("Golden Cage" by Los Tigres del Norte) provokes *contestaciónes*, or competitive responses, such as "Jaula Abierta" ("Open Cage") by Bernardo y Sus Compadres. That invisible forum or autonomous domain of self-power allows people to generate and inhabit symbolic spaces (however tentative) and to rehearse victories over all forms of social violence. Many corridos and love songs, for example, stage the inversion of established oppressive social relations.

Several songs closely identified with Lydia Mendoza are important feminist blueprints that deeply engaged (and continue to engage) our thinking about gender and sexual relations. Her first hit (1934), "Mal Hombre" ("Evil Man"), and "Mujer Paseada" ("Experienced Woman"), for example, defy academic and popular stereotypes of Latina chastity and virginity. These and other songs cemented a strong popular platform for the launching of later womanist (*mujerista*, feminist) values. Both the songs and women's practices of *historia* (discussed later in "Gendered Historia: Performing Indigenous Women's Working-Class History (A Way of Talking)" prefigure and run parallel to Chicana academic feminist discourse, which has, however, often not perceived the mujerista force within the popular traditions of song performance.

Lydia Mendoza's mother, Leonor Zamarripa Mendoza (*left*), and aunt Rosa
Zamarripa (ca. 1940s). Courtesy Lydia Mendoza Collection

Lydia Mendoza's norteño performance repertoire: performance tradition and the creation of social meaning

Wherever I walk, wherever I sing, is a blooming of
flowers, a swelling of song, and there my heart is alive.
Bierhorst, Cantares mexicanos: Songs of the Aztecs
(circa 1500s, p. 205)

How do we conceptualize the traditional song reper-
toire, musicianship, and enormous popular appeal of Lydia Mendoza? The term
norteño offers a starting place. In her historia (the segment "We Northerners:
Nosotros los norteños"), Mendoza positions herself within that sociocultural
system of shared experiences and meanings called norteño music. Lydia Mendoza rose to prominence as a self-contained singer who played her own 12-
string guitar. Yet in the course of her long musical career she also performed
and recorded in the full gamut of norteño instrumental ensembles and song
forms. Lydia Mendoza's repertoire of songs embraces a rich variety of genres
from the oral tradition of norteño song: the corrido, ranchera, bolero, *vals*,

música de antaño, tango, *milonga*, and huapango. She draws from multiple song forms, most of which have had a long-standing presence in that music sphere known as "norteño," the rich and diverse family of musics indigenous to the northern reaches of today's Mexico (especially the states of Nuevo León, Tamaulipas, Coahuila, Sonora, and Chihuahua), including what was formerly the northern half of Mexico: today's Southwest United States. Norteño is a borderlands term.[23] As a musical designation, norteño is often used interchangeably with the term *ranchera* or *música ranchera*. Terms such as norteño and ranchera enjoy varied usage—at times intersecting, overlapping, and/or diverging from one another and from other related terms such as *música tejana*, *Tex-Mex*, and *conjunto*. The norteño musical presence has expanded to physical and cultural geographies outside the "north" (today's U.S. Southwest and the north of Mexico). Norteño musical culture of the twentieth century has moved with people along the migratory worker routes to the Midwest; the western states, including the Pacific Northwest; and recently even the eastern United States and remote outposts in Central and South America. Most norteño forms and their star performers—most especially the conjunto norteño with button accordion and bajo sexto—have also been marketed to the four winds by virtue of new technologies that include everything from television to satellite communications. Many people in Central America, for example, consider borderlands norteño groups such as Los Alegres de Teran as native to their own regions. Not only have norteño musics circulated widely outside their "northern" places of origin, but also heavy migration of people *into* the northern borderlands has brought new impulses, exchanges between musical families, and cross-fertilization, which has helped shape and change norteño musical forms. The term norteño in my usage embraces a number of different yet related instrumental ensembles and a range of collective sentimiento, (see "Changing Borderlands Musical Languages") encoded and performed within the changing song repertoire.[24] But norteño is also the shared memory of that infinite number of dance halls, bars, and streets, of celebrations, tragedies, and broader social/human relations, a common circle of meanings (however divergent) that this music has cocreated.

Although tejano musics constitute only a subgroup of the larger "norteño" musical domain, much of what is U.S.-norteño has its home base in Texas. The diverse norteño instrumental ensembles include the button accordion conjunto ensemble (with its variants); the orquesta tejana (also called *onda Chicana* or *onda tejana* or *la onda grupera*); the *trio romántico*, the contemporary version which consists of three guitars (formerly it included violins and/or other string instruments); and the imported mariachi ensembles originally native to the state of Jalisco. One could also include the *banda* or *tambora* (bands that featured mainly wind instruments), which migrated north from Sinaloa. The contemporary ensembles evolved from various earlier ensemble (or solo) styles that dated to the 19th century, including the tejano harp, the tejano string bands, and even the norteño string bands with winds.

Within that richly diverse and ever-changing norteño musical culture, Lydia Mendoza represents one of the most elemental, enduring, and economical of all norteño vocal/instrumental presentational genres: the lone singer who self-accompanies on guitar. Although that was her preferred form of musical expression, she no doubt also increased her visibility, impact, and public presence through her enormous versatility: her ability to unfold her musical talents within the give-and-take of multiple norteño instrumental traditions. She performed and recorded widely with many of the leading tejano Hall of Fame musicians, composers, and diverse norteño instrumental ensembles of the twentieth century, including Beto Villa, Lorenzo Caballero, José Morante, Tony de la Rosa, and Narciso Martínez (who made the first button accordion recordings in Texas). In her long career she moved with ease between the orquesta tejana (big-band ensemble) and conjunto music (button accordion ensemble), the trío romántico (with two guitars and *requinto*), and occasional stints with mariachi backup. At times she recorded with her 12-string guitar but added another musician or musicians.[25] Early in her career, she performed in various ensemble configurations with her family members (as she describes in her historia). This creative versatility was related both to the need to generate income and to her varied musical interests and talents. As a popular performer she embodied many different roles: street singer, recording artist, itinerant vaudevillian performer of the *carpa*, family ensemble singer and soloist, concert hall artist, and musician at neighborhood restaurants, parties, and dance clubs.

Most of Lydia Mendoza's song repertoire (but not all) crosscuts in and out of the other norteño instrumental ensembles—although those song transpositions between different instrumental ensembles usually involve revisions of musical arrangements, including rhythms, and song forms (a waltz can turn into a polka, for example). Lydia herself composed only a very few songs. She performed a traditional repertoire from the oral tradition. Yet tradition is by no means static but changing, flexible, and flowing. Song forms and songs from Lydia Mendoza's repertoire have a history of steady circulation and permutation, with corresponding adaptations and arrangements arising within the diverse norteño instrumentational styles and times. One and the same song can move among diverse instrumental styles (within one region or across regions).

Changing borderlands musical languages

In her formative years, Lydia Mendoza absorbed and evolved within the musical vocabularies of that heterogeneous norteño bioregion: above all, various regional Mexican tejano musical strands but also pan-Mexican, German/Czech, and Latin American, as well as occasional Euro-American and African-American, currents in cross-pollination with one another. The nineteenth-century German/Czech colonial presence in Texas (or the Austrian one in northern Mexico), for example, brought with it the button accordion and musical forms such as the polka, *chotís* (schottische), and *redova*—today considered among the most typical of tejano instruments and song forms, respectively. Yet norteño instruments and song forms have evolved with deep localized roots in numerous other southwestern regions such as Arizona (in Tohono O'Odham "Chicken Scratch" vari-

eties, for example, or the Yaqui/Mexican norteño forms).[26] Musical languages in multiple variations are at the heart of indigenous Mexican regional and trans-regional cultures. Particularly during the colonization and resistance processes of the last 150 years, musical languages have frequently crisscrossed cultural, ethnic, class, and supposed national borders—a testimony both to the lived proximity of diverse cultures and to the transgressive magnetism of musical cultures across social boundaries of class, ethnicity, gender, sexuality, and georegion. Music has an infectious quality and thus lends itself to cross-cultural assimilation much more easily than other cultural expressions. Even though much of the social and historical interaction between people of color and Euro-Americans has been highly conflicted, music reminds us that on another level the relationship was as much one of convergences (and mutual dependencies) as of divergences.

The sociohistorical relationship of violence between Mexicans and neocolonial Germans in nineteenth-century Texas, for example, was also a relationship of musical exchanges and refunctionalizations—with elements from Mexican music finding their way into Anglo country-western music, while indigenous peoples adopted the German button accordion, polkas, chotís and other musical forms that the immigrant Germans had formerly adopted from the Czechs in Bohemia. Throughout parts of the nineteenth century, German and Spanish were the two main languages in San Antonio. (Today's Spanish language in San Antonio reflects the Mexican/German "exchange of words.") Lydia Mendoza performs such mexicanized "German" song forms, interpreting them in her individual style, thus assimilating and adapting them into the deep-rooted indigenous culture. (As she says: "We adapt the music. I adapt my music.") The world of music has often been a common ground or bridge between peoples assumed to be totally separated by a gulf of social mistrust and differences—racism, sexism, language differences, and economic exploitation. Yet in some ways the popular (and classical) ethnic musics and identities now considered "separate" were historically shaped in close interaction—exclusions and exchanges—with one another.[27]

Examples of cross-cultural musical bonding and interethnic musical conversation abound: of appropriations, of oppositions and resistances within shared musical and geographical environments. Lydia Mendoza, for example, performs a few songs in fox trot rhythm (some of them called fox-canción), while master accordionist Valerio Longoria (among the earliest tejano accordion recording artists) surprisingly includes one or two English-language songs in his two most recent albums where he performs duets with Freddy Fender. Was Longoria temporarily influenced by Chicano country-western singer Baldemar Huerta (aka Freddy Fender), whose recording career features predominantly English-language or bilingual country songs sung with ranchera intonations? Inversely, Euro-American country swing musician Bob Wills, for example, credits Mexican music as a powerful influence in his music. And although norteño fare has been the staple of the majority of raza in the Southwest, raza in Texas (particularly among the working class) have always loved, danced, performed, and developed country-western music (not to mention big-band and rock and roll)—even though dance activity remains largely racially segregated. Some prominent conjunto norteño musicians in Texas, such as accordion virtuosos Nick Villareal, Esteban Jordán (aka Steve Jordan), or Chabela and the Brown Express in California have always included country-western two-step numbers in their recordings and have performed country music at raza dances—interspersed within the predominantly *polkita* repertoire (which they imbue with blues influences). The cross-cultural and transnational flow of musical exchange also led Lydia Mendoza to perform some songs that originated in places such as Argentina, Cuba, and Colombia. Significantly, her first major solo recording hit, "Mal Hombre" (1934), was in the rhythm of the Argentinean milonga and no doubt related to the tango craze that began to sweep the United States and Mexico in the 1920s.

Lydia Mendoza's relationship to music and new musical influences was a complex process, involving change within a dynamic continuity. Diverse tejano musics exist in a vital state of change and exchange. In the segment "We Northerners: Nosotros los norteños," Lydia Mendoza describes the dynamic qualities of a tradition that continually reinvents itself through a steady process of appropriation, adaptation, innovation, and maintenance. Some might imagine Lydia Mendoza's artistic constancy over the decades was a static "traditionalism." Of course some elements of her music remained unchanged even as she appropriated new elements. Yet change was also a constant. When Lydia Mendoza did "foreign" songs, however, such as milongas or tangos, she transposed them into the tejano/ranchera vocabulary of the people for whom she performed them. Mendoza herself transposed many songs into norteño polka rhythm—songs not originally composed as polkas. There are numerous examples of songs originally composed in triple meter that Mendoza converted into duple meter. One notable example is Mendoza's interpretation and arrangement of the corrido "Delgadina."

Another example of her appropriation and innovation within maintenance is her 12-string guitar, which was not a standard norteño instrument. She refunctionalized the 12-string guitar, by tuning it to B, a perfect fourth lower than regular guitar, and tuning a minor third lower than standard 12-string tuning—a variation that was uniquely hers. Regular guitar tuning is, starting from the lowest string: E, A, d, g, b, e'. Standard 12-string tuning is D, G, c, f, a, d, with the lowest four courses in octaves, using the next highest octave and the highest two courses in unison. Mendoza's tuning was B1, E, A, d, f#, b. In essence, she adapted her 12-string guitar to emulate the double-course sound of the Texas bajo sexto, creating a guitar range between guitar and bajo sexto. She innovatively tuned her 12-string in a pitch halfway between a regular 12-string guitar and a bajo sexto—in order to achieve that booming bass sound that highlights and accompanies the expressiveness of her voice. In other words, she created a new space between the conventional boundaries of established instruments to fit her aesthetic needs.

Mendoza's process of appropriation and change within continuity always involved a double translation on her part: on the one hand, she translates songs into a collective regional tejana musical vocabulary or recognizable/audible norteño mode of expression (with wide-ranging and fluctuating parameters); on the other hand, she appropriates and transposes songs to her own personal aesthetics as a song stylist/arranger with an unmistakable voice. Lydia Mendoza's recognizable voice and 12-string guitar combined to create her characteristic solo performer style within the norteño cultural matrix. Her voice came to be regarded as quintessentially expressive of the norteño tejano collective musical vocabulary, with its repertoire of songs and languages—those modes of expression that developed over time within the communities for whom she sang. Whatever instrumental ensemble she performed with, she articulated a *sentimiento* that resonated deep within the realms of raza experiences and geographies—the Southwest, Midwest, and Northwest. Within her circle of song performance, her musical arrangements, timbre, voice, body, and spirit enacted the space of a popular collective expression. The expressiveness of her voice encodes a sociocultural matrix far beyond the surface value of the notes; her voice generates a spirit through the notes. If audiences feel, think, and identify with the expressivity of her music it is because her music—her voice and repertoire—evokes the deep-rootedness of the people: born and bred regionally. Artistic modes of regional expression (like the tejano norteño) are like mother tongues; just as you learn a mother tongue, you also absorb and understand musical language(s) with its(their) own spectrum of sentimiento. In popular usage, *sentimiento* denotes sentience and cognition (consciousness) as much as an emotional quality or sentimentality. A shared music in the Texas of the first half of the twentieth century implies a shared flesh-and-bone consciousness, instinctual awareness, and structure of feeling.

The expressivity of Mendoza's personal aesthetics is unmistakable and widely loved. It grew organically among the people, first through her watching/hearing the women in her family and then through her observing other musicians at work. As Mendoza was a musician trained in the oral tradition (called *lirica*), the mass appeal of her voice had something to do with its naturalness, clarity, strength, and lack of affectations. She never felt a need to go the route of various other popular singers who attempted to attain a supposed polish through operatic training (Jorge Negrete and Pedro Infante are two examples). Mendoza had no bel canto ambitions and sang with only a minimal vibrato. Thus her vocal inflection and tone had a straightforward and almost speechlike quality. Mendoza articulated her musical phrasing in an economical style, close to the orational style (*declamadoras*), using the inflections from daily human speech in her music. She typically avoided all the melismatic frills cultivated by singers who aimed to climb socially. Lydia Mendoza represented all the rural qualities of voice and song, which later overtook the urban sphere as well.

Her expressivity differs markedly, for example, from that of another legendary tejana: Chelo Silva. Silva's sultry and distanced intonation, droning, clamoring, and bolero repertoire, rife with sexual allusions (and even profanity), captured the diverse and changing imagination and tastes of an increasingly urban people. Silva's cool torch singer voice and Mendoza's emotive grassroots intonation formed two sides of one norteño coin. (Not to mention that they were good friends and at times traveled together, performing as part of the same show.) Chelo Silva's *cabaretera* voice and her sleek non-Mexican urban attire were honed and developed in smoke-filled "cosmopolitan" nightclubs of the 1940s and with instrumentational ensembles that distanced themselves from the visual and aural styles and preferred instruments of the rural folk. By contrast, Lydia's natural and clear voice marked a strong connection to rural roots, imagery, and singing style. Chelo's style and almost exclusively bolero repertoire also made her a beloved idol and phenomenon among the people. The popularity of a Chelo Silva alongside Lydia Mendoza is testimony to the diversity of musics within the norteño-tejano—and greater Mexican—cultural space.

During her long performance career—perhaps the longest of any American musician ever—Mendoza recorded and performed with numerous instrumental backup groups, including her sisters on various recordings. Yet Lydia's preferred mode was as a self-contained one-woman show, in some ways a throwback to the old itinerant *corridistas*. That configuration of musicianship tends to ensure a high survival rate due to the degree of independence (from other musicians) as well as flexibility and mobility. Unlike many contemporary tejana singers, Lydia Mendoza was not only a singer working with her voice; she was also a musician in possession of musical skills beyond her voice. Her high level of musicianship involved original musical arrangements and the challenge of making her voice work with the 12-string guitar. Her musical phrasing and style, her accentuations and nonaccentuations, resonate with the larger norteño musical system that emerged in the twentieth century.

Lydia Mendoza and the canción ranchera

Me gusta cantarle al viento
porque vuelan mis cantares,
y digo lo que yo siento
por toditos los lugares.

Atravesé la montaña
pa' venir a ver las flores,
no hay cerro que se me empine
ni cuaco que se me atore.

(Excerpt from "La Feria de las Flores,"
canción ranchera by Jesús "Chucho"
Monge, one of Lydia's favorite songs)

The increasingly restricted geopolitical and economic contexts of the twentieth century—most notably the environmental degradation of the planet and social degradation of its peoples—have also created the "restricted cultural spheres" or "reduced universe of social life" described by Guillermo Bonfil Batalla.[28] The canción ranchera/*norteña* and some of its close relatives have survived and thrived throughout the twentieth century, while many other briefly popular song and cultural forms have emerged and then retreated or vanished. Thus its importance is all the greater. The sheer exuberance of the canción ranchera (along with its general proliferation) needs to be understood both inside and outside that context of social constraints.

We cannot point to a sizable body of research on norteño music or its practitioners even though they have played such an important role in the everyday life and survival of working-class raza. Only the corrido has received substantial critical attention, although it has often been examined more as a source of verbal information or meanings than holistically as a musical form or living social practice. Corridos have been collected, dissected, and examined in their formal textual (and some contextual) qualities by scholars for decades.[29] In academia, however, historical corridos—as transmitters of supposedly hard-and-fast historical "facts"—have been privileged, for example, over the equally, if not more, popular love song genres, as well as over multifaceted instrumental musical genres that are not sung, such as the distinctively tejano variety of the instrumental huapango, the *vals alto*, *vals bajito*, or the redova. Many of the oral tradition's manifold and mutually sustaining musical forms—as a corpus—have been largely overlooked. There is virtually nothing written on the polka norteña, for example, perhaps the most danced and sung raza musical form of the twentieth century, nor on the canción ranchera (and the *canción de amor* generally). The important historical work of Manuel Peña on the Texas-Mexican accordion ensemble or conjunto stands virtually alone—yet he does not examine the canción ranchera.[30]

Lydia Mendoza's songs and performances feature a broad range of musical forms, instrumental ensembles, and themes. Yet the preponderance of her songs are ranchera love songs. (And she sings her corridos, for example, in ranchera style.) In order to understand the significance of Lydia Mendoza, we need to understand the musical aesthetics, expressivity, and social functions of canciones de amor, which have had such widespread popular resonance to this very day. Ignored by researchers, canciones de amor and the canción ranchera are typically only referenced in passing and dismissed as either frivolous, escapist, or apolitical. Other scholars stereotype the ranchera songs by superficially highlighting the imagery of alcohol and cruel women *mujer ingrata*. Thus these scholars easily dismiss the canción ranchera, overlooking its vast musical and poetic richness.

The ranchera love song is a living social practice within the lives of millions. It has diverse levels of meaning. Given the constraints of space, I can only sketch some significant sociodynamic aspects of the canción ranchera:[31]

1. The canción ranchera is far and away the most powerfully emotional of all Mexican song types. For those singing, listening to, or dancing a canción ranchera, the music and lyrics work together as a cultural channel of human flow and desire. There is a powerful release of deep happiness or deep sorrow, or just plain unmitigated enjoyment—often linked to other contexts in which that song was experienced or to the loved ones who cherish the song. These songs serve as a momentary and autonomous space of rehumanization. The pleasure or pain they trigger is both emotional and physical, often including dance as a component. Rancheras are not only about words; they are also about a resonance that transcends the conscious rational cerebral dimensions. The melodic lines and their interpretations by varied artists (referred to as *interpretes de la canción* within Mexican culture) have profound effects, often culminating in the ritualized *grito*, or piercing primordial scream, which pow-

erfully releases emotions. For many families these songs are an important part of what establishes linkages: the consonance of bioenergies across generations and geographies. The following anecdote illustrates one dimension of that human flow:

> I believe that there are many things which contribute to our identity and I feel that ranchera music has greatly influenced mine. As a child and even today I remember waking up in the morning to the sound of canciónes rancheras. My mother would always be playing her favorite songs by Juan Gabriel, Vicente Fernández, etc., while she cooked and cleaned in the morning. I would ask her, "Mom, can't you lower the music?" And she would respond, "No, mi'ja, sin la música me da flojera y no acabo el que-hacer." ["No, without the music I'll get lazy and won't be able to do the chores."] The music was her driving force and still is. It is not only part of her identity, but I've made it part of mine as well.[32]

Among the existential realms touched and transformed by the vibrational field of this consummately emotional music is the untold suffering and indignities experienced at the workplaces of physical wage labor. When we look at it in this way, we can only fathom the survivalist importance of musical rehumanization by examining it in the context of dehumanizing working-class jobs and chronically violent raza histories.

2. Many love songs—in particular the ranchera variety favored by Lydia Mendoza—are much more than songs about love. The love situation is always supported by a vocabulary, imagery, values, customs, landscapes, material culture, and symbols from the deep cultural matrix of Mesoamerica, the deep roots of indigenous Mexican culture, and its changing and unchanging symbols of identity. Love (and the attendant grief, disappointment, ecstasy, death, and birth) happens amid cornfields, cactus, maguey (agave), trees, rebozos, beloved geographies, aspects of the natural environment such as the open sky, sunlight/nighttime, the stars, and the deep love for the land and rural places of origin (el rancho) and all its symbols from the entire plant and animal kingdom. Significantly, the markers of popular raza spiritual practices and sacred spaces also figure prominently. From "Cuatro Milpas" to "Besando la Cruz" and "Amor de Madre," the canción ranchera circulates as a storehouse and symbolic repository of the raza cultural matrix. Although such regional music was once confined to the rural areas, the canción ranchera successfully took the cities, vesting the imagery of el rancho with new urban meanings and translations, evoking desires, dreams, and fantasies. The canción ranchera thus evokes collective memory and knowledge and remains one of the richest of raza archives and popular curricula, instructing both rural and urban dwellers. It is an important audible dimension of memory and storyworld: part of our social apprenticeship. It opens up a space of identification, the reexperience of manifold encounters, of solidarities (including bonds of enmity).

3. Taken as a body, love songs manifest a broad discursive range, serving as sounding boards for gender relations, sexual relations, and broader human relations—for creating and re-creating culture. The symbolic ranchera cultural archive serves up a heterogeneous vision of human possibilities and impossi-

bilities. Each song—its singer and listeners—rehearses a strategy of person-hood. The range is encyclopedic and you can take it or leave it. Everyone has their favorite songs and the ones they don't like. Each song provides the lis-tener, the singer, and the community of shared memory with a negotiation of personhood and social identity. The song narratives in their confluence com-prise an "art of operating" or a theory of life practices, moves, and behaviors charged with symbolic enactments within everyday activity.[33] Those who cul-tivate these songs are free to establish relationships between the domain of song and other lived domains. The body of songs thus presents a knowledge of behaviors and collectively validated concepts from which listeners negotiate the boundaries of collective and individual identities.

Love songs circulate among raza in a rich variety of musical forms, includ-ing the ranchera songs, boleros, *baladas*, lyrical love corridos, even *cumbias*, with innumerable themes and scenarios. Lydia Mendoza's repertoire spans all forms and themes, yet her preference for the canción ranchera is undeniable. Her ranchera repertoire configures, for example, familial love (particularly for the mother figure), love of place of origin or nation ("Mexico Lindo y Querido"), love of the land or lost homeland ("Cuatro Milpas"), the dispassion-ate love of old age ("Cuando Estemos Viejos"), romantic passion, love betrayal, unrequited love ("Celosa"), and even happy adoration ("Amor Bonito," which she authored) and aggrieved love due to death ("Cuando se Pierde la Madre"). Mendoza performed and recorded some of these songs over and over through-out her career (e.g., "Mal Hombre," "Cuatro Milpas," "Amor de Madre," "Be-sando la Cruz," and "El Lirio"), and many are popularly identified with her. These figured among the songs that audiences always requested from her. I once witnessed a street concert in San Antonio where Lydia Mendoza had to sing "Mal Hombre" three times—by popular demand.

Although Mendoza's live musical performance career has ended, her legacy continues in the form of musical recordings in the media of CDs, film, and radio. Her legacy also includes the innumerable Lydia Mendoza stories I have heard since childhood from a host of people from all walks of life: stories that reveal her audience's love of her and of her legendary presence among us. Sto-ries such as those from my own mother, who will never forget how she first heard Lydia's voice on the rural and remote rancho of her native Sinaloa in the late 1930s. (It was a place without electricity, before radio, television, cars, or recorded music had reached most of the world.) Lydia Mendoza's voice moved throughout rural Mexico, thanks to enterprising individuals who toted Victro-las and records by donkey to isolated outposts. The people always gathered to hear their songs coming out of the strange box. Everywhere I go I hear similar stories and recollections that concern Lydia Mendoza's presence and imprint. She is legendary. On many levels—including now that of her life-telling—she remains a cultural symbol and galvanizing force for a people in a state of siege; her voice (singing and telling) will forever remain a monument within the com-plexities of the "culture of resistance" described by Bonfil Batalla. Within that culture, the memory arts are a crucial resource of self-preservation. Groups that face neocolonial pressures control their cultural spaces as their own axis of self-definition—thus maintaining permanence (in change), identity renewal, and existence itself.[34] Lydia Mendoza's remembrances are one such collective ritual.

Gendered historia: performing indigenous women's working-class history (a way of talking)

> The world's earliest archives or libraries were the memories of women. Patiently transmitted from mouth to ear, body to body, hand to hand. In the process of storytelling, speaking and listening refer to realities that do not involve just the imagination. The speech is seen, heard, smelled, tasted, and touched. It destroys, brings to life, nurtures. Every woman partakes in the chain of guardianship and of transmission.
>
> (Trinh T. Minh-ha, *Woman, Native, Other*, p. 121)

Since time immemorial, native women have performed their histories in ways inaudible to the colonial imaginary of print culture. Print culture's heavy focus on political histories of nation-states and on supposed "world-historical" subjects, as well as the "bottom-up" grassroots progressive historiography (such as by the French *annales* school, ethnic studies historiographies, and feminist historiographies), have tended to obscure another discursive dynamic: the ways in which women have spoken history to one another within the oral tradition, the ways women have spoken to one another a knowledge of who they are as Chicana/mexicana/indigenous women. Since ancient times in what is now the Americas women elders have passed on to others like them a knowledge of the past as a tool for the present and future. In spite of the elitist appropriations of the term *history*—so narrowly circumscribed by academic convention—indigenous women continue the ancient narrativizing practices, including the speaking of historia, transmitting a strategic and tactical self-knowledge to subsequent generations. *Historia* in Spanish means both "history" and "storytelling." Outside of universities, these two categories are usually one and the same. Historia (oral historical discourse) preserves the unity of what academia has separated into "history," "autobiography," "storytelling," and "oral history" —with specialists in each domain.[35]

Working-class native women have always eloquently transmitted their own diverse systems of meanings—*una conciencia mujerista*, called feminism in English—their own knowledge and sources of theoretical and practical authority. What emerges as meaningful within historia Chicana/mexicana (such as Lydia's narrative) is the transcendent or theoretical values that guide both the practices of everyday life as well as the discursive weaving of the historia itself. *Mi historia* means my history, my story, my life, and my telling. For working-class Chicana women, storytelling and historical discourse have the same name and serve the same purposes. Lydia Mendoza's historia is a series of social paradigms for rehearsing and inculcating woman's history, woman's agency, and gender relations in their multiple configurations and possibilities. Its thrust is not to create a catalog of information but to probe and reveal processes and strategies of self-empowerment for women: for their next of kin, their daughters, for me, and for other circles who might benefit. The performance of historia is power-laden across generations, in ways Paula Gunn Allen describes: "My mother told me stories all the time, though I often did not recognize them as that. . . . And in all of those stories she told me who I was, who I was supposed to be, whom I came from, and who would follow me. In this way she taught me the meaning of the words she said, that all life is a circle and everything has a place within it. That's what she said and what she showed me in the things she did and the way she lives."[36]

It is significant that Lydia Mendoza opens her life-telling by marking her life-long commitment to her work: music. She organizes this cycle of historia around her life in music. She sets herself up as a role model, highlighting her "body and soul" dedication to her musical career. From the beginning, Mendoza asserts a distinct agency and spirit of "Sí se puede" that will traverse the entire narrative. Yet most of her narrative does not describe glory but instead offers guidance and encouragement for overcoming multiple obstacles. She aims to provide inspiration, counsel, and guidance, ultimately empowering women like herself (perhaps others as well). This is the typical trajectory of the cultural practices known collectively as consejo (genres of counsel giving and taking), which have always been deeply valued in the Americas. Consejo circulates in long forms such as the Aztec Huehuetlatolli ("words of the elders"), as historia, or as related forms such as *dichos* (proverbs).

Chicana visual artist Estér Hernández (whose stunning Mendoza portraits grace this book), for example, provides us with a vivid recollection of the lasting impact of consejo/historia that she received from an encounter with Lydia Mendoza: "Lydia Mendoza is one of my favorite people in the world. I consider her my *madrina*, my godmother. There were times in my life when I didn't know what I was doing and was really struggling. I was at a real turning point when I met her. She gave me advice about how hard life is, but if you find something you really want, then do it. She also talked about finding a partner who respects what you're doing. Her husband had been extremely supportive and proud of her. I learned a great deal from her."[37]

Lydia Mendoza's life narrative invites reflection on gender relations and on her trajectory and circumstances as a U.S.-Mexican working-class woman performer. Throughout her narrative she reconstructs her identity as a woman, both as a musical performer and within the relational complex of her extended family, particularly the female relatives. She charts the contours of her past and present predominantly through women agents and reconstitutes herself primarily in her relationship to other women. She traces her musical lineage across generations to women in her family. In spite of the public visibility of men in music (and the male presences in her own life), Mendoza sees her mother and grandmother (along with the Creator or Dios) as the roots of her own musical inspiration and training. She also refers to her mother as "artistic director" of the Mendoza family itinerant performance group in the 1920s and 1930s. Thus Lydia's narrative manifests a woman-centered and woman-

Portrait of Lydia Mendoza 1985, by Estér Hernández. Courtesy Estér
Hernández

identified consciousness although she works within an industry and world in
which economic power is usually vested in males.

The relational complex that emerges from Lydia Mendoza's discourse and
her terrain of self-identity as a woman encompasses social contradictions of
gender. Her matrifocality does not obscure existing gendered social contradictions or hide patriarchal strategies of control. These are aired, for example, in
the story about her father's drinking and familial violence; male control is also
played out in the narratives about women who have succumbed to male authority. With very few words Lydia Mendoza illustrates how her performance
career was negotiated across multiple social contradictions, including, for example, the coexisting demonization (by her in-laws) and idolization (by her
husband and parents) of women musicians. The father's position within the
family is multivalent: at times he appears dominating yet also subject to the
mother's ultimate decision-making. He prohibits schooling for the girls, yet he
fully fosters the public singing and performance careers of his wife and daugh-

ters. In this regard, it is important to contextualize the father's reluctance to send the girls to school. During the years in question, the white supremacist Texas Rangers were still lynching Mexicans and raping Mexican women with impunity.[38] Notwithstanding the father's position of power within the family, the mother carries the greater importance—and a greater power: one based in nurturing instead of in trying to control. Mendoza constructs a matrifocal narrative in which the father ultimately recedes into the background and the mother emerges as the most important authority.

Lydia Mendoza's narrative and her musical career certainly unravel standing notions of Mexican/raza women as passive and/or powerless, as silent or silenced, and as oppressed by "tradition" and a totalizing patriarchy.[39] In fact, raza women have never been silent, even if that womanist eloquence was not university-trained—or heard. In the words of writer Lorna Dee Cervantes: "I come from a long line of eloquent illiterates whose history reveals what words don't say."[40] Mendoza's narrative foregrounds the central and powerful *traditional* roles of raza women as prime transmitters of historical knowledge, as teachers of spiritual practices and of spirituality, as performers of musical knowledge—as vessels of the humanistic ethics that shape everyday life for workers who survive and thrive against the odds. Leonor Zamarripa, Lydia's mother, is also positioned as the prime teacher and transmitter of the humanistic concept of *buena educación* (the teachings of respectful action) so highly valued within mexicana/o indigenous cultures. I stress this reading of "traditional woman" over against that which I often encounter. The term *traditional woman* is widely stereotyped as indicating a subservient and passive object of oppression. Mendoza's narrative constitution of gendered/womanist subjectivity should lead us to perceive the feminist/humanist traditional powers of women that extend back through the generations.

Lydia Mendoza articulates her subjectivity and strategies of self-representation within her historia through her choice of topics, situations, and commentaries, her flows, hesitations, and stops. Her vocabulary and narrational style suggest a type of subjectivity bound to oral forms of storytelling and to the nomadic circumstances of working-class migration: it is brief, economical, delivered in nuggets for easy retention. Her historia is interspersed with songs; it is woman-centered; it is tied to a higher power or spirit. A sacred force/power guides her life and cultural production. The spirit world is a source of literal and figurative healing, from illness and from social degradation. The heart is always in conversation with a power much greater than that of humans, of presidents or bosses. Mendoza's deeply ingrained sense of identity connected to a higher power (God) or God-Self gives her the power to sustain hardship, to self-empower, to live fully and meaningfully even in the face of extreme hardship—to defy the subordinate places to which women of color are often assigned. Although Lydia Mendoza casts herself in multiple subjectivities or roles, as professional singer, responsible mother, sibling, and adoring daughter, the foregrounded role and overriding emphasis is that of the struggling collective from which she emerges as a highly successful musician grateful to her people—and other audiences.

The ways in which raza women elders speak to and with others have been largely made invisible within print culture or appropriated as quotes here and there, refunctionalized as oral history for the grist of the academic mill. Many have approached Chicanas/mexicanas/raza/indigenous women armed with academic disciplinary conventions, processing these women as "informants" and objects of research—not as articulate intellectuals knowledgeable of their own histories. Historia does not circulate as an intellectual currency among elites. Yet these self-representational practices have secured raza cultural, physical, humanistic survival through multiple narrative strategies, forms, functions, and aesthetics. Paula Gunn Allen, Leslie Marmon Silko, and Greg Sarris explore in a sustained way the ancient flow of women talking and the communicative powers of story. Trinh T. Minh-ha also theorizes women's storytelling and the relationships between story and history in *Woman, Native, Other*. Yet there is virtually no specific study of the ways in which Spanish-speaking raza working-class women elders perform historia, their own reconstructions and representations as speaking subjects.[41] In the last 20 years there has been a marked tendency to quote raza women's oral histories or survey responses, then splice, contain, regulate, and subordinate their self-articulations within a larger "scientific" discourse. The product resembles a ventriloquism in which women who do not write books are "spoken for" or "spoken about" by a class of professional writers. Thus flesh-and-blood lives are ultimately abstracted into generalized categories.

Lydia Mendoza performs Chicana working-class history. I say this not in order to designate content but more so to designate her reflexive stratagem as a means by which working-class Chicanas have traditionally reconstituted past experience in the present. Across generations, Chicana working-class history remembers and constitutes reality through storytelling and other memory arts: be it in the form of historias and *pláticas* (historical discourse) or *cuentos* (storytelling such as through La Llorona / the wailing woman) and *casos*. Lydia Mendoza's narrative historia transcends the tedium and seeming monumentality of elite Eurocentric "Western" historiographic practices and the prescriptives of dates, places, politicians, armies, governments, nations, and chronologies so indispensable to the often male-centered historical discourse characteristic of print culture. Significantly, Lydia Mendoza's life spans various "dramatic" events, from the mass migrations *al norte* (to the United States) during and after the Mexican Revolution of 1910, two world wars and the Vietnam War, and two major "repatriation" efforts by the U.S. government that sought to rid the nation of raza, to the Chicano civil rights movement. Yet such events are not markers, nor for the most part even marked, in her historia. Not one U.S. or Mexican president is mentioned; not one politician of any kind. She occludes the patriarchal political history of the nation-states (United States and Mexico)—the kinds offered in the masculinized nationalistic school history texts, which highlight and center the supposed great actors, dates, and places of "history." She does not map the contours of the nation-state. The narratives of the nation-state are almost fully absent or marginalized while she centers mexicana/Chicana historia. Mendoza's historia privileges the markers of everyday life and the strategies by which many women have survived poverty and the nation and pursued their desire. Everyday governmental politics, the affairs of state, and the markers of the nation-state's history are distant matters and not of much concern.

Working-class histories are—like any other history—necessarily useful narratives. In part, that historia is driven by the need to relegate some events (such as the political history of nation-states) to oblivion and to remember what is needed to bring into profile the pillars that sustain both physical and humanistic survival. Mendoza even occludes events from her own life that some might consider conspicuous or "important": the awarding of the kinds of institutional honors people put on résumés to impress others (such as her honors from the Smithsonian and the National Endowment for the Arts). Those events are not what Lydia Mendoza considers memorable.

If, as Rudy Acuña indicates, the historian is "an agent of social control," I would argue that Mendoza's historia is a form of history that is inherently democratic, for it is localized in one body and does not seek to exercise the kind of social control that adheres to the grand totalizing narratives or "universal" generalized knowledge (of amorphous groups) produced in print historiography. Her narrative reminds me of what Trinh T. Minh-ha has called "women's womb writing, which neither separates the body from the mind nor sets the latter against the heart."[42] Mendoza speaks and writes through her own body. There is a political consciousness at work here; it is akin to what Honor Ford-Smith surmises in the life stories of Jamaican women: "To create such tales is a collective process accomplished within a community bound by a particular historical purpose. . . . They suggest an altering or re-defining of the parameters of political process and action."[43]

Making historia/Making history

 Lydia Mendoza's historia represents a transposition from a living oral discourse to print culture. As such, it demonstrates a convergence of two contending signifying systems with very different ground rules and trajectories. Although rendered here in written form, her narrative features the style and speech forms of a performance by an elder within the oral tradition. She spoke her history (historia) to me and did so in culturally specific ways that governed our interaction. Mexicana/Chicana conventions from the oral tradition placed responsibility for structuring the historia in her hands. As the "junior" person, I was called upon to assume the role of attentive (and quiet) listener or "learner" and relinquish any controlling ethnographic impulses. She remained in control throughout, even to the extent of brushing aside any of my efforts to "structure" or probe by means of an occasional question.

Lydia Mendoza performs her historia as a series of teachings or pláticas delivered for the benefit of listeners now and in generations to come. At all times she is keenly aware of addressing, counseling, and challenging me and others who may hear her words. Her historia is delivered with prerequisite brevity and within a free form that nonetheless follows traditional oral discourse patterns of style, theme, textual structure, speech forms, and communicative functions.

Charles Briggs's important fieldwork[44] among raza elders in New Mexico and his cogent analysis of what he calls oral historical discourse bear relevance to an analysis of how Lydia Mendoza makes historia. Briggs delineates four separate but interrelated forms of oral historical discourse. One of them (which he calls pedagogical discourse and which I call historia) is the form practiced between an elder and a younger person. Some of its general features are found in Lydia Mendoza's life-telling, with variations. Briggs identifies a tripartite form of movement within the oral historical discourse of the elders: first the statement of a premise regarding bygone days (the *antes* or "back then"); then the discursive pendulum swing to nowadays (*ahora*); and finally synthesis of this "oppositional dynamic" through the explanation of an underlying principle—a basic moral value that mediates the opposition (or juxtaposition) of past and present. The elders thus exhort the younger people to internalize certain values and reflect them in their behavior. Through the past, meaning is made in the present—a meaning we hope will extend into the future. The three communicative functions at work in oral historical discourse are thus descriptive, interpretive, and exhortative.

Lydia Mendoza's historia bears a strong similarity to what Briggs describes. One example of that discursive dynamic is her discussion of a specific physical location: San Antonio, Texas. She contrasts the old San Antonio of the twenties (the antes or "before") with today's (the ahora or "now") San Antonio after urban removal. The purpose is not description of the past as facts significant in and of themselves. That story articulates the importance of preserving collective public spaces for Mexicans to gather and exercise collective will and presence. Her story articulates the need to maintain such social and cultural spaces. The antes is the San Antonio of the 1920s, which she describes as the place where "there was life twenty-four hours a day." The ahora is the current downtown San Antonio where favored sites of Mexican collectivity, of recreation, have been removed. She critiques the concepts of progress or "modern times," referring to the ahora (present) as a demolished urban geography where native peoples are dislocated: "Ahora ahí ves puro gringo paseándose" ("Now all you see there are gringos strolling about").

Mendoza does not deploy facts or events from her life if they are not needed to buttress or sustain the overarching logic and impetus toward a larger overriding point or life lesson (consejo). As with Briggs's New Mexican elders, Mendoza's narratives are exemplary and exhortative because she is trying to instill life values important for collective identity formation and its maintenance. Those life values are a cultural way of being in the world. Situational lived "facts" or life events are insignificant in and of themselves; their meaning fully unfolds only within the analytical / operational context of providing life counsel to others. Elements from the past carry importance only insofar as they can be enlisted into dialectical relationship to situations in the present and future. To her narrative Lydia Mendoza frequently brings the framing and rhetorical devices characteristic of oral historical discourse or historia: for special emphasis on a central principle there are expressions such as "Y por eso te digo"

("And that's why I'm telling you") and "Es como te digo" ("It's like I was say-ing"); for structuring the discourse there are the "antes . . . /ahora" frames. The most frequent markers of our interaction are Lydia Mendoza's fixed expres-sions as well as her gaze, generously used to question and confirm my under-standing: "¿Sabes?" ("You know?" meaning, "Do you understand?"), "Tu sabes" ("You know," meaning, "You of course know"), and "¿ves?" ("do you see?"). In our interaction these were the cues Lydia Mendoza provided for me in order to gauge whether I was following her. I was consistently called on to signal my understanding, confusion, agreement, or interest or to hint at a possible dis-agreement through the use of what Briggs calls verbal and visual back-channel signals. For the sake of readability I have removed all my "hm-hum" and head-nodding signals from the manuscript.

In spite of the usefulness of Briggs's analysis of the texts and contexts of mex-icano verbal art, I would extend it to account for gender, on the one hand, and to account for the migratory populations who are not tied to physical geogra-phies and economies in the same way as New Mexicans who have inhabited one place across many generations, on the other. Migratory populations (like Lydia Mendoza) have a fundamentally different relationship to the land. I would even argue here that Lydia's bodily terrain (her radically Mexican attire, her heart and voice full of songs) stands in for the land and as a symbol of the lost homeland.

Lydia Mendoza is concerned with "weaving that story by telling it." She weaves remembrance and the community of memory with words. The seg-ments of her performance, taken together, weave a composite web of meaning. Her narrative is like the spiderweb of oral narrative described by Leslie Mar-mon Silko: "I want you to hear and to experience English in a structure that fol-lows patterns from the oral tradition. For those of you accustomed to being taken from point A to point B to point C, this presentation may be somewhat difficult to follow. Pueblo expression resembles something like a spider's web— with many little threads radiating from the center, crisscrossing one another. As with the web, the structure emerges as it is made, and you must simply listen and trust, as the people do, that meaning will be made.[45]

Mendoza's narrative strongly resists the linearity and linear thought so prevalent in the "rationality" of print culture, such as the tendency to chronol-ogize life activity. Lydia Mendoza presents us with a shifting, discontinuous, segmented historia. A circularity is at work, evidenced in a general spiraling of language and the manner of the narrative's topical progression. The life-telling variously closes on itself: at times she first foregrounds the point she wants to make; then she will offer an extended narrative to illustrate and return to the point she wanted to bring across. This same topic or event or person will then reemerge in a later story, yet viewed with a different lens. Thus Mendoza sketches various individuals in their multiple and conflicting identities. For example, Mr. Cortéz is defined as benefactor in one segment and as an exploiter in an-other segment. In one segment she casts her father as an avid supporter of her musical talents; in another segment he emerges as an abusive, drunk spouse holding a gun to the mother. We, the listeners, must make sense of the picture in its entirety.

Lydia Mendoza (El Paso, 1983). Courtesy Yolanda Broyles-González
Collection

In her historia, Lydia Mendoza characteristically plays the past and present
off each other continually, not in an effort to only tell one woman's life but in an
effort to crystallize contemporary values, meanings, and challenges for the
community from her own life. The past only exists as "past in present." All
times are woven together in the now. It is a fragile fabric, mended and rewoven
every day by women elders. As an elder with vast maturity and experience she
weaves for us a life-fabric, with a range of conducts from which to chose. Mendoza's life reconstruction (her supposed "past") is always critique and exhorta-
tion for the present and future: all temporalities are thus collapsed through an
important human/ethical principle valid in all times. She "performs" and crafts

her life (like a storytelling) with a precise and willful focus only on specific narrative "clusters" that transmit her human legacy rooted in timeless collective values, life principles, and her personal vision for their continuation in the future. What is significant is not names, places, and dates but the transmission of human values from her lived experience: perseverance, faith in higher powers, the need for hard work and a life dream. Lydia Mendoza's relationship to facts and information resembles that of Mabel McKay in the life study undertaken by Greg Sarris. In response to Sarris's efforts at "getting the exact dates and figures that go with the stories," she responds: "It has nothing to do with dates and that. I don't know about dates. It's everlasting what I'm talking about." In another place, Mabel McKay performs a litany of informational "facts" about her life, then immediately critiques that life-telling strategy as (white) culture-specific: "There, how's that? That's how I can tell my life for the white people's way. Is that what you want? It's more, my life. It's not only the one thing. It's many. You have to listen. *You have to know me to know what I'm talking about.*"[46]

Mendoza seeks to produce *effects* (actions) and not just descriptions or ideas. Her work of interpretation, be it in the performance of her songs or in the performance of her historia, serves to constitute that powerful cohesive force of raza shared/contested meanings and collective practices known academically as affiliations of race, economic class, ethnicity, gender, culture, sexuality, and bioregion. In the words of Gloria Anzaldua: "The ability of story (prose and poetry) to transform the storyteller and the listener into something or someone else is shamanistic."[47] Lydia Mendoza's rhetorical strategies, much like her musical performance, are cultural forms and acts that function as a crucible for collective mexicana/o identity negotiation and formation. That crucible of identity is what Judith Butler describes as "an open assemblage that permits of multiple convergences and divergences."[48] Mendoza performs her own agency in combination, contrast, and comparison with that of other women—most notably her mother's and sisters'. In this economical narrative, she is not concerned with performing all the details of her life. For example, she makes only fleeting references to the topics of discrimination and other violent social dynamics and avoids opening this Pandora's box for full viewing. Is it something she does not wish to foreground within her legacy of remembrance? Does she assume I amply know those social facts: "tu sabes . . ."? Would their obtrusive reiteration interfere with her goal of narrating a self who has risen above the social obstacles of poverty and the patriarchal order? Would they interfere with her desire to explore women's options, rather than their victimizations?

This historia renders one configuration among a number of differently configured historias by Lydia Mendoza, most of them unpublished. This is not to say that this particular historia is arbitrary; it is to say that historia is usually performed across the lifetime of an elder, in varying contexts, with different needs and desires informing both the woman performing historia and what she perceives the listener needs in changing contexts. In a different time and space and with a different listener, Mendoza would have performed differently. This particular historia constitutes one of her grand reckonings with her life core: her praxis as musician and within the web of relationships that sustained her. The flow of historia as a daily practice of course makes it impossible to ever capture it in its fullness. Oral discourse and knowledge flows and cannot be contained by anyone: authorities and/or scholars. It cannot be put on a shelf. Some of it even remains unspoken—shared only with a knowing glance among women, an intimation, or a "Tu sabes . . . ," or in a conversation with the spirit world or Dios (the Creator/God). These are perhaps the "secrets" of a people living in a state of siege, what Rigoberta Menchú refers to when she states: "Sigo ocultando lo que yo considero que nadie lo sabe, ni siquiera un antropólogo, ni un intelectual, por más que tenga muchos libros, no saben distinguir todos nuestros secretos." ("Nevertheless, I'm still keeping secret what I think no-one should know. Not even anthropologists or intellectuals, no matter how many books they have, can find out all our secrets."[49])

The web of oral tradition

 The Mendoza life-telling manifests her immersion and movement within the oral tradition in various ways. Her life narrative illustrates, for example, how oral traditions (often studied separately from each other) interrelate as a system of mutually sustaining performance practices. The oral tradition is the grid through which life is lived. In this historia, the network of oral tradition is manifest with numerous song genres (ranging from historical corridos to love songs), in Mendoza's prayer and other spiritual practices, in cuentos (storytelling), and in the overall historical discourse of her life-telling (historia). With regard to both her matrilineal focus and her self-contextualization within and in relationship to the spirit world Mendoza performs her lineage within native systems of gender.[50] Lydia Mendoza, for example, lives the interconnectedness of all being, that overriding relationship of reciprocity with the powers (Dios) visible in the daily spiritual life practices within her extended family and community. Dire life problems or troubled situations are negotiated with powers from the spirit world through an exchange: paybacks for miracles or favors granted (the essence of the vow or *manda*); the spirit powers that animate her music and enabled her successful artistic work and career; the spirit world, which is summoned through her health practices, and so forth. Her relationship to Dios undergirds her entire narrative; all human endeavor is an act of cooperation between human beings and that divine source that animates the universe (*gracias a Dios*).

Mendoza's historia gives insight into various mutually sustaining spiritual domains of women's autonomous self-power: the home altar, the manda, the *peregrinación* (pilgrimage), daily prayer, belief in future miracles, invocation of past miracles, and parables that manifest ethical behavior; knowledge of the spirit world and the negotiations with the spirit world; the certainty that all that moves on the planet does so through the presence of a sustaining force, which she calls God or los espiritus; her distant relationship to the institutionalized religion of Catholicism; and women's canonization of popular borderlands saints (e.g., Nuestra Señora de San Juan). Mendoza also performs spiritual parables for us, such as the parable of the feathers, in which ultimate authority belongs to the spirit world, the place of spiritual negotiations that involve ethical self-formation and self-critique. All of these spiritual practices have the common ground of faith in higher powers.

The oral tradition is a communitizing web, and the performer physicalizes community. Each performance—through reliance on collective forms and through the presence of participatory listeners—is an act of incorporation that vies with (and supplants) the imagined supposed national communities of Benedict Anderson.[51] The performative within the oral tradition is always a renegotiation of collectivity. The practices from the oral tradition are collective both synchronically and diachronically, because the song, dicho, or story is always performed in time and across times. These performances form the most resilient contours of collective and individual identity. Being an indigenous "mexicana" is born of the shifting and mobile activity of making meanings through storytelling.

Negotiating the space and movement between orality and print culture

In completing this book I faced numerous challenges, among them the challenge of naming the discursive space of Lydia Mendoza's life narrative in this book's title. As listener, participant, collaborator, and editor I felt highly conflicted about calling this narrative an autobiography. That term is historically laden with bourgeois individualism, yet its parameters have recently widened somewhat to include myriad forms of everyday communication as well as the submerged narratives of women and people of color. Lydia's focus on the self is neither self-serving nor self-centered; nor does she engage in self-heroics or self-idealization. Within indigenous cultures it has usually been considered *mala educación* to call attention to yourself. She enlists her individual self, however, within a strong sense of communal life and communal self-understanding in order to teach and guide others, toward life teachings and life lessons, to challenge other women to self-empowerment. The segment "'Persevere! Don't Hold Back, Don't Give Up!' (Surrender to Music: A Whole Lifetime)" exemplifies the persuasive function of Mendoza's narrative—which also distinguishes it from much of what is found in classical white autobiography. (Mendoza's narrative is more an example of the "resisting autobiography" and "outlaw genres" described by Caren Kaplan.[52]) Although Mendoza is the strong individual at its center, the narrative focus is not a narrowly individualistic subject engaged in self-psychologizing, introspection, or any other techniques of intense self-description or self-scrutiny. Mendoza defines herself through her relational constructions within a large kinship network, to a community, and to the spirit world. The term *testimonio* seemed far more appealing than *autobiography*. Ultimately, however, I decided on *historia*, the term widely used by women within the oral tradition.

The recent tidal wave of autobiographical writings and the emergence of

Lydia Mendoza Restringing Guitar. Photo by Estér Hernández (1986).
Courtesy Estér Hernández

voices and formerly submerged narratives of Third World people, people of color, and women—usually referred to as testimonio—is perhaps related to the opening of discursive spaces through global decolonial movements and the critique of master narratives, including the critique of historiography. Are the discourses of the margins overtaking the center? In approaching Lydia Mendoza's historia I have combined insight from various academic domains, including autobiography research, theory of history, performance studies, gender studies, and cultural and social studies. To date Chicanas/indigenous women remain invisibilized within much of autobiographical research. The sustained studies by Genaro Padilla on nineteenth-century Mexican-American autobiography and that by Greg Sarris on the Pomo orality, as well as Ruth Behar's double autobiographical study, are notable exceptions.[53]

My own considerable editorial work always moved within the formal parameters prescribed by historia (oral historical discourse), and resisting the occasional impulse to arrange Lydia Mendoza's stories in chronological order. I at times shortened, at times lengthened, at times clarified and annotated. I could not assume the reader to have the knowledge of Mexican/Chicana/o musics that Lydia assumed I had.

In spite of editorial reworkings, the "topics," sections, and substance of her narrative were of her own choosing. This is what she considered memorable, and this is what she considered important. I deliver them here in the order in which she told them. They did not emerge in one sitting. She tended to many other things (including two concerts), cooking, conversations, music-making, and television-watching; she would invite me to turn on the tape recorder when a story came to her that she wanted included in this book. She also told me other stories that she did not want included. Her life-telling unfolded incrementally, each increment a discrete story. I took the editorial liberty of giving each story/increment a title that consisted of words from that segment that captured a focal point. (No doubt other "listeners" will find other focal points—depending also on frame of mind, circumstance, personal and social background, etc.)

Throughout this project I faced the challenges of negotiating a linguistic space between the cultures of orality and the print culture: transposing spoken testimonio to the printed page, deciding what "worked" once transposed onto the written medium—and what did not. These two systems are not always compatible. Even the initial process of transcribing the tapes triggered many questions. My first transcription had every last "hm" and "uh," groans, laughter, pauses, and repetitions that made the page seem unreadable. Working to make the manuscript into something readable required streamlining. I regularly reported on my editing to Lydia Mendoza. Out of respect for her words I wanted to ensure that the process of editing was clear to her. Yet it was obvious that she wanted to leave most of it up to me. Still, out of respect I informed her of issues and my suggested solutions. Her major concerns from the very beginning—and which she stressed many times over—were that this book contain what *she* wanted and that it be published in the Spanish language. The linguistic stipulation inspired this first bilingual publication with Oxford University Press, to whom we are so grateful.

As the arduous process of transposing Lydia Mendoza's oral historical discourse onto the written page posed many challenges for me, a word about language and style is in order. My goal of preserving the oral character of her speech on the written page required seemingly contradictory editorial processes. Lydia Mendoza's speech patterns in oral discourse include certain patterns of repetition that involve words or entire phrases. ("Luego, luego vino. Fueron a traer el doctor luego luego.") In many instances, the written page could not sustain the generous repetitions so common in spoken language. I pared down many repetitions that felt overdone on paper. Yet I never eliminated them; they are among the prime stylistic and pedagogical tools of oral performance. Maintaining just enough repetition was difficult yet crucial in maintaining the oral style on the printed page.

Other kinds of editing were needed. For example, Lydia Mendoza's tendency to bridge all her spoken sentences with the conjunction *and* required modification and trimming. However, it was incumbent upon me to leave many of those *ands*, because that is part of the oral quality of her speech. Similarly, she often started several sentences in a row with *entonces* (*then*). Although this connector works well in spoken language, in writing it has a very awkward feel. At other times what was needed was a slight linguistic augmentation to convey meaning she expressed through her body, gestures, or tone of voice.

In transcribing and transposing Lydia Mendoza's narrative to paper I have also deliberately maintained much of her tejana speech patterns and pronunciation. This necessarily involves some departure from what is at times considered "standard" Spanish. (Since all forms of Spanish are in fact local and regional, the notion of "standard" Spanish is a convenient fiction for language textbooks and royal academies.) Specific markers of Lydia Mendoza's regional tejano Spanish, for example, include her common use of the word *pos* instead of *pues* (even though she also occasionally uses *pues*). I maintained a number of tejana verb forms such as the conjugation "yo traiba" instead of "yo traía" (for the verb *traer*). I also maintained some of the dropped sounds characteristic of Texas Spanish: "pa'lla" instead of "para allá." Furthermore, Mendoza's generous use of conversational feedback signals like "¿ves?" or "¿sabes?" that require confirmation (head nodding, gaze, or yes/no answer) from her listener is rendered in writing even though such signals are not common written practice and might even appear superfluous. Some words or phrases that are strongly regional and might be unfamiliar to a Spanish speaker from a different region are annotated in the text (such as the verb *afanar*, which in Texas means "to toil," whereas in Argentina it means "to steal").

Beyond the transposition to paper, the Spanish-language manuscript then had to be translated into English. Translation into English was like a second translation. The first translation was the transcription to paper that "fixed" the historia. To me it felt like a double encasement. Historia is a communal activity; it flows from person to person, heart to heart, lips to lips. In this double translation, that which is alive in the human breath and listener becomes fixed, inert, and certainly disembodied. The absence of the body diminishes the magical powers of the telling. As Gloria Anzaldúa has noted: "For only through the body, through the pulling of flesh, can the human soul be transformed. And for images, words, stories to have transformative power, they must arise from the human body—flesh and bone—and from the Earth's body—stone, sky, liquid, soil."[54] The translation was two-phased. María Elena Gaitán and I worked with the first translation draft for weeks, sometimes through the night, debating how to render Lydia's tejana Spanish and regional expressions so tied to culture and history into a language that did not share those sentimientos. Translating it into a "regional" English would have made it appear stilted. Unfortunately, we translated before editing the Spanish. So I later retranslated that initial translation, adjusting it to the editorial changes I made in the Spanish.

I feel great joy at passing on this story to reading listeners. Sometimes I retell Lydia's stories. They are now part of my stories, along with the other ones I've inherited from women ancestors and which I retell to my children, to youth, and to adults. When I retell them they are not identical to the stories told to me; we know they always change with each telling:

> In this chain and continuum, I am but one link. The story is me, neither me nor mine. It does not really belong to me, and while I feel great responsibility for it, I also enjoy the irresponsibility of the pleasure obtained through the process of transferring. Pleasure in the copy, pleasure in the reproduction. No repetition can ever be identical, but my story carries with it their stories, their history, and our story repeats itself endlessly despite our persistence in denying it. *I don't believe it. That story could not happen*

today. Then someday our children will speak about us here present, about those days when things like that could happen."[55]

With this book a small part of Lydia Mendoza's vast historia goes into print, while the rest continues to flow, shaping face and heart (*encarnación*) among women and joining the immense flow of story told by women since the beginning of time, moving to the power of the four directions.

Notes

I   Let's weave that story by telling it

1. *Compadre* (literally co-father) and the female *comadre* are terms that denote the ceremonial kinship relationship between godparents and the child's parents.

2. Reference here is to the Rio Grande Valley (Río Bravo).

3. The term *raza* is short for *raza humana* (human beings) and is widely used as a self-identifier by native people of Mexican descent (be they U.S. nationals or Mexican nationals). Virtually all Native American tribal names signify "people" or "human beings." I consider "Mexicans," "U.S.-Mexicans," "Chicanas/os," and so-called Latinas/os or Hispanics for the most part indigenous peoples, even though the bureaucracies of the nation-states (such as the Bureau of Indean Affairs) have created false divides that separate the "Native American" from the "Mexican American." I like using *raza* also because it is a transnational term that blurs national affiliations and political borders transcended by culture.

4. The *mutualistas*, or mutual aid societies, were worker self-help groups that first emerged in the 1850s. These worker cooperatives protected the economic, legal, and social rights of their members. They continued into the 1920s and 1930s.

5. The Mexican charro and china poblana costumes have come to typify "the Mexican." They are considered "typically Mexican," although, in reality, each Mexican region has its own typical attire.

6. The reference here is to her concert at the Santa Barbara Museum of Natural History.

7. A song performed by Chelo Silva.

8. "Pancho" is a nickname for Francisco.

9. *Consejo* is the custom of giving and taking counsel; children are raised with *consejos*, words from elders. Often these are in story form.

10. Here Lydia Mendoza describes a complex process triggered by the development of diverse sound and visual media. That process involves displacements, adaptations, enhancements, and rivalries among stage performers, audio recordings, film, radio, and television. Mendoza made a remarkable transition from the home and streets to recording and radio. Live performance music was enhanced and also in part supplanted by audio recordings. Simi-

larly, movies enhanced and also supplanted the live performance within the oral tradition. Movies were then enhanced and hurt by radio and television. Home video and computers are new media that interact with all of the preceding forms. Although television eventually supplanted virtually all live performance in theaters, this process hit the Mexican moviehouses first. Also, the growing monopolization of the Latin American film industry by the U.S. film industry has led to phenomena such as distribution control and control of movie industries in Mexico and other Latin American countries. One outcome is an extremely debilitated Mexican film industry.

11. She uses the popular term *norteño*. There is great fluidity and variation in the usage of the terms *norteño, ranchera, tejana/o, Tex-Mex*, and *música ranchera*. At times, "norteño" is used as a subset of "música ranchera"; at other times, the inverse appears to be the case. At times, the two are used interchangeably. Literally, "norteño" means "from the north"—a geographical reference to the current and former north of Mexico: Texas, California, New Mexico, Arizona, Colorado, and the northern Mexican states of Tamaulipas, Nuevo León, Sonora, Chihuahua, and even Sinaloa.

12. The huapango is a song and dance form from the Gulf Coast of Mexico. In the Huasteca region of the Gulf Coast, *falsete* (falsetto) is used prominently in the singing—a kind of yodeling. "Cucurrucucú Paloma," a traditional Mexican song, is written in the huapango style and is sometimes sung using falsete.

13. Although tuning the third, fourth, fifth, and sixth courses in octaves on a twelve-string guitar is now common practice, in the period in question the twelve-string guitar was apparently tuned with each double course in unison.

14. These are the two major Mexican and U.S. Mexican independence day celebrations, marking (respectively) independence wars against France and against Spain.

II *Vamos hilvanando aquella historia: platicándola*

1. "Nicle" es la moneda estadounidense "nickel": cinco centavos.

2. Se refiere a su concierto en el Santa Barbara Museum of Natural History.

3. Chelo Silva cantaba esta canción.

4. "Mapiar" es un anglicismo chicano derivado del verbo "mop". Significa "trapear".

5. "El Wes" (the West) le dicen a la parte oeste del estado de Texas.

6. El acordeón es el instrumento central de la música norteña, de los conjuntos norteños.

7. "Rollers" es anglicismo. Significa los tubos del pelo.

III *Background and analysis*

1. I am necessarily limited by the 80,000-word limit in my contract with Oxford—not the kind of space that would allow for the type of self-interrogation done, for example, by Ruth Behar in *Translated Woman: Crossing the Border with Esperanza's Story* (Boston: Beacon, 1993).

2. An important recent working-class life-telling is *Forged under the Sun / Forjada bajo el sol* (Ann Arbor: University of Michigan Press, 1993). This narrative, however, is not performed within the oral tradition parameters of historia. The editor mentions using "long lists of questions," chronologizing the narrative, and constructing a print narrative.

3. The volume *Lydia Mendoza: A Family Autobiography* (compiled and with an introduction by Chris Strachwitz with James Nicolopulos [Houston: Arte

Público, 1993])—hobbyist in nature—displays both strengths and weaknesses. The discography is an important contribution. Given the very scant literature on Lydia Mendoza, I consider all publications on Mendoza necessary contributions. Among the problematics of this volume, however, is the complete disregard for oral historical collection and editing principles. The collection and editing process is not discussed in the volume, although it bears the imprint of numerous editorial and collection decisions. Specifically, Lydia Mendoza was responding to the presence of male interviewers with whom she did not have a relationship of confianza (trust) and whom she could not enact "woman talk" with; the five interviews with Lydia Mendoza that went into the book were conducted by five different sets of male interviewers at different times. In the book, her interviews are disjointed (taken apart by the editors), dispersed, rarranged, and juxtaposed with interview segments with other informants. Interview materials are "arranged" within chapters whose "topics" the editors decided upon. The chief compiler of the material, Chris Strachwitz, who—according to Mendoza—does not speak Spanish, was present at three of those interviews. Lamentably, there appears to be no sensitivity toward (or awareness of) the difference between conducting an interview with someone and respecting the performance of oral historical discourse.

The thrust of this volume appears to be the extraction of as much "information/facts" as possible through interview questions (which are withheld from us)—even if it means pitting the individual testimonies against one another and even obviating the subjectivity of each "respondent." One such moment of colliding stories is mediated by Lydia Mendoza when she powerfully signals to the editors (in vain) the mexicana/Chicana cultural imperative of historia: the need to respect each person's subjectivity manifest within each person's control over his or her own life story and the performance of that story: "But it's Beatriz's own life, and I'll let her tell her own story, in her own way" (p. 42). Within the volume, Lydia Mendoza's own story and her way of telling it are made invisible and marginalized amid the multiplicity of voices included in the volume and the immense scope of information gathered through interview directives (edited out but nonetheless palpable); the editors extracted facts (narrative), cut them into small pieces, and rearranged those pieces under chapter titles as they pleased—thus also disjointing and obscuring the dynamic of the interviews.

The space of historia within which a woman elder distills her own life experience vis-à-vis a younger woman is obliterated. Instead, the non-Chicano male compilers structured the narrative according to principles not revealed to readers. Lydia Mendoza was "cast" as an adjunct within her family, thus diminishing our ability to perceive her on her own terms, in her own voice.

4. For an in-depth analysis of how social science methodologies (dis)figure Mexican life stories see Genaro Padilla, "The Mexican Immigrant as * : The (de)Formation of Mexican Immigrant Life Story," in *The Culture of Autobiography: Constructions of Self-Representation*, ed. Robert Folkenflick (Stanford: Stanford University Press, 1993), 125–148.

5. Lydia Mendoza's book differs markedly from those books in form, style, and purpose. She willfully circumvents the sensational as well as depictions of any amorous or sexual experiences.

6. *Cantares mexicanos / Songs of the Aztecs*, trans. from Nahuatl, introduction and commentary by John Bierhorst (Stanford: Stanford University Press, 1985), 213.

7. Yolanda Broyles-González, *El Teatro Campesino / Theater in the Chicano Movement* (Austin: University of Texas Press, 1994), chapter 1.

8. Charles L. Briggs, *Competence in Performance: The Creativity of Tradition in Mexicano Verbal Art* (Philadelphia: University of Pennsylvania Press, 1988).

9. Studies on social functions of popular cultural practices in the raza life-world include works by Charles Briggs (on verbal performance), José Limón (on diverse elements of popular culture), Manuel Peña (on tejano musics), Norma Cantú (on collective festivities), Olga Nájera Ramírez (on *charreadas* and festivals), Richard Flores (on the *pastorela*), George Lipsitz (on popular music), and Nestór García Canclini, Guillermo Bonfil Batalla, and Américo Paredes (on the corrido and diverse cultural expressions). Their writings are too numerous to list here.

10. With the term *autonomous domains of self-power* I seek to extend Guillermo Bonfil Batalla's cogent theorizing that concerned "cultural control" and "cultural autonomy" in *Identidad y pluralismo cultural en América Latina* (Buenos Aires and San Juan, Puerto Rico: Editorial de la Universidad de Puerto Rico, 1992).

11. I am deeply indebted to the work of Michel de Certeau and seek to extend his analysis, particularly of *The Practice of Everyday Life*, trans. Steven F. Rendall (Berkeley: University of California Press, 1984).

12. Gloria Anzaldúa, *Borderlands / La frontera* (San Francisco: Aunt Lute Press, 1987), 50.

13. Mohandas Gandhi, *The Words of Gandhi*, selected by Richard Attenborough (New York: Newmarket, 1982), 50.

14. For a critique of the hierarchical academic discourses on Latin American popular cultures see Nestór García Canclini, "Culture and Power: The State of Research," *Media, Culture, and Society* 10 (1988): 467–497.

15. Devon Peña, *The Terror of the Machine: Technology, Work, Gender and Ecology on the U.S.-Mexico Border* (Austin: University of Texas Press, 1997).

16. Gloria Anzaldua, *Borderlands / La frontera*, 61.

17. Studies of the U.S. government's illegal deportation of U.S.-Mexicans include Abraham Hoffman, *Unwanted Mexican Americans in the Great Depression, Repatriation Pressures, 1929–1939* (Tucson: University of Arizona Press, 1974); and Camille Guerin-Gonzáles, *Mexican Workers and American Dreams: Immigration, Repatriation, and California Farm Labor, 1900–1939* (New Brunswick, NJ: Rutgers University Press, 1994).

18. On the war between the United States and Mexico see Rodolfo F. Acuña, *Occupied America: A History of Chicanos*, 3rd ed. (New York: Harper & Row, 1988).

19. George Lipsitz, *Dangerous Crossroads: Popular Music, Postmodernism and the Poetics of Place* (London and New York: Verso, 1994), 6.

20. California enacted laws that legalized Native American slave labor in 1850 and in 1860. Not only did the slave laws deny Native Americans the suffrage and citizenship guaranteed under the Treaty of Guadalupe Hidalgo, but they also enacted a master/slave relationship between Anglos and any persons considered "Indians." Such persons were routinely hunted, rounded up, and bought and/or sold at public auction. This forced labor relationship—often referred to euphemistically as an apprenticeship—allowed whites to enslave as many perceived "Indians" as they wished, to declare them private property. For decades—in recent human memory—the wholesale trade in Native American men, women, and children was legal and widely practiced. Many Chicana/o ancestors tried to escape the slavery provisions by "de-Indianizing": speaking Spanish and passing as Mexicans (a more general and protective Native American "identity" or label). Yet for the authorities and slave traders "Mexicans" and "Indians" were virtually indistinguishable for two reasons: on the one hand,

the Bureau of Indian Affairs (and other government agencies) had not yet imposed terminologies that differentiated between locally indigenous Indians and Mexican Indians (Indians with tribal roots in Mexico); on the other hand, California Indians had all been Mexican nationals until the United States occupied California in 1848.

21. From *Cantares mexicanos*, ms. of the Biblioteca Nacional, fol. 35r. Quoted in Miguel León-Portilla, *Toltecayotl: Aspectos de la cultura nahuatl* (Mexico City: Fondo de Cultura Económica, 1980), 427.

22. Mikhail Bakhtin, *Rabelais and His World*, trans. H. Iswolsky (Bloomington: Indiana University Press), 90–91.

23. In recent years, the writings on "borderlands" have mushroomed. Works that explore the norteño borderlands include *La vida norteña: Photographs of Sonora, Mexico*, photographs by David Burckhalter, essays by Gary Nabhan and Thomas E. Sheridan (Albuquerque: University of New Mexico Press, 1998); and Alan Weisman, *La frontera: The United States Border with Mexico*, photographs by Jay Dusard (Tucson: University of Arizona Press, 1986).

24. There is great fluidity and variation in the usage of the terms *norteño*, *ranchera*, *tejana/o*, *Tex-Mex*, and *música ranchera*. At times, the term *norteño* is used as a subset of música ranchera; at other times, the inverse appears to be the case, and at still other times, the two are used interchangeably.

25. For an invaluable discography of Lydia Mendoza see the aforementioned *Lydia Mendoza*.

26. Unlike the Bureau of Indian Affairs—and many scholars—I do not define "Mexican" (or "raza" or "Latino" or "Chicano" or "Hispanic") as separate and distinct from "Native American." Thus I consider "norteño" musics indigenous. I am aware of the historical and political events that have enabled the imagined separation of the "Mexican" from the "Indian." However, my own experience and that of my elders in the Arizona/Sonora borderlands have taught me that "Mexican" is just another name for "Indian"—and many Indians are also Mexican, by virtue of cultural practices if not by national origin. In the borderlands, the BIA labels are particularly strained and transparent as a divide-and-conquer mechanism.

27. This relational quality illustrates Jesús Martín Barbero's (and before him Carlos Monsiváis's) reconceptualization of the popular that emphasizes "the interlacing of resistance and submission, and opposition and complicity" (p. 462). Jesus Martin Barbero, "Communication from Culture: The Crisis of the National and the Emergence of the Popular," trans. Philip Schlesinger, *Media, Culture, and Society* 10 (1988): 447–465.

28. Guillermo Bonfil Batalla, *Mexico Profundo: Reclaiming a Civilization*, trans. Philip A. Dennis (Austin: University of Texas Press, 1996), 142 and 133, respectively.

29. Books on corridos published in the United States include Américo Paredes, *"With a Pistol in His Hand": A Border Ballad and Its Hero* (Austin: University of Texas Press, 1978), also his *A Texas-Mexican "Cancionero": Folksongs of the Lower Border* (Urbana: University of Illinois Press, 1976); and the more recent María Herrera-Sobek, *Northward Bound: The Mexican Immigrant Experience in Ballad and Song* (Bloomington: Indiana University Press, 1993) and *The Mexican Corrido: A Feminist Analysis* (Bloomington: Indiana University Press, 1990). Steven Loza, *Barrio Rhythm: Mexican American Music in Los Angeles* (Urbana: University of Illinois Press, 1993) provides an important generalized portrait of raza musical cultures in twentieth-century Los Angeles (and virtually nothing on the canción ranchera).

30. Manuel Peña, *The Texas-Mexican Conjunto: History of a Working-class*

Music (Austin: University of Texas Press, 1985). The University of Texas Press has also announced as forthcoming Peña's *Mexican American Orquesta*. On the horizon we can also look forward to a new generation of research into the significance of musical cultures in the formation of social meaning; that new generation of scholars includes Estevan Ascona, Candi Jaquez, and Russell Rodríguez. Some popular readings on norteño musics include Jack Loeffler and Katherine Loeffler, *La música de los viejitos* (Albuquerque: University of New Mexico Press, 1999); and Jack Parsons (photographs) and Jim Sagel (essay), *Straight from the Heart: Portraits of Traditional Hispanic Musicians* (Albuquerque: University of New Mexico Press, 1990).

The tragic shooting death of tejana singer Selena Quintanilla Pérez has occasioned an interest in the norteño music sphere—although most of it is focused on Selena's sexuality and not her musicianship. Publications include José Limón, "Selena: Sexuality, Performance, and the Problematic of Hegemony," in *American Encounters* (Boston: Beacon, 1998); Emma Pérez, "Beyond the Nation's Maternal Bodies: Technologies of Decolonial Desire," in *The Decolonial Imaginary: Writing Chicanas into History* (Bloomington: Indiana University Press, 1999), 101–125; Nick Joe Patoski, *Selena: Como la flor* (New York: Little, Brown, 1996); and Ilan Stavans, "Santa Selena," in *The Riddle of Cantinflas: Essays on Hispanic Popular Culture* (Albuquerque: University of New Mexico Press,) 3–9. Only Patoski considers Selena's musical lineage and talents.

31. For a more extensive discussion see my "Ranchera Music(s): Lydia Mendoza Performing Social Location and Relations," in *Chicana Traditions: Continuity and Change*, ed. Norma Cantú and Olga Nájera Ramírez (Champaign: University of Illinois Press, forthcoming).

32. I am grateful to UCSB undergraduate student Marlene Valenzuela—and her mother, Ursula Soto—for this anecdote.

33. See de Certeau, *The Practice of Everyday Life*, 78.

34. See Bonfil Batalla's discussion of these terms in *Mexico profundo*, chapter 8.

35. For interesting discussions of relationships between "storytelling" and "history" within the oral tradition see Angela Cavender Wilson, "Power of the Spoken Word: Native Oral Traditions in American Indian History," as well as the other essays found in *Rethinking American History*, ed. Donald L. Fixico (Albuquerque: University of New Mexico Press, 1997), 101–116.

36. Paula Gunn Allen, *The Sacred Hoop: Recovering the Feminine in American Indian Tradition* (Boston: Beacon, 1986), 46.

37. "A Conversation with Estér Hernández," in Teresa Harlan, *The Art of Provocation: Estér Hernández* (Davis, Calif.: C.N. Gorman Museum, 1995), n.p.

38. In fact, it was not safe to send Mexican girls to school or to otherwise leave them unsupervised. State violence against peoples of color at the hands of Euro-Texan law enforcement was rampant. In the words of historian Rodolfo Acuña: "To the Mexicans, the Texas Rangers were assassins" (*Occupied America. A History of Chicanos*, 4th ed., New York: Longman, 2000, p. 70).

39. Even within the Chicana feminist discourses, patriarchy has often been totalized and mexicanas/Chicanas/raza women construed as "silent" or "silenced." Academic feminism's inadvertent hubris has many times equated the post–civil rights process of "breaking into print" with "breaking the silence"—thus ignoring that within the oral tradition women have never been silent; they have been orally articulating and singing women's history for untold generations.

40. Lorna Dee Cervantes, "Visions of Mexico While Attending a Writing

Symposium in Port Townsend, Washington," in *Emplumada* (Pittsburgh: University of Pittsburgh Press, 1981), 45.

41. An important first collection of writings that examine and validate Chicana speech is *Speaking Chicana: Voice, Power, and Identity*, ed. Letticia Galindo and María Dolores Gonzáles (Tucson: University of Arizona Press, 1999). Earlier articles have provided valuable insight into the value, techniques, and interpretation of oral interviews by researchers—for example, Raquel Rubio-Goldsmith, "Oral History: Considerations and Problems for Its Use in the History of Mexicanas in the United States," in *Between Borders: Essays on Mexicana/Chicana History*, ed. Adelaida R. Del Castillo (Encino, CA.: Floricanto, 1990), 161–173.

42. Trinh T. Minh-ha, *Woman, Native, Other* (Bloomington: Indiana University Press, 1989), 40. Readers who seek a greater familiarity with the written narrative of Chicana/o history are referred to the important works by Rudy Acuña, Antonia Castañeda, Deena González, Vicki Ruiz, Emma Pérez, Arnoldo de León, George Sánchez, David Montejano, and others too numerous to name here.

43. Sistren with Honor Ford-Smith, *Lionhart Gal: Life Stories of Jamaican Women* (Toronto: Sister Vision Press, 1987), 3–4.

44. Charles L. Briggs, *Competence in Performance: The Creativity of Tradition in Mexicano Verbal Art* (Philadelphia: University of Pennsylvania Press, 1988), chapter 3.

45. Leslie Marmon Silko, *Yellow Woman and a Beauty of the Spirit* (New York: Simon & Schuster, 1996), 48–49.

46. Greg Sarris, *Mabel McKay: Weaving the Dream* (Berkeley and Los Angeles: University of California Press, 1994), 135–136 and epigraph, respectively. For a discussion of many of the issues that surround storytelling/life-telling and print culture see Greg Sarris, *Keeping Slug Woman Alive: A Holistic Approach to American Indian Texts* (Berkeley and Los Angeles: University of California Press, 1993).

47. Anzaldúa, *Borderlands*, 66.

48. Judith Butler, *Gender Trouble: Feminism and the Subversion of Identity* (New York and London: Routledge, 1990), 16. With regard to Lydia Mendoza's performance of music and historia I would also enlist Judith Butler's definition of gender (and other social categories) as an "act": "Gender ought not to be construed as a stable identity or locus of agency from which various acts follow: rather, gender is an identity tenuously constituted in time, instituted in an exterior space through a *stylized repetition of acts*. The effect of gender is produced through the stylization of the body and, hence, must be understood as the mundane way in which bodily gestures, movements, and styles of various kinds constitute the illusion of an abiding gendered self. This formulation moves the conception of gender off the ground of a substantial model of identity to one that requires a conception of gender as a constituted *social temporality*" (pp. 140–141).

49. Rigoberta Menchú, *I, Rigoberta Menchú: An Indian Woman in Guatemala*, trans. Ann Wright (London: Verso, 1984), 247.

50. For an examination of native systems of gender see the work by Paula Gunn Allen.

51. Benedict Anderson, *Imagined Communities: Reflections on the Origin and Spread of Nationalism*, rev. ed. (London: Verso, 1991).

52. Mendoza's life-telling—once transposed into print—has some correspondences to the kinds of narrative that Caren Kaplan calls outlaw genres, forms linked more to cultural survival than aesthetic experimentations and

generic rules of Western autobiography. Yet I resist applying the term *outlaw*, given the existent criminalization of peoples of color by police, media, and other institutions. See Caplan's article "Resisting Autobiography," in *De/Colonizing the Subject: The Politics of Gender in Women's Autobiography*, ed. Sidonie Smith and Julia Watson (Minneapolis: University of Minnesota Press, 1992), 115–138.

53. In the area of autobiography and/or life narratives I have derived invaluable insight from studies such as Genaro Padilla's pathbreaking *My History, Not Yours: The Formation of Mexican American Autobiography* (Madison: University of Wisconsin Press, 1993); Behar, *Translated Woman*; and Sarris, *Mabel McKay* and *Keeping Slug Woman Alive*. Other readings that were stimulating include *U.S. Hispanic Autobiography*, ed. Julián Olivares, vol. 16, nos. 3–4, of *The Americas Review* (Houston: Arte Público Press, 1988); Laura Marcus, *Auto/biographical Discourses: Theory, Criticism, Practice* (Manchester: University of Manchester Press, 1994); Carolyn Heilbrun, *Writing a Woman's Life* (New York: Norton, 1988); *The Private Self: Theory and Practice of Women's Autobiographical Writing*, ed. Shari Benstock (Chapel Hill: University of North Carolina Press, 1988); *Revealing Lives: Autobiography, Biography, and Gender*, ed. Susan Groag Bell and Marilyn Yalom (Albany: State University of New York Press, 1990); Sidonie Smith, *Subjectivity, Identity, and the Body: Women's Autobiographical Practices in the Twentieth Century* (Bloomington: Indiana University Press, 1993), particularly chapter 7; *The Uses of Autobiography*, ed. Julia Swindells (London and Bristol: Taylor & Francis, 1995); *Getting a Life: Everyday Uses of Autobiography*, ed. Sidonie Smith and Julia Watson (Minneapolis: University of Minnesota Press, 1996); *Interpreting Women's Lives: Feminist Theory and Personal Narratives*, ed. Personal Narratives Group (Bloomington: Indiana University Press, 1989); and *Storied Lives: The Cultural Politics of Self-Understanding*, ed. George Rosenwald and Richard Ochberg (New Haven: Yale University Press, 1992).

54. Anzaldúa, *Borderlands*, 75.

55. Minh-ha, *Woman, Native, Other*, 122.

The Lydia Mendoza CD Recording

The CD attached to this book is an invaluable document: the only released recording of Lydia Mendoza with a live audience. Its documentary importance lies in capturing the interactive performance circle between audiences and musicians so characteristic of the Mexican/Chicana/o/indigenous oral tradition of song. Within that community dynamic, the people embrace and cherish particular songs and collectively transmit that body of song across time; musicians of the working class apprentice by learning many cherished songs and, once they step into public performance, sing by popular demand. This performance dynamic is captured here live with Lydia Mendoza pausing between songs to take requests for the next songs.

Lydia Mendoza began learning traditional songs as a child, from her mother and grandmother. These songs are not unique to Lydia: they have been sung and recorded by many artists, as they have been sung within families across generations. What is unique to Lydia Mendoza is her style. That style is unmistakable and deeply loved among the people. Correspondingly, some collective songs are closely identified with her voice, with her interpretive powers and depth. Her signature songs are of course requested even more often. Such is the case with her 1934 hit, "Mal Hombre," which audiences requested from Lydia Mendoza at every appearance throughout her lifetime. In fact, audiences were not satisfied to hear it only once when she played. I witnessed one of her live performances in San Antonio where the public prevailed upon her to sing it twice—and wanted it sung one more time.

The CD included with this book was recorded in concert during Lydia Mendoza's last year as a performer. We recorded it in Santa Barbara, California, on April 27, 1986, the day she and I sat for the last installment of her life-telling. It was just a few days before her seventieth birthday and just a few weeks before a severe stroke ended her long performance career. It is evident from the audience's reactions that they are in the presence of a long-standing idol and legend, a singer whose voice's expressivity has only grown, even as its physical power has lessened. She is the quintessential voice of the people, of the oral tradition. Gloria Anzaldua—the only feminist writer to acknowledge Mendoza ("La gloria de Tejas / The Glory of Texas")—pays a succinct and appropriate tribute to Mendoza's presence: "These folk musicians and folk songs are our chief cultural myth-makers, and they made our hard lives seem bearable" (*Borderlands*, p. 35).

The recording that accompanies this volume was issued by Mr. Salomé Gutiérrez of DLB Records of San Antonio, Texas, after Lydia Mendoza passed her copy of our recording on to him—during recovery after her stroke. (DLB has recorded Lydia Mendoza since 1966.) Since Mendoza's copy of the recording was not marked, Mr. Gutiérrez issued it as *En Vivo desde New York* (*Live from New York*). In reality it was live from Santa Barbara. The second half of the concert—with the perennial favorite "Mal Hombre"—is due to be released soon and will be available from DLB Records. Taken together, this collection comprises a rare treasury of favorite tejano/mexicano songs heard across generations and popular to this day.

The songs that accompany this volume represent a cross section of song types deeply rooted in the Americas: the corrido (narrative ballad), bolero (a slow urban love song once popular throughout Latin America), and milonga (an Argentinean song form popular in the 1930s). Most prominent is the canción ranchera, the exuberantly passionate rural Mexican–based love song, usually in duple or triple meter. The ranchera is certainly the most popular and abiding of all Mexican/Chicana/o song types. I refer readers to my extended discussion of this soulful song type in "Background and Analysis."

The songs on the CD are as follows:

1. "Flores Negras" (Sergio de Karlo), milonga
2. "Corrido de Luis Pulido" (Cain Alfaro), corrido
3. "Pajarito Prisionero" (Lydia Mendoza), ranchera
4. "Mujer Paseada" (Daniel Garzes), ranchera
5. "Dos Palomas al Volar" (Juan Gaytan), ranchera
6. "Cuatro Vidas" (Manuel E. González), ranchera
7. "Cielito Lindo" (Quirino Mendoza), ranchera
8. "Solamente Una Vez" (Agustín Lara), bolero
9. "Por un Amor" (Gilberto Parra), ranchera
10. "Pajarillo Barranqueño" (Public domain, arr. Lydia Mendoza), ranchera
11. "Celosa" (Pablo Rodríguez), ranchera
12. "Canción Mixteca" (J. López Alavés), ranchera

Index

Silva, Chelo, 81–83, 169–171, 185, 195–196, 217n7, 218n3
Smithsonian. *See* Mendoza, Lydia
Songs
  as collective, xii, 186, 189, 190–192, 192–200
  as gift from a higher source, 47, 48, 136, 188–189
  as homeland, 182, 188
  by popular demand, xii, 43, 58, 88, 131, 145, 176, 186, 199
  printed on gum wrappers, 5, 17–18, 93, 105–106
  and survival, 182–184
  See also Bolero; Corrido; Huapango; Mendoza, Lydia; *Música de antaño*; Ranchera; Norteño
Songs mentioned in text
  "La Adelita" (corrido), 5, 93
  "El Adolorido" ("The Pained Man"), 5, 93
  "Amor Bonito" ("Beautiful Love"), 199
  "Amor de Madre" ("Mother Love"), xvi, 52, 140, 198, 199
  "Bésame Mucho" ("Kiss Me Alot"), 73, 161
  "Besando la Cruz" ("Kissing the Cross"), 57, 145, 198, 199
  "Camelia la Tejana" (corrido), 49, 137
  "Celosa" ("Jealous"), xvi, 57, 145, 199
  "Cielito Lindo," 42, 129
  "El Contrabando de El Paso" (corrido), 49, 137
  "Cuando Estemos Viejos," 199
  "Cuando se Pierde la Madr,e" 199
  "Cuatro Milpas" ("Four Corn Fields"), 5, 93, 198, 199
  "Cucurrucucú Paloma," 72–74, 79, 161–162, 167
  "Delgadina," 194
  "Espejito," 31, 119
  "La Feria de la Flores," 196
  "La Hija del Carcelero," 18, 106
  "Jesús Cadena" (corrido), 49, 137
  "Jesusita en Chihuahua," 73, 161

"Joaquin Murrieta" (corrido), xvi, 49, 137
"Ladrillo," 5, 93
"Lágrimas de Vino" ("Tears of Wine"), <qu pp>
"Lucio Vásquez" (corrido), 49, 137
"Luis Pulido" (corrido), 49, 74, 137, 162
"Luz Arcos" (corrido), 49, 137
"El Lirio," 199
"Mal Hombre" ("Evil Man"), xi, xv, 19, 30, 49, 107, 117, 137, 189, 199
"La Malagueña," 79, 166–167
"Margarita," 74, 162
"México Lindo y Querido," 199
"Los Mirlos," 80, 168
"Mis Flores Negras" ("My Black Flowers"), 80, 168
"La Mocosita," 5, 93
"Mujer Paseada" ("Experienced Woman"), 189
"Mundo Engañoso" ("Deceitful World"), 57, 145
"Noche de Ronda," 73, 161
"Nochesita" ("Sweet Night"), 73, 161
"La Pajarera" ("The Bird Keeper") 19, 107
"Pajarito Herido" ("Wounded Bird"), xvi, 57, 145
"La Paloma" ("The Dove"), 42, 81, 129, 169
"Al Pie de Tu Reja" ("At the Foot of Your Window"), xvi
"El Quelite," 177
"La Sandunga," 31, 119
"Serenata de Mayo" ("May Serenade"), 80, 168
"Soberbia" ("Anger"), 80, 168
"El Tango Negro" ("Black Tango"), 5, 93
"Todo por Ti" ("Everything for You"), 5, 93
"El 24 de Junio" (corrido), 49, 137
Soul, 47–48, 135
South America. *See* Lydia Mendoza
Spirit world, xiv, 64–65, 152–153, 178, 203, 210
  invoking spirits, 62, 150

Waltz (*vals*), 47, 135, 197
"Western" historiography, 204, 212
Wills, Bob, 193
Women
  flow of story among, 214–215
  spiritual practices of, 210
  traditional roles of, 203
  woman-centered narrative, xi, xiv,
    62–66, 151–153, 201–202
  women's autonomous domains of
    self-power, 184–186, 189
  See also Historia
Women singers, 5, 12, 54–56, 93,
    100, 142–144, 185, 195–196
Working class
  agricultural laborers, xi, xv, 14, 74,
    76, 102, 162, 188
  as auditory community, 181, 184
  Chicana women, 200–205
  Chicano/a cultural art forms, xiii,
    181, 184

historia (history), 179, 200–210
  humanism of, 183, 188
  identity formation, 181, 185–186,
    193
  native cultures, xiv, 187–189
  rural, 195–196, 198
  sentimiento, 181, 182, 195
  subjectivity, 180
  survival, 182–185, 197, 198
  urban, 195, 198
  See also Academic discourse;
    Songs; Spiritual practices

Zaízar, David, 185
Zamarripa Mendoza, Leonor. xi, xv,
  6, 10, 17, 20, 27, 32, 51, 94, 98,
  105, 108, 115, 120, 138, 139,
  190
Zúñiga, Agapito, 74, 162